As a Sword in My Bones

By

Jessica C. Joiner

This a work of fiction. Any resemblance to actual events or people, living or dead, is entirely coincidental.

AS A SWORD IN MY BONES

International Standard Book Number: 978-1-365-84260-3

Cover design by Elijah Principe

Printed in the United States of America

For more information:

Jessica C. Joiner

jcjauthor@gmail.com

https://authorjessicajoiner.weebly.com

LCCN: 2017913180

~ As with a sword in my bones, mine enemies
reproach me; while they say daily unto me,
Where is thy God? ~

Psalm 42:10

Prelude

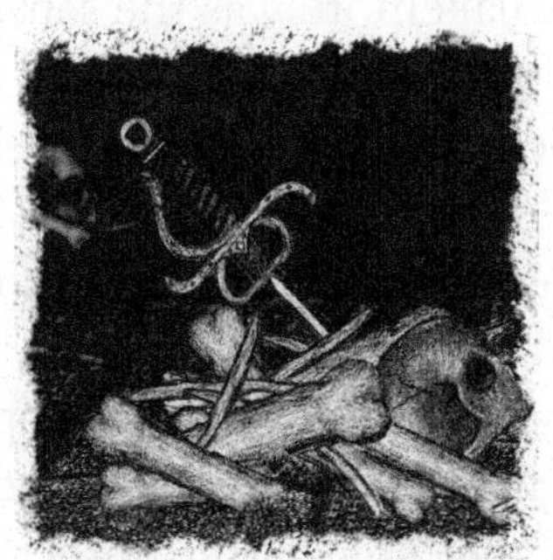

"If the Royal Council does nothing to curb my mother's cruelty, the oppressed people of Boldaria will revolt and this nation will be engulfed in a civil war," Prince Tristan Leander warned as he finished speaking before the gathered members of the twelve man Royal Council.

"You speak treason, young man." Lord Windemere stood from his chair and wagged his finger at the young prince. "Who would lead this uprising? You?"

"I oppose violence from either side, which is why I came to you. The Royal Council holds the power to check my mother's abuses." Tristan's research on the Council found Lord Windemere sided with the queen. He was not surprised by the accusation, but did not appreciate it all the same.

"Your Highness, I fear you overestimate the authority of this Council." Lord Applegate spoke with a grim shake of his head. "Perhaps when you are of age to be crowned king you can affect the changes you seek yourself."

Lord Applegate was the leader of the Council and, as far as Tristan had been able to discern, shared his dread of the impact of the queen's abuse of power.

Why will he not stand against her? Tristan wondered, clenching his fists at his side. *A word from him could sway many members of this Council.*

"How many more people will you allow her to kill in the year that remains until I am crowned?" Tristan demanded as his eyes raked the group of men. His gaze locked with Lord Blakemore's. Lord Blakemore was the same age Tristan's own father would have been, and was rumored to be a member of the resistance himself. Surely he would stand against the queen.

Lord Blakemore only scowled as he leaned back in his chair and folded his arms over his chest.

"I am sorry, Your Highness," Lord Applegate responded. He gestured to the men sitting on either side of him. "I do not see how we can do anything. Your mother's power is too great."

They fear her, Tristan realized as he took a stunned step back. Even the twelve most influential men in the kingdom did not dare oppose her publicly. "Then you had all better pray my coronation comes before she pushes the people too far." He whirled on his heels and stormed from the Council chamber.

"How did it go?" Lucas Medellin asked from where he stood leaning against the front of the building. He pushed off of the wall and scrambled to keep up as Tristan stomped past. "Not well, I gather."

"They will do nothing but wait until I am crowned." Tristan stopped in the street and turned to face his best friend. "But will the people put up with my mother's harsh rule that long?"

"They have put up with it for nearly twenty years," Lucas said with a shrug, "one more will hardly make a difference. Especially when they know they have you to look forward to as king."

"Some king I will be." Tristan raked his fingers through his black hair. "I could not even sway the opinions of twelve men, how can I rule a nation?"

"There are those of us who are concerned you will even survive to be crowned in the first place," Lucas said under his breath. "Your meeting with the Council would be enough to put your life at risk, but when you consider what I learned today..." His expression was dark with worry as he continued, "Must you return to the palace tonight? I fear it is not safe."

"Not safe?" Tristan raised a skeptical eyebrow. "Surely you do not believe my mother would retaliate against her own son?"

"Yes, actually, that is precisely what I believe." Lucas rubbed the back of his neck. "How much do you know about how your father died?"

"He became ill shortly before I was born," Tristan replied. He narrowed his eyes as he tried to determine how his father's death twenty years earlier could worry his friend today. "Your father did everything he could, but even his skill could not save him."

"I stumbled on my father's notes from that night while organizing his records today." Lucas looked around to make sure no one was near enough to overhear and lowered his voice. "King Justin was poisoned. My father suspected your mother."

"No, Lucas," Tristan shook his head. His mother may be a ruthless monarch, but he refused to entertain the suspicion that she would have murdered her own husband. "As much as I respect your father, I cannot believe she would harm my father – or me. You need not fear for me."

Lucas forced a laugh. "Someone has to, my friend. If anything happens to you, I would lose my best friend, my future brother-in-law, and my king."

* * * * *

"I think it was very brave," Aleatha spoke up as she laid a piece of rich birthday cake on the table in front of Tristan. She looked at him with twinkling eyes. "I would not have had the courage to stand before the Royal Council, knowing at least half of them are loyal to the queen."

"It was brave," Dr. Medellin agreed with his daughter. He gestured at Tristan with his fork. "I am very proud of you, Tristan. We all are. You will make a fine king."

Heat rose to Tristan's cheeks and he focused his attention on devouring the cake.

"That's what I told him," Lucas spoke up. He swallowed the bite of food in his mouth and continued, "Anyone would be better than the witch we have now."

"Lucas Gaius Medellin," his mother scolded. "In this house we speak respectfully of the queen, even if we do not approve of her actions."

"Sorry, Mother," Lucas apologized as he pushed a crumb around on his plate.

Pounding at the door shook the plates on the table. "Open in the queen's name!"

"That would be my summons," Tristan said, taking a deep breath as he pushed his chair away from the table. He never looked forward to the end of his visits with the Medellins. "Thank you all for the birthday celebration."

"Next year we will celebrate both your birthday and coronation," Dr. Medellin promised.

The front door swung open and a pair of soldiers stepped into the house.

"Let's go, Prince," one of the soldiers sneered. "The queen hates to be kept waiting."

"Allow me to say good bye, Captain Brogan," Tristan answered. The disrespectful captain of his mother's guard would be one of the first to go when he was crowned.

"Tristan, please," Lucas protested, grabbing Tristan's arm and pulling him aside. He leaned close and whispered, "It is not safe. Not after how you opposed her openly this morning. Your mother will..."

"My mother will be furious, yes," Tristan returned, "but she is my mother. She will not harm me. You worry too much."

"Of course I worry. You are my friend and the only hope this kingdom has for freedom." Lucas glanced back at the soldiers standing by the door. "At least promise me you will be careful."

"I will, Lucas, I promise." Tristan frowned. His friend's concern was catching. Though Tristan did not believe Queen Brigitte would murder him, he understood the punishment for his failed attempt to curb her excesses would likely be unpleasant. "God is in control, my friend." Tristan gripped both of Lucas's shoulders and met his eyes with a reassuring gaze. "If He wills for me to take the throne, nothing my mother does can change that."

Lucas took a deep breath and nodded, his look of concern only slightly faded. "I will not stop praying for His hand of protection on you, then. I do not think you understand how dangerous this next year will be."

He truly believes my mother will seek to keep me from the throne, Tristan realized as he regarded his friend. There would be no time now to question Lucas further, but perhaps it would be wise to keep a watchful eye at the palace. Even if his mother were not involved, he would not have made many friends among the servants loyal to her today. Danger could easily come from a direction other than the one Lucas suspected.

"You will be coming to church with us tomorrow, won't you?" Aleatha interrupted as she stood from the table and crossed the room to Tristan.

"I'm afraid sneaking out again tomorrow may not be wise," Tristan apologized as he took her hands in his. He did not deceive himself into thinking his mother was unaware he avoided her state-sponsored church, but he could not risk provoking her further by slipping away to attend the Medellins' dissenting church. "Perhaps next week. Until then, my lady, good bye." He bent and pressed his lips gently to the back of her hand.

"Ahem," Dr. Medellin cleared his throat, looking at Tristan with a raised eyebrow as he rose to stand behind his daughter. He placed a protective hand on Aleatha's back. "Until next week, Tristan, may God be with you."

Tristan released Aleatha's hands reluctantly and turned to follow the guards. Next Sunday seemed so far away.

*****

You speak treason, young man. Lord Windemere's accusation echoed in Tristan's mind as he entered his mother's chambers with his head held high. Nervousness gripped his stomach. Lucas's warnings nagged at him. His mother *was* going to be furious. While he did not fear his mother would truly hurt him, he was keenly aware he would have to pay the price for his speech this morning. A price he was certain would be calculated to make him think twice before questioning her again.

Heavenly Father, be with me, he prayed as he stepped onto the plush red carpet of the opulent room. It was excessive, like everything else about his mother. The queen herself sat on an upholstered chaise waiting for him. Her quiet regard as he approached increased his nervousness.

"Tristan, my dear son," she purred as she leaned back in the chaise, lifted her feet onto it, and crossed her ankles. "Lord Windemere told me you spoke to the Royal Council this morning. You know you could have come directly to me."

Any hope Tristan may have had of trying to explain his behavior in a softer light was clearly gone. *If only it had been Lord Applegate who had reported to the queen, rather than Lord Windemere!* Lord Windemere's accusation of treason and Lucas's worried warning clashed in Tristan's mind and a seed of real fear took root for the first time.

"Mother, I have come to you, countless times. and yet the cruelty continues." Tristan swallowed against the dryness in his mouth. "The people of Boldaria deserve..."

"The people of Boldaria deserve a strong ruler willing to do what it takes to make sure the laws are obeyed." Queen Brigitte cut him off . "And I am in no way certain you are ready to be that ruler. I knew your association with Dr. Medellin and his family was making you soft. Would they also turn you against me?"

"No," Tristan answered quickly. He was willing to face his mother's anger for his actions, but he would not have her turn her wrath on his friends. "The Medellins are faithful to Boldaria."

"But not to *me*," the queen amended with a wave of her hand. "You need not be concerned about them, the good doctor has been in my service since before you were born. I know well his feelings for me. He does not need to agree with me, so long as he does not oppose me." She propped herself up on one elbow and gave Tristan an intent look. "Fear is loyalty, Tristan, at least where the common people are concerned. You think the Medellins are your friends. They only seek to align themselves with the next king. How better than to make an advantageous match for their daughter and place their son, a member of the resistance, where he could do the most harm: by the king's side."

"Dr. Medellin has not yet approved of my attentions to Aleatha and Lucas is not a member of the resistance," Tristan argued. *Not yet, at least.* Lucas felt as strongly as he did about the queen's harsh rule; it would not be too far a stretch for him to join the rapidly swelling number of citizens resisting her reign.

"My poor naive boy," Queen Brigitte said with a sigh, "what do you think that church of theirs is, if not a cover for the resistance?" A cunning look glinted in her eyes as she sat up and placed her feet on the floor "Anything that does not promote loyalty to me *is* resistance. You wish to worship their God, marry their daughter, promote their son, and now I find you publicly condemning me at their behest. I believe 'treason' was the word Lord Windemere used." She stood and crossed to Tristan, tilting his chin so his eyes met hers. Her voice was like the blade of a sword as she asked, "What will it take to break the hold they have over you?"

Cold fear wrapped around Tristan's heart. His mother might not hurt him, but she was very capable of ordering the Medellins killed. "Please, Mother, let them be. I swear to you my speech today was my own foolishness."

"Swear your allegiance to me," Queen Brigitte demanded, her fingers on his chin tightening.

"Of course I am loyal to you," Tristan responded without hesitation. After all, she was his mother.

"No, Tristan," she snapped. "I want you to pledge your faithfulness to me above everything else. I am your mother and your queen. I will not have either the Medellins or their God taking your loyalty from me."

Tristan bit off the sharp reply that rose to his lips. To cross her now could bring death to everyone he cared about, but he could not do as she asked. Not even to save the only family he knew.

"You cannot do it, can you?" his mother sneered. She shoved his chin as she let go and returned to her chaise. "Lord Devon, come in here," she called.

An immaculately dressed man with black hair and the dark eyes of a predator stepped into the room and stood behind her. His eyes raked over Tristan as if sizing him up. "He should be no problem, Your Majesty."

"This is Lord Devon," Queen Brigitte announced. "I have hired him to turn you into the ruler this kingdom needs. His methods are a bit rigorous, but after our little discussion I am afraid they are necessary. He will take you somewhere far from the influence of the Medellins and bring you back when you are ready to lead this nation."

"If I go with him, will you swear not to harm the Medellins?" Tristan attempted to negotiate, knowing full well he had little control over what his mother did to either him or his friends. *Heavenly Father, they are in your hands.*

"The Medellins are in no danger as long as they can no longer turn you against me," Queen Brigitte assured him.

The fear that had gripped his heart turned into a hard ball of dread in his stomach. The ominous stare Lord Devon had fixed on him since entering the room left him with a sense of foreboding. *What have I gotten myself into?*

"When do we leave?"

Chapter 1

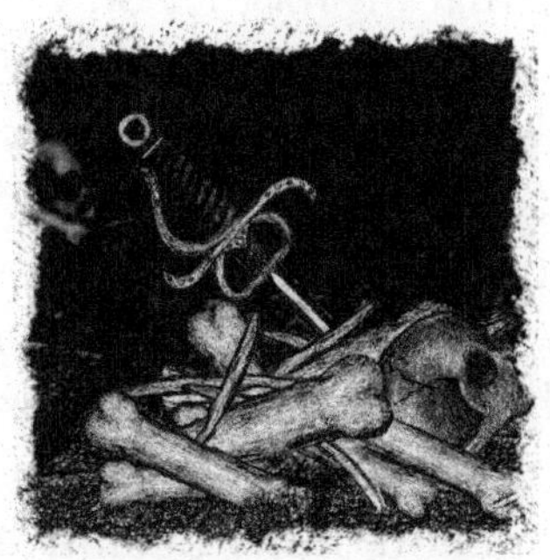

Prince Tristan lay on the night-cooled sand as the rays of the burning desert sun crept over the mountains. The thin blanket that covered his body had done little to protect him from the chill of the night and would do even less to protect him from the intense heat, but he did not dare move to push it off. The dawn itself would soon awaken Devon in the tent pitched nearby, but he could not risk even the slightest movement bringing his tormentor out sooner. These precious few moments with his Lord were the only respite Tristan had each day from the torture Devon had inflicted on him in the name of "training him to take the throne."

Heavenly Father, he prayed, *I cannot go another day. Please, I beg you; have mercy on your servant. Allow this to be the day Devon kills me.* He had prayed the same thing nearly every morning since Devon had begun his "training" in earnest. Today was different. He could not endure another day of Devon's torture. Today would be the day Devon broke him.

A faint rustle from within the tent made Tristan squeeze his eyes shut and bit his lip. Devon would be out at any moment.

My God is always faithful. Tristan moved his lips silently as he repeated to himself a mantra of the few truths he had been able to cling to. *Lucas would never betray me. Aleatha...* A sob nearly choked him. The past year had been a battle over five truths Queen Brigitte had ordered Devon to force him to embrace.

The first truth – that his mother only had his best interests at heart – was attained with minimal struggle. He wanted nothing more than to believe his mother was only doing what she thought was best for him, despite the methods she used.

The second truth – that her harsh rule was necessary to govern the difficult and rebellious people of Boldaria – well, he fought against that one a bit harder. His stand against her cruelty was the reason he had been sent away with Devon. In spite of his strong opinion of her tyranny, he had eventually been forced to agree he knew little about what it took to rule a kingdom.

The third truth – that Aleatha, his beautiful Aleatha, would always be true to him – he had clung to that truth through months of torture. Starvation, scourgings, canings, lack of sleep, lack of water, even poison: every form of torture Devon's twisted mind could invent had been utilized to rob Tristan of the confidence he had in his fiancée. Two days ago, his body battered and his mind in shambles, he had given in to the nagging doubts Devon had planted and nursed.

The final two truths – his faith in Lucas's loyalty and his faith in God – had not weakened. But if he could lose his confidence in Aleatha, he could lose his confidence in anything at all. He no longer wanted God's strength to make it through the day.

Devon's heavy boots crunched on the sand as he stepped out of the tent. Tristan forced himself to breathe rhythmically, hoping Devon would think he was still sleeping. Though nearly a year of abuse had taught him Devon would not care whether he was sleeping or not. His time was up.

"Heavenly Father, let me die!" he whispered.

The footsteps in the sand stopped beside him. "So you want to die, do you, Prince Tristan?" Devon mocked. "As you wish, Your Highness. Today I will make you believe you died and went straight to hell."

A sharp kick to his back made Tristan gasp as he rolled onto his stomach and gritted his teeth against the pain. Warmth soaked the back of his threadbare tunic where Devon's blow had reopened the wounds from the whipping he had given Tristan the day before.

"That is one truth you could never convince me of," Tristan retorted. He drew a ragged breath and continued, "The moment you kill me, I will be waking to see my Savior's face, not your hideous one!"

Another vicious kick rolled Tristan onto his shredded back and forced a cry from his lips. Devon crouched down and gripped him by the front of his tunic, pulling Tristan's face close to his own. "By the time I am done with you, you will be convinced your God would be only too happy to see you burn for eternity."

Tristan's blood ran cold. Devon's black hair, eyes, and goatee made him look like an emissary of Satan himself and lent unnatural credence to his threats.

Heavenly Father, Tristan prayed as he lay his head back against the sand, *I beg you, let him kill me today.*

Devon's mouth widened into a devilish smirk. "No answer, Prince Tristan? You grow weak."

Tristan scrambled for a reply. He could not afford for Devon to feel he was winning. His mother had only authorized Devon to try to break him for a year. If Devon failed in that time, he was to make sure Tristan would never return to the kingdom. That year was almost up. Tristan's only hope for sanity was to wait out the year. He decided to plead physical weakness. "I have eaten twice in the last week, in addition to whatever torment your deviant mind has come up with. Most men would be dead by now, and you wonder why I cannot keep up the witty repartee?"

"Most men would have broken by now!" Devon screamed, throwing Tristan back down to the sand. "A year! One whole year and you still stubbornly refuse to cooperate! What do I have to do to you? You should be a puppet in my hands!"

Cringing, Tristan tried to catch the breath Devon knocked out of him. Devon's rage had brought him to the brink of death twice before, but only to the brink. *Let him go too far today.*

"But today will be different, Your Highness," Devon said with feigned kindness as he helped Tristan to sit up. His kind tone clashed with the malice in his words. "Today is the one-year anniversary of our time together. Your mother has authorized a change. All restrictions are off."

Tristan's eyes widened as he fought the terror that thrilled up his spine. "What do you mean? What restrictions?" If the last year had been under restriction, he could not even begin to comprehend what might be in store now. *Please, God, where are you?*

"She cares for you. She wanted me to do everything in my power to turn your allegiance to her without causing permanent damage, but you have proved so very uncooperative," Devon said. He brushed the dust from Tristan's ragged tunic and gave Tristan a look of eager anticipation that promised Devon would enjoy today far more than Tristan would. "First we celebrate. Let me tend to your wounds, then I have a delicious breakfast waiting for you in the tent."

Devon applied an ointment to the cuts on Tristan's back and bandaged him. He then helped Tristan to his feet and led him to the tent. Tristan followed, dread filling his empty stomach as if with stones. Devon always fed him well, cared for his wounds and let him rest before trying a new, intense session of training. Now with all "restrictions" off…

The smell of hot food reached Tristan before he even set foot in the tent. His stomach rumbled in spite of his fear. On a brightly colored rug in the middle of the tent lay hot mince pies, fresh apples, roasted chicken, and sweet pastries.

"Eat." Devon waved his hand toward the food. "Anything you want. All you want."

As Tristan knelt beside the rug, every instinct in his starving body told him to devour as much as he could before Devon changed his mind, but a memory held him back.

"How do I know this is not poisoned like last time?" He kept his eyes on the food as if it were a viper. The poison ordeal had been one of the worst things Devon had put him through. He suspected by Devon's treatment of him afterward that his tormentor had considerable trouble bringing him back from that one.

"There really is no way to know for sure," Devon admitted as he knelt across from Tristan and traced a finger over the rosy curve of an apple. "You will just have to trust me."

But I cannot trust you. Tristan stared down at the food as he tried to decide. Devon had tried the "I am your savior, trust me with your life" method of control for two months early on. It had not worked then; it certainly was not going to work now. However, his watering mouth and growling stomach were harder to ignore than his fears. Perhaps if it were poisoned this time, it would kill him quickly. He picked up a mince pie in one hand and an apple in the other, savoring each delicious bite. He ate until he was satisfied, and then pushed the food away before he became too full. He had made that painful mistake before and was not about to repeat it.

"Finished?" Devon asked. "Good, then rest. We have a busy afternoon." Devon gestured to a corner of the tent where a pile of soft pillows lay.

Too exhausted to argue or care about what Devon was planning, Tristan lay on the pillows. He would know soon enough.

*****

The rough shaking of his shoulder awakened him.

"Wake up," Devon ordered. "We have work to do."

Blinking his eyes, Tristan looked at Devon. The bright sunlight shown through the open tent flaps behind Devon, and Tristan realized he could have only slept a couple of hours. Still, he was surprised at how good rest and food made him feel. He slowly stood to his feet, knowing he was walking straight into whatever trap Devon had planned for him, but powerless to avoid it.

"Come, Your Highness. We are going to go for a little walk." Devon handed him a robe and a pair of sandals like Tristan had seen the Bedouins wear. "You will need these."

Tristan dressed and followed Devon from the tent. Standing outside were two camels. Devon mounted one and motioned for Tristan to do the same. Tristan hesitated. Food, rest, clothes, and a camel seemed too good to be true. There had to be a catch, and usually it was a very painful one.

"We are just going for a short ride," Devon called. "You have nothing to fear."

"As long as I obey you implicitly." Tristan glared at Devon as he mounted and turned the camel to follow him.

"As always, Prince," Devon answered as he led his camel out into the desert.

They rode into the desert until they were out of sight of the camp.

"I received a letter from your mother last night," Devon commented.

"What, pray, does that mean to me," Tristan snapped. After this last year, he was pretty sure he did not want to know.

"I had written telling her of your stubbornness. I told her I thought I could convince you to cooperate soon, but I might need to take drastic measures," Devon said as if discussing something mundane, like the sweltering heat.

A chill coursed through Tristan in spite of the temperature. After a year of nearly every form of suffering a human could endure, Devon talked of drastic measures?

"She asked me to give you one more chance to accept reason." Devon turned back to Tristan and added, "She really does care for you, Tristan, in her own way. She only wishes to gain the absolute allegiance she deserves as your mother."

Tristan did not respond. He had lost that battle months ago.

"She has never given up hope on you," Devon continued, allowing his camel to drop back so he was riding beside Tristan. "She has never stopped asking about your well-being. You know she only wants what is best for you. She fears your loyalty to the faithless Medellins is leading you astray. I have been assigned to mold you into the strong monarch she knows you will have to be to guide Boldaria's rebellious people when she is gone."

"I do not question that she thinks she is doing what is best for me and the kingdom," Tristan lashed out. "That does not mean I need to agree with either her goals or her methods."

"Certainly no child agrees with his mother's methods," Devon sympathized. "Does not even your own Bible teach that God's methods of discipline can be unpleasant?"

Devon waved his hand to cut off Tristan's retort.

"At least she has not abandoned you like your 'beloved' Aleatha," Devon said, his piercing black eyes taunting Tristan, "or betrayed you like your 'friend' Lucas."

"Lucas would never betray me," Tristan returned. He winced at his own response. His unconscious omission of Aleatha's name could not fail to go unnoticed by Devon.

"But you doubt your beloved's faithfulness?" Devon cut off Tristan's reply again as he pulled his camel to a stop.

"Never mind. Your mother thought you might need some extra persuading."

"Nothing my mother would say could change my mind." Tristan reined in his own camel as he watched Devon reach into his robe and remove two sheets of paper.

"That is why she thought you would appreciate their own words." Devon grinned as he selected one of the pieces of paper and leaned forward to pass it to Tristan. "This is a copy of the banns published for Aleatha and a Marc Erosthanes. I believe you know him."

Tristan took the paper from Devon's hand, his last shred of hope dying as he read the words written there. Aleatha was to have married Marc on the fifth of February, a month ago by Tristan's closest guess. Tristan crumpled the paper in his fist and slumped over the neck of his camel in grief. Marc was the biggest rake in his mother's court. He was also Tristan's biggest competitor for Aleatha's hand. Tristan had thought Aleatha could not stand the sight of Marc. Evidently, a year could change a lot.

"I am sorry," Devon said. He drew his camel closer and laid a hand on Tristan's arm. "Your mother knew all along she was not worthy of your love. She tells me your devoted Aleatha was already with child."

Chapter 2

The mocking tone in Devon's voice reminded Tristan he had to put on a strong front, or lose everything. *Heavenly Father,* he prayed as he tried to compose himself as well as he could, *why will You not help me? I cannot take anymore of this.*

"Will you still persist in your confidence in her *faithfulness*?" Devon asked.

Willing himself to meet Devon's gaze without wavering, Tristan gritted his teeth and remained silent.

"Perhaps you are ready to listen to reason," Devon said, giving Tristan an appraising look. "Will you now abandon this foolish confidence in Lucas's loyalty? Surely if his sister could betray you, so could he. The love between you and Aleatha was stronger than the friendship between you and Lucas, was it not?"

"I do not care what you say, or what those papers you have in your hand claim," Tristan insisted through clenched teeth. "Lucas would never plot to kill me."

Devon met Tristan's stare with a challenge in his own eyes as he selected another paper and held it in front of him. "I have here a letter written in Lucas Medellin's own hand agreeing to murder you himself, for the sake of the people." Devon handed the paper to Tristan. "Who better than another Brutus? No one can get as close as a trusted friend. It's like I told you, the Medellins were only using you, turning you against your mother as a pawn of the resistance."

Tristan snatched the letter away from Devon. It appeared to be from Lucas to the leader of an underground resistance group. In it Lucas admitted Tristan had "become a danger to the well-being of the people" and further agreed he was in the best position to "mercifully end the prince's life and the threat he poses to freedom." Tristan fought to keep his hand steady as he examined the wording and handwriting more closely for some sign of forgery. He saw none. Lucas's precise, clear handwriting was as familiar to him as his own. He swallowed hard and looked up at Devon, shaken but still defiant. "If I return to Boldaria as you and my mother intend, I will certainly be a danger to the people. I can only hope Lucas would have the mercy to stop me before I become the tyrant my mother is."

"Read the letter again." Devon laughed. "Your friend Lucas does not say 'if' you become a danger; he believes you already are. Look at the date. The letter was written the week before you left with me. You mother probably saved your life by sending you out here. Breaking the hold the Medellins had over you was one of the greatest reasons your mother had for sending you out here with me. She never wished to hurt you, but their power over you was too great."

The doubts Devon was planting took root as Tristan read the letter again. *Heavenly Father, I am losing. Give me a way out!*

"You may as well just face it," Devon said, leaning forward as if sensing Tristan's weakness and moving in for the kill. "The only person who truly cares about you is your mother. Even your God has abandoned you."

"God has not abandoned me." Tristan fought to keep his voice steady even as his body began to tremble. "He will never abandon me."

"He has abandoned you," Devon insisted. He drew his camel so close that the side of the animal pressed against Tristan's leg and leaned his face close to Tristan's. "Or do you mean to tell me this past year has been evidence of his 'care?' Your mother put restrictions on what I was to do; what has your God done? What future does this 'faithful' God the Medellins taught you to worship have waiting for you? Your true love in the arms of another man and a knife placed in your back by your best friend? Your mother offers you a kingdom. All you have to do is swear allegiance to her – and only to her."

Squeezing his eyes closed, Tristan tried to fight off the wave of panic that began to overwhelm him. *My God is always faithful. Lucas would never betray me,* he forced himself to repeat. He must not give in to the doubts that were growing in his mind. *My God is always faithful. Lucas would never betray me,* he repeated again, this time with more confidence. *Give me the strength to conquer my doubts.*

"What is your answer, Prince Tristan?" Devon pressed, with victory in his voice.

Taking a deep breath, Tristan opened his eyes and gave the only answer he had left to give. He spat in Devon's face, still inches from his own and replied, "You can give that answer to my mother."

Devon's face grew purple with rage. His hand shot out, grabbed Tristan by the front of his robe, and flung him from his camel to the burning sand. Before Tristan could get to his feet, Devon had dismounted and was standing over him with a short dagger in his right hand. "Your mother has authorized a final attempt to persuade you. Personally, I hope you can resist this one as well. I would love nothing more than watching you die!"

One more test, Heavenly Father. Tristan fell back against the sand. *Help me pass it, then please let me die.*

"And I would not go wishing for death." Devon knelt and yanked Tristan to his feet. "I can assure you the death I have planned for you will be more agony than anything you have endured so far.

"Take off your robe and sandals," Devon ordered, gesturing at Tristan with his dagger.

"Do you think I am mad?" Tristan rebelled, crossing his arms over his chest.

Devon drew back his hand and struck Tristan across the face with enough force to knock him back to the ground. "Do not think you can goad me into killing you now. It will not work and you will only cause yourself unnecessary pain. Take off the robe and sandals."

Tristan allowed the robe to fall to the sand and sat on it to keep from burning himself as he removed his sandals. He had a pretty good idea what Devon had planned. Without a robe and sandals, Tristan would be exposed to the sweltering afternoon sun. He could not survive long in the heat of the day without protection. And without water, which he somehow doubted Devon would provide.

"And your tunic." Devon held out his dagger and pointed it at Tristan's tattered shirt.

Tristan paused halfway through unlacing one sandal and looked up at Devon. "Surely you jest."

With a swift motion, Devon severed the laces on the front of Tristan's tunic, cutting through the bandages he had put on him earlier. The point of the dagger sliced a shallow cut along Tristan's breastbone.

Letting out his breath with a hiss, Tristan pressed his hand to the cut. It was not bleeding much, but it stung from the sweat soaking his body.

"Your tunic," Devon repeated, his voice threatening.

He had no other option, so Tristan pulled his tunic over his head and stood up on the robe. Throwing the tunic and the loose bandages to the side, he turned back just as Devon finished pounding the last of four long stakes into the sand.

He did not have time to wonder what Devon was doing. Devon pulled several lengths of rope from the pack of his camel and shoved Tristan backward onto the sand. Tristan cried out in pain as the sand seared the wounds on his back. He lifted himself onto his elbows, but was driven back to the ground as Devon yanked his right arm from under him and straight out to his side.

"What are you doing?" Tristan gritted his teeth against the pain. Fear welled up inside him as he struggled against Devon's iron grip.

Without answering, Devon looped one length of rope around his wrist until it bit into the skin and tied the ends to the rope to one stake. When he was satisfied Tristan was secure, Devon went around to Tristan's left side and repeated the process on that arm.

The stake held fast as Tristan yanked his right arm as hard as he could. He dropped his head back with a groan. Devon meant to give him more than a sunburn or a bad case of dehydration. He meant to bake him alive. The sun beating down on his exposed face and chest was scorching his skin already.

After staking out Tristan's legs as well, Devon stood and surveyed his work. "I think you will not be walking away from this one."

"What are the rules to this game, Devon?" Tristan asked. He could not actually see his tormentor. Not only did looking up at Devon cause the blinding sun to glare into his eyes, but sweat was running into his eyes as well. "Same as usual? I agree to cooperate, beg you for mercy, and you come and rescue me?"

"Not this time." Devon crouched beside him and snorted as he said, "Do you think I would be crazy enough to stay out here without protection during the hottest part of the day? I will be back in an hour. If the heat has not made you completely ready to cooperate by then…"

"You leave me here," Tristan finished. His mouth was dry, either from the heat or from the fear coursing through him. He was ready to die, but he did not welcome the slow, painful death offered to him by Devon. Still, what else should he have expected?

"Happy Birthday, Your Highness," Devon mocked. The sand crunched as he took a step toward the camels. "Your mother said to be sure to mention it was not too late for a coronation celebration when we get back. If you get back, that is."

Birthday. Coronation celebration. A light went on in Tristan's mind. He wetted his lips as well as he could with his parched tongue. "That is what this past year was about, was it not, Devon? I am twenty-one today. If I were home, I would be crowned king tonight. My mother would lose her power."

Devon's footsteps returned to his side and Tristan felt a slight change in temperature as Devon's shadow fell across his face. He opened his eyes to see Devon kneeling over him again. The sun glowed around him, making him look more shadow than human.

"She cannot have someone in power who will undo all the work she has accomplished over the last twenty-one years," Devon answered.

"You mean she cannot have someone in power she cannot control." Tristan squinted to get a better look at Devon reaction. He did not look pleased. "She told you to break me, create me into her puppet, or not to bring me back at all. This was all about her power!"

Devon scowled. Tristan blinked the sweat out of his eyes. His outburst had given him strength. He prepared himself for one final question, a question he hoped would explain the previous year of torment. "Were you there when she killed my father?"

"How old do you think I am?" Devon scoffed. "That was all her doing."

A strange rush of emotion filled Tristan. Elation at finally catching Devon off guard, of gaining one point on him in his twisted mental game. Grief and pain at the confirmation of the rumor he had refused to believe. His stomach churned. "My father would not be controlled by her either. She killed him just as she is having you kill me."

"Prince Tristan," Devon said, his voice like silk as he recovered, "whatever gave you the idea she killed your father? She loved your father."

"Just as she 'loves' me?" Tristan was surprised at the depth of bitterness in his voice. He licked his lips again. "Lucas told me the day before you took me out here that she had killed my father. He warned me she would never let me live to claim the throne from her. Lucas was right."

He stopped, frozen by his own words. He repeated them to himself, "Lucas *was* right."

Rage passed across Devon's face, a rage greater than anything Tristan had seen over the last year. Still, Tristan pushed on. He had nothing to lose and his sanity to gain. "Why would he have warned me of my mother if he were planning to kill me himself? Lucas and his family have always looked after me as if they were my own family. You have lost, Devon. Everything you have worked for this last year is gone. My mother was looking after her own interests, not mine. Her cruelty and manipulation is a crime, not a necessity. Lucas did not betray me. And my God may have allowed me to suffer this last year, but he has given me the strength to defeat you." His speech had left him drained, but it had been worth it.

"You forget Aleatha, my prince," Devon returned, his voice trembling and his teeth clenched. "She abandoned you and married another. Or do you have some magic way of disputing the banns I read you?"

The banns could have been faked, but Tristan had no way to be sure. He sighed, closed his eyes and turned his head away from Devon. "If she is married, it is because she thought me dead. Which will be true in a couple of hours anyway, will it not? I wish her happiness, if not through her husband, then through her child."

With a roar, Devon stood and kicked Tristan in the side. Tristan cried out in pain when his body was forced away from the stake that held him down and his arm was wrenched from his socket . Without a word, Devon turned and stomped toward the camels.

"Do not bother returning in an hour," Tristan said, panting from the heat and the pain. "My answer will not change."

"Do not worry, Your Highness," Devon said, his voice distant as he rode away. "I will be back, if only to watch you die."

If I last that long, Tristan thought. He had nothing to drink since that morning and he was already lightheaded from lack of water. The pain in his exposed skin was excruciating, and he found himself eager for the end.

Heavenly Father, be merciful, he prayed, gritting his teeth and focusing on his prayer to avoid thinking about his pain. *Thank you for sparing my sanity. I beg you to allow death to come easily. Bless Lucas and Aleatha.* He paused. He felt cold and clammy and found it increasingly difficult to concentrate. *Give them happiness. And, please, Lord, send someone to bring peace to Boldaria and end my mother's reign of tyranny.*

Lord. Welcome me. To your kingdom. His pain ended as he succumbed to the heat.

*****

A sharp pain to the left side of his face, and another to his right dragged him back to consciousness. The pain from his burned skin flooded over him as he squinted his swollen eyes to see Devon standing over him. This time he had chosen to stand out of the way of the sun, so its rays continued to pound Tristan's already seared skin.

"I told you I would be back, Prince Tristan," Devon taunted. "Do you have an answer for your mother? Or do I get the pleasure of watching you die?"

Tristan moved his mouth to answer, but no sound came out. His tongue felt thick and cottony and his throat was cracked and dry. He tried again. "Tell her I won," he rasped, his voice little more than a weak whisper. "I defeated you. She cannot control me."

"I hoped you would say that. I will be returning immediately to give her your message." Devon drew a dagger from beneath his robe. "But first, I want to leave you with something to remember me by."

With a quick motion, Devon brought the dagger down and plunged it into the taut flesh near Tristan's left shoulder and pulled it back out again. Tristan's cry of agony was only a weak croak as he strained against his bonds. Moaning, he settled back on the sand as the warm blood ran down his parched skin. He slipped back into unconsciousness.

Devon struck him across the face, jolting him back awake. "You will not go that easily, Prince," Devon hissed. "You have little time left, but I mean to make sure you enjoy every moment of it."

Pain and dehydration left Tristan's mind too fogged to answer. Soon, nothing Devon could do would wake him. The pain in his shoulder and across his burned body was unbearable. He was slipping away again. Devon grabbed him in a choke hold and tried to shake him back to consciousness, but no effort could keep him awake. Peace flooded over Tristan as he passed out for the last time.

* * * * *

Devon dropped Tristan's limp body back onto the sand and stood in disgust. Tristan's chest still rose and fell in barely perceptible breaths, but he was as good as dead.

A cloud of dust on the horizon drew Devon's attention. He shielded his eyes with his hand and tried to determine the cause. Still a good way off was a caravan. Swearing, he looked back down at Tristan. He did not want to be caught anywhere near the body when it was discovered.

Mounting his camel, Devon glanced back at Tristan. He watched for a moment, needing to be certain the prince was dead. The shallow motions of Tristan's chest slowed until he could no longer see any motion at all. Satisfied with his work, Devon turned his camel and hurried out of the path of the caravan. He had everything he needed from the campsite; he was free to report to the queen.

She would be happy to hear her throne was now secure.

Chapter 3

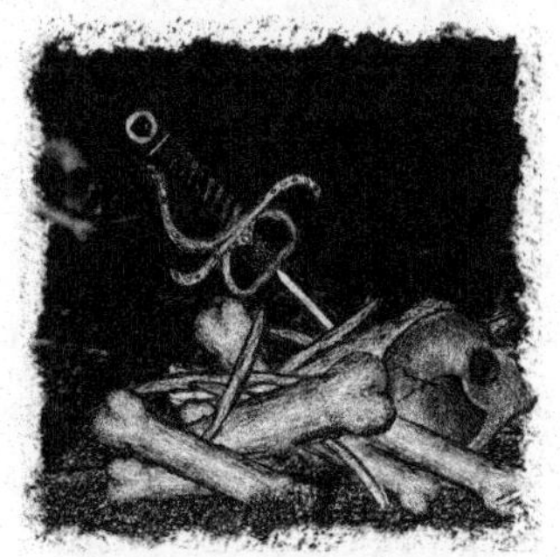

Lucas Medellin slipped into his father's medical chamber beside the queen's bedchambers, closed the door behind him, and leaned against the door. He rubbed his hands over his face and through his hair, thankful to escape the clamoring courtiers and servants. He hated the intrigues and imagined illnesses of the palace. His real passion was for the charity work he did in the city.

The previous night, once he had finished working with his father, he had gone to the worst part of town as he often did. A desperate mother had begged for his help with her small son. The little boy had tried to climb the family's market stall and had fallen, breaking his arm. It had been a simple break, easy to set, but the relief and gratitude in the mother's eyes stood out in his mind. How he wished he were there now. At least there the gratitude was real, and evil was recognized for what it was. He compared that memory with disgust to that of the beautiful courtier who had just tried to entice him when he went to check on her feigned illness. Ever since Tristan had left, Lucas awaited his daily visits to the palace with dread. However, as his father's apprentice, he still had a few more months before he would be free to do as he pleased.

Dr. Gaius Medellin's tiny medical chamber was attached to the queen's personal quarters. There was little room for both Lucas and his father to work together in the cramped space. A intricately engraved door separated them from the queen's bedchambers. The wall to his left was lined with a long table for mixing medicines below a row of cabinets full of flasks and boxes containing herbs, minerals, and other things his father had collected from renowned physicians and apothecaries the world over. Stepping away from the door, he went to the table his father used to prepare his medicines. Each night he was tasked with setting out the vials his father would need to mix the queen's sleeping draught. His father, the queen's personal physician, was the only one allowed to actually mix the medicine, but Lucas had been setting out the vials for three months now.

One by one he took down the vials, pausing only to look at the vial of Passion Flower Extract his father purchased from some Spanish Missionaries returning from the Americas. It was the most potent ingredient in the elixir, only a few drops were needed to help the queen sleep through the night, more than that and she would never awaken.

Lucas's brown eyes scanned the row of vials he had set out on the tabletop, double-checking to be certain he had all of them. He knew all the correct proportions, but the queen feared poison more than anything. The only person she seemed to trust was his father.

The sound of the door opening behind him caused him to turn. His father stepped in and closed the door to the hall.

"You did well today, Lucas," Dr. Gaius Medellin said, laying an appreciative hand on his son's shoulder.

A smile brightened Lucas's face as he looked down at the shorter man. Compliments from his father were rare, especially over the last year. "I really do appreciate the training, Father."

He was not as thankful, however, for the necessity of spending everyday at the palace. The queen seemed to take a perverse pleasure in all things evil, often feeling no need to hide her actions from him or his father. His disgust over her wickedness had caused no little tension between him and his father. Lucas turned his attention back to the vials. Anytime they talked about their medical work, it ended in a fight. He was not in the mood for another tonight.

His father looked at him as if determining if Lucas truly was grateful. Deciding in his son's favor, he relaxed and said, "I know you do, son."

"Dr. Medellin, are you in there?" the queen's musical voice called from her quarters. "Come here, please."

Dr. Medellin turned in the cramped chamber and pushed the door open. Lucas followed close behind.

The ornate decor of the room contrasted sharply to the functional medical chamber they left behind. Queen Brigitte lounged on a chaise. Her knee-length, ebony hair was braided with a gold ribbon and she wore a shimmering gold dress. Even at nearly fifty, she still possessed a stunning beauty that brought even much younger men to their knees. Lucas had ceased to be impressed many years ago. The first week he had come to the palace with his father, he had witnessed her slit the throat of a messenger who had brought her upsetting news. He and his father had been forced to clean up the mess before anyone else came into the room. Lucas shuddered as he pushed the graphic memory out of his mind. Was it any wonder he hated coming to the palace?

"Doctor, I am expecting a special visitor tonight." The queen rose to her feet and crossed the room to a large mirror mounted on the wall. She examined herself in the mirror, smoothed away a few stray hairs, and adjusted the ample skirt of her dress. "I will not be needing my sleeping potion right away. Please wait in your chamber until I call."

"As you wish, my Queen." Dr. Medellin bowed his acknowledgment.

Queen Brigitte turned her attention to Lucas. "Young man, your name is Lucas, I believe?"

In the nearly seven years Lucas had been his father's apprentice, the queen had never acknowledged his presence, much less addressed him. He swallowed hard and bowed low, as he had seen his father do a thousand times, "Yes, Your Majesty."

"You may be interested in what my visitor has to say." The corner of her mouth twitched upward with a hint of sadistic enjoyment. "You were a special friend of my son, were you not?"

"Yes, Your Majesty." Lucas felt his heart pounding. *News of Tristan?* He tried to hide his excitement. He feared the queen was toying with him, as he had seen her do with so many others.

"Devon is coming to report to me tonight." The queen turned with a swish of her long, full skirts and sat back down on the chaise. She lay back in a relaxed position and said, "I hope for some good news."

"Good news, Your Majesty?" Dr. Medellin asked, his voice hard. "Good for whom?"

Lucas winced. Sometimes his father could be freer in his opinions to the queen than he would like. Prince Tristan's frequent stays at their house before the queen sent him away with Devon had made him a favorite of the entire Medellin household.

Queen Brigitte chuckled, taking his comment in the same good humor she usually took with him. "Why me, of course. Is not anything good for a queen, good for her kingdom?"

"I was thinking about your son, Prince Tristan," Dr. Medellin continued. "I hardly think Lord Devon's treatment over the last year has been 'good' for him."

"I know you rarely approve of my methods, but even you have to admit this country needs a strong ruler. I intend for my son to be that ruler. Anything that attains that goal will be good for him in the long run. You coddle him, Doctor, treat him as one of your own. He was born to be a powerful king, not a compassionate physician." The queen turned at the sound of a knock at her door. "That must be Devon now. You may be dismissed to your medical chambers. I will call for you when I am finished."

Dr. Medellin whirled on his heels and stormed out of the queen's bedchamber. He stomped into his medical chamber and jerked the door closed behind him, slamming it into Lucas who scuttled in after him.

"'Good news,'" Dr. Medellin mocked, gesturing to the door behind him. He turned to Lucas, his voice filled with hatred. "Not for Prince Tristan, certainly. She never loved that boy! She has only used him for her own ends, no matter what the cost. Is it any wonder he sought refuge at our home?" He gripped his hands behind him and began to pace the tiny room. "He was like a son to your mother and me." He stopped and looked at Lucas. "And a brother to you and your sister. Now that witch has the audacity of suggesting that we might be interested in her 'good news'?"

"Not so loud, please," Lucas pleaded. "If she hears you…"

"What will she do? Kill me?" Dr. Medellin laughed. "No, son, she needs me… and fears me." He turned to the vials lined up on his table in preparation to mix her nightcap, rested his hands on the edge of the table, and leaned over them. He picked up the tiny vial of Passion Flower Extract and turned it in his hand. "She knows how easy it would be for me to mix these in just the right proportions. Just a few drops too much of this and her wickedness would end forever." Dr. Medellin stared at the vial in his hand and murmured, "The Good Lord knows how many times I have been tempted to do just that."

"Never, Father." Lucas stepped forward, alarmed. "You would never harm anyone, even Queen Brigitte."

"Would I not?" Dr. Medellin turned to him with a haunted, remorseful look in his gray-blue eyes. "Where do you think she got the poison she used to murder King Justin? She stole it from me, and I was too slow to realize her intent until the king was lying dead before me. Now she intends to kill her son also. Perhaps we would all be in a better situation if I had given in to my temptations long ago."

"But perhaps Tristan lives." Lucas laid a hand on his father's shoulder. "She said she hoped for good news, after all."

Dr. Medellin shrugged his son's hand off his shoulder and glared at him. "Do you not realize after the last year of her taunting that the only 'good news' for Prince Tristan would be his death? If he is to return as she intends, it will be only as her puppet, a pawn to work her wickedness through for another lifetime." He turned and stormed to the door leading out to the hall. As he prepared to go, he turned back to Lucas and delivered a parting shot, "For all our sakes, including Prince Tristan's, I hope the only news Lord Devon brings is the news of Prince Tristan's death."

*****

The slamming door rang in his ears as Lucas sat on the padded bench in his father's medical chamber and put his head in his hands. Perhaps his father was right, but he could not abandon slim hope that Tristan might be returning to them.

Dear Lord, he prayed for the thousandth time since Tristan had left, *be with him, wherever he is.*

"It is over then?" Queen Brigitte's normally cold, emotionless voice seemed almost regretful as it drifted through the door separating her from Lucas.

Lucas edged closer to the door and nudged it open a crack.

"I am sorry, Your Majesty," a deep, suave male voice apologized. "I am afraid he was just too stubborn. As you said, if you could not have his complete loyalty, he could not be allowed to return. For the good of the kingdom."

Lucas froze with his hand on the door, torn between the need to hear news of Tristan and the loathing to hear about more of the queen's cruelties. There were nights he had trouble sleeping with the knowledge of her atrocities to strangers; he doubted he could handle hearing of her treatment of his best friend. The desire to hear news of Tristan won out as he dropped his hand to his lap and leaned closer to the gap in the door.

"In your last letter you told me he was about to break," the queen said. Her voice was edged with steel. "How could you fail? Failure is inexcusable."

"His faith, Your Majesty." Devon's voice remained calm and unruffled. "We did not anticipate the depth of Prince Tristan's faith in his God."

Thank you, Lord, Lucas prayed, relieved Tristan had at least stayed faithful to God, whatever else may have happened.

"I sent you out there to break him, not kill him. You swore you could break him!" the queen said, her voice rising to a frenzied pitch.

Perhaps listening was not such a good idea, Lucas realized as his stomach clenched. She had taken that tone right before she had killed the messenger, and nearly every other time she had committed some gross act of cruelty. Lucas felt the bile rise in his throat at the flood of memories. Her violence made him sick, and the fights with his father over returning to the castle renewed with a vengeance each time. He stood to his feet and turned to go.

"Break him or eliminate him," Devon reminded her. "It was the last resort, but I can assure you your son is no longer a threat to your throne."

"He is dead then?" the queen asked, her tone uncertain. "You are sure?"

That question had driven Lucas to eavesdrop in the first place, and it kept him from leaving now. He knew he should go, he did not really *want* to know anything more, but he needed to be sure of what had happened to his friend.

"Absolutely sure," Devon assured her. "I killed him with my own hand."

Reality hit Lucas as if a fist had punched him in the gut, even though he thought he had prepared himself for the news of Tristan's death. *How do you really prepare yourself to hear your best friend was murdered by his own mother?*

There was a pause before the queen responded, her voice calm and resigned, "How did he die?"

That was it. Lucas left the suffocating room. He was not about to sit around and listen to the gory details of his best friend's death. Even if the queen reveled in that – which he was sure she did – he certainly did not.

Without stopping, he dashed out of the castle and directly to his horse. He was done here. He was going home. Aleatha needed to know, and he needed to be out of this evil place.

And he wished to heaven he would never need to return again.

Chapter 4

The Medellins' city home was an imposing stone structure, near enough to the castle for Dr. Medellin to assist the queen at a moment's notice, but distant enough to give them a little privacy.

Far too little, Lucas thought. His eyes burned as he dismounted and threw the reins to a waiting servant. Lucas nodded his thanks absently. The houses on either side nearly touched theirs and people seeking his father's advice came and went throughout the day. *Perhaps I could persuade Mother and Father to take a trip to our country estate for a few months. Even if Father refuses to go, they may at least allow me to take Aleatha. She will need the time away after the news of Tristan's death.*

He sucked in a breath, steeling himself for the unpleasant task ahead. That she would take it badly was certain, the question was how badly? Father had warned them both

Tristan would not be returning, but she had been clinging to hope, just as he had been. He had been Tristan's closest friend, but she and Tristan had been planning to be married as soon as he was crowned king. *Lord, give me the strength to be there for her.*

"Lucas, is that you?" his mother called from the kitchen. Even though they had several servants to help with the housework, she always insisted on helping make dinner for her family. She came out drying her hands. "Dinner is nearly ready. Is your father… What is wrong?"

With his lip clenched between his teeth, Lucas took in a ragged breath. "It is Tristan, Mother. Lord Devon returned today, without him."

Lady Joanna Medellin pressed her fist to her mouth to hold back a sob. Lucas embraced her and let her cry on his shoulder. He waited until she calmed down a little before asking, "Is Aleatha home?"

"She is in the garden, I believe." She looked up at him, sniffled, and wiped at her eyes with the towel she had used to dry her hands. "Lucas, you know your father is right. It is better…"

"No, Mother." Lucas raised a hand to stop her. His barely suppressed emotions surged to the surface. His voice boiled with all of the hatred, anger and grief he was feeling. "I cannot believe this is better for anyone but that hateful Queen. If I ever have to return to that horrible castle, it will be too soon."

"Please, do not let your father hear you say that," his mother pleaded. "You know how he feels about your attitude toward the castle. I hate to see you two argue."

"Then perhaps you had better tell him I will not be down for dinner," Lucas snapped, "and I seriously doubt Aleatha will either."

He spun away from his mother and stormed up the stairs. *How I wish Father had poisoned the queen as he had suggested! In fact, I cannot swear I will not do it myself if Father forces me back to that evil place.* Guilt pricked his heart at his vengeful thoughts. The last thing he ever wanted was to sink to the queen's level. Yes, it would be better for them all if he never set foot in that wretched palace again.

The rooftop of the Medellins' home contained the most beautiful garden in the city. Even the royal gardens could not compare with its serenity and beauty. Lady Medellin and Aleatha spent many hours tending to it lovingly; weeding, pruning, watering, and enjoying the blooms. The variety of flowers rivaled the variety of Dr. Medellin's medicines. Each place he traveled, he brought back another lovely plant for his wife to add to her collection.

Lucas stepped onto the rooftop and paused. The smell of fragrant blossoms, though usually welcome to him after a hard day at the castle, seemed cloying and oppressive. The radiance of the fiery sunset and the bright rainbow of flowers mocked the darkness he was feeling. Aleatha stood with her back to him, humming to herself as she watered a cluster of tulips. The sun glimmered on her sleek, brown hair and lent a glow to her fair skin.

"Aleatha," he said, loath to interrupt her happiness.

"Oh, Lucas, welcome home!" She turned to him with a joyful expression that faded when she saw his face. "Whatever is the matter?"

"It is Tristan," he said. The words tumbled from his mouth. Any plan he had to break the news to her gently went with them. "I am sorry, but he is… he is…"

He never got any further. He did not need to. Aleatha began sobbing. She dropped the watering can with a clatter and sagged to the ground, unmindful of the puddle spreading around her.

Lucas sat beside her, put his arm around her, and let her cry. His own tears streamed down his face as they grieved for the death of their friend.

*****

Laying on his bed and staring at the ceiling, Lucas listened to the muffled sounds of his sister's sobs penetrating the wall between their rooms. Three weeks had passed since he had broken the news of Tristan's death to her. For three weeks she had cried herself to sleep every night. Not that it was keeping him up; he would have been unable to sleep regardless. Grief mingled with the dread of his inevitable return to the castle stole his sleep every night. Father had not pressed the issue yet, but it was only a matter of time before the argument would come.

Aleatha's sobs quieted. At least she had found some sleep. Lucas rolled over in his bed. *Now, if only I could.*

A muted knock at his door roused him. He threw back the covers, crossed the cold floor to the door, opened it a crack, and peered into the dark hallway.

"Master Lucas, a boy is here to see you," Addis, his father's manservant, said. "He says it is urgent."

"To see me?" Lucas whispered. "Are you sure he does not want Father?"

"He specifically asked for you."

"Give me a minute to dress." Lucas closed the door. He did not bother to light a lamp, dressing only by the moonlight. *Perhaps the boy has come from the Shambles.* All his spare time was spent giving medical aid to the people who could least afford it. His father did not approve; he had better hopes for his son than for him to become a poor common doctor. Still, it was nearly an hour's walk to the Medellin's estate from the city; he could not imagine anyone making the trip this late at night.

He strapped on his sword, grabbed his medical bag, and slipped out of his room, through the hall, and down the stairs to the door. A dirty boy of about eight or nine stood twisting his tattered hat in his hands and staring at the Medellins' home as if he were standing in the castle itself.

"You Lucas?" the boy asked as soon as Lucas stepped into view. The boy's eyes widened in recognition. "Doc?"

"I am," Lucas affirmed. Only the people of the Shambles called him that. "How did you find me?"

"The man said you'd be here." The boy jerked his head out the open door into the night. "C'mon, there's not much time."

"What man?" Lucas grabbed a lantern, struggling to light it as he followed the boy. "Much time for what?"

The boy did not answer, but simply turned toward the road to town.

"Wait." Lucas grabbed the boy by the arm. "We will take my horse."

He set the boy on his horse, mounted quickly behind him, and urged his horse into a gentle gallop. A quick explanation to the gate keeper was all it took to allow them to pass into the streets of the city, where the boy slid off Lucas's horse and dashed down the street.

"'Urry up, e's bad sick," the boy called over his shoulder, not slowing down as he wove his way through the dark streets. "Mightn't make it 'til we get there."

Weaving through the narrow, debris scattered street on horseback, made it difficult to keep up with the boy in the dark. Every so often the boy would pause, glance behind him, and call, "Got to 'urry, not much time!"

The buildings lining the street were dingy and dilapidated. Litter lay in the streets and trash filled the gutters. The smell of human filth weighed down the air around them. A large rat scurried across his path, causing his horse to shy and whinny. Lucas leaned forward and whispered gently to his horse, bringing him under control as he looked around. Unlike the streets in the part of town he lived in, which were quiet and vacant by this time of night, people milled about the Shambles at all hours. He never liked to come here during the night. Not that he was afraid any harm would come to him; over time the people of the Shambles came to respect what he did. Some even seemed to like him. None would dare harm the kind "Young Doc" that helped heal their children and bind up their injuries. No, he did not fear harm. Even so, the Shambles was intimidating enough during the day, much less at night.

I've lost the boy, Lucas realized with alarm. *There.* He was squeezing through an opening in a sagging, battered building. Lucas raised his lantern. The building looked like it could collapse at any moment. The entrance was little more than a hole where two thick beams kept the rest of the wall from touching the ground. *I doubt anyone would live in a place like this, no matter how desperate.*

The boy stuck his head out the opening in the wall and beckoned for Lucas to follow. Lucas tied his horse to a broken beam and dismounted. Ducking beneath the beams, he followed the boy down a flight of roughly cut stone steps into the cellar. Like the rest of the Shambles, it was filthy, if possible, even more so. The number of rats and other vermin covering the floor made it seem as if this were the source of all the rest of the pests in the Shambles. The smell of decay and refuse and the soft material squishing beneath his feet indicated the abandoned building served as something of the neighborhood dump. He reached the bottom of the stairs and turned. A large bundle of rags lay on the floor against the stairs. The boy knelt next to the rags and waited for Lucas.

In the dim light of his lantern, Lucas could barely make out the features of the man lying motionless on the rags. He appeared to be about Lucas's own age, with a dark, scruffy beard and stringy, shoulder length black hair. A stained rag served as a blanket to warm the man's body. The dirt streaking the young man's face stood out in stark contrast to his pale, bloodless skin. Lucas eyed his patient critically. The unfortunate young man seemed to have passed beyond his help.

Lucas turned to ask the boy what was wrong with the man, but the boy had already disappeared. Shaking his head, he turned back to the man and lowered his lantern to get a better look at his patient. With a cry of astonishment, he dropped to the floor beside the man.

"Tristan!" he cried, his voice filled with fear and disbelief as he pressed a trembling hand to Tristan's jugular. Devon had said he had killed Tristan out in the desert. Surely he had not somehow survived to make it this close to help, only to die now. Lucas breathed more easily when he felt his friend's weak, but steady, pulse. *Perhaps I am not too late after all.* He gently laid his hand on Tristan's shoulder, only to withdraw it with a start. He looked down at his wet, sticky hand in the light of the lantern. It was smeared with his friend's blood.

His heart pounding, Lucas pulled back the blanket and tore Tristan's bloody tunic away from his shoulder, uncovering a deep, oozing wound in Tristan's chest. It was in the flesh near his shoulder, too far from any vital organs to have done any mortal damage. Still, it looked like it had been bleeding a while, and loss of blood would take Tristan's life if he could not get the bleeding stopped.

Lord, guide my hands. Lucas reached into his bag, pulled out a roll of bandages and a container of ointment his father used to clean wounds, and glanced up at Tristan's face. He had used the ointment enough to know it would burn intensely as soon as he applied it to the wound. Using a clean cloth from his bag, Lucas dabbed the ointment on the wound and the surrounding area. Tristan stiffened and stirred, but did not waken. Lucas finished applying the ointment and bandaging Tristan's shoulder before he examined the rest of his body for any further injuries requiring immediate attention. Even in the dim light of the lantern he could see the bruises and scars that covered Tristan's body, and his anger at the queen and her assassin returned with a fervency he had not felt since the day Lord Devon had reported Tristan's death to the queen. Some of the scars had already begun to fade, indicating the abuse had gone on for some time.

"What did that monster do to you?" Lucas demanded as he satisfied himself Tristan did not currently suffer from any broken bones and rolled his friend over to examine his back.

Anger flamed to hatred. There also, well-healed scars beneath the fresh ones indicated multiple whippings over a span of time.

Lord, punish the woman who would allow such pain to be inflicted on her own son, much less authorize it!

Seeing there were no additional injuries that required his immediate attention, Lucas lay Tristan back down and checked his friend's bandaged wound again. Assured the bleeding had been stanched, he turned his attention to his second concern: Tristan's raging fever. Tristan's body was so warm Lucas could feel the heat even a few feet away. Raising his lantern, he glanced around the room. Not far from where Tristan lay, he found a bucket of what appeared to be drinking water. Lucas stood and brought the bucket closer to Tristan. It was nearly full of cool, cloudy water. He doubted it was suitable for drinking, but right now he needed it to bathe his friend's fevered body. He would look for a purer source of drinking water later.

He dipped another cloth from his bag into the water and laid it across Tristan's forehead, and paused. He did not have enough cloths to cool Tristan's entire body. His eyes fell on the blanket beneath Tristan. *No good. I will need that if Tristan's fever turns to chills.* Tristan's tunic would be a better choice. It was no longer fit to wear anyhow. He would have to bring Tristan some of his own clothes from home. The thought of home made Lucas wince. His family would worry about him when they discovered him gone, but he could not leave Tristan now until he was sure he was out of danger. He would just have to explain whenever he got back. They would most certainly understand.

Chapter 5

Dawn was beginning to glow through the windows of the cellar when Tristan's fever finally broke. Lucas sagged against the gritty wall with relief and exhaustion. It had been a rough night. More than once he had feared Tristan would not survive until morning, but their merciful God had seen fit to spare him.

Lucas frowned at his sleeping friend. Tristan had never regained consciousness and Lucas was now forced to admit a new concern. The damage done to Tristan's body over the last year had been extensive; he could only imagine the damage done to his friend's mind. Tristan had been delirious much of the night, and his anguished cries still echoed in Lucas's ears. Lord Devon had failed to twist Tristan to the queen's desires; that was why he had tried to kill him. Still, Lucas feared his friend's sanity might not have survived the ordeal intact.

He was very tempted to stay until Tristan awoke, in case his friend was unfit to be left alone, but his parents would worry if he were not present for breakfast. Perhaps he could slip away later and check on Tristan. Scrawling quickly on a scrap of paper from his bag, he left a note beside Tristan in case he woke up before he could return. His instructions were simple: drink plenty of water and rest until he returned after nightfall with food and clothes.

Satisfied he had left everything the best he could, Lucas carefully pulled the dirty, tattered blanket over his friend to keep him warm, mentally adding a clean blanket to the list of things he needed to bring.

When Tristan is well enough to be moved, I will bring him home to be cared for in a healthier, safer place. Aleatha will most certainly like that, Lucas decided. *Should I tell them about Tristan today, or wait until he is stronger?* Lucas stood. He could make up his mind on the way home.

"Lucas?" Tristan's voice was only a raspy whisper. "My friend, I knew I could count on you."

Startled, Lucas dropped down beside him. "Tristan? How do you feel? Are you in pain? Is there anything I can get you?"

"Weak. Very tired," Tristan said. "Hungry. I do not remember when I ate last." At least Tristan was lucid enough to answer his questions.

"I will bring you some food and clean clothes when I return tonight." Lucas laid a gentle hand on Tristan's arm. "Until then, drink the water I left you and rest."

"Please, tell no one I am alive." A look of concern flashed across Tristan's face. "I am in no shape to defend myself if someone were to find me here."

"No one?" Lucas asked. He thought Tristan would have wanted Aleatha to know, at least. "What about my family?"

"Please, no one," Tristan insisted, his dark, haunted eyes pleading. "They need only to slip to a trusted friend or be overheard by a servant. I cannot expect you to protect me at all times, and I can do nothing to protect myself. Only for a short time."

"I will tell no one until you give me permission," Lucas promised. Tristan's point was valid, besides, it would allow him time to evaluate his friend's condition more closely. "I will be back after nightfall. Rest well."

*****

Dawn had broken by the time Lucas reached his home, and his empty bed had surely been detected. Resigned now to a confrontation, he headed to the dining room to join his family for breakfast.

Dr. Medellin stood to his feet when Lucas entered the room, nearly knocking his chair over. "Lucas Gaius Medellin! Where have you been? Why did you not return home last night? Your mother and I have been worried sick." Lady Medellin laid her hand on her husband's arm to calm him, but Dr. Medellin's voice continued to rise. "If I find you have been with some woman…"

"Do you think I would actually…" Lucas felt heat flame to his face at the accusation.

"What are we supposed to think?" his father roared. "You do not get home until morning, disheveled and unkempt, and Addis reported he believed you went to the south quarter last night. You tell me what you expect us to think!"

"Lucas," Aleatha cried, interrupting their father and pointing at Lucas's shirt. "Is that blood?"

Lady Medellin gasped as Lucas looked down at the front of his tunic. A smear of Tristan's blood stood out against the pale yellow cloth.

"I had a patient. A charity case," Lucas began the explanation he had rehearsed on the ride home. "A beggar boy came and brought me to him last night. He was a stabbing victim and delirious with fever. I could not leave him until his fever broke this morning."

"It is so dangerous over there," his mother protested. "Did you have to go alone? You could have taken your father with you."

"It was an urgent case. Besides, I am nearly twenty-one. In eight months, I will be old enough to be out on my own." He was treading a fine line. One wrong word could bring back up his ongoing argument with his father. "Let me clean up, then I will be back for breakfast."

His father opened his mouth to argue, but his mother's gentle hand stopped him. He sat back down with a grunt. "Fine, but go quickly. You are coming with me to the palace today."

Lucas had known his respite could not last long. He hated the idea of going even more now that he had seen what the queen had done to Tristan, but arguing would be useless. *I will look forward to tonight, when I can return to care for Tristan.* Until then, he would just have to hold back his opinions of the palace evils and their petty "illnesses," a task that was hard on a normal day.

This was far from a normal day.

*****

Once it was dark, Lucas returned to Tristan's hiding place. Since he had told his family he was caring for a charity case, there was no need to hide his actions from them, but he felt it best to be cautious. The rowdy clamor of voices and fetid smell of squalor assaulted him as he neared the Shambles. A gaudily dressed woman beckoned to him, but he kept his gaze ahead of him. His father's accusation from earlier that morning rose up again. Indignation rose up with it.

Surely Father has a better opinion of me than that. I know Father does not approve of my work in the Shambles, but at least he can trust me not to get into trouble. Lucas sighed. Nothing he ever did seemed to satisfy his father. At least he could not criticize his helping Tristan, not once he knew what he was really doing.

Let no one take my horse, Lord. He dismounted and tied his horse as securely as he could to a splintered wooden post. *And please help me heal Tristan.*

He ducked through the opening in the building and down the stairs. Tristan lay as he had left him that morning. Lucas knelt beside his friend and laid a hand on his forehead, hoping his fever had not returned. *Cool. Good, and his breathing seems steady.* Tristan stirred at his touch and opened his eyes.

"Lucas," he said. He started to sit up, but sagged back with a moan.

"Easy." Lucas supported his friend's head with his hand and gave him some water. "You have been through a lot."

Tristan looked away and clenched the rag covering him tightly in his fist.

"We thought you were dead," Lucas said as he checked Tristan's wound. "Lord Devon told the queen he had killed you himself."

"He tried." Tristan drew in a sharp breath when Lucas applied the ointment and continued, "He thought his dagger and the desert sun had finished the job." He lowered his eyes to the clean bandage Lucas was applying to his shoulder and whispered, "I had hoped it would."

It came as no surprise that Tristan had wished for death after his treatment. The wistfulness in his voice bothered Lucas, though. It was as if his friend still wished Devon had killed him. "I brought some food. Do you feel up to eating?"

"I have not eaten since…" His eyes darted to the bags Lucas had brought. "Since I was on the ship. I have no idea how long ago that has been."

Reaching into the bag of food he had brought, Lucas pulled out two thick slices of fresh bread and a chunk of cheese and handed them to Tristan. "Just a little, too much after not having eaten in a few days could make you sick."

"Trust me, I will not make that mistake again." Tristan grunted as he pushed himself up to recline against the stone wall. He took a small bite of bread, chewed slowly, and swallowed before taking another.

Dear Lord, Great Physician, heal him where I cannot, Lucas prayed. Tristan seemed so frail; so broken. He offered Tristan a bottle of water. "How did you survive?"

Tristan stared at the chunk of cheese, turning it in his hand.

"Lord Devon's final attack, I mean," Lucas clarified. He set the bottle of water on the floor between them and added, "You need not talk about it if you do not want to."

"I had won. By some miracle of God, I had held out against Devon's torments." Tristan answered, his eyes shifting to the bottle between them. His voice trembled and his breathing quickened as he continued, "I was content to die. I welcomed it after... everything." He touched his left shoulder gingerly. "After he gave me this, I passed out.

"I do not remember much until I woke up nearly a week after Devon left me. I had been picked up by some Bedouins. They had bandaged my wound and put salve on my burns," he said, laying aside the half eaten chunk of cheese and the last slice of bread.

"One day, the servants who were caring for me seemed excited. They brought me nice clothing and helped me shave and bathe. I asked them what was going on. They told me the sheikh had visited while I slept. He recognized my ring." Tristan looked down at his hand and twisted his signet between his fingers. "He knew who I was, and planned to return me to my mother. He hoped his act of kindness in rescuing me would bring peace between his people and my mother, or at least a reward." He looked up at Lucas, his eyes haunted. "I could not go back to her, not after…"

"Perhaps you had better get some rest now." Lucas wrapped the leftover food tightly in a cloth and tied it back inside the bag to keep it away from the rats. He covered Tristan with the clean blanket he had brought. Tristan's harrowing story could wait until he was stronger.

"No, I am nearly finished," Tristan said. He reached a shaking hand for the bottle of water and took a long drink. "I could not cross the desert myself, so I waited until we were in town. I found my moment as they were readying the ship to sail. While everyone was occupied, I slipped away. They searched for me for hours, but I had hidden in the hold of a merchant vessel preparing to sail. I had no idea where it was going, but I hoped it was far from my mother, the sheikh, or Devon. I slept in the hold unnoticed, eating only what I could find during the night. Three days passed, and I was awakened by the sound of the ship scraping into a harbor. Before I was even fully awake, a shout from one of the sailors told me my hiding place had been discovered. I ran. The ship had not yet cast anchor, and there was no place for me to go, so I dove overboard. Either none of the sailors could swim, or they simply did not care to go after me, but I made it to the dock unmolested. It was only then I realized the ship had taken me to the one place I did not want to be, back here. My little swim had reopened my wound, and I felt faint and dizzy from my exertions. I needed a place to hide and ended up here. That is when I sent the boy to get you."

"I am glad you did. Perhaps God brought you here to remind you that you still have friends," Lucas said. "Now rest. I will be here when you wake up."

"Thank you, my friend." Tristan closed his eyes closed as his voice trailed off. "I should never have doubted you, not even for a moment."

What cause would he have to doubt me? Troubled, Lucas looked down at his sleeping friend. *What torments has he been through? More importantly, do I have the skill necessary to undo the damage Devon has done?*

Chapter 6

A cry woke Lucas from his light sleep. He sat up and turned to look at Tristan. Tristan cried out again and tossed in his makeshift bed. Lucas lit the lantern beside him and knelt to check on his patient. Tristan seemed to be asleep, but his tossing and cries grew more frantic. Lucas laid a gentle hand on Tristan's good arm and called to him, "Tristan! Wake up, it is just a dream."

Tristan's body stiffened briefly and became limp and still. Alarmed, Lucas set the lantern down and leaned closer to his motionless friend. His breathing was slow and shallow, as if he had fallen back to sleep, and his pulse was strong and steady. Relieved, Lucas sat back on his heels and let out a long breath.

"Did I wake you?" Tristan asked, looking up at him ruefully.

Lucas blinked once before answering, "I thought you were asleep."

"A defense I developed over my time with Devon." Tristan pushed himself up a little against the wall. "It was often in my best interest if he did not know I was awake."

"You cried out," Lucas responded to Tristan's question. "You were having a nightmare."

"Yes," Tristan said, his face reddening with shame. "They have been very frequent, and intense, ever since I awoke with the Bedouins. I never had them the whole year I was with Devon. Perhaps because my waking hours were nightmare enough."

"Tristan…" Lucas hesitated. Tristan had been reluctant to share any details about the past year. "How did you not give up? No man could have suffered a whole year without giving up."

"I did give up, several times," Tristan admitted. He took a deep breath and bit his lip. "For two months, I would end each day crying for mercy and swearing I would say anything Devon wanted if he would only stop." Tristan's voice became husky. "That was not what he wanted. It was not enough for me to give up. Devon knew I would only return to my old views when the pain ended. He wanted complete and unconditional surrender; every one of my most deeply held beliefs abandoned from the bottom of my soul. He wanted to destroy me completely and rebuild me into the puppet my mother wanted me to be." He closed his eyes and hung his head. "I doubt even Devon knows how close he got."

A dark, menacing silence hung between them as Lucas began to be more worried about healing his friend's mind than his body.

"I am sorry. Sometimes I feel as if Devon still has power over me." Tristan shook his head as if clearing it from the dark thoughts that filled it and forced a thin smile. "Even though I won in the end, it seems as if I cannot escape the things he said and did. "

"Let me bring my father here," Lucas recommended. Tristan needed more help than he was capable of giving. "He has had some skill with…" He paused, knowing how he was about to sound, but unable to find a better term. "… illnesses of the mind."

"No, my friend, I can assure you I am not mad." Tristan's smile turned more amused than forced, but the shadows lingered in his eyes. "Devon brought me to the brink, but the Lord brought me back. It will be a hard journey, but with you as my physician and the Lord to heal my mind, I will make it, eventually."

"Get some rest, Tristan," Lucas advised, not at all convinced. "It will be dawn in a few hours, then I will need to be going again."

*****

The next day, Lucas performed his regular duties at the castle in moody silence. Tristan's insistence he tell no one of his survival weighed heavily on him. His father would be much better able to help. He could tell his father was displeased with his lack of focus, but Dr. Medellin did not say a word to him until they were on their way home.

"I am very disappointed in you." An undercurrent of anger flowed through Dr. Medellin's words as they mounted their horses. "You have done nothing but sulk all day. I know you care little for the castle, but you need to correct your attitude immediately. I am giving you an opportunity other young men would kill for."

"What?" Lucas looked at him with surprise. "No, Father, I was not sulking. I was just… preoccupied… I guess."

"Is it about Tristan?" Dr. Medellin lowered his voice and he looked at his son with compassion as they passed through the castle gates and into the city.

Lucas started in alarm, then realized his father was talking about his friend's supposed death. "I have a… patient." Lucas segued into his problem. Perhaps his father could lend advice on a nameless case. "He has suffered greatly. I think I have been able to treat his outward injuries, but his mind is tortured and I do not know how to help him."

"Your charity case." Dr. Medellin grunted. "Perhaps I could go down with you and see him."

"No!" Lucas winced at his sharp reply. His father was only offering to help. "He has insisted I tell no one where he is."

"It is not enough you insist on spending your free time in the Shambles," Dr. Medellin asked, his voice hard, "now you have taken to caring for criminals and fugitives?"

"A fugitive, not a criminal," Lucas returned, his tone matching his father's. They were going back to the same argument they always had, and he felt powerless to stop it. "Besides, do fugitives and criminals not deserve medical care also?"

"Not by my son!" Dr. Medellin thundered. Passersby glanced at him and he lowered his voice, though the intensity of emotion was still there. "I am training you to be the physician of lords, the healer of royalty, not the doctor of the gutters. I have given you every advantage, the best training, even the opportunity to follow in my footsteps, and you have chosen to go to the rabble!"

"I am not you," Lucas snapped. "I, at least, have no desire to spend my life condoning the actions of that queen or others like her!"

Dr. Medellin glared at him for a few silent moments, took a deep breath, and said, "In spite of what you may think, I do love you, son. I worry about you. the Shambles is not a good place for a young man to be. I admire what you want to do there, but I feel you would be better off serving here in the castle. Safety, affluence, prestige – what more could a man desire for his son?"

The anger drained from Lucas. His father had never acknowledged his point of view before. He, also, was more composed when he spoke. "The wickedness and pettiness of the castle wear on me. I cannot imagine spending the rest of my life in the presence of the queen, as witness to her evil."

"And the people of the Shambles are not just as wicked?"

They were. It just seemed different, somehow.

"I know what you mean, though. It is worse." Dr. Medellin nodded to the sentries as they left the city, then looked back at Lucas with a grim expression on his face. "You would like to believe the lords and ladies in the castle represent the best Boldaria has to offer, but you expect no better from the people in the Shambles. The power of the queen, wielded for evil, is greater than all of the evil in the Shambles."

It was as if his father understood the thoughts even he himself had not.

"All this time you thought I was willingly blind to her ways? More concerned about my own life than the evil she has been pushing on this nation for the last twenty-one years?" Dr. Medellin asked. He held up a hand to stop Lucas's protest. "And I have been, in the past. But even I have a limit." A muscle tensed in his jaw. "That limit was reached three weeks ago. That is why we are not going home tonight."

"Where are we going?" Lucas had been so focused on his argument with his father, he had not noticed they had turned from the road heading to their estate.

"Odell Chapman's," Dr. Medellin said, a conspiratorial twinkle in his blue-gray eyes. "I joined the night the queen received her visit from that devil. There will be another meeting tonight. I have decided it is time you joined also."

"Joined what?" Lucas whispered. Fire raced though his veins. He had heard rumors of an underground resistance group gathering strength against the queen's atrocities, but would never have dreamed his father would be part of it.

"The Friends of Naboth," Dr. Medellin returned. "The enemies of Jezebel."

Chapter 7

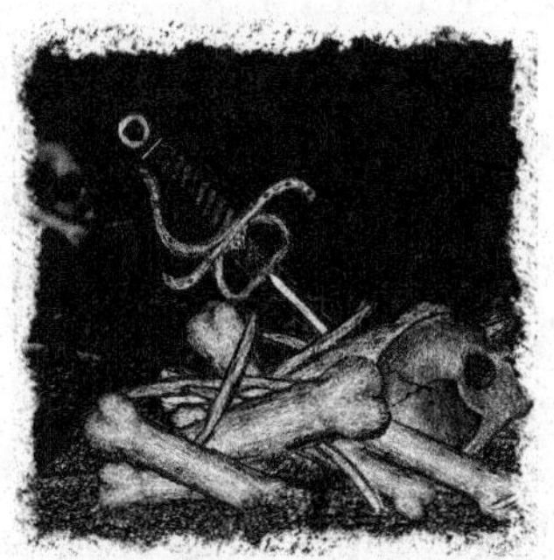

The Medellins' household was asleep for the night by the time Lucas and his father returned from their clandestine meeting. As Lucas scrambled to gather the supplies he needed for Tristan, his mind raced from the night's activities. The revelation that his father had joined the underground resistance and his own acceptance into the group still had him reeling. He would have never guessed his father would dare stand against the queen. He chuckled to himself as he scooped up his own dagger and added it to the bundle in his arms.

I wonder what my newfound friends would say if they knew who I was hiding. Tristan could be the salvation they are all looking for. Lucas bit his lip. If only he could help him become stronger in mind and body.

Once he arrived at the Shambles, he tied up his horse in front of Tristan's hiding place and dismounted. Taking a critical look around him, he descended the stairs to the cellar. Getting Tristan out of this dank, dirty hole might improve his chances of recovery.

"Good evening, Lucas." Tristan still looked gaunt and worn as he greeted him.

"How is my patient?" Lucas asked cheerfully as he checked Tristan's wound. It looked good. Perhaps another day or two and they could find him a better place to stay.

"Sore. Hungry. Thirsty," Tristan said, groaning as he stretched. "Mostly sore. My whole body aches."

"That means you are alive," Lucas pointed out. "You should be grateful even for that."

"I am trying to be grateful." The haunted look Lucas had seen so frequently returned to Tristan's face. "I simply cannot imagine why God did not allow me to die out there."

"God had a purpose in sparing you, Tristan." Lucas laid a hand on his friend's shoulder, "Even Lord Devon is powerless against the purposes of God."

"I know what you say is true," Tristan said, dropping his gaze from Lucas's face, "but I wish God would have let me die rather than spare me. What purpose could he possible have for me? Devon took everything from me. Every last vestige of my former life, my health, nearly my very life itself. All I have managed to cling to is my faith in God and your friendship."

Lucas frowned at Tristan's glaring omission. He had noticed it before, but had not been sure how to approach Tristan about it. *Aleatha.* Tristan had not asked about her or even mentioned her at all since he had revived. Lucas thought he would have been desperate for news. "Do not forget Aleatha. She never gave up on you, even when others had lost hope."

A flash of light that reminded Lucas of the old Tristan filled Tristan's eyes at the mention of Aleatha, only to be replaced by the same dark look they had held since Lucas had found him. "You mean she still… She is not…" Tristan broke off in confusion.

"Is not what, Tristan?" Lucas's eyes narrowed. He had not truly believed the damage done by Devon could have been this extensive. "What did Lord Devon tell you?"

Tristan hesitated. He did not look at Lucas when he answered and his voice filled with grief, "I had been told... Your father never did approve of us. Devon said she married Marc Erosthanes." He looked back at Lucas as if his very life depended on his answer.

The idea of his sister marrying Marc made Lucas swallow back his amusement. Tristan was deadly serious, and his friend's feelings were no laughing matter.

"No, she is not married. Though, this time, I cannot say your fears were not justified. Father tried very hard to convince us both you were not coming back. That if you did it would only be as the queen's pawn and would marry who the queen decided. Though, in all honesty, Father would never have approved of Marc either. Aleatha refused to believe him or to marry anyone until she had conclusive proof of your death."

Satisfied he had allayed his friend's fears and seeing Tristan was exhausted, Lucas turned his attention to preparing food for Tristan.

"Lucas, please understand," Tristan said, his voice rising weak and thin from the makeshift bed, "I must know the truth."

Alarmed by both the weakness and tone of his voice, Lucas turned his attention back to Tristan. *What could be more dreadful than the question I just answered?*

"Aleatha..." Tristan's voice faltered then gained strength as if steeling himself for the most difficult question of his life. "Is she still... Has she kept herself..."

Outrage flared in Lucas's chest as he realized what Tristan was trying to ask. "Has she kept herself, what, Tristan?" he snapped. "Spit it out."

Closing his eyes as if he were afraid to face his friend's wrath, Tristan whispered, "Please, is she still... honorable?"

"How dare you, of all people, question my sister's honor," Lucas seethed, his voice rising as his anger got the better of him. "Look at me when I speak to you! Aleatha has believed in you, waited for you, kept herself *for you* for the last thirteen months and you have the gall to doubt her purity? It would be within my rights to leave you here to die for your insinuations!"

Lucas's heart froze when he realized what he had said. Tristan lay on the blankets at his feet, motionless and as pale as death. His eyes were filled with a frightening mixture of terror and grief as he looked up at the only person left he trusted. The person who had just threatened to abandon him to die alone in a dank cellar in the worst part of town.

"Tristan, I…" Lucas sought for the right words. He could see by the fear on Tristan's face that he had just come dangerously close to doing in thirty seconds what Devon had been unable to do in twelve months; break Tristan's faith in his best friend's faithfulness. "I would never…"

"I know," Tristan said, the lingering fear in his eyes belying the relief in his voice. "When Devon found I refused to believe Aleatha would be unfaithful to me, he tried a new tactic. He spent the next three months trying to convince me your father had given her to another, to Marc. By the end of the three months, I was close, so very close, to believing him. Your father never did approve of my attention to Aleatha anyway. I did not let Devon see my doubts, though, and he grew frustrated. Determined to break me, he forced me to watch as he wrote a letter to Marc ordering him to do whatever it took to persuade her to consent to marry him."

"But," Lucas broke in, "Aleatha would never agree to marry Marc, of all people. Surely you know that."

Tristan held up his hand. "I told Devon that. He simply assured me Marc would have all the time he needed, since I would not be going home anytime soon. Besides, I had already seen that, with time, a person could be convinced of nearly anything."

"How long did he keep that argument up before you were convinced?" Lucas realized now that Tristan had just been voicing the doubts Devon had pounded into his head over the last year. It was no wonder he had not mentioned Aleatha since his return.

"Only a week." Tristan's face flushed with shame. "I knew Marc's reputation and I had already been persuaded to believe so much I had never thought I would. I could not see how Aleatha could fare any better. I kept defying Devon a week longer. He thought he had failed to break me. He knew Aleatha's faithfulness was one of the last three truths I held to. Since he thought he had failed there, he felt he had failed completely. The next day, he gave me this." Tristan motioned to his bandaged shoulder with his right hand and continued, "and left me alone in the desert to die."

Left me alone… to die. Tristan's words echoed in Lucas's head, mirroring the ones he had just spoken. "Tristan, I am so sorry. I did not mean what I said. Can you ever forgive me?"

Tristan smiled at Lucas weakly, all trace of fear gone from his eyes. "Of course, my friend. I did not cling to my faith in your friendship through twelve months of torture only to lose it now to a few words hastily spoken and quickly regretted.

"Besides," Tristan said. His grin widened. "You have given me back my faith in Aleatha. Perhaps there is still a chance I could win her hand."

"More than just a chance," Lucas said. "Just wait until I tell her you are alive! She will…"

"She will beg to be brought to see me. When you refuse, she will follow you alone into this slum." Tristan shook his head. "No, you cannot tell her. Not yet. I do not want her to come here, and I do not want her to see me like this."

"Then we will move you. You need to be in a safer place anyway."

"As my doctor, do you think I am ready to be moved?" Tristan countered. "I do not even have the strength to walk yet."

"Probably not yet," Lucas admitted, "but certainly in a few days."

"Then in a few days, you can tell her," Tristan said with a resolute shake of his head. "As much as I would like to see her, a few more days will not hurt any of us."

*****

By the time Lucas left, Tristan was sleeping peacefully. It was as if their conversation about Aleatha had taken a weight off his soul. Lucas was beginning to feel more confident in his friend's chances of making a full recovery.

He took a few moments in his room to change and freshen up before heading down to join his family for breakfast. He passed his father's private medical chambers on the way. The door was open and he could see his father sitting at his desk.

"Lucas! Come in." Dr. Medellin looked up from his desk and beamed. "Take a seat. I have wonderful news for you."

"What news?" Lucas asked as he entered the small room and took a seat opposite his father.

"Your mother and I have found a suitor for Aleatha." Dr. Medellin clasped his hands and rested them on the desk in front of him. "Dale Blakemore. I will announce their engagement at Aleatha's birthday celebration next week."

Tristan… Lucas's heart dropped into his stomach. "Aleatha agreed?"

"Happily," Dr. Medellin answered, not seeming to catch the displeasure in Lucas's voice. "I am sure you have noticed he has been hanging around a lot this past year. He came to me last week and asked for her hand. Your mother and I approve of him heartily, but we agreed to allow Aleatha have the final decision. She agreed this morning."

"Does she… love him?" Lucas stammered. *Why could she not have waited a couple more days?*

"She cares for him," Dr. Medellin said, raising an eyebrow. "She will come to love him. What is wrong with you? I expected you to be happy for her. Do you have an objection to his suitability as a husband for your sister?"

Only that Tristan lives, Lucas wanted to shout. He bit his lip to keep silent. He had promised Tristan not to tell anyone yet, though he doubted that promise held now. "No, Dale is a good man, but…"

"Tristan's dead, Lucas," Dr. Medellin interrupted. "You heard the report yourself. Even if he were not, the queen has had him for a year. If he were to return, he would no longer be a suitable husband for your sister. She needs to move on. You need to move on. He has been gone over a year, and they never were engaged. They never could be. You have no right to expect her to ignore Dale over him."

Suspicion narrowed Dr. Medellin's eyes as he looked at Lucas. "Unless you know something I do not."

"I will go congratulate Aleatha. Dale is a good man." Lucas stood without meeting his father's gaze. "With your permission…"

"You may go." Dr. Medellin frowned as he stared after his son.

Nearly stumbling over his chair, Lucas hurried from the room. He had to see Aleatha before he returned to Tristan. He needed to know from her where things really stood, whether there was any hope for his friend.

Chapter 8

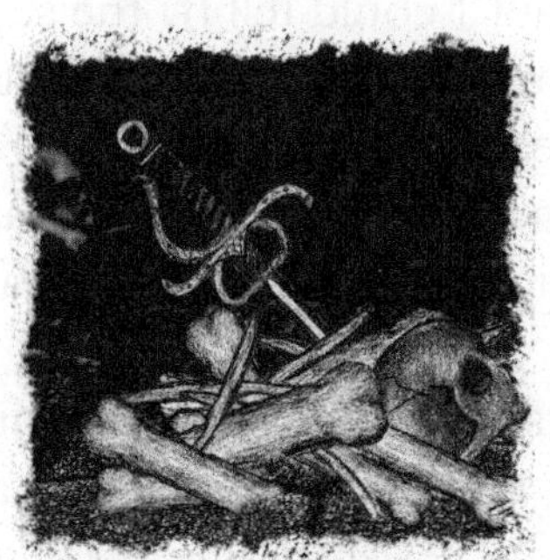

Footsteps on the stairs to the cellar woke Tristan. As silently as a cat, he snatched the dagger Lucas had left him off the floor beside him and rolled to a crouch in the shadows. The sudden movement made him dizzy, and a wave of nausea hit him as he put his hand against the cold, stone wall to steady himself. His visitor was nearly to the bottom of the stairs. Tristan decided he would try to stay hidden if possible. He was not even a match for a boy in hand-to-hand combat, much less a man. Lucas had said nothing about being back before nightfall and the footsteps sounded heavier than Lucas's. A man dressed in a dark cloak stepped tentatively into the cellar, turned his hooded head, and scanned the room. The figure knelt where Tristan had been lying only moments earlier. Tristan held his breath as the man examined the blankets and the remains of his breakfast carefully. The intruder was only a few feet away from his hiding spot; even a deep breath could give him away.

"I know you are still here." The man pulled the hood down away from his face. "I am no danger to you. I just wish to speak with you."

Dr. Medellin? Tristan started. *What is he doing here?* He stayed as still as possible. Dr. Medellin may know Lucas was caring for someone and still not know who that someone was. He was not ready to reveal himself to anyone until he was stronger. Even a friend could slip a careless word.

"I followed Lucas here last night. He told us he was caring for a charity case, but I could tell by the supplies he is taking from our house that his patient was more than that." Dr. Medellin took a breath. "You do not bring a simple charity case your own dagger, as I saw Lucas do last night. He is obviously protecting someone. I have already guessed who that might be."

A chill of fear raced down Tristan's spine. If Dr. Medellin could follow Lucas and figure all that out, anyone could. He was no longer safe here. *Perhaps Dr. Medellin guessed wrong.* Tristan remained hidden. He would allow Dr. Medellin to make the first move.

Standing, Dr. Medellin removed his cloak and turned in a slow circle. "I am unarmed, Your Highness. I have only come to speak with you about Aleatha. I assure you I am no danger to you."

"You guessed right, Doctor." Tristan took a deep breath and stepped from the shadows, the dagger still clutched in his right hand. "However, only news of Aleatha would draw me from hiding. The fewer people who know I am here, the safer I am."

Dr. Medellin looked startled to see Tristan so close, but recovered quickly. He looked Tristan over critically, his trained eye quickly assessing Tristan's condition, and stepped back away from the blankets. "Please sit, Your Highness. You make a show of strength, but even I can see how weak you are.

Lucas mentioned his patient was gravely wounded. I see he was not exaggerating."

"Why did you come here, Doctor?" Tristan asked as he lowered himself onto the blankets. His strength was gone and he was beginning to feel lightheaded. "Surely you have more faith in Lucas's work than to need to check up on him."

"Ordinarily I would agree." Dr. Medellin scowled as he glanced around the filthy cellar. "Though I cannot imagine how he could allow any patient to stay in this filthy pest hole. I thought I had trained him better than that."

"I insisted on staying here. I could not think of a safer hiding place and do not feel up to moving yet," Tristan explained. "What about Aleatha? You said you came to talk about her." He was already getting tired and needed Dr. Medellin to say what he came to say and leave.

"Yes, my dear Aleatha." Dr. Medellin laid his cloak down on the cellar floor a few feet from Tristan and sat down on it. "You care for her, do you not, Prince?"

"Very much, sir," Tristan responded, not daring to guess which direction this conversation was headed.

"You would even claim to love her, would you not?" Dr. Medellin pressed.

"I do love her, sir." Tristan frowned. He did not appreciate the insinuation his feelings for Aleatha might be insincere.

"Hmm, as you say," Dr. Medellin said with a shrug. "Then you would want what is best for her? For her future and her happiness?"

"What do you mean?"

"Simply this." Dr. Medellin leaned forward. "Aleatha has grown tired of waiting for you. She will announce her engagement to Dale Blakemore at her birthday celebration one week from today. Her mother and I both approve of the match. Dale will be a much more suitable husband for Aleatha than you could ever be."

Tristan felt as if all the life had been sucked out of his body. He quickly forced his mind into the same mode he had used when facing Devon. Pushing aside all emotion, he prepared himself to face Dr. Medellin's statements one at a time. "What would be unsuitable about me as a husband?" Tristan managed to keep his voice steady. He would not allow Dr. Medellin to see how shaken he was.

"Come, Prince, you are too weak to care for yourself, much less a wife." Dr. Medellin said. "Even if you do recover, do you think the queen will ever allow you to live in peace? If she allows you to live at all? Aleatha has already grieved your death once when Lord Devon claimed to have killed you, do you want her to have to grieve for you twice?"

"I will recover from my injuries soon, thanks to your son's expert care," Tristan responded. "As far as my life is concerned, no one is guaranteed tomorrow. Even Dale may die of the plague or be robbed and murdered by bandits. Mother has no power over my life beyond what God allows."

"Does she? Perhaps she has a greater hold on you than you wish us to believe," Dr. Medellin charged. His eyes traced over Tristan as if assessing a threat.

"What do you mean?" Tristan demanded, taking offense at the accusation in Dr. Medellin's voice.

"We both know why the queen sent you out with Lord Devon. You were not to return unless he could change you into a loyal follower of the queen." A sneer played at the corners of Dr. Medellin's mouth. "You may have fooled Lucas, Highness, you may even have been able to fool Aleatha, but you cannot fool me. I can tell you have changed. I can see it in your eyes. Lord Devon would not have allowed any man to live without compromise."

"I left here as a boy, innocent even in my opinion of my mother." Tristan clenched his fist tightly around the hilt of the dagger he still held in his lap. "A man cannot endure the things I have and retain the innocence of a boy. Yes, I have changed, but I have no agreement with either Devon or my mother."

"Do you know how your father died?" Dr. Medellin asked. "Your mother killed him. Everyone believed her innocence, but I knew the truth. For twenty-one years I have kept silent, fearing for my family's safety. I will not sit back and allow my daughter to fall victim to the same fate."

"You fear my mother would harm Aleatha?" Tristan had a fair idea that was not what Dr. Medellin meant at all, but the abrupt change in topic confused him. Fatigue and the throbbing pain in his shoulder made concentration difficult.

"Not the queen, Prince Tristan, you." Dr. Medellin nodded toward the dagger clenched in Tristan's fist. "Do not think to use that on me, I can easily see you have not the strength to stand, much less kill a man. But that will change, will it not? I know the true monster your mother has raised you to be. You may hide it now, just as she did for so many years, but eventually it will have to come out. I will not allow you to hurt Aleatha. I will not allow her marriage bed to become her death bed!"

Indignation choked Tristan. "You… You think I would… that I could ever…" He could not bring himself to finish the sentence. He swallowed hard and began again, his voice quivering with fury. "Doctor, you do not know me nearly as well as you believe you do if you think me capable of harming Aleatha."

"Perhaps not, but I am unwilling to gamble her life and happiness on your character." Dr. Medellin stood and bent to pick up his cloak. "Aleatha has agreed to marry Dale. He is a good man and she cares greatly for him. If, as you say, you truly do care for her, do not get in the way of her happiness. You have nothing to offer her but pain and misery. Any interference on your part would only indicate your own selfishness. As far as Aleatha is concerned, you are better off dead!"

With those parting words, Dr. Medellin turned and stormed out of the cellar, leaving Tristan to ponder everything he had said.

Perhaps he was better off dead after all.

*****

Lucas found Aleatha in the garden quietly sitting on a bench and staring at their mother's carefully tended flowers. Her expression was grave and she was deep in thought.

"Aleatha?" Lucas spoke up as he came closer. She had not noticed him and he did not want to startle her. "Can I join you?"

"Lucas!" Aleatha greeted him eagerly. She slid to one end of the bench and patted the seat next to her. "Certainly, there is plenty of room."

"Why so serious? Father told me the news about Dale." Lucas tread lightly into the subject, trying to ascertain Aleatha's feelings. "I would expect you to be a little more lighthearted. Maybe singing among the flowers like you did as a girl."

"I guess I do not feel like singing," Aleatha said with a small sigh. "I should, but I just do not know how I feel."

"Do you not love Dale?" Lucas prodded. "He is a good family friend and a nice man."

"He is a wonderful man. A man any girl should be glad to marry." Aleatha looked down at a daisy she held in her hand, absently picking the petals off the head. "But I am not sure of my own feelings. I do care for him. I am certain I will come to love him."

"What about Tristan?" The topic might hurt his sister, but he had to know her feelings before he faced Tristan tonight.

"Father says it is time I stop grieving. Now that we know he is not coming back." She looked down at the mangled flower in her hands as a tear dropped into her lap. "He has been gone over a year, and it is not like we were officially engaged. I have no right to ignore Dale over him."

Those are Father's words in Aleatha's mouth. Lucas leaned forward. "What if Tristan were still alive, Aleatha? Would it make a difference?"

"Lucas Medellin, do not dare even ask me that!" Aleatha stood, her face white and tears streaming down her cheeks as the daisy petals fell at her feet. "Tristan is dead. You told me yourself that hateful queen murdered him. I will not pine after him, even if he was your best friend. I will not let his memory… Ohh." With a sob, Aleatha covered her face and ran from the garden.

That went poorly. He had not aimed to upset her, but he needed to know the truth. For Tristan's sake and for Aleatha's future.

Chapter 9

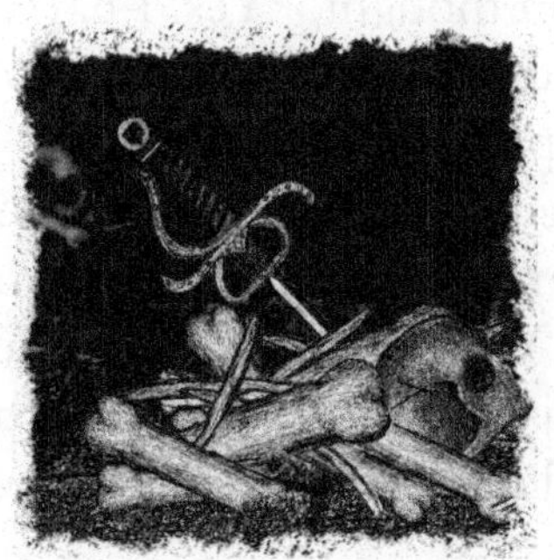

Filled with apprehension, Lucas descended the steep stairs to the cellar that evening. He needed to tell Tristan of Aleatha's upcoming betrothal, but he did not know how to break the news to him. *How does a man tell his best friend the woman he loves will be marrying another?* After their discussion last night, he feared how Tristan would handle it. The prince was still very weak from his ordeal – mentally, emotionally, and physically. The toll it had taken on his emotions was apparent, especially where Aleatha was concerned. Lucas had barely been able to convince Tristan of her steadfastness earlier, now this.

As he turned the corner, Lucas shone his lantern into the cellar. *I also have to persuade Tristan it is not safe for him to stay down here. He is not strong enough to defend himself if someone were to…*

He lifted the lantern higher. Tristan's makeshift bed was empty. Fear gripped his heart. *Am I too late? Has someone already discovered Tristan's hiding place?* He played the light around the room, searching for some sign of his friend. Tristan was too weak to go far by himself.

Tristan stood on the opposite side of the room with his hands clasped behind him, staring out the hole in the wall that served as the cellar's only window.

"Tristan," Lucas cried out in relief and surprise. "You are up!"

"Hmmm?" Tristan turned and looked at him blankly, as if he had been deep in thought. "Yes, I have been up several times today to build my strength. I have to find another place to hide as soon as possible."

"What happened?" Lucas raised his eyebrows at Tristan's sudden change of mind. At least that was one battle he would not have to fight. "Were you discovered here?"

With a sigh, Tristan sat down against the wall beneath the window. He closed his eyes and rested his head back out of sheer exhaustion.

"Did someone find you here?" Lucas repeated. He set the lantern on the floor next to Tristan and knelt to check his condition. He did not know how long Tristan had been up, or what else had happened during the day, but if Tristan was already exhausted, moving him tonight might not be wise. After he heard how pressing the danger was, then he would decide if moving was worth the risk to his friend's health.

"Your father was here this afternoon," Tristan answered. He opened his eyes and watched Lucas for his response.

"My father!" Lucas sat back on his heels and stared at Tristan in disbelief. "How did he find you?"

"He said he followed you here last night. He figured by your behavior your patient was more than just a charity case." Tristan rubbed the back of his neck with his good arm. "If he could follow you, so could someone who might really wish to harm me."

"What did he say?" Lucas asked. He could not decide if he should be glad his father broke the news to Tristan, or concerned about the damage his father's version might have done.

"He said he was shocked his son would allow a patient to stay in such a filthy pest-hole." Tristan attempted to sound lighthearted, but the lightness in his voice did not mask the pain in his eyes. "He said he thought he had trained you better."

Clearly it was time for some damage control. "No, Tristan, you know what I mean. What did he say about Aleatha?"

"The long or the short version?" Tristan closed his eyes and leaned back again.

"First tell me what he said," Lucas advised. "We will deal with how he said it later."

"He told me Aleatha tired of waiting for me and would announce her engagement to Dale Blakemore at her birthday celebration in one week." Tristan pulled himself up a little straighter, as if drawing strength for the difficult conversation. "He said both he and your mother feel Dale is a better match for Aleatha and she is consenting to the arrangement. He told me if I truly cared for Aleatha's happiness, I would not interfere with her marriage to a man who could make her happier than I could ever dream to."

Tristan paused, his dark eyes searching Lucas's face for either confirmation or denial of his summary. "I can tell by your expression my facts are accurate."

"Your facts are accurate," Lucas confirmed slowly. "However what will or will not make Aleatha happy is purely my father's opinion."

"Then Aleatha has consented?" Tristan raked his trembling fingers through his tangled, greasy black hair. "She willingly agreed to marry Dale?"

"Hear me out," Lucas began. Here was where things got complicated. "Yes. Aleatha willingly agreed to marry Dale, but she believes you to be dead. Father told her it was time for her to move on. If she knew you were alive, I doubt she would go through with the betrothal."

A cautious hope sparked in Tristan's eyes, only to be clouded again. "Does she love him?"

"She cares for him and is certain she will come to love him," Lucas answered, careful to use the exact words Aleatha had used when he had questioned her earlier, "but she still has not gotten over the news of your death."

"Lucas, as much as I value your father's opinion, I value yours more." Tristan looked away apprehensively, as if he were struggling over how to frame his next question. When he finally looked Lucas in the eye, his expression was grave. "Please answer my next question honestly, as Aleatha's brother, not as my friend. Do you find any objection to my marrying your sister?"

"That is unfair," Lucas protested. "I am both Aleatha's brother and your friend. You cannot force me to put one over the other."

"Then you do have objections as a brother you feel would jeopardize our friendship." Tristan pressed his lips into a tight line as he looked hard at Lucas. "Do you agree with your father then?"

"My father's objections have always been more concerned with your mother than you," Lucas snapped, irritated that Tristan had trapped him into discussing a topic he had wanted to avoid. "I have always defended your case for Aleatha's hand to him in the past. Though, I will admit your current situation gives me cause for concern. What brother would be thrilled by the prospect of his sister being engaged to a man who is likely to leave her a widow before she is even a bride? Of course I have objections, but I am also your friend, and I want the best for you as well as her." Lucas did not know the depth of his father's objections, but he realized the ones he had given himself were strong enough to stir up the doubts already buried in Tristan's mind.

As Tristan weighed Lucas's words, he stared down at his hands in his lap. The prince's voice was unsteady when he finally spoke, "She would be better off then? If I were to allow her to marry Dale, would she have a better chance at happiness?"

Would she? Lucas thought his answer over carefully. What he said now would have a huge impact on both Tristan and Aleatha's futures. There was no doubt his friend would take his advice to heart, especially in his current condition. He looked at Tristan, who sat before him in anxious, grim silence. The objections against Tristan were great, but Aleatha and Tristan's feelings for each other were great also. *Are the objections enough for me to lay their feelings aside? Do I even have a right to do that?* There were many positive things about Tristan his father usually overlooked. *More than I can come up with for Dale.* He took a deep breath and said, "What are the components of a happy marriage?"

Tristan gave Lucas a startled look. Lucas was referring to a conversation they and Aleatha had with the Medellins' pastor shortly before Tristan had left with Devon. "Two people who love each other, love Christ, and are seeking to follow Him. There are other considerations, Lucas."

"Forget that right now." Lucas shook his head. "Father fears you may have changed since you left. I believe you have, but I have seen enough the last couple of days to know not all change is bad. Your faith in Christ has strengthened, not weakened, over the last year. So has Aleatha's. Waiting for you has forced her to put a greater dependence on Him. Your love for Aleatha is very clear. She still loves you, even if she thinks you are dead. Yes, there are other, practical objections, but I think the two of you should seek the Lord's leading through them together. It is not my place to choose God's path for you."

"Your father may never approve of us marrying," Tristan whispered. "His objections are much greater than you realize."

"You will not even have a chance to change his mind if you do not try." Lucas made a mental note to talk to his father later about what "greater" objections he had. "I think you should see her as soon as possible. Perhaps I can even bring her to see you tomorrow."

"No!" Tristan nearly shouted in horror. "You cannot bring her here, no decent lady comes to this part of town. Besides, I do not want her to see me like this."

"Do not worry, I do not mean here." Lucas suppressed a chuckle at his reaction. "You mentioned finding a new place. I already have somewhere in mind. We have an old gardener's cottage behind our house. No one has used it in years. You will be safe there and easier for me to look in on. As far as your condition, I can get you a change of clothes, a razor, or anything else you need to make yourself presentable."

"A bath and a hair cut would be nice." Tristan made a wry face. "It has been weeks since the last time I have had either."

"It is settled then." Lucas stood. "Just before dawn, I will bring a wagon to take you to the cottage. I will have everything waiting for you there. Meanwhile, you try to rest."

*****

Well before sunrise, Lucas returned home and slipped out to the stables. He hoped to be gone and to get Tristan safely to the cottage without anyone noticing. He hitched a horse to small wagon the servants used for carrying supplies to and from the market, mounted the horse, and headed to town. A full moon lit the road clearly, making a lantern unnecessary. *Another small blessing.* Lucas glanced back at the house. No one seemed to notice his departure. *Please let us be as successful on the way back,* he prayed.

As Lucas guided the horse into the Shambles, he allowed his right hand to rest on the hilt of his sword. If anyone recognized Tristan as he brought him out of his hiding place and reported him to the queen, they would both be in incredible danger. *Keep Tristan and me safe,* he prayed as his eyes darted around him. *Help me get him back without discovery.* It would be dawn soon and he was cutting their margin of safety close. Soon the streets would be full of people.

As he descended into the dark cellar, Tristan's eager voice greeted him,

"I thought you would never get here!" Tristan stood, shifting his feet and looking at Lucas anxiously. He was wearing a cloak Lucas had left him. The blankets he had been using for a bed were neatly folded on the floor beside him and the few items Lucas had brought for his comfort were piled on top of them.

"First I cannot convince you to leave this rat-hole, now you cannot wait to leave," Lucas said, feigning amazement as he stooped to pick up the pile on the floor. "I wonder what, or who, you could be so excited to see."

"I wonder." Tristan smirked. He pulled the hood of his cloak over his head. "Can a man not just be anxious for a bath and a shave?"

"Is that all you want?" Lucas teased as he led Tristan back up the stairs. "I could have sworn a certain sister of mine might have had something to do with your excitement."

The banter trailed off while Lucas tossed his stuff into the back of the wagon and helped Tristan up. His friend's expression was grim. "What is wrong, Tristan?"

"What if Aleatha does not want to see me?" Tristan said as he pulled the hood of his cloak further over his face, "Let us be honest, my appearance is not going to make her life any easier."

"That decision is for her to make," Lucas checked his frustration as he spoke, remembering all his friend had been through, "though I really do not think you have anything to worry about on that score."

The road to the estate was rough, and Lucas did not want to jostle Tristan anymore than he had to. His caution made it take twice as long to get home as he had taken to travel to the

Shambles to begin with. He looked with concern at the glow on the horizon. They would barely make it to the dilapidated cabin behind the house before the servants awakened. Once he got Tristan settled, he would have to try to get Aleatha out of the house unnoticed.

Chapter 10

Lucas knocked gently on Aleatha's door. He hoped to rouse her without alerting any of the servants that were already up preparing for the day.

"Aleatha," he whispered, his mouth near the door frame. "It is Lucas."

"Just a minute," she answered, her voice muffled by the thick door.

Soft noises came from inside her room. It seemed like an eternity before she opened the door a few inches and looked out at him.

"What is wrong?" She rubbed her eyes and blinked at him. "It is too early…"

"Just be quiet and let me in." Lucas pushed the door open, slipped past her, and eased the door closed behind him.

"Lucas Medellin, you get out of my room." Aleatha glared at him, her hands on her hips. "You may enjoy being up at all hours, but I do not. Besides, I am not dressed."

"It is not like I have not seen you in your nightgown before. For goodness sake, I am your brother," Lucas hissed. "Now be quiet and listen to me."

"Be quick." Aleatha cocked her head, still scowling. "I have half a mind to kick you out of my room and go back to bed."

"Look, I know you are still angry with me for what I said yesterday, but I had my reasons. I needed to know if you still had feelings for Tristan."

"I refuse to talk to you about Tristan," Aleatha said. "Why do you insist on bringing him up? I am… I am trying to move on." Her eyes flashed and her voice rose. "He is dead, Lucas!"

"Would you be quiet!" Lucas grabbed her by both arms and squeezed hard. He put his face just inches from hers and whispered, "He is not dead, and if you have not drawn the attention of the whole household, I can take you to him."

"Tristan is alive?" Aleatha stared at Lucas with a dazed expression on her face. "But you said…" Her eyes narrowed suspiciously. "Is he really alive?"

"And waiting to see you," Lucas said as he released her, "but you must hurry, we have to be back by breakfast so no one suspects."

"Get out. Give me five minutes to dress." Aleatha sank to her bed as tears glittered in her eyes. "Oh, Lucas, Tristan is alive!"

"Just do not tell the whole world yet. He is in a lot of danger, and in no condition to defend himself."

"No condition?" Aleatha looked hard at her brother. "Is he all right?"

How do I even begin to answer that question? He sighed. *She needs to be prepared for the truth.* "No, but I will explain as we go see him. Hurry up."

Leaving Aleatha to change, Lucas slipped back to his room for a few more things to make Tristan comfortable. He tucked the bundle under one arm and met his sister halfway down the hall. She looked excited and anxious at the same time. She had dressed in a pink and cream dress Lucas recalled was one of Tristan's favorites. Her hair was pulled back with a simple pink ribbon, and her face was flush with excitement.

"Just act like we are going out for an early morning walk," Lucas whispered. He paused to nod casually to Collis, the hostler, as they left the house. "Once we reach the woods, I will tell you more."

Aleatha bit her lip, but kept silent. Her back was rigid and her wide eyes darted around her.

I hope no one is paying attention to her. Lucas shook his head. His sister looked as if he was taking her out of the house at knife point.

They reached the walking path into the woods behind the house. Lucas took one more glance around him to be sure no one was following them.

"We are clear now," Lucas assured Aleatha. "It does not look like anyone followed us."

"Where are we going?" Aleatha demanded. Her impatience made her questions tumble over each other. "And why the secrecy? Is Tristan all right? You promised you would explain as we went."

"First, where we are going." Lucas moved aside some brush to reveal an overgrown fork in the path before continuing, "You remember the old cottage out here we used to hide in when we were younger?"

"How could I forget? I think that cottage saved you many whippings." Aleatha's eyes twinkled. "There were a few times you were gone so long, Mother and Father were too worried about you to remember to punish you. I do not believe anyone ever discovered it."

"I am counting on it." Lucas helped his sister through a particularly dense part of the path. "The longer Tristan's mother believes him to be dead, the longer he can heal."

"What is wrong with him, Lucas?" Aleatha looked at her brother with concern. "Has he been this 'charity case' of yours all along?"

"I wanted to tell you, but Tristan insisted I tell no one about him until he was stronger."

A hurt look crossed Aleatha's face. "Not even me? What are you not telling me?"

Dread settled in Lucas's stomach as he pressed his lips into a thin line and motioned toward a tree that had fallen across the path. "Sit. I will tell you what I know, which is not much."

Aleatha sat, her face pale with worry.

She probably thinks Tristan is horribly disfigured or something. Lucas furrowed his brow. *It is a lot more complicated than that.* "When Lord Devon took Tristan away a year ago, his goal was to break him, to force him to swear complete allegiance to the queen. If that did not work, he was to kill Tristan so he could never return to be crowned."

"You told me that," Aleatha said as she tapped her fingers on the bark of the tree. "Back when you told me he had killed Tristan."

"Lord Devon thinks he has killed Tristan." Lucas clasped his hands behind his back and began to pace nervously as he spoke. His words rushed out nearly on top of each other. "By a miracle of God, one I am not sure I fully understand, Tristan survived. Barely. When I was brought to him four days ago, he was bleeding, feverish, and on the brink of death. With God's help, I was able to bring him back. His body is healing quickly, at least well enough I felt I could finally move him out of that rat-trap I found him in. But his mind… that may take a while longer."

"His mind? What do you mean?" Aleatha looked at him with alarm. "He is not… mad, is he?

"Oh, no," Lucas assured her. He sat on the log next to her and looked her in the eye. "But he was tortured, physically and mentally. Lord Devon spent the last year using every method imaginable to cause Tristan to doubt everything and everyone he knew – me, you, even God Himself – and pledge loyalty to the queen. Not even I know the extent of what he went through. All I can see are the results."

"But he failed," Aleatha said. Her eyes begged for reassurance. "Lord Devon would not have tried to kill him if he had succeeded."

"He failed," Lucas confirmed, "but only because Tristan's faith in God was stronger than Lord Devon realized. Tristan's confidence in us is sorely shaken. He tries to hide it, but I am not certain he entirely trusts me yet."

"And me?" Aleatha looked down at her hands. "What lies did Lord Devon tell him about me?"

If only she had not asked the question like that! Lucas took a deep breath and let it out slowly. He had hoped to avoid particulars. Still, perhaps it was better Aleatha knew the whole truth going in. "That you were unfaithful to him. That you had married another. It took me a long time to convince him that you still cared for him. Then Father came and told him about Dale…"

Aleatha sucked in a breath. "I never would have agreed to that if I knew Tristan was alive. You have to believe me."

"I know, and I told Tristan that," Lucas said, as he took Aleatha's hand and stood to continue down the path. His voice hardened as he remembered what his father had done. "But Father told him you would be better off without him. I think Tristan believes him. His prospects are not good, I will not hide that from you. As long as his mother reigns, he is a fugitive only a step away from death."

"I do not care about that." Aleatha stood, a determined look in her eye. "I love Tristan, no matter what. We can get through this together."

"I knew that was what you would say. I told Tristan to give you a chance to decide what you wanted."

They rounded a bend in the path. The cottage now stood about a hundred yards away.

"You are keeping him in that? It looks as if it is about to cave in!"

"It is worlds better than where he was before," Lucas said. *Leave it to a woman to find fault.* "It is clean and safe from detection. Besides, I did not have much choice."

The frown on Aleatha's face told him he was not convincing her. He shook his head and continued toward the cottage. If she had any better ideas she was welcome to share them.

He stopped in front of the cottage and turned back to Aleatha. "I want you to wait outside until I call for you. Tristan does not know I am bringing you now. Let me make sure he is ready."

Leaving Aleatha outside the door to the decaying shack, Lucas entered and found Tristan asleep on the bed. At the squeal of the door closing behind him, Tristan's body tensed slightly.

"It is only me," Lucas said gently, remembering Tristan's habit of pretending to sleep until he was assured that he was safe.

Tristan relaxed and rolled over to face Lucas. He stretched and yawned. "I did not know when you would be back, so I took a bit of a nap."

"You look good. Almost like you did before." Lucas said. The prince had dressed, cut his hair and pulled it back into a short ponytail at the back of his head, and shaved the dirty stubble off his face.

"Amazing what a bath and a shave will do."

"Do you think you might be up to some company?" Lucas asked. "Aleatha is outside waiting to see you."

"Aleatha is here, already?" Tristan looked up at Lucas with astonishment. "She wanted to see me?"

"More than anything," Lucas answered. He grinned. "She told me she loves you and she never would have agreed to marry Dale if she had not believed you to be dead."

"Thank you, Heavenly Father," Tristan breathed, lying back in the bed. "I did not think it was possible. Please bring her in, right away."

Sticking his head out the door, Lucas motioned to Aleatha. "You will have to keep it short, we cannot afford to be missed at breakfast."

With a nod, Aleatha pursed her lips and stepped gingerly over the threshold, as if she were afraid to even enter the cottage.

"Aleatha," Tristan greeted her. His face glowed with excitement, but his voice was filled with uncertainty.

"Oh, Tristan!" Aleatha abandoned her fear of the shack and ran the last few steps as Tristan rose to stand beside the bed. She threw her arms around his neck and buried her face in his chest. "I thought you were dead," she choked through her tears.

Tristan's eyes darted to Lucas as he awkwardly wrapped his arms around Aleatha to soothe the crying girl. His embrace relaxed around her as his concern for Aleatha overcame his discomfort. "I am here now," he whispered. "God protected me."

"Lucas told me you were hurt." Aleatha pulled back a little and looked into Tristan's eyes. "You look pretty good to me."

"And you look beautiful to me." Tristan ran his fingers through her soft, brown ponytail. "I never thought I would see you again."

Lucas cleared his throat. "Sorry to break up the reunion, but we need to be back by breakfast. We cannot afford to have anyone asking questions."

"Why can he not come back to the house with us?" Aleatha asked, never taking her eyes off Tristan.

Alarm filled Tristan's eyes as he glanced at Lucas, but he covered his fear and released Aleatha. "I doubt that would be a good idea."

"Why not? You always came to us when there was trouble before." Aleatha's eyes narrowed. She had not missed his change in expression. "What is changed now?"

"Father," Lucas answered for Tristan. "He is not thrilled Tristan has returned. I am pretty sure he will not want Tristan home, and especially not around you."

"Nonsense," Aleatha said. She dismissed Lucas's objection and turned back to Tristan. "You have been a part of this family since you ran away from home the first time when you were eight. Father never had any problem with you coming around until you started showing interest in me. We all know he was just trying to keep me from the wickedness of the court."

"His objections go a little deeper than that now," Tristan said. A muscle tensed in his jaw. "He fears I have changed."

"I would think so. We all have." Aleatha said. "Perhaps if you stay with us he will see he has nothing to worry about."

"There is also Tristan's safety to consider," Lucas spoke up. "If one of the servants slips that he's staying with us…"

"The servants all love Tristan as much as they do us," Aleatha argued as she placed her hands on her hips. "If we warn them of the danger, they will protect him with their lives."

"Besides, he still needs medical care," she continued. "Would he not be better off at home, where we can all look after him? No offense, Lucas, but this does not exactly look like the most healthy place to care for a patient."

"It is better than where I was before," Tristan said. A smile twitched at the corner of his mouth.

"That is what Lucas said." Aleatha rolled her eyes. "No more discussion. I will talk to Father at breakfast." She batted her eyelashes as she said, "He always gives me what I want."

"If you can convince him to let me stay at your house, you are a miracle worker," Tristan said. His voice was soft and worry lit his eyes.

He never had a problem coming to our home before his time with Devon. Lucas raised an eyebrow. *Quite the opposite, he always sought our home as a refuge.* Perhaps it was related to his father's visit. Still, maybe Aleatha was right. *What better way to prove to Father that Tristan was not the danger he believes him to be?*

"It is settled then." Aleatha turned from Tristan with a swirl of her skirts and flounced toward the door. "Pack your things. This evening, you will be moving again."

Chapter 11

At the breakfast table, Lucas pushed the food around on his plate. He glanced at his sister sitting across from him. Aleatha was glowing. Her cheeks were flushed to match her dress, and a wide grin stretched across her face. She had spoken of nothing but Tristan as they had walked back to the house. She was so sure their father would agree to let Tristan stay. Lucas was not.

"You look lovely this morning, dear." Lady Medellin commented to Aleatha as she smoothed a napkin over her lap.

"Perhaps it is a boy," Dr. Medellin teased. "I have not seen you this happy in a long time."

Aleatha blushed deeply, but kept her silence until after her father had said grace. When she spoke, it was with all the serenity as if she had been discussing the weather. "Mother, this bread smells divine. You know how much Tristan loved it. I will have to be sure to take him some after breakfast."

The room grew deathly silent. Lucas bent his face closer to his plate and began shoveling food into his mouth to avoid eye contact.

"Aleatha, dear." Lady Medellin's voice quivered as she gained her tongue. "Are you feeling all right?"

"Of course, Mother." Aleatha flashed her a dazzling look. "I have not felt this good in, oh, more than a year."

Dr. Medellin's face turned a deep shade of red as he glowered at his son as if he blamed Lucas entirely for this fiasco. Lucas slumped lower in his chair and focused on his plate.

"You meant, Dale, sweetie," Lady Medellin corrected. "You mean to take *Dale* some bread, right?"

"No, Mother," Aleatha said, buttering her bread as if she were unaware of the chaos she was causing. "I saw him this morning – Tristan, I mean. He would definitely love some of your homemade bread. Perhaps I could bring him some pastries, too. He always enjoyed those."

"Gaius, please." Lady Medellin pleaded with her husband, but kept her eyes on Aleatha as if she were sure her daughter was going quite insane. "Aleatha, dear, you must have dreamt about the prince last night. It is perfectly natural to…"

"You mean you did not know?" Aleatha paused with her buttered knife in mid air and turned to her father in feigned amazement. "Father, you did not tell her?"

All eyes went to Dr. Medellin, who simply grunted and mimicked Lucas's concentration on his meal.

"Prince Tristan is dead." Lady Medellin glanced in confusion around the table from one face to the next before setting back on Aleatha. "How could you possibly have seen him?"

"He was just badly wounded, Mother." Aleatha's eyes glowed as she set the knife and the bread on the table. "Lucas has been caring for him in the Shambles for the past few days.

Father went to see him yesterday, and Lucas took me to see him this morning." The glow in her eyes was replaced by a concerned look. "He is so weak, Mother, and scared, too. Lucas has been doing his best to nurse him back to health and keep him hidden from the queen, but the conditions he has to endure…" She trailed off with a pathetic shake of her head.

Rubbing his napkin over his mouth to hide a grin, Lucas leaned back in his chair to watch his sister artfully weave a net around their father.

"Lucas Medellin, is this true?" Lady Medellin demanded. "Have you been hiding Prince Tristan while treating his injuries?"

"Well, yes, Mother." Lucas tried to seem appropriately contrite, but feared he was failing miserably. His sister's look of displeasure confirmed it. He coughed. "Tristan made me promise to tell no one. Besides, his health has been very unstable."

"Gaius, have you seen him?" Lady Medellin tilted her head to the side and frowned. "Why did you not tell me Prince Tristan was alive?"

"I was trying to think about Aleatha's happiness." Dr. Medellin placed both hands on the table and leaned forward. "Dale is a much better match for her." He looked meaningfully at Lucas. "I had hoped the prince would see that."

"You left that poor boy in the filth of the Shambles because you think Dale is a better suitor?" Lady Medellin clucked her tongue with disapproval. "I think your time in the palace has affected you, Gaius." She turned to Lucas. "As soon as he is well enough to move, you bring him here."

Too late, Dr. Medellin realized the trap had been sprung. He stood to his feet, his gray-blue eyes flashing. "Absolutely not! I will not have that…" He bit off the word he was about to use. "I will not have him bringing danger to this home. If the queen finds out he is alive, this is the first place she will look."

"Then we'd better have a plan to hide him." Lady Medellin put her napkin back on the table and stood. "Frankly, dear, I am disappointed. Tristan has been part of this family since he was a child. How could you abandon him when he needs us most?"

Dr. Medellin opened his mouth, then snapped it shut again. He gave Lucas a withering glare, whirled, and stormed out the door.

As he watched Dr. Medellin leave, Lucas felt a little sorry for his father. He never really had a chance.

*****

Just before nightfall, Lucas returned to the shack with the wagon while his mother and Aleatha prepared for Tristan's arrival. Tristan lay in the bed with his hands folded behind his head. The prince's hand darted for the dagger lying on the bed beside him as Lucas slipped inside and shut the door behind him.

"How did it go?" Tristan relaxed and laid the dagger back down.

"She did it," Lucas said. He shook his head in admiration. "You should have been there. Father never saw it coming."

"He agreed?" Tristan's eyes widened.

"He had no choice." A smile split Lucas's face as he began gathering up some of the things he wanted to take back to the house with him. "Aleatha had Mother on her side. I do not think Aleatha ever even asked to bring you home. Mother did it for her."

"But your father still does not want me there." Tristan's eyes clouded as he sat up and swung his feet over the side of the bed.

"No, but this is your chance to convince him you are worthy to win Aleatha's hand." Lucas crossed the room and laid his hand on Tristan's shoulder. "You will see, he will come around. He just needs to see the queen has no hold over you."

The look in Tristan's eyes darkened as he stood and slid the dagger beneath his belt.

"God brought you out of that desert for a purpose, Tristan. You trusted Him in the desert, why can you not trust Him now that you are home?"

A blush of shame flooded Tristan's face and he looked down. "You are right, Lucas. It is so much easier to forget now that clinging to that truth is not a matter of life or death. Pray for me, my friend. I still have a long way to go."

"I do pray for you." Lucas bent to pick up a bundle of bedding. "I think you will find the atmosphere of our house much better for your temperament also.

"Of course the attentions of my beautiful sister cannot hurt either." Lucas called over his shoulder as he carried his load to the door.

The only response he got was a boot thrown at his back.

*****

As Lucas pulled the wagon up to the back door to the house Tristan pulled the hood of his cloak further over his face. Lady Medellin was supposed to have warned all the servants to keep quiet about their important guest, but he was taking no chances. One hand clutched the hilt of Lucas's dagger hidden beneath the folds of his cloak as Lucas helped him from the wagon and they entered the kitchen. The servants cleaning up from breakfast continued on as if nothing was happening, only stealing an occasional glance in his direction. To the left of the servants' stairs, Dr. Medellin leaned against the wall, his arms folded tightly across his chest and his eyes boring holes into Tristan's. The sound of heavy footfalls behind him as Tristan mounted the stairs indicated Dr. Medellin was close behind.

"Mother thought it would be best if you did not stay in the room you used to use when you came here, for safety's sake," Lucas explained as he led him to a rarely used guest room. He shot a glance at the man behind Tristan. "Father thought it best you were on the opposite end from Aleatha and suggested we post a guard outside your door."

"Also for safety's sake." Dr. Medellin's voice was low and threatening.

"Oh, good, you are here," Aleatha greeted them as they entered the room, She rushed to Tristan and took both of his hands in hers. "We just finished. What do you think?"

Conscious of Dr. Medellin's eyes on him, Tristan extracted his hands from Aleatha's grip before looking around the room. The first thing he noticed was that it was clean. Not that he expected anything else; it was just a stark contrast to where he had been. A crisply made bed sat against the wall to his right with a small table beside it. A chair sat in the corner to his left and the window was open, allowing the evening breeze to bring in the luscious scent of the Medellins' expansive gardens. His throat tightened. *How much I missed this place!*

"It is perfect, Aleatha," Tristan murmured. "Thank you."

"You need to rest, Prince Tristan," Lady Medellin said as she shooed her children to the door. "There will be plenty of time to visit later. In fact, I will send Aleatha up with some dinner for you in a little while."

"I will be back in a little bit to check on you," Lucas promised as he followed his mother and sister out the door. "It is good to have you back"

Keenly aware that Dr. Medellin remained, Tristan untied the strings holding the cloak around his neck and threw it over the back of the chair. The looks Dr. Medellin had been giving him left little doubt the older man had just been waiting for the appropriate moment to confront him.

"So you have them all fooled, do you?" Dr. Medellin asked bitterly as soon as the others were out of hearing.

"The only person deceived here is you, Doctor." Tristan sighed as he lowered himself into the chair. "I do not pretend to be the same as I was a year ago, neither am I the monster you believe me to be."

Gripping the front of Tristan's tunic, Dr. Medellin pulled him up out of the chair until their faces were inches apart. "If you so much as touch Aleatha, or anyone else in this household, I will finish the job your mother started."

The feelings of helplessness Tristan felt during his time with Devon swept over him. *He is not Devon. He is only trying to protect his family.* He pushed himself to his feet, squared his shoulders, and met Dr. Medellin's gaze. "If you fear me so much, why even allow me into your home?"

"I knew my children would continue to visit you behind my back. Here I can keep an eye on you. That guard outside your room is not only here for your protection."

"So I am a prisoner then?"

"No, you are absolutely free to leave, and welcome to." Dr. Medellin sneered bitterly as he released his grip on Tristan. "However, as long as you are in my house you will be under both my care and my watch."

"Then you will see I am not the man you think I am."

"All I expect to see is a devil clothed as an angel," Dr. Medellin shot back as he put his hand on the door to leave. "Remember, if you as much as touch Aleatha, you are a dead man."

Chapter 12

The dawn woke Tristan the next morning without filling his heart with terror for the first time in over a year. Lady Medellin and Aleatha had seen his every need fulfilled before assigning one of their own servants to stand guard outside his room. Forget the kingdom; he only needed one more thing to be truly happy.

Heavenly Father, please help me to win Dr. Medellin's approval to marry Aleatha, he prayed silently. *I do not want to go against his wishes, but I truly love her. Please help me to show him I am not the monster he thinks me to be.* He had no idea how he would do that, but perhaps being in the Medellins' home would give him an opportunity to show Dr. Medellin he was no threat to Aleatha.

A knock at the door interrupted his thoughts. *Probably Lucas checking on me. Still…* He threw his tunic on quickly before calling out, "Come in."

"Tristan? Are you ready for breakfast?" Aleatha asked as she poked her head into the room. "We will be leaving for church soon, and I wanted to be sure you were taken care of."

"Good morning, Aleatha." Just seeing her again felt so good. "After dinner last night, I doubt I will ever need to eat again."

"I can take it back to the kitchen," Aleatha teased, backing into the hall. "I am sure Lucas would be willing to have seconds."

"I think I might be able to try a little," Tristan admitted, as he pulled himself up to sit on the bed. "I need to build my strength, you know."

At that, Aleatha swung the door open the rest of the way and sailed into the room followed by a serving girl carrying a tray loaded with food.

How could I have ever doubted her faithfulness? Tristan wondered as he admired the grace of her movements and enjoyed her beauty while being careful not to stare overtly at her. *I feared I had lost her forever, now I never want to let her out of my sight.*

Halfway across the room, Aleatha tripped over one of the boots Tristan had carelessly tossed to the floor the night before and lurched forward with a cry. In one movement, Tristan tossed aside his covers and swung his legs over the bed. He dove forward and caught Aleatha in his arms before she could hit the floor.

"Are you all right?" he asked as he lifted her to her feet. His sudden exertion made the room spin, but at the moment his only concern was for Aleatha.

"Yes, thank you. I…"

"Aleatha?" Dr. Medellin called from the doorway. His questioning tone turned to a roar of rage as he lunged toward the couple, grabbed Aleatha by the arm, and tore her away from Tristan. With his other hand, he gripped Tristan by the throat. "Get your filthy hands off my daughter, you…"

"Father, stop!" Aleatha cried. "It is not like that. Please…"

"Take her to her room." Dr. Medellin shoved his daughter toward the frozen serving girl. "You will be lucky if I do not toss you out on the street for not watching them more carefully."

"Aleatha tripped." Tristan's heart thundered in his ears. He had to get Dr. Medellin to calm down and listen to reason. "I caught her. That is all that happened."

"Do not lie to me!" Dr. Medellin slammed Tristan against the wall beside the bed.

Pain shot through the prince's still healing shoulder wound, causing him to groan. *Heavenly Father, would he truly kill me?*

"I warned you what would happen if you touched my daughter, you monster." Hatred, rage, and fear mixed in Dr. Medellin's eyes.

"Dr. Medellin, if you would just listen for a moment," Tristan tried again, hiding the panic that flooded over him. If he could not pacify Dr. Medellin, he might just make good his threat.

"Listen to your excuses? Your lies?" Dr. Medellin wrapped his other hand around Tristan's neck. "I will not have you seducing my daughter in my own house."

"That is not what happened, Father, " Lucas's voice interrupted from right behind his father. "If you would just calm down long enough to listen to anyone, you would know the truth."

"You defend this beast?" Dr. Medellin turned to his son, his face livid. "Over your own sister's honor?"

"Aleatha told me what happened. Her story was supported by Annette." Lucas laid a hand on his father's shoulder. "Aleatha ran to me as soon as you threw her out. She is afraid you will do something you will regret later."

"I am not so sure I would regret it later." Dr. Medellin turned his blazing eyes back to Tristan as he spat, "This is far from over."

With those parting words he shoved Tristan roughly against the wall again before releasing him and storming past Lucas out the door.

Thank you, Heavenly Father, once again. Tristan let out a long breath, closed his eyes, and leaned back against the wall.

"Are you all right?" Concern filled Lucas's voice as he stepped to Tristan's side.

"I will be fine," Tristan assured him. He turned his gaze to his friend. "Thank God you got here when you did! I could not get him to listen to me."

"I have never seen him so angry before." Lucas shook his head as he helped Tristan back to the bed. "When Aleatha told me Father was going to kill you, I thought she was exaggerating. But to see him like that… I hate to think what might have happened if I had not come."

As he shakily lowered himself onto the bed, Tristan scrambled for a response. As glad as he was for Lucas's support, he did not want to come between Dr. Medellin and his children. "But you did, and I am fine," he said, determined to downplay Dr. Medellin's behavior as much as possible. "Would you not be mad in his place?"

"Maybe." Lucas gestured to Tristan's shoulder. "Take off your tunic. I want to get a look at your wound, to make sure he did not do any damage."

This is not going to help me win over Dr. Medellin. Tristan admitted as he obeyed his friend. *How will I ever convince him I am not a danger to Aleatha now?*

"Your shoulder looks fine." Lucas sounded relieved as he bandaged Tristan back up. Biting his lip, he took a step back and regarded his patient.

"What is it?"

"Father overreacted a lot," Lucas began. "I know he does not approve of you and Aleatha, but just now I could have sworn he hated you."

"Perhaps he does." Tristan looked away from Lucas's searching gaze.

"For what?" Lucas asked. "He never had a problem with you before."

"People change," Tristan said with a shrug. He winced at the pain in his shoulder and looked up at Lucas. "As far as your father's reasons are concerned, I think you had better ask him."

"Do you know his reasons?" Lucas narrowed his eyes and searched his friend's face. "You do know. Are they valid?"

"I suppose they are not entirely unfounded," Tristan admitted reluctantly as he swung his legs back up in the bed and lay back. "Although they are false. Let us just say it would take a miracle for him to ever approve a marriage between me and your sister."

"I will talk to him. Perhaps I can get to the bottom of his fears." Lucas laid a reassuring hand on Tristan's arm. "I will have Aleatha talk to him, too. She loves you, and I know her feelings count for something to my father. Maybe the two of us can persuade him to change his mind."

Only if you can erase my parentage and the entirety of the last year, Tristan thought. He closed his eyes to keep Lucas from seeing the tears gathering in them. "Thank you, Lucas. I really appreciate all your help."

"No problem," Lucas said. He headed toward the door. "You get some rest now."

* * * * *

You failed, Devon. Failure is inexcusable.

Queen Brigitte's rebuke echoed in Devon's mind as he tossed in his bed. He had never failed at anything before, especially not at the thing he was best at. Torture was his forte. Had been his forte. He had never been out matched before. He turned in his bed and punched his pillow. *I had been confident the young prince would break in the first week; surely in the first month. But to hold out a year!* The worst Devon had thrown at him had not been enough. It was obvious he had shaken the prince's faith in his friends by the end, but nothing seemed able to breach the faith Prince Tristan held in his God. Devon snorted and rolled over again. *So, I have been defeated by God. Small consolation, at least. It took deity to outlast me.*

"Sir?" a pensive voice from outside his door interrupted Devon's brooding.

"What is it?" Devon snapped. Who would dare interrupt his sleep at this hour of the morning? The sun had not even risen yet.

"A messenger," the stranger answered nervously, "with important news."

"It had better be," Devon growled as he threw aside the covers and stepped on the cold floor. He tossed on the clothes he had discarded the night before, stomped to the door, and flung it open to reveal a quaking peasant standing in the hall. Devon's eyes narrowed. He did not recognize the man as one of the palace staff. "How did you get in here?"

The man swallowed his fear. "Me… me brother's the porter. 'e let me in. I 'ave some very valuable news for you."

"If you are wasting my time, you will not have to worry about finding a way out of here."

"It is worth your time," the man hastened to assure him. A crafty look passed across the man's face. "If you're not interested, I know the queen would be more than willing to pay for what I know."

"If it is that good, I will pay." Devon's interest was piqued. He closed the door behind the man. "If not, you will. Make it quick."

Nodding, The man licked his lips. "It's about Prince Tristan."

"Prince Tristan is dead, since you have not heard." Devon grunted. "No information you have about him could interest me."

"Except, 'e's not dead." The man relaxed, as if feeling safe knowing something Devon did not know.

Heat flooded to Devon's face. "Impossible!" he roared. He gripped the man by the throat with his right hand. "I watched him die!"

"I swear it, me lord," the man croaked, his eyes bugging with fear. His hands latched onto Devon's wrist as he struggled to get free. "'E is staying at my master's house. I saw 'im myself."

The blood ran cold in Devon's veins just as quickly as it had run hot. *Perhaps if Prince Tristan's God helped him overcome torture, He could help him overcome death as well.* "How do I know you are not mistaken?" Devon shook the man, his hand still tight around the man's neck. "How would you know the prince if you saw him?"

"'E often came to my master's house, before you … um, before," the man trailed off, fear stopping his tongue.

Devon swore and threw the man aside. *The Medellins' home.* If Prince Tristan indeed lived, and still sought the company of his former friends, he had failed on more than one front. He turned back to the man cowering on the floor. "You serve Dr. Gaius Medellin?"

"I take care of the horses," the man answered, rubbing his neck.

"You swear to me you saw Prince Tristan alive?" Devon took a threatening step closer. He could not afford false rumors to surface now.

The man bobbed his head rapidly. "I swear! I saw Miss Aleatha and Master Lucas bring 'im into the house a day ago. 'E's been there ever since."

Devon cursed again. He needed time to think, which meant he needed to be alone. He crossed the room, drew a handful of gold out of a sack on the table by his bed, and threw it at the man sniveling at his feet. "Watch him. Report to me if anything changes and there will be more like it. Go."

The traitorous servant scrambled to his feet and scurried out the door, slamming it behind him.

Devon began to pace the room, considering his options. *Prince Tristan lives!* Not only had he failed to break him, but he had ultimately failed to kill him as well. One thing was certain: Prince Tristan would have to be eliminated before the queen found out. Devon could not afford another failure.

As the queen said, failure was inexcusable.

Chapter 13

The day passed uneventfully for Tristan. Lucas and Dr. Medellin spent the day at the palace. Aleatha and Lady Medellin took excellent care of him, bringing him breakfast and lunch and making sure he got plenty of rest. At least, they made sure he was left alone to rest. While he obeyed Lucas's orders to stay in bed, he found it difficult to actually rest. As he lay on his bed with his arms folded behind his head and stared at the ceiling, Dr. Medellin's accusations spun through his head.

If I do nothing to stop my mother, am I as bad as she is? But what could he do? A year ago, when he stood before the royal council and accused her of abuse of power, harsh treatment of the people, even of murdering those who opposed her, the council had failed to act. He had stormed out of the council chambers vowing that he would change everything when he was crowned king. Unfortunately, that same council was in charge of his coronation. His mother would see that they never crowned him, and without the crown, what good could he do?

A knock at the door interrupted his melancholy thoughts. "Come in."

"Dinner. How is my patient?" Lucas came in carrying a tray of food, a wide grin splitting his face.

"I could get used to this treatment." Tristan pushed aside his thoughts and smiled at his friend. "Beautiful women waiting on me hand and foot, my own personal doctor, and a bodyguard at my door, what more could a prince ask for?"

"How about his own sword?" Lucas's face brightened even more. He set the tray of food on the table beside Tristan's bed, swept aside his cloak, and gripped the ornately jeweled hilt that stuck out from his own plain leather scabbard. He drew the sword almost reverently and laid the perfectly balanced, glistening silver blade in his opposite hand. Dropping to one knee, he offered the sword to Tristan. "Your sword, Your Highness."

"How did you ever get that out of the palace?" Tristan stared at Lucas in disbelief. He swung his legs over the side of the bed and ran his fingers gently over the intricate filigree of the hilt and traced his family crest engraved into the base of the blade.

"I know how important it is to you, especially since it was your father's. While I was on my rounds in the palace, I left my sword in Father's chambers, slipped into your room, and slid it into my scabbard," Lucas said with a smirk. "I am afraid I had to leave your scabbard behind. There was no way I was carrying that jeweled monstrosity around without getting caught. It was hard enough to hide the hilt under my tunic."

Chuckling, Tristan took the sword in his hand, stood, and began to swing it in a wide figure eight. Lucas always teased him that the jewel encrusted scabbard would make him a clear target if he ever needed to go to battle. "Thank you. You ran no little risk stealing this from the palace. If you had been caught, I doubt even your father could have helped you."

"Do not mention it," Lucas said as he dismissed Tristan's concern with a slight shaking of his head. "How is your shoulder doing?"

Tristan stopped swinging his sword and rotated his left arm. He winced slightly. "Getting better."

"Obviously," Lucas said with a short laugh. "Let me take a quick look at it before I go. Father is probably getting impatient."

"You are going back out?" Tristan tried to hide his disappointment. He had hoped to talk to Lucas about his troubling thoughts.

"Umm hmm," Lucas replied as he examined Tristan's wound. "Looks like it is healing nicely. How do you feel?"

"As much as I love your house, I feel like I need to get out," Tristan answered. "At least for a little bit. I need some fresh air."

"Fine," Lucas said as he replaced Tristan's bandages. "Try not to stay out too long, you do not want to tire yourself. And for safety's sake, wait until dark and make sure you are wearing a cloak. I am not sure when Father and I will be back, but I will check on you one last time before I go to bed for the night."

"Where are you going?" Tristan persisted, a little surprised. Midnight excursions were not common in the country, since bandits were more of a danger and reasons for leaving home were few.

"The underground resistance is meeting tonight." Lucas lowered his voice and glanced at the closed door. "The Queen's men were 'collecting taxes' in Dragonshire today. They burned three homes and killed a farmer protecting his crops. The farmer was a member of the resistance. Father and some of the others think he was targeted. They're meeting to form a plan of action against the queen."

Lucas truly is a member of the resistance? Tristan took a deep breath and pushed aside Devon's returning accusations of Lucas's treachery. "How long have you been with the resistance?"

Lucas raised an eyebrow at Tristan's tone, but did not pursue it. "Only for a couple of days. Father and several of the nobles joined the night after we found out you had supposedly died. There are still people loyal to you, Tristan. When your mother had you killed, no matter how she tried to disguise it, that was a step too far for many, even many members of the council."

If members of the council are now part of the resistance, perhaps there is hope after all. Tristan looked at Lucas sharply. "Too bad they did not see it when I spoke to them a year ago. We might have all avoided some misery."

"Your speech before the council has become a bit of a rallying cry among the members of the resistance." Lucas stood to leave. "There is a printer in Pimley who is secretly printing handbills of it to distribute to the people. Your 'death' has been a call for action."

Lucas turned and began to open the door, then stopped. He took a sharp breath. "Perhaps…"

"Perhaps what?" Tristan sat up straighter in the bed. "What is it?"

As Lucas closed the door slowly and turned back to face Tristan, his face was ruddy with excitement and his eyes shone. "Yes, I think that would be a great idea," he said. He stopped, evaluating Tristan with a physician's eye. "If it would not be too much, that is."

"What are you talking about?" Tristan said in exasperation. "What would be too much?"

Putting his hands on the arched footboard of Tristan's bed. Lucas looked him in the eye. "Look, you want to go out right? What if you came with me?" His words came out in a rush. "Your words have already given so much purpose to the people, what would they do with you as their leader? The legitimate heir to the throne, one who has already proved himself a man for the people and the enemy of the queen. Who could resist following you?"

I can think of at least one, Tristan thought.

"There are already multitudes of young people who would be ready to stand behind you as one of them," Lucas continued, "and the older men could not dispute the advantages of supporting the rightful king. And no one can argue you do not have the people's best interest at heart. Everyone knows that is why you were sent away to begin with." Lucas paused for a breath and finished more soberly. "But I do not want to push you to do something you are not ready for. I am first and foremost concerned about your health. I only want you to do this if you feel up to it. There will be other meetings."

Perhaps there is a chance. Tristan looked down silently at the sword lying in his lap as he thought about Lucas's words. His friend's excitement had lit a spark of hope inside him. *Perhaps there is something I can do to stop my mother's wickedness.* He closed his eyes tightly. Just as the doubts Devon had planted in his mind about Lucas and Aleatha still haunted him, Devon's excuses for his mother's behavior persisted also. *You know she only wants what is best for you. She is depending on me to mold you into the strong monarch she knows you will have to be to guide those rebellious people when she is gone.* Devon was wrong. No people deserved the cruel way his mother ruled. He knew the things she did, both to him and her subjects, were wrong, but still the doubts came. Perhaps he was wrong to try to stop her. What did he really know about running a kingdom?

No, she was the one that was wrong, he knew that absolutely, in spite of his doubts. The doubts did concern him, though. How could he rule a nation if he could not even rule his own thoughts?

As if he could sense Tristan's internal war, Lucas circled the bed and laid a hand on his shoulder. "Perhaps this is the reason God spared your life in the desert. You are uniquely prepared for this."

Hope… and purpose. Tristan needed those things as much as the resistance did. He looked up at Lucas and nodded. "I will come."

"We will take horses." Lucas's face lit up with excitement. "If at anytime you feel like it is getting to be too much for you, we can come right back here. I will send Father on ahead, it will take us a few minutes to get ready and I am sure he is already getting impatient."

Dr. Medellin would not be pleased if he knew what Lucas has in mind, Tristan thought as Lucas left. Dr. Medellin would be the least of his worries now. He lay back and closed his eyes, trying to catch a few minutes rest before Lucas returned. He was going to need all the strength he could for the war he was preparing to enter.

*****

Lucas returned with another cloak and dark clothes for Tristan as well as a spare scabbard and sword to complete arming them both. Tristan strapped the belt of the scabbard on over his surcoat and slid his sword into the scabbard with a satisfying hiss. It felt good to wear his own sword again. He threw the cloak on over his shoulders, tied it loosely around his neck, and pulled the hood over his head. Self-consciously, he twisted his signet ring on his finger. *Persuading the members of the resistance I am who I claim to be is going to be a difficult task. I hope my ring and sword will help convince them.*

The rest of the Medellins' household was asleep for the night, and they did not wish to rouse them. Tristan and Lucas appeared to be no more than two shadows drifting down the stairs and out the back door to the pair of horses Lucas had readied after his father had left. The horses were also dark, completing the shadowy disguise. They headed away from the house and down a road lined with trees so dense, the light from the moon barely penetrated the leafy ceiling. Once they were out of sight of the house, Lucas slid aside the darkening panel on the lantern hooked to his saddle, illuminating the road ahead of them.

Half a mile later, a rustling sound in the woods ahead of them made Tristan's heart race. He gripped the hilt of his sword and urged his horse ahead until he was riding abreast of Lucas's mount.

A glance from Lucas indicated he had heard it also. The young doctor leaned forward over his horse's neck as if preparing to send his horse into a gallop and gestured for Tristan to do the same. He raised three fingers, putting down one, then another in a countdown to making an attempt to dash past whatever danger lurked in the woods ahead of them.

When Lucas's final finger went down, Tristan drove his heels into the sides of his horse, sending him forward like a streak of lightning. They only made it a few yards before a man carrying a lantern and a sword stepped into the road in front of them. Tristan gripped the reins tightly as his horse reared in fright, gritted his teeth against the strain on his shoulder, and squeezed his legs around the horse's flanks. A loud whinny, followed by a dull thud and a low grunt, told him his friend had not been so lucky. He fought his panicking horse back under control and turned in his saddle to check on Lucas. He lay on the ground beside his horse, elbows propped behind him, glaring up at a bandit holding the tip of a sword to his chest. Another bandit held the reins of his horse to keep it from bolting.

"What 'ave we here, boys?" a low voice jeered. "It looks like we've got ourselves a pair of peacocks ripe for the plucking."

Turning again, Tristan faced the bandit blocking the road. "Let us go, we have nothing worth stealing."

"I wouldn't call that sword of yours 'nothing', young sir," the bandit said with a chuckle. "I could see it glinting in the moonlight. Anybody who carries a piece like that has got to be carrying plenty more a man like me might find worth taking." Pointing with his sword to the man holding Lucas's horse. "Grimbold, search them and their horses."

With a flash of steel, Tristan slid his sword out and pointed it at the bandit ahead of him. Since he was still mounted, the other man did not stand much of a chance against him. "I would recommend you change your orders to 'back off' unless you would like to become very closely acquainted with the sharp end of my sword."

"Unless you want my man to gut your young friend there, I would 'recommend' you hand your sword gently to Grimbold," the head bandit sneered. "Perhaps if you cooperate, I might let you live."

Chapter 14

Holding his sword steady, Tristan glanced back at Lucas. His friend had sucked in his stomach away from the sharp point pressing against his belly. Fear glinted in his brown eyes as he looked back at Tristan, but his jaw was set in defiance. He shook his head slightly, darting his eyes back to the head bandit.

He wants me to take him out. Tristan realized. They both knew the fate that waited for Tristan when they discovered his signet. Ransomed back to the queen, or worse yet, to Devon, who could not afford for the queen to discover his failure. In either case, the only thing Tristan could look forward to would be a slow, painful death.

Ice threaded through his veins. He was not going back to Devon, not alive anyway, but he was unwilling to stake his future on Lucas's life. He could easily take out all three men, but not before Lucas was murdered. His only choice was to take his chances the bandits would spare them, and perhaps not recognize the significance of his ring.

With a deep sigh, he lowered his sword, turned it in his hand until he was holding the cross guard, and offered it to Grimbold. The bandit looked up at him with a triumphant smirk Tristan would have loved smacking off his smug face. Glaring as the man grabbed the sword's grip, Tristan maintained his own grip on the sword for just a moment longer as his eyes met the bandit's.

"You there! Halt, in the name of the queen," an authoritative cry, accompanied by the hoofbeats of several horses, interrupted the exchange. All five men looked up to see a company of the queen's soldiers approaching. The captain drew his sword as he galloped toward the little group blocking the road.

Grimbold dropped his hand from Tristan's sword as if it had suddenly grown red-hot, ducked behind Tristan's horse, and disappeared into the darkness. The bandit standing over Lucas sheathed his sword and ran toward the woods, while their leader melted into the shadows.

"After them! A reward to the man who brings me their leader," Captain Brogan cried to his men.

As seven of the soldiers turned to follow after the bandits, their captain lead two more to check on the victims.

The bandits were bad enough; the queen's men are worse. Tristan slid his sword back into its scabbard, drew his cloak further over his face, let his long sleeve fall over his hand to hide his signet ring. He might have dared to try to fight off the bandits, but his only hope now was to make himself as inconspicuous as possible.

The captain raised his lantern as he drew near Lucas and Tristan. "You there. Are you all right?" His eyes widened as the light shone on Lucas. "Master Lucas?"

"Captain Brogan," Lucas acknowledged as he struggled to his feet. "We are fine. It seems you and your men arrived just in time."

"We were returning from a special assignment for the queen in Dragonshire. Lucky we happened along when we did. You and your friend would hardly be a match for three armed bandits." He narrowed his eyes at Tristan. "Who is your friend?"

"One of my patients," Lucas answered. His voice was cool despite the dangerous situation. "From my charity work in the Shambles. He has been quite ill and needed… er, special attention."

"Not the plague?" one of the other soldiers piped up with a tremor in his voice.

"Nothing so bad as that," Lucas assured him. He took his horse's reins in his hand, then added, "Though I will say, close association with him at this time could lead to death."

Tristan bit his lip to keep from laughing at his friend's audacity as all three soldiers took a step back. They were no longer interested in the identity of the young doctor's charge. In fact they seemed to be much more interested in how quickly they could get away.

"I think we'd better catch up to our men, to see if they caught those bandits." Captain Brogan backed his horse away. "We will get them, Master Lucas, don't worry. They'll not bother you again."

"Thank you, Captain," Lucas called after them. "May God be with you.

"And thank you, Lucas," Tristan said once the soldiers were out of earshot. "That was a brilliant diversion."

"I was entirely truthful," Lucas said as he mounted. "If the queen or Lord Devon find out you are alive, being with you could be deadly." He turned his horse and headed back toward Odell Chapman's estate. "Come on, the meeting must have started by now. If we hurry, we might get there before everyone leaves."

*****

When they arrived at Odell Chapman's estate, everything was dark. At first, Tristan thought their delay on the road might have caused them to miss the meeting altogether, but he dismissed that thought. They were not delayed that long. Perhaps the meeting place had been changed at the last minute and Dr. Medellin had not bothered to tell Lucas. He glanced at his friend. The lifelessness of the estate did not seem to bother him in the least as he led them to the stables at the back of the house. They left their horses with the waiting stable boy and crept across the beautifully trimmed lawn to a large building at the back of the estate. Tristan assumed it to be Chapman's winery, since his wines were famous throughout the kingdom, even the queen preferred them. This building, too, was dark.

By the dim light of the moon, Lucas led him around the building. He knocked gently on a door in the back. A female voice floated to them through the door. "Who is there?"

"A friend of Naboth," Lucas called back.

Naboth was a biblical character killed by the wicked Queen Jezebel for standing up for what was right. Tristan recognized the name and nodded appreciatively. It was a fitting reference to his mother and her crimes.

The door swung out, opening a torch-lit stairwell leading to the wine cellar. A well-dressed girl with a golden blond braid reaching to her waist held the door.

"Lucas," she welcomed him in, her sky blue eyes dancing. "Your father said you would be late, but I was beginning to wonder if you were coming at all."

"Celia! I did not expect to see you here," Lucas responded, obviously glad to see she was. "I thought you would still be at the castle."

Celia Chapman was Odell Chapman's daughter and one of the queen's ladies in waiting, Tristan remembered as he kept his head down as he pulled the door closed behind him. He watched his friend's enamored expression with approval. It appeared Lucas had found himself a girlfriend while he was gone. A good one, too, from what he could remember. She was one of the few ladies in the court who seemed to have any character.

"Who's your friend?" Celia gestured to Tristan as she turned and led them down the stairs.

"A man who has tasted Jezebel's wickedness firsthand," Lucas said. He leaned toward her and whispered, "His position in the kingdom makes him fear to show his allegiance with the resistance."

Celia looked admiringly at Lucas. "You and your father have influenced more of the nobility to join us than anyone else. The resistance has you especially to thank for the growing number of young nobles joining our cause."

Embarrassment tinted Lucas's face, but he was clearly pleased with her praise. He cleared his throat and changed the subject, "What have I missed?"

"More arguing." Celia rolled her eyes to the ceiling. "About the only thing they can agree on is that something must be done. You heard about Dragonshire?" Lucas nodded as Celia continued, "Father believes they need to organize the people to put pressure on the council to try the queen for her crimes and choose a new king. Lord Blakemore believes they need to appoint a member of the resistance who can get close to the queen to kill her, just like she did King Justin. He already has several volunteers."

"No matter how wicked the queen is, we cannot allow ourselves to stoop to her level," Tristan said, deepening his voice a little.

"That is what my father said." Celia hesitated before looking back at Lucas. "I am pretty sure your father sides with Lord Blakemore, though."

Lucas glanced at Tristan in surprise. Tristan simply shook his head grimly. That revelation may shock Lucas, but Tristan could have guessed that was the side Dr. Medellin would take. His feelings against Queen Brigitte were very strong.

They stopped before a door at the bottom of the stairs. Voices raised in heated argument could be heard coming from the other side.

"How is the group divided?" Lucas whispered, his hand on the door.

"It is hard to tell," Celia said with a shrug. "Lord Blakemore's group seems small, but passionate. They could persuade many of the undecided members." Her eyes twinkled at Lucas as she said, "Many of the undecided are the young people that look up to you. I think they are waiting to hear what you say before making a choice."

The noise level jumped as soon as Lucas pushed the door open. The trio entered the crowded room and wove through the buzzing crowd as they made their way toward a table in the center of the room. Tristan kept his hood low as he attempted to scan the crowd for familiar faces. There were several. Wealthy merchants, noblemen, soldiers, farmers, even a few servants from the palace. It was evident the queen's cruelty had managed to unite members of both ends of the social spectrum. Many of them would recognize him in a heartbeat, but would they be happy to see him? If Dr. Medellin feared him, others probably would, too.

As they neared the center of the crowd, Tristan saw two men standing on either side of the table, a printed handbill lying on the table between them. Lord Bryce Blakemore, tall and thin, with faded blond hair and eyes that reminded Tristan of a sword's blade, was Dale's father and a member of the royal council. He stood on one side, red-faced, shaking his fist at the man opposite him. Several other noblemen stood behind him, including Dr. Medellin. Odell Chapman, short and heavy, opposite his opponent in appearance as well as ideas, stood on the other side of the table, his normally jolly face dark and his full lips set in a tight line. Two other councilmen and handful of merchants stood behind him, eyeing Lord Blakemore and whispering to each other.

At that moment, Lord Blakemore raised his voice and turned to the crowd. "There is no other choice! The council will never defy the queen and depose her; she wields too much power. Once she is dead, we councilmen who value a free kingdom can push to crown a man with the interests of the people at heart."

The buzzing of the crowd rose to a roar as arguments broke out between the supporters of the opposing viewpoints scattered throughout the room. Lucas and Tristan finally pushed their way into the open circle at the center. As Lucas approached the table, Tristan stood back against the crowd. He did not want to draw attention to himself until the time was right. With the crowd on the edge of riot, this certainly was not it.

Disappointment was clear on Lucas's face as he nodded acknowledgment to his father and took his place behind Chapman. Dr. Medellin responded with an equally curt nod and a slight blush to his cheeks, but never noticed Tristan.

Chapman took a step toward the crowd and raised his hands over his head. "Gentlemen, quiet please. No matter the queen's wickedness, we cannot advocate cold-blooded murder." The roar was reduced to a buzz, so he continued, "We all agree that the queen holds great power over the council, but if we can gather the people to put pressure on the council, perhaps we can break that power without violence." He picked up the handbill. "In his final speech, the prince encouraged the council to dethrone Queen Brigitte peaceably; he would have never encouraged bloodshed."

"This is a war, Odell!" Lord Blakemore slapped his hand on the surface of the table and leaned across it, his face right in Chapman's. "Do you think Greyson's family would appreciate your restraint? The queen's men showed him none!"

The buzz rose again. Blakemore's words had their intended impact. Many people looked thoughtful and a few were nodding their heads. Fear gripped Tristan's stomach. As much as he hated his mother's actions, he knew what an assassination would bring: full-scale reprisals and an even more horrible ruler, King Devon. Many, many lives would be lost and no freedom would be gained. He clenched his teeth. *I need to put an end to this.*

He shot a glance to Lucas, who gave him a half smile and a short nod. Clenching his fists beside him, Tristan stepped to the center of the room. *Give me courage, Heavenly Father.*

"Lord Blakemore, Master Chapman, may I have a word with the people?" This time he did not bother to disguise his voice.

The room grew silent as the crowd focused their attention on the cloaked stranger who dared to interrupt the debate.

"Who are you?" Lord Blakemore snapped, squinting his eyes as if trying to get a glimpse of his face beneath his hood.

"He is my guest, sir," Lucas spoke up. "One who would have first hand knowledge of the issue at hand."

"Lord Blakemore, I hardly think this is a good idea." Dr. Medellin stepped forward. He flashed a sharp look at Lucas, his face flush with anger.

"Let him speak," Chapman commanded, sending both Dr. Medellin and Lord Blakemore back to their places with a look. He turned to address Tristan. "Which side do you fall on, young man?"

"Reason," Tristan answered. He turned to the crowd. "Esteemed freedom-fighters. Do we come here tonight to shake off the chains of Queen Brigitte's oppression and violence only to lower ourselves to her level in the process? If you kill her, do you not think Lord Devon would have himself crowned and initiate a slaughter against the innocent people of this kingdom to avenge her death? You would gain nothing and lose even your own integrity."

A hum rippled through the crowd, but only among the common classes of people. The nobles and councilmen who had heard him speak before stared wide-eyed as they tried to convince themselves it was impossible for them to be hearing the voice their ears told them they were hearing.

Lord Blakemore licked his lips uncertainly, but pressed on, "What would you have us do? Let the queen and her men kill us and burn our homes? The council will not defy the queen, and crown another. Not while she lives. We only have one hope: kill her ourselves and force the council to crown the man we choose."

"If you cannot persuade the council to crown your man now, they will only be more divided after her death," Tristan argued. "Demand the council banish the queen and crown the rightful king."

The room became deathly silent. The noblemen who before were silent were now completely colorless. Only a young farmer dared to speak up. His voice was filled with confusion. "Who would that be?"

Tristan pulled the hood down from his head. "Me. Prince Tristan Leander."

Chapter 15

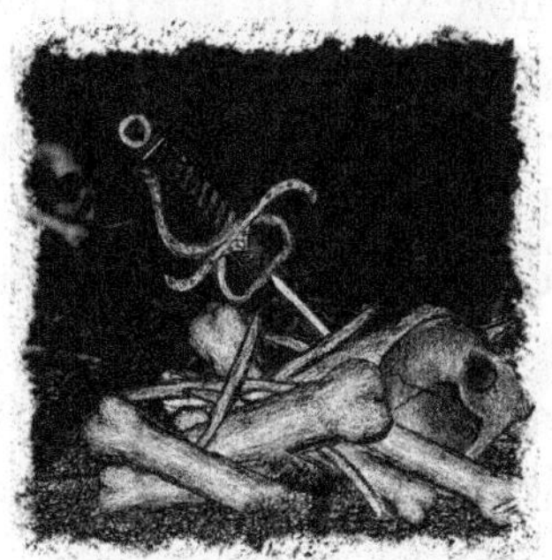

"By law the council was required to crown me king on my twenty-first birthday." Tristan lifted his voice against the rising clamor. "That day has passed. I am the rightful king." He took a deep breath. "My mother is a usurper, she no longer has any power."

Cries of astonishment and disbelief filled the room.

"Impossible!"

"He is dead!"

"The prince?"

"Prove it!"

At once, every voice stopped as if it had been cut off. All eyes went to Lord Blakemore. He stood behind Tristan with his hands on his hips. "How do we know you are not an impostor?"

"It is a good question," Odell Chapman agreed. "How do we know you are who you say you are? According to Lord Devon, Prince Tristan died during their travels."

"We should be so lucky." Tristan could have sworn he heard Dr. Medellin grumble.

Ignoring the glowering man, Tristan strode to the table, pulled his signet from his hand, and laid it on the table. He drew his sword and laid it beside his ring. "Examine them," he said with calm assurance. "I believe they will end any dispute.

Chapman and Blakemore took turns examining the ring and the sword, Chapman with a merchant's eye for quality and authenticity, Blakemore with the eye of familiarity, having seen both plenty of times before. After several minutes, Chapman laid down the sword he had been examining and looked at Lord Blakemore. "I am satisfied."

Lord Blakemore simply grunted his grudging assent as he slammed the signet down.

Turning to the attentive crowd, Odell Chapman called, "Gentlemen, I present to you Prince Tristan Leander, the true king of Boldaria!"

*****

An urgent summons in the middle of the night is never a good sign. Devon paced outside the door to the queen's chamber. Surely she had not discovered Tristan still lived. Where were his men? They should have been back over an hour ago to report that they had finished the young prince. Surely the Medellins were not guarding him that well. Perhaps they would still show up before the queen called him in. He had already been waiting nearly twenty minutes for her.

Too late. The door swung open and a dour-faced manservant faced him. "Lord Devon, Queen Brigitte will see you now."

Devon drew himself to his full considerable height. There was no way he was going give the queen the satisfaction of seeing him nervous. Besides, he could not be sure she knew anything yet, and he was not going to give her any indication something was wrong.

The queen lay reclined in a plush chaise, a table filled with food to her left and Captain Brogan standing at attention to her right. Devon felt beads of sweat beginning to form on his forehead. Captain Brogan's presence at this meeting did not bode well.

"You summoned me, Your Majesty?" Devon bowed low.

"Captain Brogan brought me some disturbing news," Queen Brigitte said, her soft, musical voice grave. Mock concern turned down the corners of her painted lips. "He and his men caught a band of bandits attacking some of my subjects this evening."

"Bandits are a curse of any wealthy kingdom." Devon straightened, a droplet of sweat running down the side of his face. "This would not be the first time a nobleman has lost a few baubles to them."

"But they were not looking for baubles," she purred as she sat up and leaned toward him. "Captain Brogan tells me they were looking for *someone* very specific. Who do you think they were looking for?"

She knew, and he was as good as dead. "How would I know, my queen?"

"Because they claim you hired them." Her calm voice was edged with steel and a deadly rage gleamed in her eyes. "They claim they were hired to kill my son and make it look like a robbery."

She leaned back in the chaise and picked up a pastry from the table beside her. "But that cannot be right, could it, Lord Devon? My son is dead. You killed him with your own hand." She took a careless bite from the pastry and looked at him, her eyes daring him to contradict her. "Or so you told me."

Devon debated his options. He could deny her accusations, pitting his word against Brogan's, but when she confirmed Tristan lived, her rage would be all the greater for his having lied to her. He could admit his failure and fall on her mercy, but she was known for having none. His only choice was to try to spin the events in his favor and blunt the force of her anger as much as possible.

"I believed him to be, Your Majesty," Devon said. "How he survived, I have no idea, perhaps his God resurrected him. In any case, I was prepared to rectify the situation. He would truly have been dead if your man had not interfered."

"You are the one who will be dead if the situation is not rectified immediately," the queen hissed. "First you fail to turn him, then you fail to kill him. Must I do everything myself?"

"I will kill him myself; I will kill the whole household while they sleep if I must." Devon turned to leave before the queen could stop him, but a knock at the door interrupted his escape.

"Who dares disturb me at this time of night?" Queen Brigitte roared, pushing herself upright in her chaise.

"Celia Chapman, Your Majesty," a soft, nervous voice answered through the door. "I have important news."

"Come in, and make it quick," the queen snapped. She tossed a meaningful glance toward Devon. "I have other more important things to deal with."

Celia opened the door and peered into the room. "Queen Brigitte, the underground resistance held a special meeting tonight to discuss your, uh, tax collection in Dragonshire."

"Come in, Lady Celia, and close the door," the queen barked. "They are always meeting about something, but they never actually do anything important. I hope this is as urgent as you claim. Your brother's life depends on relevant information about the underground. Or I could have Captain Brogan assign Lieutenant Chapman to one of our galleys."

Paling at the mention of her brother, Celia stepped inside and closed the door behind her. "Please, Your Majesty, don't hurt my brother," she begged, her blue eyes filling with tears. "I do have important information. Prince Tristan returned tonight. He spoke to the resistance and rallied them behind him."

"It seems your little failure is wasting no time in making an annoyance of himself," Queen Brigitte snarled at Devon. "My son has ever been popular among the people. His bid for the throne will gain strength each day he is permitted to live."

Desperate to redeem himself before the queen, Devon turned to the fearful girl, grabbed her forearm tightly, and yanked her toward him. "Where are they meeting?" he snarled in her face.

"At my father's, in the cellar of his winery," Celia squeaked, trembling.

Dropping Celia's arm, Devon bowed to Queen Brigitte. "I will take twenty men and eliminate all who would gather against you. I personally swear to bring you Prince Tristan's corpse. I will end this threat to your throne once and for all."

"No, please, Your Majesty!" Celia cried, terror filling her face. "My father… all my friends…"

"Do you think I could not have sent my men to disrupt their little meeting if I chose to?" Queen Brigitte said disdainfully. "Thanks to Lady Celia and her brother, I know all their names and all their plans. The underground resistance is no threat to me. Only my son can threaten me."

"Then I will set upon him as he leaves." Devon cast an accusing glance at Captain Brogan. "Without interference, I can finish what I set out to do. This time I will bring his body to you as proof."

Queen Brigitte thought for a second. "Captain Brogan, you are dismissed." She gave Celia an appraising look. "You did well, my dear. Your brother and his family should be proud of your loyalty to your queen."

She turned back to Devon after Captain Brogan and the now weeping girl left and frowned. "You will bring my son back to me, alive. I never wished to see him dead, only to have him rule beside me. Perhaps I can do what you failed to do. I will give him one more chance to pledge his loyalty to me, if he still refuses, you can do what you want with him. Besides, he is popular among the people, a feat I have never quite been able to accomplish. With him ruling beside me, no one could stand before me. Go! You may consider this your only second chance. Fail me again and I will make the torture you put my son through look like heaven compared to what I will put you through myself."

Devon bowed again and left. He hoped the young prince would refuse his mother's final offer. He would make him pay for humiliating him in front of the queen. He would get his revenge.

*****

Tristan stood beside the door of the winery cellar as people trickled past him. He was exhausted from standing the last two hours, but pleased with the outcome. Chapman had put the resistance to a vote: support Prince Tristan's claim to the throne or Lord Blakemore's plan to assassinate the queen. The vote had gone overwhelmingly in his favor. Only a few men had voted with Lord Blakemore. Many of those were powerful men in the kingdom, but the most notable were Dr. Medellin and Dale Blakemore, neither of whom Tristan really expected to support him; Dr. Medellin for political reasons, Dale for personal ones.

On the other hand, Lucas was clearly bothered his father and one of his friends had sided with Lord Blakemore's plan. Tristan glanced at his friend standing beside him. He had been silent and moody since the vote and his expression grew blacker when his father refused to speak with him before he left. The room was nearly empty now, the men each bowing in respect or snubbing Tristan openly as they left, depending on their vote.

The elderly man who had led the council since Tristan was a child bowed low as he passed, taking Tristan's hand in his and placing his lips on his ring. "I am sorry, Your Highness, for not being bold enough to support you a year ago. This nation would not be in the state it is if those of us who loved Boldaria had not allowed our fear of the queen to rule us."

"That time is passed, Lord Applegate." Tristan laid his hand on the older man's shoulder. "I thank you for your support now. Perhaps you can influence others in the council to support my claim in spite of the queen. I know there are other honest men in the council who only need a little prodding to do what is right."

Lord Applegate bowed again and gave way to the next man in line. Dale Blakemore stood before Tristan, his head held high. He was the mirror image of his father, tall, blond, proud, but with the lithe build of a sportsman. He met Tristan's gaze with a defiant glare.

Lucas came alive at that moment. "What is wrong with you, Dale?" he growled, grabbing Dale by the forearm. "Do you not even have the decency to pay your respect to the rightful king of Boldaria?"

"This is not the way, Lucas," Tristan admonished as he laid a restraining hand on Lucas's shoulder.

Dale yanked his arm away from Lucas's grip. "I have come to love your sister, Lucas. If you think I will support my competition for her hand in his bid for the throne, you are mistaken."

"You will support your father's murderous plan instead?" Lucas seethed. "I thought you supported a peaceful change."

Unwilling to meet Lucas's accusing stare, Dale traced a line on the floor with his foot. "All I know is I will not support *him*. My concern is Aleatha." He turned back to Tristan and rested his hand on the pommel of his sword. "Even if I have to fight you for her."

Chapter 16

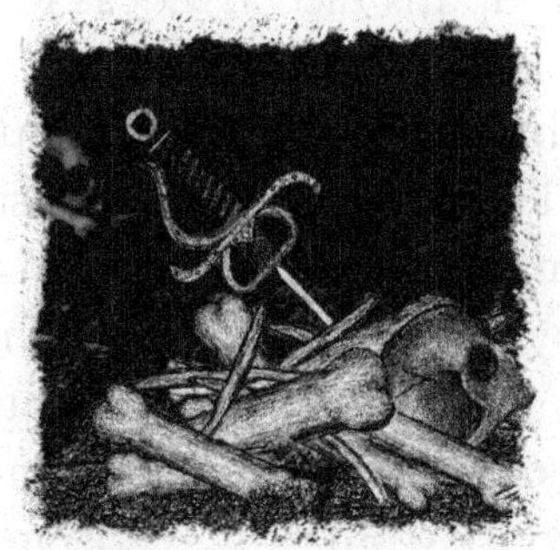

The room grew silent as the few people remaining watched to see Tristan's reaction. As much as he found Dale's impudence insulting, he was not going to duel him over it, even if he did feel up to it, which he was certain he did not. He pointed to the door and said simply, "Go home, Dale. Aleatha is a grown woman. Let her make her own choice."

Glaring at Tristan and the people around him, Dale dropped his hand from his sword and balled it into a fist. "We will meet again, Prince. I swear it." He turned sharply and stomped up the stairs.

"Let him go, Lucas. Give him some time to calm down." Tristan tightened his grip on Lucas's shoulder to keep his angry friend from following. "I think it is time we left, too. I am getting tired."

Lucas's anger cooled to concern. "Has our night out been too much for you?"

"A little," Tristan admitted. His legs felt weak as he realized just how tired he was. "I think I will be fine if I can just get some rest."

With a nod, Lucas scanned the few people in the room. When he failed to spot the face he sought, a frown creased his mouth.

"I'm sorry, Master Lucas." Chapman stepped forward and gestured to the house. "My daughter went to bed some time ago. Can I give her your regrets that you missed her?"

A blushed crept up his face as Lucas looked to the house. "Please. Though it is not quite the same."

"No, I would think not." Chapman chuckled.

"No, indeed." Tristan allowed a small smile to turn the corners of his mouth as he and Lucas turned to leave.

"Do not say anything," Lucas warned him as they mounted the stairs. "I have often seen you and Aleatha behave the same way, and do not even think about telling me it is different."

"I would not even dream of it," Tristan assured him easily as he pulled his hood up. "There is no difference at all. In fact, I plan to return your teasing just as equally as you gave it."

The pair fell silent as they stepped into the dark of the night. Keeping to the shadows, they glided across the moonlit lawn to the stables. The hair on the back of Tristan's neck rose as they entered the pitch-black stable. He glanced around for some sign of the intangible fear that had alarmed him. The stable boy was nowhere to be seen and the horses pawed their hoofs against the ground and whinnied nervously. Something was not right. A step ahead of him Lucas had stopped, too. He tossed a worried glance over his shoulder at Tristan. Tristan nodded back to the door and they tiptoed backward over the straw-strewn floor toward the exit.

"Do not take another step, Prince," Devon's voice warned from the darkness in front of them. The hiss of two swords being pulled from their sheaths only a few feet behind them lent credibility to the warning. "My men are right behind you."

Devon! Tristan froze as a feeling of panic gripped his chest. In one fluid motion, he drew his own sword and turned to face the men behind him in spite of his fear. There was no way Devon would take him without a fight. Lucas had drawn his sword also and was crouched in a defensive position beside Tristan. Lucas's swordsmanship was only passable, but perhaps if there were only three of them they would have a chance.

"Show yourself, Devon," Tristan called into the darkness, keeping one eye on the soldiers that stood by the door. "Unless you fear to face my sword."

"You know you are no match for me, Your Highness." Devon's voice dripped with contempt as he stepped out of the darkness into the small patch of moonlight the door let in. His sword was in his hand, but he held it loosely at his side. "As much as I wish it, your mother has given me express orders not to kill you, otherwise you would have been dead by now. She wishes to have a meeting with you."

"Tell her we are busy," Tristan mocked, fear infusing his tired body with renewed energy as he took a step toward Devon. "Since she already knows you failed to break me, then failed to kill me, I am sure she will be more than understanding when you fail to bring me back to her."

"You have humiliated me before the queen once," Devon snarled, his look of studied carelessness replaced by one of utter rage. The knuckles on his hand turned white as he clenched his fist around the grip of his sword. "If you do it again, I swear to you that your death will be as slow and painful as I can possibly make it."

"Take them," Devon commanded his men, his face still a mask of hatred. "Hurt them if you can, but do not kill them."

The soldiers jumped into action and in a moment both Lucas and Tristan were engaged in a frantic sword battle. Tristan parried his foe's sword as if it had been a practice match. He could have taken the ill-trained soldier with one quick blow, but his attention was divided. He did not dare let Devon, who was far more dangerous than either soldier, out of his sight.

He risked a quick glance at Lucas. Sweat beaded on Lucas's brow as he was backed against a horse's stall by a soldier more than his match. The horse occupying the stall nickered and skittered nervously as the flashing swords crowded closer to his space.

Knowing Lucas would soon need his assistance, Tristan turned his full attention to the man he was fighting. His sword flicked out and the soldier's sword flew out of his hand and over the wall of a nearby stall. As his opponent scrambled after his sword, Tristan turned to Lucas's aid. He quickly engaged the soldier that had pinned his friend down and drew him away. A few quick movements and he disarmed the second soldier.

"Lucas, go!" Tristan pointed his sword to the unguarded door. As Lucas ran to the door, Tristan scanned the stable for Devon. He had lost track of him during the fight.

"Tristan, behind you!"

The urgency in Lucas's voice caused Tristan to snap his head around. He was too late. A hand shot from the darkness and clamped down on his wounded shoulder. Tristan cried out in agony and sank to his knees as Devon dug the tips of his fingers into the wound.

With an angry cry, Lucas rushed forward to help his friend. The two soldiers stepped from the darkness and grabbed either arm. The one to Lucas's right wrenched his arm behind his back and forced him to drop his sword.

"Let him go." Tristan gritted his teeth against the pain radiating from his injured shoulder.

"I only have orders not to kill you, Prince." Devon leaned his face close to Tristan's ear. "The Queen said nothing about the traitors that harbored you. She certainly said nothing about not forcing you to watch me kill the young doctor."

A nod from Devon signaled one of the soldiers to raise the blade of his sword to Lucas's throat. Tristan smashed his head into Devon's face and jerked his shoulder free. He barely scrambled to his feet before Devon leaped on him with a roar of pain and rage. Devon dug his fingers into Tristan's shoulder again, sending Tristan to his hands and knees. Dropping to one knee beside Tristan, Devon increased the pressure on the wound until Tristan felt tears spring to his eyes and darkness began to creep into the corners of his vision.

"Tristan!" Lucas called, fear and worry mingled in his voice. "Stop, you monster, leave him…" His demand was cut off as the soldier pressed his sword into his neck, the sharp blade drawing a thin line of blood.

"Beg me not to kill him, Prince." Devon punctuated his demand by digging his fingers in again.

Tristan bit back another cry of pain, turning it into a low moan. The room appeared to be tipping around him. If his time with Devon had taught him anything, it was that giving in to Devon's torture accomplished nothing. He would do what he wanted with Lucas no matter what Tristan did.

"What good would that do?" Tristan panted. He was beginning to feel his consciousness slipping.

"Plead for his life, you stubborn fool!" Devon cursed as he pressed his fingers deeper into Tristan's shoulder.

The intense pain forced Tristan to the ground with a cry. *Heavenly Father, spare Lucas,* he pled desperately with the only One who could help as he lost his battle with the dizziness and darkness and passed out on the dirty stable floor.

*****

Each beat of Tristan's heart sent pain radiating down his arm as he awoke, reminding him of the abuse he had received from Devon.

Lucas. Guilt and grief mingled in his mind. Had Lucas's association with him cost him the ultimate price after all?

Tristan had little hope Devon had spared Lucas's life. He certainly would not have done it out of mercy. God had spared him in the desert, perhaps He had seen fit to spare Lucas as well. *He is in your hands, Heavenly Father.*

With a moan, he rolled over onto his side and was greeted by the sleek texture and soft rustle of silk bed sheets. Peeking through slitted eyelids, he looked about the lavishly decorated room at the familiar deeply colored velvets and gold accents. He closed his eyes tightly again and lay his head back on the pillow. Without looking further, he knew the headboard was elaborately carved with his family crest and overlaid with gold. He was in his own room at the castle. Devon had made good his threat to return him to his mother. *Why would You allow this to happen?* He had finally found some hope, now this. It was all so hard to understand. *I do not think I can go through it all again. Help me, I beg you.*

The squeak of the door opening put him on the defensive. He went for his sword, then for the dagger Lucas had given him. Both were gone.

"Good morning, Your Highness, are you ready for a bite to eat?" A dignified, gray-haired servant entered carrying a covered tray. His personal valet set the tray on the table beside the bed just as he had done every morning since Tristan was little. It was as if nothing had changed since he had left.

"What is going on, Jackson?" The throbbing in Tristan's shoulder intensified as he pushed himself up to sit leaning against the headboard.

Jackson lifted the lid off the tray, allowing the delicious scent of Tristan's favorite foods to waft into the air. His voice was somber as he answered, but he did not look at Tristan, "We thought you were dead, Your Highness, but late last night, your mother announced to the palace staff that you had been found, badly wounded, and had been in the care of Dr. Medellin until you were strong enough to return. This morning, I was informed you were home and I was to attend you just as before. She suggested I prepare you some of your favorite foods."

As the steam rose from the hot food, Tristan's stomach begin to growl. Boiled eggs, baked apples, and rich pastries filled the tray. He reached for a chocolate drizzled pastry, but stopped short.

"My mother told you to bring me this?" Tristan asked, his eyes never leaving the food.

"Yes, Your Highness. Is there anything else I can get you?"

"No, thank you," Tristan said with a sigh as he let his hand drop back on the bed beside him. There was no way he could eat anything here, no matter how delicious it looked.

"I took the liberty of laying out some clean clothes while you were sleeping. The queen told me you had been borrowing Master Lucas's clothes during your stay at the Medellins' home."

How did his mother know so much about where he had been and what he had been doing? Tristan looked down uneasily at the dusty surcoat he was wearing.

"What is really going on here?" he demanded in a low voice. "You know Mother never showed this much concern about me before, surely you do not believe she is going to start now."

His servant hesitated, and finally met Tristan's gaze. "No, Your Highness, but there are those of us who are concerned about you. She told us we are to give you the best the palace has to offer and make sure you have everything you could possibly want. She did not say why, and I did not ask. It was one order we were more than happy to follow."

"Is there anything else she did tell you?" The idea that there were still some people loyal to him in the palace comforted him a little, perhaps he could use it to his advantage.

"Only that she requests an audience with you first thing this morning," Jackson said with a shrug, "and that she has appointed five of her best men to make up a bodyguard for you. They are waiting outside your door now to accompany you to her chambers."

Chapter 17

"Bodyguard, my eye." Tristan snorted as he swung his legs around and set his feet on the plush rug beside his bed. "More like a prison guard." He stood and crossed the room to where his clean clothes were hanging. Stripping off his dirty clothes, he pulled on the layers of items courtly etiquette dictated he wear, layers he had gotten used to going without. Finally, he yanked the fashionably cut scarlet satin surcoat down over his head, ran a comb through his hair, and turned to look at himself in the mirror hanging nearby. The effect was startling, as if he had gone from renegade to royalty overnight. It was also strangely pleasant, like he was back the way he was supposed to be. As he stood in front of the mirror, Jackson reached around and strapped his empty scabbard around his waist.

"I am truly sorry, Your Highness, but it seems your sword went missing while you were gone. I know how much it meant to you."

"It is all right, Jackson, it was not your fault," Tristan assured him. The jeweled scabbard at his hip brought to mind the risk Lucas had taken bring him his sword. Concern for his friend's well-being overcame him again. *Heavenly Father, please help me discover Lucas's fate soon.*

A moment later, Jackson gently placed his coronet on his head. It was a simple braided circlet of solid gold with a trio of jewels set in the front – two large rubies flanking a larger diamond – wreathed by intricate gold filigree. Tristan's brow furrowed, his guard raised again. He never wore his coronet except to especially high affairs of state, and visiting his mother certainly did not qualify.

"Your mother's idea," Jackson responded to Tristan's suspicious look. "She requested it in honor of your return from the dead, as it were."

Queen Brigitte was up to something far more sinister than honoring her son, the Heir Apparent to the throne she had killed to obtain. Tristan bit back a snide remark and took a deep breath. "Let us get this over with, Jackson."

Jackson opened his mouth as if to comment, then shut it quickly. Grim concern shadowed his face. "Very well, Your Highness." He opened the door and bowed as Tristan passed. "May God be with you, Prince Tristan."

"He has been, Jackson." Tristan laid a reassuring hand on Jackson's arm. "Thank you."

Four soldiers lined the hall, snapping to attention as Tristan stepped out of his room. The fifth, Captain Brogan, leaned against the wall, sneering. "You look good, Prince, better than when we met last night. I did not recognize you as one of the young nobles we rescued from the bandits."

"Your timing was fortunate, Captain," Tristan replied. He kept his tone haughty and his posture stiff and tall, trying to look as authoritative as he could. If his mother insisted he dress like a prince, he would do his best to behave like one. "I am grateful for your intervention."

"Fortunate for your mother," Captain Brogan scoffed as he shoved himself away from the wall and stood in front of Tristan. "Not so much for you, since it got you brought back here."

Shaking his head, Tristan pushed past Captain Brogan and continued down the hall. Four soldiers fell into step with him, one on either side of him and two behind, with Captain Brogan scrambling to get ahead of him.

"Now wait here, young prince. Did Jackson not tell you we are supposed to be your bodyguard?" Captain Brogan asked, feigning surprise. "That means we are to stay with you at all times."

"Jailers, you mean," Tristan corrected with a scowl. This whole charade was ridiculous, his mother knew he had never gotten along with Captain Brogan. *The only purpose of having him here is to make sure I do not escape again, and perhaps to spite me in the process.* "I assure you I need no help finding my way down the hall to my mother's chambers."

"Your Highness, you are in more danger than you realize!" Captain Brogan affected an exaggerated look of offense. "As the Crown Prince, you are a target to any rebel or anarchist that might seek to prevent you from taking your rightful place on the throne. Your mother has pledged to make sure you are protected at all times. She could not bear to lose you again."

"Who are you trying to fool, Captain?" Tristan asked, laughing outright at the idea his mother would be saddened by his death. "We both know this is all a farce, if I am in any danger it is from you or Devon at my mother's command. Just take me to her so we can get to the real purpose of her summons."

"As you command, my prince." Captain Brogan bowed low before turning to lead Tristan down the hall. He stopped only a few yards away, opened the door to the queen's chambers, and ushered Tristan in. The room was even more elaborately decorated than Tristan's. The very walls were covered with gold foil and the bedstead was encrusted with jewels.

Captain Brogan gestured formally to three luxuriant armchairs forming a triangle around a thick rug. "The Queen asked for you to wait for her there."

Tristan took a few cautious steps into the room as Captain Brogan closed the door behind him. He appeared to be alone, but appearances were most likely deceiving. Whatever his mother's plans, he was sure he was under surveillance at all times. The only thing he could do was wait until his mother made her grand appearance. Perhaps then he would finally get to the bottom of this hypocrisy and get the answer to the one question that burned in the back of his mind: what had happened to Lucas? Whatever his mother's plans, he would not allow himself to show any weakness she could use against him.   Clenching his fists in determination, Tristan strode toward the sitting area. He was close enough to the nearest chair to touch it when a glitter of light to his left caught his eye. He cast a wary glance to the side and reached instinctively for the empty scabbard. On a gilded pedestal in front of one of his mother's many large mirrors sat the elaborate crown used in the coronation ceremony. Tristan caught his breath as he turned toward the pedestal. He had seen the crown several times among the crown jewels, but never this close up before. It was beautiful, covered in more precious and semiprecious gems than he could count. Several of the jewels made the three in his coronet look like pebbles in comparison to their size and luster. His finger traced one of the four half-arches that met over the deep blue velvet cap of the crown. At the point where the half arches met, a huge sapphire was set, the setting encircled by diamonds, each at least a carat in size. The weight of the crown was legendary, with a tale of one of his ancestors having to remain seated during the coronation because he did not have the strength to carry it. Curiosity tempted him to test it, to see if the legend was true.

Reverently, Tristan slid his hands beneath the thick circle of solid gold and lifted the crown off the velvet pillow that cradled it. It was heavy, even heavier than he had anticipated. The idea of placing such a weight on his head seemed almost absurd.

As he caught his reflection in the crown's polished gold, he finally understood what his mother was up to. It was all a bribe. If Devon's threats of punishment had not worked, perhaps promises of all the rewards of submission would. The rich foods, lavish comfort, physical safety, and the power of a king – at least as much power as his mother would allow him as she ruled behind him. There only lacked one thing to make his mother's array of temptations complete: some beautiful, morally deficient princess offering her hand in exchange for the political favors of another realm. His mother had never approved of Aleatha's social status, or, he suspected, that his marriage to her would not tie him more permanently to his mother's will.

Lowering the crown back to the pedestal, Tristan set his jaw with new-found determination. His mother had meant for the sight of the crown to remind him of all he had to gain by pledging his allegiance to her; he saw it as a reminder of exactly why he could not afford to do just that. He would never consent to aligning himself with her wickedness, lending legitimacy to her heavy-handed reign, and signing his name to her evil deeds. His meeting with the resistance had done nothing if not seal that in his mind. He let his hands linger on the crown for a moment as he prayed, *Heavenly Father, grant me the strength to resist whatever evil my mother and Devon have in store for me. And if it is Your will I take this crown up again as Boldaria's rightful king, help me to rule with righteousness and grace.*

"Go ahead, Prince Tristan, try it on," a sweet, lilting voice encouraged from behind him.

Releasing his grip on the crown, he turned apprehensively to the door. He had not heard it open, or his new companion enter, and he chided himself for lowering his guard. Here in the castle, especially, such an oversight could mean death.

"It is rightfully yours, after all." A young lady with perfect alabaster skin wearing an elaborate, but modest, dress made of pink satin and white lace, glided into the room. Her long, golden curls brushed against her shoulders as she walked.

It was tempting to try it on, but that would only strengthen his desire for the crown, a desire his mother would be more than willing to manipulate. He took a step back and turned toward the sitting area. His voice was tight and guarded when he addressed the girl, "Please, take a seat, my lady."

"Princess Mercia, daughter of King Lionel of Parona." She curtsied, then gracefully picked up her skirts and took the chair he had motioned to. "I think you would look simply dashing in it. I mean, not that you do not look dashing now, I mean, oh dear." She blushed and looked down at her hands. "I am sorry, Prince Tristan, that did not come out at all like I had planned."

The girl's nervousness took the edge off Tristan's own anxiety as he sat down opposite her. He was vaguely familiar with Parona's location on the map, but was completely unfamiliar with the character of its royal family. So far its princess was unlike any his mother had recommended to him before.

"It is all right, Princess, no offense taken." He kept his voice cool as he spoke to her. There was no point in letting either her or his mother get any ideas.

"Do you think we are truly alone?" Princess Mercia relaxed.

"I would not count on it," Tristan responded. "Mother is surely watching to make sure you behave as you are supposed to, and that I respond the way I am supposed to."

"So you know it is all staged?" Princess Mercia giggled. "I am to be bait – I suppose a reward sounds better – if you cooperate. Your mother and Lord Devon coached me on what to do and say. They fought for hours on the perfect dress." She made a wry face as she looked down at herself and smoothed her dress. "I am glad Lord Devon won out in the end. I felt the queen's dress was a bit less…" She trailed off and laughed again. "Well, just less."

Tristan could only imagine, and was having a very difficult time not doing just that. The realization was unsettling. He had prepared himself against the unchaste "ladies" he was used to his mother suggesting. He found her artlessness and unpainted beauty uncomfortably alluring. He forced himself to focus his thoughts like he had against Devon. She was, after all, just another one of Devon's weapons. "What exactly did they tell you to do?"

"I am quite sure I am not supposed to tell you that," she said demurely as she sat on the chaise next to him. She folded her hands in front of her and looked at him, her lovely face growing slightly troubled. "Marry you, I suppose. Or rather convince you to marry me. They fought over exactly how I was supposed to do that also. The Queen wanted me to behave rather... unseemly. Lord Devon told me to just be friendly, that I was specifically chosen for my 'compatibility and charm', as if I were some sort of quaint cottage or something," she said gleefully. "Now I have a question, what exactly am I to tempt you to do?"

Her laughter was contagious, just as her ingenuousness was refreshing. Tristan bit his lip as a smile creased his face. "Since I have not actually seen my mother since she had me brought here, I can only guess. Swear allegiance to her in exchange for all the benefits of the throne, I assume."

"And am I supposed to be one of those 'benefits'?" Princess Mercia pushed a wayward ringlet of golden hair out of her face, clearly amused by the thought.

"Yes," Tristan answered ruefully, "and, I will admit, a very tempting benefit, if it were not for the fact I love another."

"That is too bad." She pouted. "Though I think the queen told me your young lady's father had no intention of letting you marry her."

Again his mother knew more about his life than she should. While Dr. Medellin had always discouraged his attentions to Aleatha, he had never been out right opposed to them before he had returned from his time with Devon.

"How would she know that?" he managed to ask.

"She did not say." Princess Mercia shrugged. "She did tell me you were 'too honorable' to marry her without her father's consent. What would you do if he refused to give it?" She looked uncomfortable again. "Sorry, Prince Tristan, her question not mine."

His mother's question touched a fear he had been refusing to face himself. Tristan felt a chill run down his spine as he looked down at his hands. What if he was not able to convince Dr. Medellin to give his consent, an outcome that looked more and more likely each day? He swallowed hard and pushed back his fears. "I pray by the grace of God not to have to make that decision." He stood abruptly, his cold tone and stiff posture signaling the end of the interview.

Princess Mercia stood also, curtsying low before looking him in the eye. "My only request is, in that unfortunate event, you would consider me as your second option." She turned to go, stopped, and turned back to Tristan. She leaned toward him, kissed him on the cheek, and whispered in his ear. "And I sincerely do mean that."

A red-hot blush burned Tristan's cheek where she had kissed him as she slipped out the door and closed it behind her. Even as he refused to consider that possibility, he knew he might be tempted to do just that. Tristan scowled and pushed aside the thought even as it formed. This was still part of his mother and Devon's ongoing battle for his mind.

"Her Majesty, Queen Brigitte," Captain Brogan announced as the door swung open again. He stood to the side, holding the door as Queen Brigitte sailed in.

Now began the real battle.

Chapter 18

He bowed slightly as his mother crossed the room to him with a counterfeit smile spread across her face.

"My son!" she gushed. She placed her hands on either side of his face and kissed him on the forehead. "We thought you were dead. You can only imagine my surprise when I found out you had survived your terrible ordeal in the desert."

A sharp retort sprang to Tristan's lips, but he bit it back. He was in enough danger already without provoking her further. "What is this all about, Mother? What did Devon do to Lucas?"

"Lucas will be fine." His mother gave him an exaggerated look of disapproval as she lowered herself into one of the chairs. "I simply wanted to welcome you back. Can a mother not rejoice over the return of the beloved son she thought dead?"

"Not when she was the one who ordered his death," Tristan spat, all of the anger and betrayal of the past year packed into his words.

"Surely you do not believe that, Tristan. I have only ever wanted what was best for you. Lord Devon was a little overzealous in his devotion to me, but I never ordered him to hurt you, and certainly not to kill you. I had no idea your loyalty to the Medellins was so strong. Do you really think that little of your own mother?" Queen Brigitte asked, her tone hurt. "Have the Medellins and their resistance so poisoned you against me?

Conflicting emotions chipped away at the anger inside him. He wanted to believe the best about his mother. He really, truly wanted to believe she had only good intentions toward him. She was his mother, after all. Devon's "training" in the desert came back to him, *She really does care for you, Tristan, in her own way.* Perhaps Devon was right, perhaps his mother really did want what was best for him. He felt his resolve slipping and closed his eyes. *Heavenly Father, help me to hold onto the truth.* He took a couple of deep breaths to clear his mind. "Enough, Mother. You killed my father and you tried to kill me. This is not about my best interests, the Medellins, or the resistance. It is all about your need to control me. Come to the point."

Dark anger passed across her face, and Tristan feared for a moment he had been too blunt, but she quickly contained her anger and plastered another smile across her face. "Do not be disrespectful. I simply thought after the past year you would be ready to take your rightful place in the kingdom." Her eyes sparkled as she warmed up to her subject. "I believe you just celebrated a birthday, your twenty-first. That means a coronation is in order."

She paused, looking at Tristan as if seeking some sort of response. He gave her none, mastering his face to avoid even the slightest change in expression.

"How was your meal? I had Jackson bring you your favorites," Queen Brigitte changed the subject. "Did you enjoy sleeping in your own bed again, and wearing your own clothes?"

"Yes, thank you." Tristan's words were polite, but his expression was rigid and distant.

"You know, son, there are certain benefits of royalty. Unsurpassed comfort and protection; a beautiful, advantageous wife; and the power to change the lives of your people for the better." She stood and laid her hands on his shoulders. He flinched slightly, his memories of Devon's hand on his shoulder the night before still fresh. She did not seem to notice, instead she looked him in the eye and said firmly, "I only ask one simple thing. It is not much really, not in exchange for all the benefits of the throne."

"Loyalty." Tristan's mouth went dry. *Here it is. Will she kill me herself when I refuse?* "Complete and unreserved loyalty to you."

"Sworn on the cross of the Savior you hold so dear." A cunning look filled Queen Brigitte's eyes. "No, I will not deny you your religion, as long as you remember your loyalties belong to your mother before your God."

Tristan's stomach clenched at his mother's blasphemy. He pulled himself free of her grip and stepped back. "No, Mother."

A look of warning flashed across the queen's face. "I own you, Tristan, everything you have is mine. Your fine clothes, your title, who you marry, even whether you will be allowed to live – everything about you is in my control. You owe me your allegiance."

"You have no power over me that God does not allow," Tristan snapped. He felt a rush of boldness. "You may control my circumstances, but you cannot control who I am. I am Crown Prince Tristan Leander, rightful king of Boldaria. You cannot change that!"

Queen Brigitte crossed the gap between them, her hand raised to strike Tristan across the face. She clenched her fist, drew it back to her side, and spoke through clenched teeth,

"Your God has abandoned you into my power. I would take some time to think it over if I were you. Refusal will have grave consequences for you and your rebel friends." She spun on her heels and stormed to the door, her skirts rustling in time to her hurried gait. "You have one week. Captain Brogan will see you to the city gate."

*****

"He is more dangerous to our cause than his mother ever was, Odell," Lord Blakemore's low, strident voice pierced the fog that enveloped Lucas's thoughts. "Through him the people might be persuaded to accept a reign that will be at best only a puppet rule for Queen Brigitte."

Lucas moaned. His head pounded where one of the soldiers had struck him with the pommel of his sword. Memories of the fight in the stable flooded back to him. The last being of Tristan lying prostrate on the stable floor and Devon commanding his men to kill him as he had told Tristan he would do. He obviously was not dead, but…

"Tristan!" he cried and struggled to push himself up to a sitting position.

A firm, gentle hand pushed him back down. "Relax, son," his father admonished. "You are safe here."

He blinked twice to clear his blurred vision. He was lying on a bed in a dark room, a single candle flickered on a table nearby. Dr. Medellin sat in a chair beside him, relief evident on his face.

"What happened?" Lucas closed his eyes. Even the effort of talking made his head hurt worse. Still he pushed on, his voice no better than a whisper. "Where's Tristan?"

"Dale and I heard noise in the stable." Lord Blakemore stepped into the tight circle of light cast by the candle with Dale and Odell Chapman right behind him. "We turned back to investigate just in time to hear Lord Devon order his men to kill you. I guess we startled them. One of the soldiers hit you over the head and they all ran out the back."

"What about Tristan?" Lucas persisted. He wondered if the growing nausea in his stomach was from the headache or from fear for his friend.

"They took Prince Tristan with them," Dale scoffed. "Presumably back to his mother."

"If they took Tristan back to the castle, there is a good chance we will never see him alive again." Lucas ignored the insinuation in Dale's voice, choosing instead to voice his own grim fears.

"And if he does return, I still say that is proof he is conspiring with the queen," Lord Blakemore snapped at Chapman, returning to the topic they had been arguing about when Lucas awoke. "Surely she would not allow an enemy to leave her grasp alive."

"Tristan is not conspiring with the queen." Lucas clenched his teeth against the pain in his head and stomach. "She ordered Lord Devon to kill him."

"Then why is he not dead?" Lord Blakemore folded his arms across his chest, confident Lucas could not give an answer that would satisfy him.

"That is enough, Lord Blakemore." Dr. Medellin stood and ushered the other three men away. "Lucas needs to rest, upsetting him will not help him heal."

"You know you agree with me, Gaius," Lord Blakemore threw back at him, his voice hushed. "You know the danger the prince poses."

"My political views are not as important as my son's health. We can talk about it later."

A light knock interrupted, drawing all eyes to the door.

"Who is it?" Chapman stepped toward the door and laid his hand on the knob.

"It is Celia, Father," a dulcet voice floated in. "It is really important."

The sound of Celia's voice made Lucas's heart flutter. No matter how badly he was feeling, he could certainly take a few minutes to see her.

"Make her say the pass phrase," Lord Blakemore growled.

"That will be all, Bryce," Chapman rebuked sternly. "It is my house and my daughter, you can take your paranoia elsewhere if you like."

Lord Blakemore grumbled to himself as he and Dale sat at a table partially obscured by the darkness. Chapman opened the door to allow Celia in. She leaned in through the doorway and whispered in her father's ear, gesturing to something behind her as she spoke. Chapman looked at her, then behind her in surprise. He whispered back to her, pointing toward Lucas with a look of warning on his round face.

Ducking under her father's arm, Celia smiled at Lucas and crossed the room to him, her skirts in her hands to avoid tripping. "Oh, Lucas, I have been so worried about you! When Father told me you were hurt, I wanted to come, but your father insisted I wait until you woke up."

"How long have I been out?" Lucas glanced at his father.

"Nearly four hours." Dr. Medellin glared at Celia, obviously considering her arrival an intrusion on Lucas's recovery. "I really must insist Celia keep her visit short. Lucas, you simply must rest."

"I will go. I am just glad you are all right." Celia leaned forward and kissed Lucas on the forehead, her hand ruffling his dark brown hair at the same time. "I will be back later." She grinned impishly at Dr. Medellin. "Though I doubt Lucas will be resting much when he sees his other guest."

Glancing back toward the door, Lucas noticed Chapman talking to a cloaked figure in low tones, a grave expression on his face. Dale and Lord Blakemore looked daggers at the stranger from their seats at the table.

The stranger turned and crossed the room toward Lucas. As he passed into the ring of light cast by the candle, he lowered the hood of his cloak. The circlet of gold and gems resting on his head glittered in the flickering candlelight.

"Tristan!" Lucas shouted with relief and surprise. "They told me Lord Devon had you."

"See here," Dr. Medellin said. He seemed disconcerted by the prince's regal appearance, but still stood to block his way to Lucas. "It is your fault my son is hurt in the first place, at least have the decency to allow him to recover in peace."

The room grew silent as its occupants waited for Tristan's response. Lucas watched Tristan's face closely as a look crossed Tristan's face he had not seen since Tristan's return, a look of strength and authority, an expression of power to match the symbol of his rank that now rested on his head.

The prince's voice was cool as he looked into Dr. Medellin's eyes without wavering, "Let me by, Doctor. I promise I will only take a moment of Lucas's time. I wish for him to recover as much as you do."

Hesitating as if considering his options, Dr. Medellin gave the coronet on Tristan's head another glance and stepped aside, apparently deciding he was not ready for a showdown with royalty.

Concern filled Tristan's eyes as he slipped around the doctor and bent over Lucas. "Are you hurt badly?"

"Only a severe headache, thank God." Lucas touched his head gingerly. "If Dale and Lord Blakemore had not shown up when they did, who knows what Lord Devon would have done. What about you? How did you escape?"

"Mother let me go," Tristan answered, his grave voice barely above a whisper. He touched his coronet and shook his head. "She offered me all the benefits of the crown, then sent me back to think about it. Seven days, then she comes after me and my friends."

"How did she know where to find you?" Lucas felt the strength of the headache returning.

"Her spies are everywhere," Tristan said with a shrug as he stood and took a step back from the bed. "I will leave you to rest now."

"Remember you need to rest also," Lucas called after him as he crossed the room. "Tell Aleatha she is in charge of making sure you are taken care of until I get back."

"With pleasure." Tristan turned, flashed him a wide smile, raised his hood, and disappeared out the door.

For a long moment after Tristan left, Dr. Medellin stared at the door, the wrath and hatred on his face evident to everyone in the room.

Chapter 19

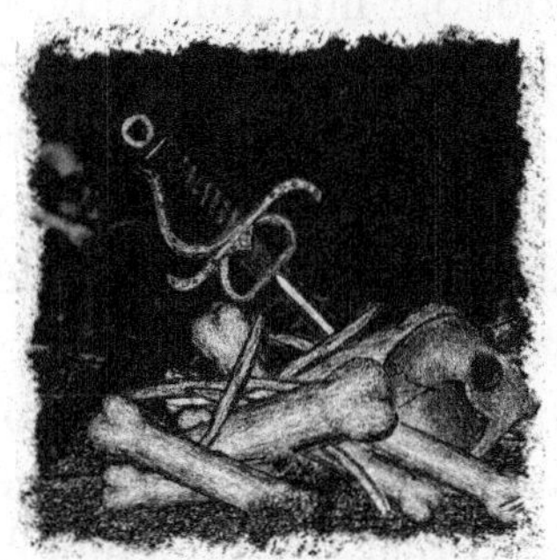

Relieved Lucas was finally sleeping, Dr. Medellin left the wine cellar and pulled the door closed behind him. Odell Chapman had given permission for Lucas to stay in the room in the wine cellar for another day, although he would more than likely be feeling much better by evening. He needed to rest; he had been pushing himself too hard the last week caring for the prince. Not to mention his part in the fiasco last night.

If I could, I would make him stay longer, he thought as he mounted the stairs, *but Lucas will insist on returning home.* He made his way up to the large barn above the cellar used for the processing of the grapes into wine. Since it was not time for the grape harvest, the building was unused and empty. Dr. Medellin had agreed to meet Lord Blakemore there as soon as possible to discuss the problem of Prince Tristan in private. By the dawning sunlight streaming in through the dirty windows of the barn he saw a cluster of men circling one of the large presses near the back of the barn. Lord Blakemore was addressing the group in his passionate way, while Dale stood to his right, his face grim.

As Dr. Medellin scanned the crowd, he set his mouth in a tight line. Though there were several respectable businessmen and farmers, he recognized many of the men as belonging to a baser class of rebels, thieves, bandits and murderers that had attached themselves to the underground resistance.

"Ah, Dr. Medellin, right on time." Lord Blakemore gestured for Dr. Medellin to join them. "I was just explaining to the men here about our little difficulty. I thought you might be able to help, considering your unique opportunity to observe the prince since his convenient return."

"What do you wish to know?" Dr. Medellin licked his lips. He had a vague feeling he was getting in deeper than he wanted.

"Prince Tristan wants to pass himself off as a hero," a rugged, tanned man Dr. Medellin recognized as the city blacksmith said. "Lord Blakemore here tells us he is more dangerous to our cause than the queen. He has been staying at your house. What do you think?"

"I believe he is a danger." Dr. Medellin nodded. "He is at best a pawn of his mother. He will gain our confidence and simply enslave us deeper under her control."

"What proof do you have of that?" a soft-spoken farmer called from the back. "He was always on the side of the people before."

The blood rose to Dr. Medellin's face as he warmed to the subject. "During the last year, he was subjected to intense persecution and torture with the intent to align him with his mother. If the fact she allowed him to return alive from that is not proof enough that she accomplished her goals, the fact he returned, more regal than ever, from her presence just last night should silence all doubts."

As the men murmured among each other, Dr. Medellin raised his voice and his hands. "I also have witnessed first hand the changes in the prince since his return. He is suspicious and brooding, with a darkness in his eyes that shows his experiences with Lord Devon have affected him deeply. Yes, I do believe he is dangerous, with all my heart."

"Tell me, good doctor," Dale spoke up, conflicted emotions on his face. "How can you justify betraying a man you raised as your own son for years?"

Dr. Medellin grew pensive. He had battled that question every night since he had learned Prince Tristan lived. He remembered the prince as a young boy playing with his children, crying as the soldiers came and summoned him back to his mother yet again; and the pride he himself felt as he watched the prince, now a godly young man, take a stand against his mother's wickedness during his final days before Lord Devon took him away for his training. Those memories were replaced by more recent memories of a haggard, suspicious fugitive clutching a dagger as he hid in the slums, Prince Tristan's attempt to seduce Aleatha only a few days earlier, and his return in royal glory from the castle just this morning.

"He is not the young man I raised," he answered with conviction. "He is now completely poisoned by his mother. He is a danger to my family, to Aleatha especially. Surely you of all people should be able to appreciate that."

"It is decided then," Lord Blakemore spoke up, "Prince Tristan must be eliminated."

I have signed Prince Tristan's death warrant, Dr. Medellin realized as his heart began to pound, *but I only told them the truth.* Still, he did not like what he had taken part in.

"My men and I can take care of him. The next time he goes out, we will get him." A swarthy man with a long scar running on the left side of his face from his ear to the corner of his mouth stepped forward, his mouth twisted in a grotesque smile. "I can even get a hold of some soldier's uniforms and we can blame the queen for killing her own son."

Prince Tristan is not likely to go anywhere without Lucas. A quick thought flashed into Dr. Medellin's mind. "And if my son is with him? Promise you will not harm Lucas!"

The ugly man's grimace widened, making his face look even more hideous. "What if he fights back? My men and I have to defend ourselves. Collateral damage, I say. Besides, if it was to appear the queen killed the city's darling 'Young Doc', imagine the people who would flock to our cause. Not only all the young nobles that hang on his every word, but hundreds of outraged citizens from the Shambles would join us in our resistance against the queen."

"Bryce, stop this!" Dr. Medellin turned to Lord Blakemore, his voice and eyes pleading. "Make him swear to Lucas's safety."

"There is another way, Gaius, a way that would carry no risk to your son." Lord Blakemore stroked his chin as he considered Dr. Medellin. "You could take care of the prince. It should be easy. He is staying in your house. I am sure a clever doctor such as you can devise a way to direct suspicion away from you and onto the queen. Perhaps a poison?"

"I absolutely will not!" Dr. Medellin blanched. "I am not a murderer."

"Do you question the righteousness of our cause?" Lord Blakemore demanded. "Do you have doubts in the Prince's guilt?"

His thoughts swirling, Dr. Medellin paused. In answer to the first question, perhaps a little, but to the second he had no doubt. "No, but I will not kill him in cold blood."

"I guess if you will not, we will have to go with Holt's plan." Lord Blakemore turned back to speak to the scar-faced man, "Holt…"

"Father, this has gone too far," Dale interrupted. He was silenced by a glare from his father.

"Holt," Lord Blakemore continued, "Take your men…"

"No, Bryce, I will do it," Dr. Medellin said through gritted teeth. "For Lucas's sake, and for my family's sake."

"And for the kingdom's sake, do not forget," Lord Blakemore added. "You will go down in history as one on the heroes of our resistance. You will not regret this."

I already do. Dr. Medellin sat down on the edge of the wine press and placed his head in his hands. As the men around him dispersed, he knew he would regret today's decision every day for the rest of his life, just as he did for the part he had in King Justin's murder over twenty years earlier.

*****

After breakfast the next morning, Lucas returned home. His stomach no longer hurt and his headache was nearly gone. More than that, he needed to see Tristan, both as his doctor and his friend. He needed to make sure Devon's abuse during the clash in the stables had not re-injured Tristan's shoulder and return his sword Chapman's servant had found half buried in the hay scattered on the floor of the stable. Besides, he was dying to know what had happened at the castle.

Dashing into the house, Lucas nearly breezed past his mother in his haste.

"Lucas!" she called out, reproof and surprise in her voice. "Your father told me about what happened. I've been so worried about you!"

"I'm fine, Mother," he assured her. He gave her a quick hug and a peck on the cheek. "I had the best doctor in the kingdom looking after me."

Leaving his mother looking after him in bewilderment, he mounted the stairs two at a time to the floor where the family's chambers were located. He turned down the hall and pulled up short to avoid crashing into Aleatha as she came out of Tristan's room.

"Good morning, Aleatha," Lucas greeted her with a wide smile. His humor changed quickly as he noticed the full tray of meat and vegetables in Aleatha's hands. "Is that from last night?"

"I am worried about him, Lucas." Concern written on her face, Aleatha looked down at the tray and back up at her brother. "He has not eaten or drank anything since lunch yesterday. Even then he ate little." She shrugged. "He does not make a big deal out of it, but none of it is gone by the time I come to remove the dishes. And he seems weak. After he joined us for breakfast yesterday morning, he did not leave his bed again." Her voice caught a little as she glanced back at the door, "He seems so sick, worse even than when he came here."

Lucas chewed his lip, staring at the door as if he could see through it. "He seemed fine when I saw him early yesterday morning. Did you ask him why he is not eating?"

"I did, but he just said he was tired and not to worry." She gripped Lucas's arm and looked into his face. "But it is more than that. He is worried, I can see it in his face. He knows something is wrong, but he does not want me to be concerned about him. Please go to him, maybe he will tell you."

"He will tell me." Lucas squared his shoulders as he headed for the door. He turned back to reassure his sister. "Do not worry, Aleatha, he will be fine. He has me for his doctor, remember."

Troubled by his sister's report, Lucas opened the door to Tristan's sickroom. Tristan had been recovering fine a couple of days earlier, or Lucas would not have allowed him to go out to the meeting. Perhaps everything had been too much for him, or more had happened at the castle then he had let on. *Still, that does not explain his refusing to eat. I will figure out what was wrong before I leave his room again.*

His concern grew as he surveyed the room. Tristan's breakfast lay untouched on the table beside his bed, as Aleatha had told him. Tristan himself was still in bed, motionless and pale.

After placing Tristan's cloth-wrapped sword on the chair with his clothes, Lucas crossed to the side of the bed and laid his hand on his friend's forehead. It was cold and clammy. Lucas furrowed his brow. *Perhaps I should get Father in here for a second opinion. If he will come.*

"Lucas?" Tristan stirred and opened his eyes. His voice was strained as he struggled to push himself up. "Did Aleatha send for you? She seemed concerned I did not eat my dinner last night."

"Or anything else since yesterday morning," Lucas scolded. "Why? Do you feel ill?"

"I was fine until yesterday morning," Tristan averted his gaze. "I came straight here after I left you, caught a couple of hours sleep, and joined the family for breakfast. Soon after breakfast, I started to feel ill. I went back to bed and I have not even had the strength to get out of bed since."

"Why did you not send for me?" Lucas's voice rose, "or Father, one of us would have come. Do you think I would have let a little headache stop me from coming? I am your friend as well as your doctor."

"I needed to be sure, Lucas," Tristan said, squirming as he still avoided meeting Lucas's eye. "That is why I quit eating the food Aleatha brought."

"Sure of what?" Lucas's eyes narrowed. *Aleatha is right. Tristan does know what is wrong with him.* "Do you suspect what is wrong with you?"

Blowing out a long breath, Tristan looked up at Lucas with a hard expression. "I have been poisoned. Someone is slipping small doses of poison into my food or drink. Maybe both. I cannot tell."

"Poisoned!" Lucas exclaimed, his eyes widening with shock. "Are you sure?"

"I recognized the symptoms almost immediately. Devon used poison several times while I was with him." Tristan pushed himself higher up on the bed. "I simply stopped eating. I have noticed a difference already. I am getting stronger, slowly, but I am."

"But, poison, Tristan." Lucas dropped into the chair beside the bed as he stared at Tristan in disbelief. "In our house? Who would do such a thing?"

Tristan stared back at Lucas with probing eyes.

"Surely you do not suspect me." Lucas paled as his heart dropped to his stomach.

"Not you," Tristan reassured him. "I am confident you and Aleatha have been doing your best to help me get better."

"Who then?" Lucas was both relieved and exasperated. "Spit it out, man. Do you think I would still be sitting here talking if I had figured it out on my own?"

"Who else in your household is experienced in medicines?"

"Father?" Lucas answered incredulously. "Are you serious? I know he lost his temper the other day, but I hardly think he hates you enough to commit cold-blooded murder."

"If your father knew of a man he believed to be entirely evil, who would bring your sister only pain, misery, and eventually death. A man who he believed to be seducing your sister to believe she actually loves him and poisoning you to trust his lies." Tristan paused, pain evident on his face. "If your father truly believed this man intended only to use your family to his ends, then destroy them, could he kill such a man?"

"If he believed such a man existed, perhaps," Lucas admitted. He began to feel sick as he realized the plausibility of Tristan's words. He pushed the accusation out of his mind. "But surely you do not believe that is what he thinks of you."

"He has said as much." Tristan lay back in his bed and closed his eyes. "He said he believes me to be just like my mother, hiding my true colors until it is too late for anyone to do anything. He especially fears for Aleatha."

"He fears you would kill Aleatha like the queen killed your father?" Lucas choked back the bile that rose in his throat. He rubbed his fingers on his temples as the pounding in his head returned. The growing conviction his own father had tried to murder his best friend was nearly too much for him.

"If he truly thinks me to be like my mother, murder is one of the nicer things he thinks me capable of. He would do anything to protect you and Aleatha from such a monster." Tristan paused and added in an undertone, "I know I would in his place."

"As would I," Lucas agreed, his expression troubled. "But we have to prove it was him. Surely he will deny an open accusation."

"I have thought of a way, with your help." Tristan lifted himself on one elbow and looked at Lucas, a hint of doubt in his eyes. "Are you willing?"

"Of course I am," Lucas confirmed, laying his hand on Tristan's arm. "You know I would never condone this. Besides, if it is not my father, we need to figure out who is trying to kill you. What would you have me do?"

"Go to your father and describe the way you found me here. Ask him to prepare a medicine to help me. Watch carefully what he does, but do not let him see you. If what he prepares is harmless, my suspicions are wrong. But if what he prepares is dangerous…" Tristan shrugged.

"That is easy enough." Lucas stood to carry out Tristan's suggestion. "If he is innocent, he never needs to know we suspected him."

"Would you also be kind enough to bring me something safe to eat?" Tristan frowned at the plate of food beside him. "I am starved."

"I will go down to the kitchen and prepare it myself, at least then I will know it is safe."

Lucas turned quickly to leave Tristan, praying fervently his friend was wrong, but knowing in his heart he most likely was not.

Chapter 20

Perhaps this is all just a mistake. Lucas knocked on the door to his father's chambers. If he were fortunate, the apprehension on his face would just come across as concern for his friend. *When I finish speaking to Father, we can both go back to Tristan and brainstorm over which of the servants might be poisoning him.* He hated the idea of any of the servants being a traitor, but it was better than accusing his father.

"Come in," his father's voice answered from the other side of the heavy door.

"I need your help. Tristan is ill." Lucas said as he closed the door behind him. His father was at his desk looking over some papers and did not even look up as Lucas approached his desk. "I know how you feel about his being here, but would you mind coming to take a look at him?"

"I am busy right now." His father still did not look up, and Lucas thought he detected a slight tremor in his voice. Perhaps it was just his imagination.

"He is really ill," Lucas tried again. "Aleatha's worried about him. His symptoms seem so vague, I just thought you might be able to help."

His father grunted as if irritated over the interruption. He looked up at Lucas. "What are the symptoms?"

"Extreme fatigue, loss of appetite, weakness," Lucas listed, watching his father for a reaction. There was none. "Aleatha says he has not been out of bed since breakfast yesterday. I thought he was finally getting better, now… I just do not know what to do."

A slight change came over Dr. Medellin's expression, as if an idea had come to him. "I have just the thing for him. You stay here, I will prepare it for you."

Dr. Medellin rose from the desk and walked to the alcove where he kept his medicines. He turned his back to Lucas, shielding his view with his body.

Father does not usually try to keep me from watching as he prepared medicine. Lucas felt his suspicions grow. *Just the opposite. He usually pushes me to learn every possible concoction for every possible disease. Perhaps Tristan is right.* Lucas shook his head. He just needed to get a better look at what his father was doing. He moved a little to the left, trying to look as if he were simply wandering aimlessly while he waited. His father shifted his position slightly to the left as well. Dread gripped Lucas's stomach. Surely it was just a coincidence. His father poured some liquid into a small vial. If Lucas could not get a glance at the bottle he held before he put it back, it would be too late.

Beside his father sat the mortar and pestle he used to grind herbs to make medicines. The mortar was silver, a gift from a wealthy patient. In the shiny bowl, Lucas could see the bottle his father held. His father's hand covered most of the label, but he could see the bottom of a red skull indicating poison. He felt his breakfast rise up in his throat. Swallowing hard, he regained his composure. Many of his father's medicines were poisonous if not used correctly. He needed to see the rest of the label. Perhaps when his father… Sure enough, his father finished measuring out the medicine into the vial and double-checked the label, just as he always did. Lucas could see it clearly now. *Passion Flower Extract.*

"Give this to him in a glass of wine," his father instructed, as he turned to hand Lucas the vial.

"Are… Are you sure you want me to give him *all* of this?" Lucas could barely force a whisper through his parched lips. If he followed his father's instructions, Tristan would be dead before Lucas even left the room. *There has to be a mistake. Surely Father would not…*

"Did you come to ask me for help, or to insult me?" Dr. Medellin turned his attention back to his papers as he sat back down at his desk. His voice wavered a bit as he spoke, but his words were firm, "Either do as I instruct, or take care of him your own way. Now, go."

Surely this can not be happening. Lucas swallowed hard against the churning in his stomach. He needed to leave. He was desperate to leave. *My father could never become a murderer.*

But the proof was clutched in his shaking hand as he turned and hurried from the room.

* * * * *

Feeling lightheaded, Lucas paused at a doorway and gripped the frame for support. He needed to warn Tristan, but he felt too ill to continue. He turned into his room. *How could Father sink so low as to attempt to murder Tristan, no matter the supposed justification?* He bent over his chamber pot and lost his breakfast.

Lord, what am I going to tell Aleatha?

He bent over the chamber pot and retched again. *Pull yourself together.* He wiped his mouth on a handkerchief and stood. His stomach hurt and his legs felt weak. He did not know what to do about his father, but he did know what he needed to do next. *I must get Tristan out of the house and make arrangements for another, safer, place for him to stay.* His stomach churned again and he eyed the chamber pot warily. *It is my fault Tristan is in this danger, I need to get him out before it is too late.*

Dumping the contents of the tiny bottle of poison into the chamber pot, he hid the bottle among his clothes and slipped out of the room into the hall. He quickly made his way down to the kitchen for food, and returned to Tristan's room. With a nod to the servant at the door, he let himself in.

"Lucas?" Tristan stirred and sat up groggily. "What did you find out?"

"You were right." Lucas placed the tray of food on the table beside Tristan's bed, then dropped into the nearby chair with a groan. "He had the gall to prepare a poison powerful enough to finish what he had started in minutes." He rested his elbows on his knees and put his face in his hands. His headache was back with nearly blinding force. "What I am going to tell Aleatha and Mother? I cannot believe Father actually tried to kill you!"

"Tell them nothing," Tristan advised, throwing the covers aside. "I will go. If I am not here, your father will no longer have the opportunity to do anything. Besides, as long as I stay, I represent a danger to your family if my mother or Devon decide to come for me again."

"Where else would you go?" Lucas protested as Tristan swung his legs over the side of the bed. "You cannot go back to any of the old places; Father already knows about them."

As he put his weight on his weak legs, Tristan grabbed the bedpost to steady himself. He did not answer as he concentrated on taking a few wobbly steps toward his clothes sitting neatly folded on another chair across the room.

"Perhaps the greater concern is whether you are even strong enough to leave," Lucas said as he watched Tristan struggle to cross the room. He had not realized how truly weak his friend was.

"I did not think I was still this bad," Tristan admitted, sitting on the edge of the chair with his clothes to rest. "If I could only get some food and a few hours rest before I go, I think that would make a huge difference."

"Father is going to think the poison he gave me finished what he started. He will not try anything else, at least not until he discovers you are alive in the morning." Lucas helped his friend back to the bed. "I will even tell the guard he placed at the door to let me know if anyone tries to enter. Just before dawn, we will go to Odell Chapman and see if he knows anywhere you can hide."

Doubt flickered across Tristan's face at the mention of trusting Odell Chapman. "I guess I do not have much choice. Perhaps with a good meal and a little sleep, I will be ready to go. However, I absolutely must be out of here before the household begins to wake up."

"I will be here. Meanwhile, you rest."

"After I eat." Tristan eyed the food Lucas had brought him. "I really appreciate your bringing me this." He slid the tray of food off the table onto his lap and bit down into a crisp, juicy apple.

"I am sorry about all this," Lucas apologized as he sat back in the chair next to Tristan's bed. "I had no idea you would be in danger here. It was clear Father did not approve of your attention to Aleatha, but I had no idea he would try something like this."

Tristan turned his half-eaten apple in his hand and stared down at it.

"You did, did you not?" Lucas leaned forward to see his friend's face. "You need not hide anything from me now."

"That day your father came to the cellar, I could see the hate and fear in his eyes. I was not even sure I should come here, but I was so certain he would refuse that I said nothing." Tristan returned Lucas's searching gaze and continued, "When he gave in to Aleatha and your mother, I did not know what to do. I have been on my guard ever since, especially since that incident with Aleatha. Otherwise, I would be dead by now."

"You are not making me feel better." Lucas scowled. "I saw the anger in Father's eyes after he caught you and Aleatha together. I heard his threats. I could have done something then. Deep down I simply could not believe he would really do anything."

"It is not your fault. I knew there might be a risk." Tristan laid a hand on Lucas's shoulder and added wistfully, "I guess the temptation to be closer to Aleatha was just too much for me."

"Once we get you settled in a truly safe place, I will bring Aleatha to see you," Lucas promised as he stood. "Rest, I will be here early."

"See you then." Tristan nodded as he turned his attention back to his food.

Chapter 21

Late that night, Tristan awoke to a noise in his room. He remained still, keeping his eyes closed and his breathing regulated, as he listened carefully. The noise had come from the direction of the window. It sounded as if someone were forcing his way into the room. He moaned and pretended to stir in his sleep, settling onto his side facing the window and slipping his hand under his pillow to grasp the dagger he had tucked there. *Please, Heavenly Father, do not allow the effects of this poison to hinder my ability to defend myself*, he prayed as he steeled himself for an attack.

Soft footsteps crossed the room to the side of his bed. Tristan peered through slit eyelids at a dark figure standing over him, staring down as if trying to come to a decision. With a faint sigh, the shadow decided. His hand crossed his body to grip the hilt of the sword at his side. Before the man slid the sword half way out, Tristan had the point of his dagger pressed against the man's belly.

"Remove it slowly and place it on the floor," Tristan whispered. He was unwilling to rouse the whole house just yet.

The man trembled as he pulled the sword the rest of the way from its scabbard and laid it on the floor, never taking his eyes off the blade of Tristan's dagger as he did so.

Not a soldier or a trained assassin, Tristan mused as he watched the frightened man. *Who wants to kill me now?*

Keeping the dagger in his right hand pointed at the man, Tristan turned up the lamp on the table beside him with his left hand. He grunted in frustration as the flickering light from the lamp revealed the identity of his would-be assassin.

"Dr. Medellin, I could have killed you," Tristan said through clenched teeth. *He probably still expects me to*. Tristan shook his head and pointed his dagger to the chair next to his bed. "Sit."

Trembling, Dr. Medellin obeyed while Tristan swung his feet over the edge of the bed and kicked the sword under it.

"Explain yourself, Doctor." Tristan stared at Dr. Medellin in anger and disbelief, but still kept his voice steady. "Everything, or I will wake the whole household for you to explain it to them."

"You should have been dead already," Dr. Medellin complained. "That medicine I mixed for Lucas was more than strong enough to finish the job."

"Fortunately Lucas is a better doctor than you give him credit for. I did not take your medicine."

"You still should have been too weak from the effects of the poison I have been slipping you in your meals." Dr. Medellin shifted in his seat. "I should have found you too weak to move, much less fight back."

"If I was already supposed to be dead, why the sword?" Tristan rose to his feet. He was weak, certainly too weak fight off Dr. Medellin if he decided to make another attempt. He was not too weak to fake it though. Without taking his eyes off Dr. Medellin, he crossed the room to his clothes. *It is time to go. I will tell Lucas where I am later.* He certainly could not wait until Lucas came for him in the morning. "Wait. Let me guess. Sneaking through the window and stabbing me was supposed to make it look like my mother hired an assassin to kill me."

"It was not my idea." Dr. Medellin looked down at his hands nervously. "The others persuaded me to do it."

"What others?" Tristan laid his dagger on the chair with his clothes and paused to pull his tunic over his head. "And why would they want to kill me?"

"Certain members of the resistance have agreed the kingdom will only ever be safe if the entire royal family has been overthrown," Dr. Medellin answered, calming as he realized Tristan did not intend to kill him.

"I am sure you did not protest too loudly when they appointed you to do the job." Tristan forced down his rising bitterness and kept his voice mild as he pulled his boots on. "Or did you volunteer? Remove a threat to your family and gain favor with your friends all in one blow."

"It is not quite like that, Prince, though I admit you were more of a threat to my family than even you realize," Dr. Medellin said, a defensive note creeping into his voice. "They were going to kill Lucas as well."

"Lucas? Why?" Tristan asked, raising an eyebrow. "What does he have to do with this?"

"Lucas carries a lot of influence with the younger members of the resistance. They saw the way the young people responded to you and Lucas's dream of a glorious national restoration with you as the young hero." Dr. Medellin looked up at Tristan, resentment smoldering in his eyes. "Ninety percent of the underground resistance is made up of young people. The others were going to make it look like the queen had killed both of you and rally the youth around their cause. It was either I kill you myself, or they would kill Lucas. The choice was obvious."

As he strapped his sword on and slid his dagger under his belt, Tristan sensed Dr. Medellin's agitation return. Nausea gripped him. He had practically grown up in this house. Dr. Medellin had been the only father he had ever known. Tonight he could feel Dr. Medellin's cold, desperate fear of him. Fear desperate enough to bring a man who claimed Christ down to the level of cold-blooded murder. Now he clearly believed Tristan would wreak his vengeance on him.

"Please, Your Highness," Dr. Medellin's voice quivered as he begged, "My family… I was only thinking of them."

"And what of the Savior you taught me about?" Tristan felt a surge of anger. He turned to face Dr. Medellin, his eyes flashing. "Did you think of Him before you decided to take matters into your own hands? To become a murderer?"

"P-Prince?" Dr. Medellin spluttered, confusion flooded his face, followed quickly by a red-hot blush of shame.

"I still place my trust in the Christ you led me to nearly ten years ago, even if you do not," Tristan snapped as he scooped up his coronet and the rest of his meager belongings and gave Dr. Medellin an accusing look. "Remember the story of David and Saul, Doctor. You seek the blood of an innocent man. Contrary to what you may think, I do not wish either you or your family harm. I will go through the window, so I do not wake the others. What happened between us tonight will remain between the two of us."

"Your mother would never have allowed me to live. Not if she were in your place," Dr. Medellin said as if doubting Tristan's words.

Tristan swung one leg over the windowsill and took a deep breath to calm himself before responding. "How many times must I tell you?" he forced through clenched teeth. "I am not my mother. I am not *like* my mother. You and your family raised me more than she did. If that frightens you, perhaps you ought to take a closer look at what you have become."

"This changes nothing as far as Aleatha is concerned." Dr. Medellin insisted as he followed Tristan to the window. "You may not be your mother, but you certainly cannot hope to escape her. There is nothing you can offer my daughter but more grief. You are not welcome to see her again and you are not welcome to return here, not Saturday, not ever. I still stand by what I told you earlier, if you truly feel any love for my daughter, you will leave her to marry Dale and give her a real chance at happiness."

Saturday. Aleatha's celebration. Tristan's heart grew cold in his chest. He had hoped to convince Dr. Medellin by then that he was not the monster he feared, but had not succeeded. His mother was right, he would never dare marry Aleatha without Dr. Medellin's permission. Permission he now would never have. Aleatha's engagement to Dale would still be announced in only two days. Without replying, he dropped to the ground. He would find Lucas in the morning. Right now he needed to find somewhere safe to rest. To think. To calm his tortured emotions.

To pray.

* * * * *

A vague feeling of dread woke Lucas just before dawn. Rising quickly, he threw on some clothes. He needed to check on Tristan before his father awoke and decided to make sure of the effects of his poison. There was no telling what his father would do if he found out he had not succeeded in killing Tristan after all.

As Lucas approached Tristan's room, the guard looked down at the floor nervously. Lucas's dread increased. He swung the door open quickly and stepped inside. Dread turned to fear as his eyes swept the room. Tristan was gone. The bed sheets were tangled and the window was open. The lamp beside Tristan's bed burned brightly. Lucas's eyes rested on the empty chair where Tristan's things had been. He forced himself to think clearly even as fearful thoughts swirled in his mind. Tristan had likely left under his own power. If he had been carried out, his abductor would not have bothered to stop for his clothes. Which also indicated he had left alive. A murderer would also not have bothered to take his body with him.

The guard knows something. I just hope his discomfort does not come from falling asleep on the job.

"Did you see or hear anything last night?" Lucas kept his voice low, but firm, as he confronted the servant. Few people in the house were up yet, and he wished to keep it that way.

"Master Lucas, I…" The man grew more uncomfortable. "Well, I cannot explain it, sir."

"Then just tell me what happened and I will try to figure it out."

"In the middle of the night, I heard low voices coming from the room. Just as I turned to check, your father left the room."

"My father was in there last night?" Lucas's heart began to race. *What has Father done?*

"Yes, sir. But…" The guard stopped again. "I never saw him go in, sir. I was not asleep. I swear it, but I would also swear he never passed me in the hall either."

"I will ask him about it." Lucas turned toward his father's room. He paused and turned back to the servant. "Do not let anyone into the room until I get back." If his father was less than forthright with him, he might need to come back and look for some clue to what happened to his friend.

Outside his father's bedroom, he raised his fist to knock, but hesitated. If his father was not there, he would risk having to explain things to his mother. He still hoped to keep his father's behavior away from Aleatha and his mother as long as he could. Instead, he headed for the stairs. He would check his father's medical chambers first, before he would risk waking his mother.

The door to his father's chambers was locked, so Lucas knocked firmly. There was no answer. He knocked again, louder this time. "Father, if you are in there, it is Lucas. I must speak with you." He heard a rustle from behind the door, followed by the click of the lock being disengaged. The door swung in slowly. His father peered out at him, his face drawn and his hair wild. Lucas stared at the haunted, guilty look that filled his father's eyes.

"What is wrong?" Fear rushed over Lucas. He was certain now his father had something to do with Tristan's disappearance. *Lord, please make him not to have…* "What have you done?"

Dr. Medellin opened the door wider and silently motioned for his son to come in. He closed and locked the door behind him and sat down at his desk, his head in his hands.

"Father, what have you done?" Lucas repeated. He forced himself to calm down. His father had no way to know Tristan had not drunk the poison the previous night. His guilt could be from that. He may not have had anything to do with Tristan's disappearance. Still, he had been in Tristan's room last. "Where is Tristan?"

"I have brought shame on our entire family, Lucas." Dr. Medellin moaned; his voice muffled by his hands. "Your father is nothing more than a murderer."

"What…" Lucas felt his body grow numb. His voice caught in his throat. He cleared it and forced himself to speak. "Tristan did not drink the poison you prepared for him last night. He suspected and had me watch you."

"I know, he told me last night." Dr. Medellin still did not look up. His voice grew nearly imperceptible. "I went to his room to finish the job."

Lucas gripped the edge of his father's desk with both hands for support as his legs threatened to give out beneath him. Surely his father was not capable of cold-blooded murder. And yet, the poison proved he was. *This is my fault. I never should have persuaded Tristan to stay the rest of the night.* "What… What did you do?"

"Last night, after everyone was asleep, I went to his room, through the window to make it look as if one of the queen's men had broken in and killed him. I went to side of his bed and drew my sword. And…

Please, no. Lucas bit his lip until he tasted blood. His head swam. If his father had murdered Tristan, he had lost both his best friend and Boldaria's final hope. *Tristan cannot be dead!*

"He stopped me, Lucas." Dr. Medellin finally looked up at him. "He was awake the whole time. He stopped me and let me go."

"Tristan… lives?" Relief flood over Lucas as he sagged against the desk. *Praise the Lord!* "Where is he?"

"He left, through the window, so he did not alarm the rest of the family." Dr. Medellin's haunted eyes sought Lucas's own. "I tried to kill him, and he was concerned about my honor before my family. As he left, he compared me to Saul in the Bible – told me I sought the blood of an innocent man. He is a better man than I am."

"Then tell him that," Lucas pleaded. "Let me bring him back here. Apologize. Tell him you see the truth now."

"Let him marry your sister?" Dr. Medellin scowled. "What if you are wrong? What if I am wrong? Do I dare risk her future on that boy?"

Give me words to speak, Lucas prayed as Dr. Medellin allowed his head to drop back into his hands.

"What if I am right?" Lucas asked, bending over the desk closer to his father. "What if Tristan and Aleatha will be truly happy together? If you know him to be a man of character, how can you justify wronging both of them?"

Dr. Medellin did not answer. He did not look up or even move at all.

"You may object to his circumstances, but you can no longer object to his integrity," Lucas insisted.

"No. I cannot object to his integrity or his character." Dr. Medellin let out a long, deep sigh. "But I can and do object to his circumstances. And since there is little hope of any positive change in that area, my decision stands. For everyone's sake, especially your sister's, I forbade him to show his face around here again. She will grow to love Dale, and if Tristan has any feelings for her, he will leave her alone and give her the chance to do so. You may tell him I am sorry, but it changes nothing." His voice took on a hard edge. "I will do whatever it takes to protect my family from danger, and whether you like it or not, he is still a danger to us all."

"I had better go find him then. Since he is no longer welcome here, he will need to find another safe place to stay." Lucas's heart sank. He had hoped to be able to change his father's mind. He straightened up.

"I am sorry, Lucas," his father called after him. "Please, tell him I am sorry, for everything."

"I will tell him," Lucas said as he paused by the door and turned back to his father, "but you get the responsibility of telling Aleatha. I will not. You can tell her why Tristan is gone and why he will not be coming back."

Leaving his father alone again, Lucas sped from the room. He needed to find Tristan before anyone else did. The kingdom and his best friend's life depended on it.

Chapter 22

Hidden in the shadows from the first rays of dawn, Tristan closed his eyes and leaned his head back against an overgrown tree at the edge of the Chapman estate. He had spent the last couple of hours wandering the woods behind the Medellins' home trying to reach a decision about what to do. He was tired from little sleep and still weak from Dr. Medellin's poison. Eventually, he had decided to go to Odell Chapman. Lucas had sworn to his loyalty and he could not go back to any of his old places. Now that he was within sight of Chapman's home, he was having second thoughts. Dr. Medellin had indicated that members of the resistance had put him up to murder. Tristan had assumed that meant Lord Blakemore and his followers, but he was not sure if he should risk it.

Perhaps I ought to try to contact Lucas first. He needed to talk to Lucas; his friend would be worried by now. In all his wanderings, he still had not determined what to tell him… or Aleatha.

Aleatha… Despair's icy fingers tightened their grip on his heart. Though he may have escaped the Medellins' household with his life, he had lost any chance of winning Aleatha's hand. In less than two days she would be betrothed to Dale Blakemore.

Focusing on his one hope to hold back the darkness threatening to swallow him, he fought his exhaustion and pushed away from the tree. The resistance was the only chance he could see of gaining Aleatha's hand. Perhaps if he could prove to Dr. Medellin that he was more than a doomed fugitive, the doctor would be persuaded to abandon any further doubts he had about his character. It was a slim chance, yes, but the only chance he saw of having any future with Aleatha. Truly, it was the only chance he had of any future at all.

Pulling the hood of his cloak forward to cover his face, he crossed the lawn to the door of Chapman's home, knocked, and stepped back to wait for an answer.

"May I help you?" Chapman's butler answered.

"I need to see Odell Chapman on an important matter of business." Tristan kept his head down. Lucas had sworn to Chapman's loyalty, but not to the servants' loyalty. It would be best to only reveal his identity to Chapman himself.

"Who shall I tell him is calling?" The butler looked Tristan over with a disdainful sniff.

"A friend of Naboth," Tristan answered, recalling the password Lucas had given.

The butler's frown deepened, but he stepped back to allow Tristan to pass. Without a word, he led Tristan to a large library, motioned for him to sit in one of the plush chairs facing a massive mahogany desk, and stepped out.

A few minutes later, Chapman entered. He looked Tristan over before asking, "Well, friend, what can I do for you?"

Tristan stood from his chair and pulled back the hood of his cloak.

"Your Highness!" Chapman bowed low. "To what do I owe the honor of your visit? And where is young Medellin?"

"I have come to ask your assistance. Lucas swore to your loyalty. I did not know who else to trust."

"Anything you need." Chapman rounded the desk and motioned for Tristan to sit back down. "If it is within my power, it is yours."

"I need a safe place to stay." Tristan lowered himself into the plush chair. "Somewhere unknown even to the other members of the resistance."

"That is a difficult request," Chapman said, rubbing his chin thoughtfully. "Were you not staying with the Medellins? Was your location compromised?"

"There is a faction within the resistance that wants me dead." Tristan watched Chapman's expression harden with displeasure. "They nearly succeeded in killing me last night."

"There are those of us who fear you could just be another Queen Brigitte, but I never guessed they would stoop to murder." Chapman shook his head, and stared out the window. After a moment deep in thought, he looked back at Tristan. "There is a place. It recently came into my possession. The former owner fled the kingdom to seek a safer place for his family. Only… it is right in town. That is why we have not used it yet. Coming and going would be noticed too easily."

"Only you know of this location?" Tristan asked. It would be risky, but not nearly as risky as continuing to stay with the Medellins.

"Well, there is one other," Chapman admitted. "Lord Bryce Blakemore."

The animosity in the way Lord Blakemore had looked at him was clear, though the source was not. Did he resent Tristan as his son's rival for Aleatha's hand or did he espouse the same fears Dr. Medellin did? Either way, had he been the driving force behind Dr. Medellin's decision to poison him?

"Did I hear my name?" a deep voice interrupted from the doorway. "Sorry to interrupt, Odell, but when you did not return, I thought I would come see what was so important."

"Come in, Bryce," Chapman said, gesturing to another chair. "We were just discussing the house the Morrisons left. Prince Tristan seems to be in need of a safe place to stay."

Lord Blakemore started visibly at the sight of Tristan, but replaced his surprise with a dark scowl. He bowed stiffly. "Your Highness."

Tristan gestured mildly for Lord Blakemore to sit. He felt safe in interpreting his reaction to indicate that Lord Blakemore was part of the plot to kill him. However, he was in no position to confront him. Not before Chapman, and certainly not without proof.

"What about the Medellins' home?" Lord Blakemore looked to Chapman. "Was he not staying there?"

"It is no longer safe for him there," Chapman said. "I was just telling him about the Morrisons' place. Only the two of us know of the location. I am prepared to swear my secrecy." He looked at Lord Blakemore meaningfully. "Are you?"

"Odell, you know where my allegiances lie, and my feelings about this… boy." Lord Blakemore threw a glance at Tristan. "There are those of us who feel he is a threat to this kingdom."

Chapman opened his mouth to object, but Tristan waved him off. He was tired of people thinking he was just like his mother. "On what grounds? Do you object to my claim to the crown?"

"No man could object to that." Lord Blakemore grunted. "It is your parentage we object to."

"My father, King Justin, was one of the most beloved rulers of Boldaria," Tristan countered as he drew himself up and squared his shoulders. "It is through him I inherited my right to rule."

"You know I meant Queen Brigitte," Lord Blakemore snapped. "Your father did not raise you, she did. We believe you will be just as wicked as her."

"What have I done to merit that reputation?" Tristan asked, measuring his tone to keep his rising emotions in check. "Was it the aid I gave to the common people last year? Or my call for reforms before the council? I believe you were there, Lord Blakemore. Or was it the fact I refused to countenance your murderous plot to remove my mother from power?"

Lord Blakemore's face reddened as Tristan's point went home, but he pressed on, "Dr. Medellin testified to your changed character since your time with Lord Devon. He told me he firmly believes you to be a dangerous man."

"Did you bother to question Lucas or Aleatha or any of the others who have been with me since my return?" Tristan knew the answer was no, Lord Blakemore was uninterested in anything that did not further his views.

"Their opinion would be biased. Lucas is your friend and everyone knows you intend to marry Aleatha. Even though her father has forbidden it." Lord Blakemore added, trying to get in a barb of his own.

"My intentions toward Aleatha are subject to my changing her father's mind," Tristan answered, his voice still carefully controlled. He would not let Lord Blakemore see any sign of weakness. "Instead of going to my friends for their opinion, you went to my enemy instead. You did not seek justice, only approval for what you had already decided to do."

Working his mouth noiselessly, Lord Blakemore flushed a deep purple at Tristan's indictment.

"I do not ask for your support, I do not even ask for your loyalty," Tristan continued before Lord Blakemore could compose himself. "I only ask that you swear you will not do anything to hinder the path chosen by the vast majority of the resistance."

"It appears Prince Tristan inherited his father's skills at debate as well as his father's throne," Chapman said, clapping

Lord Blakemore on the back. "Let it go, Bryce. The least you can do is promise him that much."

"I promise I will not betray his location to any who wish to harm him," Lord Blakemore assented. He shook his fist at Tristan. "I will still do everything in my power to expose him as the danger he truly is."

With a parting glare, Lord Blakemore stormed out of the room.

"It has been a long time since I have seen anyone get the better of him," Chapman said almost happily as he turned to Tristan. "I will take you to the Morrisons' house as soon as it is nightfall. Until then, you would be safest here, at least temporarily."

"I only request that you have someone deliver a letter to Lucas letting him know I am safe," Tristan said. Lucas and Aleatha had to have discovered his absence by now. They, Lucas especially, would be sick with worry.

"Fine. I will have one of my servants deliver it," Chapman promised. He slid a sheet of paper and a pen across the table to Tristan.

Tristan wrote quickly, assuring Lucas he was safe and promising to get in touch with him as soon as he could.

As soon as he was finished, Chapman called for a servant, "Take Prince Tristan to the guest room. Make sure he is comfortable. Then deliver this message to young Lucas Medellin."

The exhaustion from the past couple of days hit Tristan like a ton of bricks as he followed the servant from the room. He felt like he could sleep for the rest of the day. He would need all the rest he could get. Between the resistance and the problem with Aleatha, he was in for the fight of his life.

Chapter 23

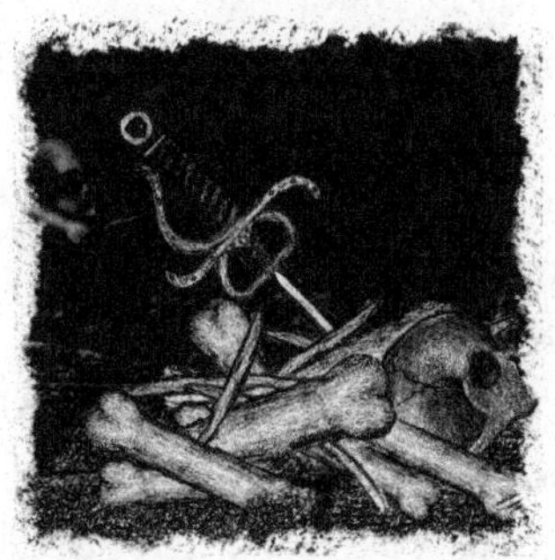

"Lucas!" Aleatha shoved the door of his bedroom open without so much as a knock. "Tristan's gone!"

Scowling, Lucas looked up from the letter he was writing. Tristan certainly was gone, and he was getting concerned. He had spent several hours searching for any sign of Tristan, but found nothing. It was now late morning and he had expected Tristan to contact him before now.

"Do you know where he went? Why would he leave?" Aleatha fired one question after another to her brother. The angry edge in her voice faded as she asked, "Why would he not come see me first?"

"He left in the middle of the night." Lucas tried to reassure her. "He probably did not want to wake us. I am sure we will hear from him soon."

"You mean he did not tell you where he was going either?" Aleatha blanched. "What would make him leave so suddenly?"

"You will have to talk to Father about that," Lucas said sullenly.

"Father?" Confusion clouded Aleatha's face. "Why would Tristan have told Father and not us?"

"Like I said, you will have to talk to Father." The events of the last several hours had made him feel very cross, especially where his father was concerned.

"I did," Aleatha said, her voice wavering. "He said Tristan left because he felt he was bringing danger to our family. He did not want to put us at risk."

Father skirted that issue neatly. Lucas grunted and went back to his letter.

"Lucas, we have to find him." Aleatha leaned on the desk in front of her brother. "He is not strong enough to be out there alone. He needs our help."

"Tristan is stronger than you realize, Aleatha." Lucas put his pen down and looked her in the eye. "I do not know why he has not contacted us yet, but I am sure he has his reasons." He was pretty sure his father's behavior last night was one of them, with his father's orders about Aleatha being another. "I have been looking for him since dawn, I was just preparing a letter to send to some friends I have in the city who might keep an eye out for him. Other than that, we will just have to wait until he is ready to contact us."

"Father sent him away, did he not?" Aleatha asked, her golden brown eyes flashing.

Picking up his pen, Lucas began to write again. He was not interested in starting that conversation, the chance he would tell his sister more than was prudent was far too great.

"Answer me." Aleatha snatched the paper out from under Lucas's pen. "Father sent him away because of me, did he not? He told Tristan he was not welcome to see me anymore."

"Among other things," Lucas answered, bitterness creeping into his voice.

"You have to bring him back here." Tears welled up in Aleatha's eyes. "You know how he respects Father; he is likely to obey him."

"What do you think I have been trying to do?" Lucas shouted, his frustration with the whole situation coming out on his sister. He grabbed at the paper she still held in her hand. "Now, give me that paper so I can finish my letter."

Aleatha's tears spilled down her face at Lucas's tone as she handed the paper back to him and headed toward his door.

"Aleatha, look, I am sorry." Lucas rubbed his face with his hands. Fighting with his sister would not solve anything. "Just because I am angry with Father does not mean I should take it out on you."

"Why are you angry with Father?" Aleatha turned to him, her red-rimmed eyes narrowed. "Because he sent Tristan away, or something else? I'm not blind, Lucas. Something more is going on."

He had done it now. Returning to this conversation was the last thing he wanted. Lucas pressed his lips into a tight line. What was he going to tell her, since his father obviously had not admitted to anything?

A knock at the door gave him a temporary reprieve. "Can you answer that, Aleatha?"

Aleatha's displeased look promised to pick up the conversation later as she turned and opened the door. Addis stood stiffly on the other side. "Master Lucas, a messenger has arrived with a letter for you."

"Did he say who from?" Lucas stood from his desk and crossed the room.

"He did not, sir, though the seal is quite unmistakable." He handed Lucas a folded piece of paper sealed with wax.

Lucas seized the piece of paper from Addis' hand and glanced at the signet. The impression made by the Tristan's ring was unmistakable. He broke the seal and read the note. "Tristan is fine, and with friends, but he does not say where."

"Is the messenger still here?" Lucas demanded Addis as he passed the note to Aleatha.

"I asked him to stay in case you had an answer."

"I do." Lucas retrieved his cloak from off the bed where he had thrown it when he had returned home from searching for Tristan earlier. "He is going to take me to Tristan."

"I am coming, too." Aleatha laid the letter on Lucas's desk with a determined look on her face and began to follow.

"No. It is unsafe, what if he has went back to the Shambles?" Lucas said firmly. *Besides, I will not get straight answers out of Tristan if Aleatha is present.* "I will be back as soon as possible to let you know how he is, but you are not coming with me." He turned to Addis. "Make sure she does not follow me."

His sister's voice called after him as he shrugged his cloak on and hurried down the hall.

*****

The sun was beginning to set when Tristan awoke and rolled over with a moan. He had hoped resting would help, but pushing himself the night before had brought back the symptoms of Dr. Medellin's poison. After he'd sent his note to Lucas, he'd asked Chapman for a bed. In spite of getting hours of sleep, he still felt weak.

"It is about time you woke up," Lucas's relieved voice pierced the fog that still surrounded his brain. "I was beginning to wonder if you would sleep until tomorrow."

"I feel like I could, too." Tristan blinked at his worried friend.

"Too little sleep, too much exertion after your injuries, and Father's poison will do that to you," Lucas commented sardonically. He examined Tristan's wound and replaced the bandage, a satisfied look taking the edge off his grim expression. "Other than that, how do you feel?"

"Just a little sore." Tristan rolled his wounded shoulder in a slow circle. "Truly, Lucas, I am fine. Just exhausted, and maybe a little hungry."

"I will personally bring you some food before I leave." Lucas promised and changed the subject. "Why did you leave without coming to me? Aleatha and I have been worried sick looking for you."

Looking away, Tristan considered his answer. As far as he was concerned the doctor's part in last night's events would remain a secret, but he still owed Lucas some explanation for his sudden departure. "My situation at your house took a sudden turn for the worse during the night." He looked back at Lucas and continued, "I meant to see you after I had sorted some things out, but I guess I was more tired than I thought. I did send a note as soon as I was settled here."

"I spoke to Father. He told me what happened last night." Lucas pulled the chair closer to the bed and sat back down. "For what it is worth, he said to tell you he was sorry."

A glimmer of hope lit Tristan's eyes. "Did he say anything about Aleatha?"

"Sorry, he is still set against you marrying her." Lucas shook his head. "He did say it is no longer personal, he simply objects to your prospects."

"That is little comfort with Aleatha's celebration a day away." Tristan leaned his head back against the pillow and closed his eyes. When he spoke again, his voice was husky with emotion. "My only chance was to convince your father to change his mind. Instead he tries to kill me and forbids me to ever see Aleatha again. What am I to do?"

"I know what Aleatha would want you to do," Lucas said, his eyes twinkling. "Sneak into the celebration tomorrow, sweep her off her feet, steal her away to a secret wedding, and live happily ever after."

"And prove to your father once and for all that I truly am the cad he believes me to be," Tristan finished bitterly. "No thank you."

"Father tried to kill you, I do not think his opinion of you matters anymore," Lucas said, exasperation filling his voice. "Aleatha is the one you have to think about now. What will she think of you if you leave her to marry Dale?"

"If that is what is best for her after all, like your father believes, perhaps it really does not matter what she thinks of me either." Tristan's voice was low, but his eyes flashed as he pushed himself up in the bed. "Maybe it *would* be better if I disappeared from her life."

"We have been over this." Lucas scowled as he tried to keep his growing irritation under control. "Aleatha loves you, in spite of the risks." He paused as a thought hit him. "Have you spoken to her about this?"

When Tristan did not reply, Lucas continued, "It is getting dark and you need to rest. There will be no way you can see Aleatha before the celebration tomorrow, but once the guests arrive, we might be able to get her to slip away so you can talk for a few minutes before Father's announcement. For now, promise me you will not make any decisions before you talk to her."

"I promise, for Aleatha's sake." Tristan nodded, his mouth set in a grim line. "Though I am still not comfortable defying your father like that."

"I know how much you respect him, but Father's wrong this time." Lucas sighed as he stood from the chair. "I know he is doing it out of concern for his family, but he is dead wrong. You need to do the right thing for you and Aleatha, no matter what Father does."

With that parting admonition, Lucas left a somber Tristan to his thoughts and returned home.

Chapter 24

The light of the nearly full moon coupled with the torches encircling the Medellin's spacious yard lit the clearing with a gentle glow. Tristan kept to the shadows of the underbrush at the edge, avoiding exposure as he waited for Lucas. Streamers, flags, and colored paper lanterns flapped in the gentle breeze. Laughter and music filled the air. Brightly dressed noblemen and women danced and chatted gaily. Most of the guests would have arrived by now.

As Tristan scanned the crowd, he recognized many of the young people from balls held at his mother's court. A couple carrying a gift passed a few feet in front of him. He drew further back into the shadows, pulling the hood of his cloak further over his head. It was Marc and his latest wench. Tristan shook his head at the reminder that not so long ago he had thought Aleatha capable of loving that rake. Shifting his feet, he waited until they passed before edging forward and searching the crowd again. He could not see the one person he longed to see: Aleatha. Or the person he was waiting for either.

"When will Lucas get here?" he muttered under his breath. Lucas had helped him move to his new hideout at the Morrison house early that morning, bringing with him a change of clothes and a bit of charcoal. He told Tristan to use the charcoal on his face to look like a beard and mustache to complete his disguise, agreed to meet him at the edge of the clearing after the celebration started, and left hurriedly to help his family prepare. The charcoal looked surprisingly good, probably more so in the failing light of the evening, but Tristan still felt safer with the hood of his cloak shadowing his face. He was mostly concerned about the Medellins' servants. Lucas had warned him that Dr. Medellin had offered a day off to any servant who turned him in.

"Sorry I am late," Lucas said from behind him.

Tristan spun to face his friend. Lucas was flushed and out of breath.

"Mother kept me busy up until the last moment preparing for the celebration," Lucas said. His words came in a rush. "I think she suspects something. She kept hinting that she wished you would come in and sweep Aleatha off her feet at the last minute. Mother always did like you. Too bad Father does not agree. That will make things a little hard for you and Aleatha at first, but it cannot be helped."

"Lucas, I am here to speak to Aleatha, as I promised," Tristan cut in, he set his jaw grimly, but doubt gripped his heart. "And I have not made any decisions, as I also promised. I will do what is best for Aleatha. What that is remains to be seen."

Lucas bit his lip as if he were holding back a sharp response. Finally, he took a deep breath and simply reminded his friend, "Just remember, the only person who can truly decide what will make Aleatha happy is Aleatha herself.

"You will need to hurry, though." Lucas looked out toward the celebration. "Father wants to make the announcement before the servants bring out the food, and I happen to know the food is nearly ready."

Tristan took a deep breath. "How do I look?"

"Good enough. No one would recognize you unless they looked closely. And you have to remember not everyone knows you are alive and most of those who do are going to be too busy with the celebration to pay any attention to you. Just try not to do anything to draw attention to yourself."

"Like sweep Aleatha off her feet at the last minute?" Tristan quipped. He shook his head. "My goal is to be long gone before your father stands to make his great announcement."

"Do you have your sword?" Lucas asked. His eyes darted to Tristan's side. "I hate to think you might need it, but there are going to be several guests loyal to the queen. You need to be prepared in case you are discovered."

"I am not going in armed." Tristan's voice was soft, but firm.

"You *cannot* go in *unarmed*," Lucas hissed at Tristan in exasperation. "Are you truly mad? Did you forget my own father tried to kill you? What if you are exposed? How can you hope to escape if you have no way to defend yourself?"

"I cannot run the risk of hurting someone Aleatha cares about," Tristan countered. "What if your father or one of your family servants does try to stop me? I am afraid the temptation to draw on them would be too great. If I harmed a member of your household, Aleatha would never forgive me."

"What if one of your mother's household discovers you?"

"Mother has already shown she knows where to find me. My actions tonight will not change that one way or another." Tristan shook his head. The expression on his face allowed for no arguments. "The greatest threat is from the members of your household. I cannot run the risk of hurting them."

"I see your point, though I cannot say I agree. Just be very careful." Lucas glanced around warily before stepping out of the underbrush. "I have to go. If I am gone too long, people will start to look for me. I will be nearby. Please, take no chances."

Once Lucas was out of sight, Tristan followed, searching the elaborately decorated gardens hoping to catch a glimpse of Aleatha among the growing crowd of guests. He needed to slip through the crowd, find her, and slip back out as quickly as possible. He still had not decided exactly what he was going to say to her, only that, either way, he needed to see her before her father's big announcement.

Forcing himself to relax and look as nonchalant as possible, he headed toward the center of the action. So far no one had given him a second look. The night was a bit cool, so he was not the only guest wearing a cloak and everyone seemed more intent on joining the celebration.

The crowd parted just enough for him to see Aleatha about fifty yards ahead of him. She was wearing a shimmering sky blue dress trimmed with white lace and pearls. The bodice was fitted and the full skirt swirled around her as she turned to speak to a nearby guest. Her long, brown hair cascaded down her back from a pearl barrette. Her golden brown eyes lit up as she laughed at something her guest had said.

She looks so beautiful, so happy. My appearance can only serve to upset her. His eyes darted to the woods to his left. *Perhaps it would be better if I just left.* He took a breath and steeled himself. Lucas was correct, the only right thing to do was to talk to Aleatha now, before her father had a chance to make his announcement. He pulled a note he had written out of his pocket. It asked her to meet him at the edge of the woods as soon as possible. All he had to do was slip it into her hand. Setting up the meeting was the easy part, making the right decision afterward would be infinitely harder.

Give me wisdom, Heavenly Father, to know the right thing to do. He clenched his teeth in determination as he took a step toward Aleatha. This night had the potential of turning out very badly for both of them. *And the strength to do it, however hard it may be.*

Before he had gone three steps, a firm hand gripped his left shoulder from behind and a sharp point dug into his back. He took a deep breath and arched his back away from the pressure of the blade. His attacker leaned forward until his mouth was beside Tristan's ear, his familiar voice deep and deadly, "Dr. Medellin warned me you might make an attempt to steal Aleatha from me tonight, Prince. I see he was right."

"I am not here to 'steal' anything, Dale," Tristan said evenly, slowly lifting his empty hands away from his body to show he was not a threat. He doubted Dale would hurt him, but he would never have guessed Lord Blakemore or Dr. Medellin would have tried to kill him either. He turned to face Dale, trying not to do anything that might be perceived as threatening. He glanced at the dagger Dale held, the tip now inches from his chest. "Put that thing away before you make a scene."

"Oh, I intend to do more than make a scene," Dale retorted. He slipped the dagger back into his belt and rested his hand on the hilt of his sword, "I intend to finish this here and now. A duel for Aleatha's hand!"

"And embarrass Aleatha at her own birthday celebration?" Tristan hissed. Out of the corner of his eye, he could see a crowd beginning to gather around them. "Not here. Not now. Allow me to leave in peace. I give you my word I will not attempt to see Aleatha tonight."

"Your word is not good enough." Dale drew his sword and touched the tip to Tristan's chest, his determined voice loud enough to be heard by the gathering crowd. "I demand satisfaction. Draw your sword!"

It was too late to avoid a scene now. Still, Tristan had one more chance to diffuse the situation. He removed his cloak, allowing it to drop to the ground as he turned slowly before Dale and the crowd. "I have no sword. Surely you would not dare duel an unarmed man." *Heavenly Father, protect me.* He was taking a huge risk by revealing he was unarmed. Even if Dale did let him go, he would be open to attack by anyone as he left. However, it was the only chance he saw of even getting an opportunity to leave.

Dale looked a little taken aback. He obviously had not expected a fugitive to go around unarmed.

"You can use mine," a voice called from the crowd.

"Or mine," called another, soon half a dozen people had generously offered their swords to Tristan.

"I am not going to duel you, Dale." Tristan shook his head.

"You refuse to give me satisfaction?" Dale challenged. "Do you fear my swordsmanship?"

In spite of the gravity of the situation, Tristan swallowed back a laugh. Dale might be stronger than he was, but even Lucas was a better swordsman than Dale. Tristan could have easily disarmed Dale with a strong stick; he had no fear of a duel with him. Still, he was not going to duel Dale, or anyone else if he could help it, at Aleatha's birthday celebration. He scanned the crowd, looking for a spot where he might be able to slip away. His gaze stopped at a familiar face just on the outside edge of the crowd encircling them. Dr. Medellin stood there, grimly observing the conflict, but making no move to intervene. Tristan set his jaw as he quickly scanned the rest of the crowd. Stationed at various points around the edge of the crowd, stood several of the Medellins' faithful servants. That was it, then. Tristan turned his attention back to Dale. There was no way he could escape through the crowd.

"Duel or die," Dale growled. "You have your pick of swords, or I can take you with my bare hands."

"Let it go." Tristan crossed his arms over his chest and looked him in the eye. "I am not going to fight you, sword or no sword, and we both know you will not kill me. Not in front of all these people."

"I could kill you with impunity; the queen has issued a reward for you. Dead or alive." A nervous light danced in Dale's eyes. Tristan was pushing him farther than he was prepared to go. Perhaps a little more and he would cave in.

"Do it, then," Tristan challenged. He was calling Dale's bluff. He hoped.

The crowd grew silent. All anticipation of a fight leached from them, they were in no way sure they wanted to witness a cold-blooded murder. Dale's eyes darted to the side. Tristan kept his eyes on Dale's face, still challenging, but he knew who he was looking at. His opponent was getting his cues from Dr. Medellin.

"Dale Blakemore, what is going on here?" Aleatha's angry voice interrupted the silence. "I was told you were going to duel someone."

She pushed her way through the buzzing crowd and stopped just inside the circle of guests. A grim faced Lucas was close behind.

"Tristan?" Aleatha said, her voice a mixture of pleasure and confusion, "Father told me you would not be here."

"He is not supposed to be," Dr. Medellin broke in. His was face red and his voice was hard as he elbowed his way to the center of the crowd. "Prince, I forbade you to come here again. Ever. I knew you could not be trusted. Dale was supposed to be on the lookout for you.

"Though I did not tell you to duel him just to keep him away from my daughter!" Dr. Medellin threw a withering glare at Dale.

"Lucas," Aleatha said, forcing a gracious smile and turning to her brother. "I believe Mother has the food ready. Please show the guests to the table. Father, Dale, Tristan, and I will just be a minute."

As Lucas herded the reluctant guests away, Tristan watched Aleatha. She was the picture of poise and control, but he could see the anger surging below the surface. She smiled and nodded at the guests as they filed by, offering a kind word here or there. He had never seen her so composed, or so angry. His heart sank as he realized some of that anger would be justly directed at him. *I never should have come.*

Chapter 25

After Aleatha waved off the final curious guest, she turned her attention to the three men, her eyes flashing with anger. She glared silently at one offender, then the next, as if trying their guilt and deciding their fate.

Her cold gaze stopped on Dale first. "What were you thinking? Did you think that by dueling Tristan you would somehow secure my favor? Or were you more concerned about besting a rival in public?"

"Your father told me Prince Tristan would try to steal you from me." Dale's eyes pled for understanding. "I… I know how you feel about him. I was afraid he might be able to do just that. I guess I was a bit too impetuous."

"Dale, you are a good man," Aleatha responded, "but my heart belongs to Tristan."

Relief washed over Tristan. He had feared his part in the chaos of the night may have ruined his relationship with Aleatha.

"Aleatha," Dr. Medellin's voice rose in angry protest.

His daughter cut him off with a fiery glance, and turned back to Dale. "I think it would be best if you left."

"But Aleatha," Dale spluttered, "our engagement… what about the announcement?"

"There will be no engagement. Not tonight, not ever. Good night, Dale, go home."

Dale opened his mouth to protest again, but the determination on Aleatha's face stopped him. He threw a deadly look at Tristan as he passed him. "This is not over, Prince," he hissed under his breath as he slammed his sword back into his scabbard.

I can add another name to the long, growing list of people who wish me dead.

Once Dale had left, Aleatha's gaze flickered to Tristan. She looked at him, indecision written on her face, before turning back to her father. The full force of her anger was packed into her tight tone as she said, "Go back to the guests. You have much to explain about your actions these last few days, but I am not going to allow this to ruin my birthday celebration. We will have a long talk tonight, after everyone is gone."

"I am not leaving you alone with *him*." Dr. Medellin looked at Tristan coldly.

"Fine, stay then," Aleatha said, her eyes flashing, "though I doubt you will appreciate what we have to talk about."

She stepped between Tristan and her father, turning her back to her father. "Why did you leave without seeing me first?" She looked up at Tristan with a mixture of anger and hurt on her face. "Why have you not tried to see me before now? None of this would have happened if you had come sooner."

"I left rather suddenly, and in the middle of the night." Tristan glanced over her shoulder at Dr. Medellin. He would keep his promise. The matter was between Dr. Medellin and Aleatha. "As far as coming sooner, it would have been impossible for me to see you at your house. I had hoped to be able to see you undetected among the other guests."

"Why leave at all? Surely you were *safer* with us than wherever you are now."

Something in the way Aleatha said "safer" caught Tristan's attention. *She knows. How? Lucas would not have told her.* "I felt it was best for me and your family."

"Why? Because Father was poisoning you?" Her voice rose. "I am not the fool you and Lucas believe me to be. I saw the way Father has looked at you ever since you came. I saw the hate in his eyes when he caught us in your room. It did not take much for me to put it together."

Tristan looked back over her shoulder at Dr. Medellin. His head was hung in shame.

"I will get an explanation from him later," Aleatha said. "Right now I want one from you. Why did you not come to see me?"

"I meant to return at daylight, but I was not certain what I would say," Tristan admitted. "Once I reached a safe place, the effects of the poison took their toll. I am afraid I slept most of the day yesterday."

"You risked a lot to come here tonight," Aleatha said as fear played across her face. "You must have decided something by now."

"No, Aleatha, that is why I came." Tristan flicked his eyes toward to Dr. Medellin's dark, threatening face. He had not wanted to have this conversation with Dr. Medellin present. *There is no helping that now,* he realized. "Lucas persuaded me to talk to you before I made up my mind." He took both of her hands in his, ignoring Dr. Medellin's low, guttural warning.

"I love you, but you have to understand what I am. I am not the dangerous monster your father thinks me to be, but I am a fugitive. Even my friends want to kill me. I have no home, no money, and nothing to offer you." He shrugged.

"There is the slight possibility the resistance could succeed and I could be crowned before the end of the year, but there is a better chance I could be dead by the end of the week. Is that the kind of life you want, Aleatha? A walking widow? A temporary princess? A beautiful target for my enemies? As much as I would desire to spend the rest of my life with you, however long or short it may be, I cannot ask that of you."

"You need not ask," Aleatha said. Her voice wavered and tears edged her eyes. "I am offering. Please allow me to be your wife, in spite of all you said."

"Aleatha Rose Medellin." Dr. Medellin stepped forward, his face livid. He pulled her away from Tristan. "This is over. We are going back to the celebration." He turned a hateful gaze back to Tristan. "Leave, and do not return. I will protect my home and my daughter in any way necessary."

"I will send Lucas to make sure you get home safely," Aleatha called back over her shoulder. "Good-bye, Tristan."

"Good-bye, Aleatha," Tristan whispered as he watched Dr. Medellin drag her out of his life one more time.

*****

No one watching Aleatha glide from one guest to the other, chatting gaily with her friends, or smiling graciously at compliments and well-wishers, could have guessed the turmoil that raged beneath the surface. It was only after all the guests had left and she was alone with Lucas and her parents that she allowed the mask to drop.

"Did you tell Dale to kill him, Father?" she demanded, her hands on her hips as she stood in front of him. "How many attempts would that make, including the poison?"

"He is a threat to you, Aleatha," Dr. Medellin snapped back. He sat back in the plush chair he occupied by the fire in the Medellins sitting room. Lady Medellin stood behind him with her hands on his shoulders, a look of concern on her face. "I will admit my methods were a bit… excessive, but I will not allow any son of that monster near my daughter. I have every right to protect my family."

Lucas watched soberly from where he stood leaning against the wall beside the fireplace with his arms crossed. It was clear his father did not like his actions being questioned by Aleatha, in spite of his remorse only the day before.

"Not by killing an innocent man who came to our house for help and protection." Aleatha's voice rose. "You tried to poison him!"

"I was there when his mother killed King Justin." Dr. Medellin gripped both arms of the chair and leaned forward. "I was not about to risk my daughter's life on his integrity." He tossed a meaningful look at Lucas. "Or my son's life either."

"Gaius, please," Lady Medellin protested, her hands gently rubbing his shoulders as if to calm him. "You know Prince Tristan loves our family like the one he never had. Do you not think you're exaggerating?"

"Tristan is not going to hurt me or Aleatha, Father," Lucas said. Father and Aleatha rarely fought, but when they did, it was usually far worse than any of his little spats. This one was shaping up to be a bad one if he could not get the two of them to calm down. He arched an eyebrow at his father. "Surely his actions the other night proved that."

Dr. Medellin quailed a bit, before replying defensively, "But everything before that pointed to him as the same monster as his mother."

"Father!" Aleatha's eyes grew wide. Her voice was strident with indignity. "How could you ever think he could be like his mother? You know him as well as anyone."

"That was before," Dr. Medellin shook his finger at his daughter. "Before his mother sent him away to be brainwashed. He is different now, surely not even you can be so blind. Even if you are both right and he is not a monster, he is still a fugitive. More than likely, he will be executed within a few days time."

"Or the resistance could succeed and he could take his rightful place as king," Lucas pointed out. "You should at least give him time to prove himself."

"Lucas is right, sweetheart." Lady Medellin massaged his shoulders more vigorously. "There's no need to rush to judgment."

"I will not be dictated to by my own family!" Dr. Medellin shouted, shrugging his wife's hands from his shoulders. "I have made my decision, I expect it to be obeyed."

"But you are wrong," Aleatha shot back. "You have no right to treat him like this!"

"Last time I checked, I was still the head of this household. As for you, you shamelessly threw yourself at him tonight. Fine. Choose your prince. I will have no daughter of mine marrying into that family." Dr. Medellin rose from his chair purple with rage. "You are no longer part of *this* family! Go to him, but do not come back to me when your heart is broken."

"Gaius, no!" Lady Medellin stepped back, aghast.

"Father!" Lucas stepped away from the wall, his eyes wide. This had gone way too far. "This is ridiculous."

"My decision is final. Take her to her handsome prince." Dr. Medellin gestured at the dumbstruck Aleatha. "She is his responsibility now."

With that, he stormed out of the room and slammed the door behind him. Lady Medellin followed quickly, tearfully calling after her husband.

* * * * *

A knock on the door of the Morrison house woke Tristan out of a fitful sleep. Startled, he grasped the dagger under his pillow in his right hand and rolled out of bed with a fluid motion. He crouched for a second to assess the situation. The knocking was persistent, but light. It did not sound like anyone trying to beat down the door. He left the bedroom and crossed the small living space to the door. He placed his left hand on the doorknob, the dagger still gripped in his right, and whispered, "Who is it?"

"Lucas. I need to speak to you."

Tristan quickly threw back the bolt on the door and let Lucas in, then closed the door and bolted it behind him. He surveyed his friend's tense face, dread growing in his mind. "What is it?"

"It is about Aleatha," Lucas said. "After the celebration she and Father had a fight."

"I am sorry." Tristan slid the dagger into the waistband of his pants and frowned. "It seems I only bring trouble to your family. I should not have gone to the celebration."

"Aleatha made her choices, too." Lucas sat down at a small table and leaned back. "That was what the fight was about. Father still hates you, passionately. He blames you for coming between them. Any approbation you gained with him the other night is gone now. Aleatha chose you. He disowned her and threw her out of the house."

"Disowned her?" Tristan's eyes widened in alarm. "Where is she now?"

"She is safe, I took her to Chapman's. Celia is taking care of her for tonight," Lucas assured him. "I think she is still in shock, she did not say a word the whole way there."

"I should go to her." Tristan reached for his cloak draped across the back of the other chair. "This is all my fault."

"Not tonight." Lucas laid a restraining hand on his friend's arm. "Aleatha will still be there in the morning. A midnight rendezvous is not going to look good for either of you. Tomorrow I will go find a minister and then the two of you can spend as much time together as you want."

"A wedding? Tomorrow?" Tristan's eyes flicked back to Lucas's face. "Is that not a little quick?"

"Let us be honest." Lucas shrugged, his face grim. "You and Father were both right about one thing: Aleatha's connection to you puts her in danger, especially now that she is no longer under Father's protection. What better protection could she have than a loving husband?"

"What about your mother? What if she persuades him to take Aleatha back?" Tristan wanted nothing more than to marry Aleatha; he just was not sure this was the way he wanted to do it. "Will your father not regret what he said and change his mind once he calms down?"

Lucas leaned forward and clasped his hands on the table in front of him. He stared soberly at his hands for a long time before he looked up at Tristan ruefully. "Not unless Aleatha changes hers. I think he already regrets having said it, but he is too proud and stubborn to take her back now, regardless of what mother or I say. Not that we have not tried."

"She deserves better." Tristan sighed. "A real wedding, fit for a princess, not just a quick ceremony."

"All she wants is you." Lucas stood and clapped his friend on the back. "You can make it up to her by giving her a coronation, if you are all that worried about it. Now get some rest. Tomorrow will be a busy day."

Chapter 26

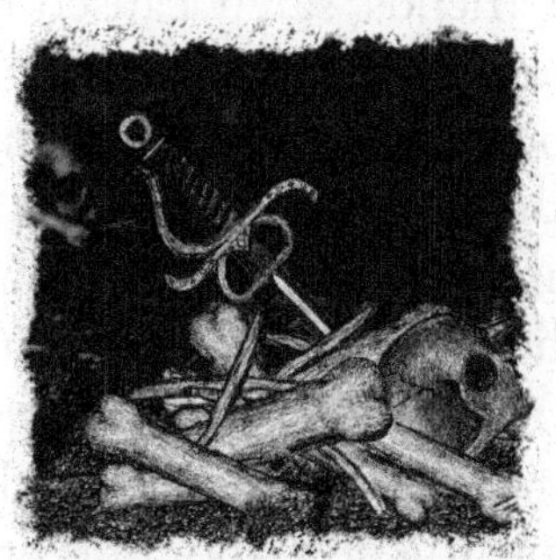

Early the next morning, Tristan arose from his bed, having spent the second half of the night more restlessly than the first. He swung his legs over the side of the bed and stood. The effects of the poison seemed to be gone; he felt stronger than he had in days. He rotated his arm slowly. He suspected his shoulder would hurt for a long time to come, but it was no longer bad enough to keep him from using it. He dressed and completed his toilet quickly, strapping his sword to his side and slipping Lucas's dagger into his belt. He needed to see Aleatha as soon as possible. Things had gotten out of hand. As much as he wanted to marry Aleatha, this was not the way he wanted to do it. Entering the main living area of the Morrison house, he scooped his cloak off the chair and threw it around his shoulders. A glint of gold caught his eye. His coronet lay on the table where he had left it.

His mother's warning echoed in his ears. *Refusal will have grave consequences for you and your rebel friends… You have one week.* His time was up. Foolishly, he had nearly forgotten his mother's threats in all that had gone on. He needed to warn Chapman immediately, though he had told the resistance leader of his suspicions about a spy in the resistance movement when he had returned from the castle. Unfortunately, the identity of the spy had never been discovered. However the queen knew the things she did, one thing was certain, no one willing to associate with him was safe, least of all Aleatha.

Concern for his friends' safety caused him to push his horse forward as he wound his way through the narrow streets of the city and through the open gates. Once on the road, he dug his heels into the horse's sides, urging it into a gallop, his cloak flapping behind him as he tore down the dusty road.

He pulled up short of the Chapman estate, led his horse a little way from the road, and tied it in a copse of trees at the edge of the estate. He did not know who the spy was, and wanted as few people to know about his arrival as possible. At the door of the house, he knocked and gave the countersign when prompted. Chapman's manservant, Terence, opened the door and motioned him in.

"Master Chapman is in his study," Terence said as he turned and headed down the hall. "This way please."

As he fell into step behind the servant, Tristan lowered the hood of his cloak. He would have plenty of time to see Aleatha, but warning Chapman of his mother's threats had to come first.

"Your Highness." Odell Chapman stood from his desk and bowed. He gestured for Tristan to take a seat and asked cheerfully, "Here to see your lady friend? Young Medellin told me to expect you this morning."

"Actually, yes." Tristan returned the merchant's easy smile, though his own was tight with concern over the other reasons for his visit. "But first I must warn you that my mother gave me an ultimatum to submit to her or everyone around me would face her vengeance. The ultimatum expired last night. Anyone she knows to be connected to me or the underground resistance is in danger."

"Especially Master Lucas and Miss Aleatha, I would wager." Chapman's expression sobered.

"She knows I am most vulnerable through my friends," Tristan agreed, his lips pulled into a tight line.

Chapman squeezed behind his desk and lowered himself back down into his chair. He picked up a quill pen and began to write swiftly. "I will send a note to several of the key members of the resistance warning them of the increased danger. I will also take a few of my personal servants off their regular duties to keep Miss Aleatha safe." He looked up at Tristan. "Would you like me to place a couple of my servants under your command to protect you as you come and go? She may decide to make another attempt for you."

It is probably only a matter of time, Tristan thought, even as he shook his head. "Not necessary. My best bet for safety right now is that no one knows where I am staying. More men privy to that knowledge increases the chances my mother could find me. Thank you, but no."

"Is there anything else you need?" Chapman paused from his writing and looked up at Tristan. "Otherwise I am sure Miss Aleatha would be more than happy to see you."

"Is she up already? I do not wish to disturb her." Tristan asked pensively, the circumstances of his visit weighing down his anticipation of Aleatha's presence.

"We just finished breakfast. I believe Celia is in the gardens with her now. I will have Terence take you to her." Chapman motioned for his servant who had retreated to the door. "I expect Master Lucas to be here before lunch. He said he had a few errands to run this morning. I will send him back as soon as he gets here."

"Thank you, sir." Tristan turned to follow the silent butler as he led him out the door of the study and through a circuitous path out the back of the house to the gardens. He scanned the elaborate gardens looking for the girls. A movement behind a cluster of bushes caught his eye. Celia emerged, ducking beneath a low-hanging tree branch.

"Welcome, Prince Tristan. Aleatha's waiting for you. She is putting on a brave face, but she is clearly upset about everything that happened last night. I think a visit from you will be just what the doctor ordered." Her eyes glittered as she glanced behind Tristan. "You did not happen to bring a certain handsome young doctor along, did you?"

"Your father said he expects Lucas sometime before lunch." Tristan appreciated her boldness. "He apparently had some errands to run this morning."

"Celia, who is there?" Aleatha stepped from behind the bushes. Her face was pale and wan and her voice was tired. "I thought I heard… Tristan!"

She crossed the distance between them quickly and threw her arms around his neck, burying her face in his shoulder. She did not cry, but simply clung to him for several minutes without speaking. Tristan stroked her soft, brown hair with his right hand as he held her.

"Lucas told you about last night?" she asked, her voice choked with emotion.

"I am sorry. I never meant to cause trouble for your family," Tristan apologized.

"You are not responsible for Father's actions." Aleatha pulled back slightly to look him in the eye, her hands still resting on his shoulders. "I just wish it did not have to be this way."

"I do not want things to be this way either." Tristan took her hands off his shoulders and held them in his own. "Your father is the only father I ever knew. It pains me to go against his wishes like this." He took a deep breath. "That is why we need to delay the wedding. You need to make one last attempt to be reconciled with him. He may never give his blessing, but perhaps he will at least accept you back as his daughter."

A look of relief crossed Aleatha's face, but was supplanted by one of concern. "He is not likely to be too willing to talk to you. He was very angry about last night."

"So were you, if I recall." Tristan suppressed a wry grin. "Lucas says your father regrets the outcome of last night's argument as much as you do. I will have him take you home tonight, after your father gets back from his duties at the castle."

"My brother probably will not be very excited about the delay," Aleatha teased, taking Tristan's hand and leading him into the garden. "I think he is out this morning making preparations for a hurried wedding tonight."

"Perhaps not," Tristan agreed with a broad grin, "but I think he will be satisfied it is just a short delay."

*****

Tristan, Aleatha, and Celia spent the rest of the morning walking through the gardens and talking. Tristan tried to savor the time as a foray into a less complicated past, but his mother's threat echoed in his ears as lunch came and went and there was no word from Lucas. As the afternoon wore on, he became more and more withdrawn, allowing the girls to carry the conversation.

"Tristan, did you not hear Celia?" Aleatha asked him. "She has asked you the same question twice now."

I thought I was doing a better job hiding my preoccupation. Tristan blushed sheepishly. He focused his attention back on Celia. "I am sorry, what did you say?"

"Are you are worried about Lucas?" Aleatha cut in.

"I am sure he is fine," Tristan said without thinking. No, he was not sure at all. "I simply expected him before now."

"Frankly, I am worried about him, too," Celia said. "He promised me he would be here for lunch. He has never stood me up before."

"Perhaps he had trouble trying to find a minister that would marry Aleatha and me. I will go see if Master Chapman knows where he might have gone," Tristan reassured them. He turned to Aleatha, the deep concern in her eyes revealing she had not accepted any of his assurances. He gently took her chin in his hand and leaned toward her, his dark eyes locked on her golden brown ones. "I will find him, Aleatha, I swear. You stay here with Celia." He dropped his hand and stood from where he had been sitting on the lush lawn, loath to leave the tranquility of the garden. He only hesitated for a moment, then turned toward the house. As he neared the back door to the house, he noticed for the first time a servant standing to the left of the door. He also noted the servant was armed. Chapman had evidently taken his warning seriously.

Nodding grimly to the servant, he entered the house and retraced to the best of his ability the twisted route Terence had taken him on the way out to the garden. His memory served him well and he only had to backtrack once. He rapped on the closed door to Chapman's study.

"Come in," Chapman's muffled voice answered from the other side of the solid wood door.

Tristan pushed the door open, raising his hand to stop Chapman even as he started to rise from his desk to bow. "You may remain seated. I simply wanted to see if you had heard anything from Lucas."

"I am sorry, Your Highness." Chapman's somber expression confirmed what Tristan feared. "I have heard nothing. I also was getting concerned, so I sent out a few servants to make discreet inquiries. So far they have turned up nothing."

"Do you know where he was planning to go this morning?" Tristan asked. He crossed the room and stood before Chapman's desk. "Perhaps he was simply delayed."

"Perhaps, though I find it doubtful he would not at least send word." Chapman looked up at Tristan sharply. "And I can see by your expression you doubt it, too."

"My mother's spies are everywhere." Tristan's expression darkened. "Lucas would make a good target for her vengeance."

"If we have still heard nothing by nightfall, I will gather my men and we will scour the city." Chapman set his jaw. "If anyone can tell us what happened, we will find out."

"Let me know as soon as you hear anything." Tristan added with grim determination on his face, "And, Chapman, if you do go out in search of Lucas, I will come with you. If he is in trouble, it is my fault, and I will do what I can to help him."

* * * * *

Dinner was a morose, silent affair as the Chapmans and their guests brooded over Lucas's absence. Aleatha and Celia only stared with red-rimmed eyes at their plates. Tristan forced himself to eat, knowing he would need his strength for whatever the night held. All glanced toward the door frequently, as if hoping Lucas would walk through it at last.

When the meal ended, Odell Chapman pushed his chair away from the table and stood. "Come, Prince Tristan, it is time we started to look for Master Lucas. Celia, take Aleatha to your room tonight. I will have Terence sleep in the hall near your door. Call him if you need anything. We will be back by morning, sooner if we find Master Lucas."

Relieved to finally be able to do something to locate his friend, Tristan stood, turned to Aleatha, and took her hand in both of his. She looked up at him, her eyes filled with apprehension. "We will find him, do not worry."

"Be careful," she pled, her voice quivering.

"I will, I promise." Tristan lifted her hand to his lips and laid a lingering kiss on it before turning to go.

Heavenly Father, protect us all, he prayed as he hurried after Chapman, *and please allow us to bring Lucas back unharmed.*

Chapter 27

The search party returned at dawn, tired and frustrated from a fruitless night. Grim thoughts threatened to consume Tristan as he reigned in his horse outside the Chapmans' stable. No sign of Lucas anywhere in the city held only one possibility in his mind: his mother or Devon had gotten to Lucas and planned to use his best friend to get to him. He knew first hand what they were capable of, and it made his stomach clench to think it was his fault Lucas was in their clutches to begin with.

He shoved aside his morbid thoughts as he passed the threshold of the house. Aleatha would be waiting for a report and he would not allow her to see the depth of his concern for her brother. She needed him to be the strong one now, no matter that he did not feel very strong at the moment.

He strode determinedly into the house, Chapman and the rest of the search party right behind him. Aleatha and Celia were waiting in Odell Chapman's study. Their wan, exhausted expressions telling they had not slept at all that night as they waited for some word about Lucas.

As the little group entered, Aleatha and Celia stood from their chairs and rushed across the room; Aleatha to Tristan, Celia to her father.

"I am sorry, my dear, we found no sign of him." Chapman looked down at his daughter, a pained expression on his face.

Celia lay her head on her father's chest and began to weep. Chapman wrapped his arms around his daughter, holding her close to him as if she were still a little girl.

Aleatha gripped Tristan's arm and looked up at him imploringly, her lower lip caught between her teeth.

Tristan shook his head and laid his hand on hers as he tried to sound confident. "We will find him. Do not worry."

She took a deep breath, gathering strength to ask the one question no one had dared vocalize. "Tristan, do you think your mother's men might have…" She trailed off. "Do you think he is still alive?"

"I am sure he is still alive," Tristan assured her sardonically. "My mother and Devon would have spread the news immediately if he were otherwise. They would count on the news demoralizing me and the resistance."

"But captured, Tristan," Aleatha persisted. "Could he have been captured by the queen's guard?"

Tristan glanced at Chapman.

"You think that is what happened," Aleatha cried as tears filled her eyes. "Oh, Tristan, Lucas is better off dead than in the hands of those monsters!"

Placing his hand on Aleatha's shoulder, Tristan met her teary gaze with a determined look of his own. "If we find he is a prisoner of my mother, I swear I will do everything in my power to rescue him."

At that moment, a man stepped into the room. Glancing apprehensively at Tristan and Aleatha, the newcomer whispered to Chapman, who still held the softly sobbing Celia in his arms, and handed him a note.

"News of Lucas?" Tristan demanded, alarmed by the man's uneasy behavior.

"Yes, Your Highness." The man swallowed and bowed deeply.

"What is it?" Aleatha begged, "Please tell us."

The man looked to Chapman, who simply nodded as he unfolded the note.

"He has been captured by the royal guard, my lady," the man answered, still hesitant.

"Oh, Tristan!" Aleatha cried.

"Has my mother acknowledged his capture?" Tristan asked with a hard voice as he squeezed her hand.

"Yes, My Lord." The man shrank from Tristan as if fearing to be the bearer of bad news.

"And?" Tristan prodded. His mother was known to kill those who brought her bad news, but he had no time for the man's fears. "Speak, man, you have nothing to fear from me."

"The queen announced he will be burned at the stake if her conditions are not met by dawn tomorrow." The man was trembling now.

"What conditions?" Tristan clenched his teeth. He had a fair idea what the conditions would be, and he did not see how he had any other choice but to comply. He slid his arm around Aleatha's waist and pulled her to his side.

"Tristan," she choked, as if she, too, had guessed.

"Your life, my prince." The man knelt with his face touching the ground before Tristan's feet. "In exchange for his."

"No!" Aleatha turned and gripped his tunic with both hands. "You cannot, there has to be another way!"

"I must, Aleatha." Out of the corner of his eye, Tristan noticed Chapman saying a few words to the prostrated man and dismissing him. He wrapped his arms around Aleatha. "No one has ever escaped the palace dungeons. Lucas would do the same for me."

"Lucas would not want you to do this. The resistance needs you." Aleatha buried her face in his chest. "I need you. Is there not something else we can do?"

"Prince Tristan," Chapman interrupted, his tone grave.

Looking up, Tristan saw he was flanked by two heavily armed men from the search party. He rested his right hand on the hilt of his sword, keeping his other arm around Aleatha, ready to push her away from him in a moment if it appeared they meant violence. "What is this, Chapman?" he asked coldly.

"The messenger also brought a letter from Master Lucas."

"My brother?" Aleatha cried. "Please, let me read it."

"He said you would readily agree to the exchange." Chapman obligingly handed the letter to Aleatha, never taking his eyes off Tristan.

"He knows me well." Tristan glanced at the two men on either side of him. "That does not explain them."

"He also told me under no condition am I to allow you to trade your life for his," Chapman continued, ignoring Tristan's comment. "He wants you to give your word you will not make the exchange."

"If Lucas truly wrote that note, he would know I would never do that." Tristan blanched. *That is precisely the reason he would write such a letter.*

"He wrote it," Aleatha replied, her voice shaking. She looked up at him with tear filled eyes. "He knew you would refuse. He says Chapman is to do everything in his power to keep you from surrendering. Even use force if needed."

That explains the armed men. Tristan felt the blood rush back to his face with a burning heat. "Let me see that letter."

He snatched the letter from Aleatha's hand and ran his eyes down the page. The body of the letter was exactly as Chapman and Aleatha had said. Lucas recommended Tristan be forcibly restrained for the good of the people. Tristan scanned through a postscript addressed to Aleatha where Lucas assured her he loved her and he was confident Tristan would take good care of her. He also assured her he would see her in heaven. A second postscript addressed to Tristan followed.

"Tristan, please try to understand the necessity of my instructions. You are the final hope for Boldaria. You of all people ought to understand the importance of hope. I am expendable, but if anything happens to you, the people will be condemned to a lifetime of abuse from your mother. The people need you. Aleatha needs you. She has given up everything to be with you. Take care of her and remember I am always your faithful friend, Lucas."

"There has to be another way," Tristan protested, his mind racing for another option. "Surely you cannot expect me to stand by and allow my mother to execute my best friend."

"Can you think of another way that would not put you at risk?" Chapman demanded. When Tristan did not respond, he continued, "This letter should be regarded as Lucas's final wishes. As difficult as it may be, I have to agree with him. You have two choices. Either you can pledge to honor his wishes, or my men will be forced to take you into custody. Which will it be?"

There was no way he would stand by and let Lucas be horribly murdered by his mother, but both Lucas and Chapman knew there was also no way he would use his sword against his allies either. Tristan clenched his teeth and balled his fists as desperation gripped him.

"Father, please," Celia sobbed. She clutched her father's shirt in her fists and looked up at him with pleading, tear-filled eyes. "We have to do something. We cannot just let him be killed!"

"I am sorry, darling." Chapman smoothed his daughter's hair and said remorsefully, "There is nothing anyone can do.

No one has ever escaped the castle dungeons before. Master Lucas is in the hands of God now."

Anger and frustration churned inside Tristan as he spun on his heels and stormed out of the study, aware that the two armed men followed closely behind. *I have to do something to save my friend, no matter the personal cost. Lucas is in this mess because I refused to submit to my mother.* He stopped in the foyer. The men behind him would never allow him to leave the house. Turning sharply, he entered the family's sitting room, dropped himself into a chair, and rested his head in his hands. The house that had lately been his sanctuary had effectively become his prison; and the price of his imprisonment would be his best friend's life.

* * * * *

Left alone by everyone except his constant guards, whose watchful eyes took in his every move, Tristan brooded in the sitting room. By late morning he had turned his chair away from the window so he did not have to watch the sun measure what was left of Lucas's life across the sky. By noon he had started to pray. Surely God could find a way to spare Lucas. By early afternoon he had begun pacing the room. There had to be a way to rescue Lucas that did not require him to surrender himself to his mother.

No one has ever escaped the castle dungeons before. Odell Chapman's ominous words echoed in his mind. Unfortunately, he had to agree that was true. The castle dungeons were built to hold the kingdom's most dangerous criminals and political threats. Not one prisoner in the history of Boldaria had escaped their iron and stone confines. He stopped pacing in the middle of the room as realization hit him. No one had escaped the dungeons, the castle itself was another thing. He had escaped the castle undetected innumerable times as a child through the catacomb of secret passages hidden in the walls of the castle. He doubted even his mother knew of the passages.

The seeds of a plan to rescue Lucas began to form in his mind. It would be risky, of course, very risky, but not suicide. If only he could convince Chapman. Masking his excitement, he crossed the room to the men standing guard.

"I need to see Chapman and Aleatha," he said as he passed between them and headed toward Chapman's study.

"Miss Celia and Miss Aleatha are in Miss Celia's room," one of the men answered as they scrambled to catch up to him.

"Please send them down to Chapman's study." Tristan stopped at the door and softened his imperative tone as he said, "It is important I see them at once. I have an idea that might save Lucas Medellin."

The two men looked at each other, then split up, one heading toward the stairs, the other taking his position on the outside of Chapman's study.

Tristan knocked firmly, turning the knob even as Chapman's voice answered from the inside. Chapman was bowed over his desk, pouring over the letter clutched in his hands, his face grim and haggard. Hopelessness was written in his stooped back and sagging shoulders. Chapman stood and bowed as Tristan entered the room.

"Your Highness," Chapman acknowledged him a little gruffly as he slumped back into the chair. "If you are here to try to persuade me to allow you to sacrifice yourself for young Medellin, I am afraid we are all agreed on that front. You are far too important to this kingdom to allow you to sacrifice yourself for anyone."

"Do not worry, I am not here to persuade you of that." Tristan crossed the room and stood in front of Chapman's desk. "I have a plan that might just save Lucas."

Chapter 28

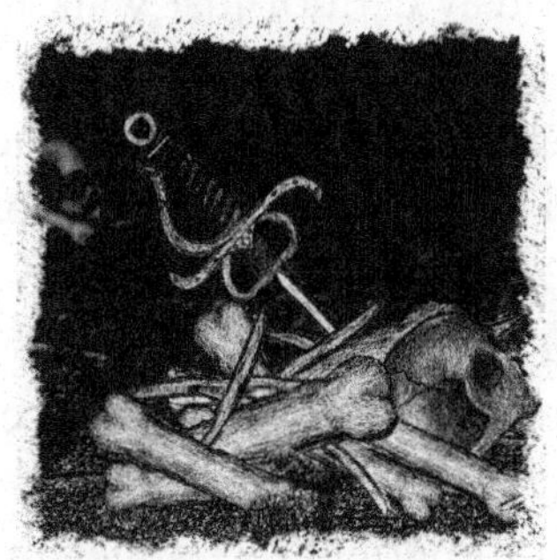

"Do you really think there is a chance to rescue Lucas?" Aleatha pushed open the doors to the study without knocking. Celia was close behind her.

Tristan allowed himself a wry smile at her enthusiasm. He could only hope she still had some left after she heard his plan. "There is a system of passages hidden in the walls of the castle leading to an underground tunnel that exits outside of the city walls. It was built to ensure the royal family's escape if the castle were ever besieged. It has been largely forgotten now. I am not even sure my mother knows about it. I discovered it by accident when I was young and used it to escape many times."

"Like when you would run away to our house," Aleatha interrupted.

After a quick nod, Tristan continued, "One of the openings to the passages is located in the guards' room in the dungeons. With the right distraction, we could slip Lucas out of the dungeon and into the passages before the guards knew what happened."

"Just how do you intend to get him out of a locked cell?" Chapman asked skeptically.

"You forget, the castle used to be my home. That will be no problem at all." Tristan assured him.

"Do you really think it will work?" Celia asked, hope lighting her eyes.

Tristan nodded again, more slowly this time. "There is one catch, the door opening to the woods is locked from the inside. Since I obviously cannot just walk into the castle, I will need help."

"If the queen really has spies among the resistance, like you said, then we are all suspect," Chapman pointed out. "Even if one of us did have access to the castle, her guards would alert her the moment we stepped inside."

"There is one member of the resistance who has always had unlimited access to the castle," Tristan said. This was the critical part of his argument. The danger in what he was about to propose would be obvious to everyone in the room, since Dr. Medellin had made no attempt to hide his animosity toward him. However, only he and Aleatha knew the full extent of the danger trusting Dr. Medellin would bring. "My mother relies on him so completely I doubt even her knowledge of his involvement in the resistance would change that."

"My father?" Aleatha's eyes widened and her voice rose an octave. "Surely you are not…"

Tristan cut her off with a sharp motion of his hand. He had never told Chapman who had tried to kill him. If he knew, he would surely refuse this final effort to save Lucas as too dangerous.

"It will still be very risky." Chapman leaned back in his chair and folded his hands in front of him as he considered the plan.

You have no idea. Tristan placed his hands on the desk and leaned across it toward Chapman. "Think of it as a compromise. I do not turn myself in, which would be as good as suicide; and I do not just sit around and do nothing to save my friend, which, as far as I am concerned, is as good as murder."

Chapman looked at Tristan silently, as if weighing his words. Suddenly he laughed. "Your Highness, I pity the men who will have to face you across the table of diplomacy after you are crowned king. Fine, go. I will have some of my best men stationed around the castle. If anything goes wrong and you need help, find one of them. You or Dr. Medellin will recognize them all readily."

"Thank you, sir." Tristan reached out his hand to shake Chapman's. "I will send you word when we are free. Do not expect to hear from me until at least tomorrow morning."

"God be with you, Your Highness." Chapman stood and gripped Tristan's hand tightly, pumping it up and down vigorously.

Celia stared at him with glowing eyes, as if he were a godsend. Only Aleatha did not look thrilled. As he walked out of the room, she fell in step close behind him.

"Are you mad?" she demanded under her breath as soon as the door had closed behind them.

"Shh." Tristan put a finger to her lips and took her arm. His eyes darted to the two men still standing guard over him. "Not here. Let us go to the garden. We can talk there."

He led her out to a bench under a grove of fruit trees and sat down beside her.

As soon as she saw the men following Tristan had stayed by the house, Aleatha spoke again. Her voice was low, but her words flowed in an angry torrent, "What are you thinking putting your life in my father's hands? He would just as soon turn you over to the queen himself!"

"For whatever else he has done, your father still cares about you and Lucas," Tristan argued calmly. Even though she was probably right, he was not about to admit that to her. "I am willing to bet I can make him realize turning me over to my mother will do nothing to guarantee Lucas's safety."

"And what is to keep him from betraying you to her once Lucas is safe?" Aleatha shot back, her words laced with venom toward her father's faithlessness. "Or worse, trying to finish what he has already attempted and killing you himself?"

The risk was great; a faithless ally was far more dangerous than any foe. He simply could not see a better option. "It is the only chance Lucas has. Your father is the only one who can get into the castle freely."

"I am going with you." Aleatha crossed her arms over her chest and set her jaw.

"What? No. Certainly not." Tristan's expression hardened and his tone was firm. "It is much too dangerous."

"Are you asking me to sit by while nearly everyone I love is in danger?" Aleatha snapped. "I think not. Besides you need someone to keep an eye on Father to make sure he does not do anything underhanded."

As much as he hated placing her in harm's way, Tristan knew Dr. Medellin would be much less likely to try anything in front his daughter. "Fine, but you will follow the plan exactly, and your sole job will be to make sure your father does the same."

"Thank you, Tristan." She leaned over and kissed him on the cheek. She turned his face toward her and looked into his eyes with concern. "Are you upset with me?"

How could he be, when she had simply expressed what he had been feeling only an hour before? Still, if anything happened to her, he would never forgive himself. He shook his head and forced a bleak smile. "Ask me again tomorrow morning when we are all back here safe and sound."

*****

Shortly before sunset, Tristan and Aleatha left the Chapman estate. Aleatha had remembered that her parents had hurriedly departed for their city home after the argument. It would save Tristan and Aleatha time, but required that they wear some form of disguise to navigate the busy streets without detection. They were on foot, dressed as peasants and carrying a baby doll wrapped in a blanket. Tristan wore a hood in the common style to hide his face and Aleatha wore a simple shawl draped over her head. Beneath her peasant's garb, she wore her regular clothes so she could change quickly for her visit to the castle. She held the "baby" and sang to it softly, rocking it in her arms as she walked. Periodically, Tristan turned toward her and checked on the baby, as if to see if it was all right. They forced themselves to focus all their attention on the doll and each other, barely glancing at the road around them.

Please allow anyone watching us to think we are two desperate parents preoccupied with taking our sick baby to see the doctor. Tristan prayed. Their constant focus on the "baby" had been Chapman's idea. He had pointed out that real parents with a baby sick enough to make an emergency visit to the doctor would care for little else. Tristan did not doubt that, but being unable to scan the areas around them for potential threats left him feeling exposed.

Heavenly Father, protect us. Help us to get Lucas out, he continued as they passed through the city gates. Good. Getting through before the gates were closed at sundown was critical. The next step was just as important. Dr. Medellin went home for dinner most nights before returning to the castle to give the queen her sleeping draught. *Don't let Dr. Medellin change his routine tonight.*

They reached the Medellins' home unmolested. Tristan gave Aleatha one more concerned glance, this one real, before he knocked on the outside door to Dr. Medellin's medical chambers. There was no answer.

"Ring the bell," Aleatha whispered, as she bent to kiss the doll in her arms. "If they are eating, they may not hear the knock."

Ringing the bell nailed next to the door, Tristan felt at the moment no father of any ailing child could feel more anxious than he did. The longer they spent at the Medellins', the more risk they had of being discovered and the less chance they had of pulling off Lucas's rescue in time.

After a moment, they heard footsteps. Addis opened the door, gave them a cursory glance and waved them over to a worn couch off to the side. "Dr. Medellin will be with you shortly."

Now came the hard part. Once Addis left, Tristan yanked the hood off his head; there was no purpose in it now. He began to pace the small room, his hands clasped behind him. Aleatha remained bowed over the doll, her eyes closed and her lips moving in prayer. A good idea, one he adopted.

Several minutes passed before Dr. Medellin appeared. He was patting his mouth with a napkin, his face solicitous and kind as he entered. "What can I do for you?" His voice turned into a snarl as Tristan turned to face him, "You! You have the audacity to dare show your face here, after all you have done to our family. You steal my daughter…" His eyes fell on Aleatha, then on the "baby" in her arms. A look of abject horror passed across his face as the blood drained out of it and rushed back in a hot rage. He took a step toward Tristan, choking on his words. "You… You…"

"Easy, Doctor," Tristan held his ground, his voice mild and firm. "It is only a doll. Surely a doctor of your skill knows it takes more than two weeks to father a child. We needed a way to see you without my mother's spies getting suspicious."

"I do not want to see you! Get out of my house." Dr. Medellin dropped his gaze back to Aleatha, and added with less conviction. "Both of you."

"We are here about Lucas, Father." Aleatha set the doll on the couch beside her and stood. "Tristan has a plan to rescue him."

"If it were not for the prince, he would not need rescuing," Dr. Medellin said through gritted teeth, glaring venomously at Tristan. "Perhaps I should offer to turn you over to the queen myself in exchange for Lucas's life."

"Do you really believe my mother would honor that deal, knowing as she does that Lucas plays an influential role in the resistance movement?"

Dr. Medellin's face flushed as he spun away from Tristan. He stomped across the room and stared out the small window, his shoulders heaving with deep, angry breaths.

Crossing the room, Tristan stood beside Dr. Medellin, being careful not to expose himself in the window. He stood silently for a moment as he struggled to gain mastery over the sudden surge of heartache he felt at the breach Dr. Medellin's suspicions had formed between them. His voice was laced with emotion when he finally brought himself to speak, "Have you really come to hate me so much you cannot even abide working with me to save your own son's life?"

The man he had regarded as a father did not respond, did not even look away from the window. Tristan's heart sank. *Is his hatred for me really so great? I had banked so much on being able to get him to see reason, a feat I have yet to accomplish about anything.* Tristan set his jaw and squared his shoulders. He would go after Lucas himself, if he had to, though he held no delusions about the outcome of a solo attempt. Perhaps he could at least persuade Dr. Medellin to forgive Aleatha. That way, if he were killed, she would have somewhere safe to go.

A gentle hand on his tense shoulders stopped him before he had a chance to speak. "Let me talk to him," Aleatha offered.

Tristan backed several steps away from the window to give Aleatha and her father room. Aleatha's voice was low, so he could only catch snippets of the conversation, but her passionate, pleading tone was evident even across the room. Pretending to be interested in the bookshelves lining Dr. Medellin's wall, Tristan surreptitiously scanned Dr. Medellin's face, hoping for some sign Aleatha's words were cooling his fiery anger. Dr. Medellin simply stood as still as a statue, deaf to his daughter's pleas.

There was a moment of silence and Tristan glanced back at Aleatha. She held a small slip of paper in her hand, offering it to her father. When he refused to take it, she began to read it aloud. Tristan turned his attention back to the books. He did not need to hear to know what she was saying. She was reading Lucas's letter to Dr. Medellin. She got about halfway when Dr. Medellin snatched the paper out of her hand and began to read the letter swiftly. Dr. Medellin threw a glance at Tristan when he was finished, and shot an angry reply back at Aleatha.

Dr. Medellin's low comment did not reach Tristan, but Aleatha's tear-filled answer did, "He was willing to sacrifice himself for Lucas, Father!"

"Then why does he not now?" Dr. Medellin growled, turning his angry glare back on Tristan, his voice raised and his words clearly directed to him. "You do not need my help to do that."

Heavenly Father, allow a loving daughter to do what I found impossible. Tristan clenched his teeth to bite back a sharp reply, turning away as Aleatha quietly continued her argument.

After a few more moments of tense whispering, the room grew silent again. Tristan turned, sensing the outcome of Aleatha's arguments had finally arrived.

"Is it true?" Dr. Medellin's voice was gruff, his expression was distrusting, but an undercurrent of respect flowed beneath his words.

Tristan glanced at Aleatha for help. He had been so focused on his prayers he had not heard anymore of their conversation.

"I told Father you had encouraged me to get things right with him," Aleatha explained.

"Is that true? Did you tell her to come back to me and try to make things right?" Dr. Medellin demanded. "When I sent her away, that was your chance to marry her. My authority had ended. Why would you send her back to me?"

"I love Aleatha, Doctor, and I want nothing more than for her to be my wife," Tristan responded. "But I never meant for things to be this way. I never meant to hurt your family. I wanted her to make one last attempt to reconcile things with you."

Eyes narrowed, Dr. Medellin searched Tristan's face as if trying to discern whether he was trying to trick him somehow. "What is this grand plan?"

Highlighting his need for Dr. Medellin's help, Tristan outlined his plan. He stopped short of telling Dr. Medellin he believed this was Lucas's only chance, both because he did not want to sound melodramatic and because he feared Dr. Medellin might not have completely abandoned his own plan to sacrifice him to his mother as an alternative.

"I will do it," Dr. Medellin agreed, "but only for Lucas's sake and because I trust your mother less than I do you. Hear me though, if it comes to a choice between my children or you, I will abandon you to your own resources with no regrets. Understood?"

"Father!" Aleatha protested, her eyes wide and her hands on her hips.

"Understood." Tristan extended his hand to Dr. Medellin, his face a grim mask. Dr. Medellin's distrust hurt deeply, but for now it was enough they would finally be on their way to help Lucas.

*****

After agreeing to rendezvous at the market, Tristan and Aleatha donned their disguises again and left, hoping to quell the suspicions of anyone watching the Medellins' home. They kept up their ruse for three moon-lit blocks before turning down an alley. Tristan gripped Aleatha's hand and led her down a circuitous route of side streets to the rendezvous point. They slipped down the alley beside the bakery. A bright glow of a lantern at the end illuminated the man that carried it. The man shifted his weight from one foot to the other, occasionally sticking his head out of the alley and peering into the main thoroughfare as if looking for someone, then ducking back into the alley for cover. Careful not to allow his feet to brush against the rubbish strewn on the ground in the alley, Tristan led Aleatha closer to the shadowy figure.

"We are here, Doctor," Tristan whispered as Aleatha removed her shawl, carefully wrapped the doll in it, and shoved it into the darkness of the alley. She pulled the simple peasant's dress up over her head and cast it into the pile also.

"Good." Relief showed on Dr. Medellin's face. "I sent Joanna to Chapman's, in case the soldiers come looking for us after we get Lucas free. We need to hurry, or the queen will begin to wonder why it is taking me so long to return. "

Stepping past Dr. Medellin, Tristan peered into the market place himself. There were few people on the streets this time of night, since all of the vendors and many of the customers had hurried to leave the city before the gates closed. He looked back at Dr. Medellin. "I will give you an hour to get in position."

"How will we know when you are ready?" Aleatha stepped out of the shadows, taking her father's arm from behind. She looked at Tristan with concern written on her face.

"If I have done my job right, you will know." Tristan was struck by how quickly she had transformed herself from lowly peasant girl to a lovely lady of the court. She wore a deep green velvet dress trimmed with gold ribbon with a thin knitted shawl of gold thread thrown over her shoulders. Her long brown hair was braided and tied back with a length of gold ribbon. She blushed and looked down toward her feet at his lingering gaze. Tristan felt a flush of color heat his cheeks as well. He hadn't meant to stare, but she was just so beautiful. Suddenly, grave misgivings about her participation in this rescue asserted themselves in his mind, but this was neither the time nor the place to revive that argument. Instead, he simply forced what he hoped was a reassuring smile, turned his attention back to a glowering Dr. Medellin, and extended his hand. "Good luck, Doctor. I will meet you at the other end of the tunnels. Chapman will have horses waiting for us to make a quick escape."

Their eyes met as Dr. Medellin took his hand. Tristan paused, surprised by something unexpected he saw there. Grudging gratitude, perhaps? It was only a flicker, gone as Dr. Medellin pushed past him into the road and drew Aleatha behind him. Tristan and Aleatha's fingers brushed against each other as she passed. He had not wanted to worry her with his plans for a distraction, and she had not bothered to ask, but they would both face much danger before the night was out. He could only pray hers would be far less than his, since he would be drawing the whole attention of the palace guard upon himself.

[illegible]

Chapter 29

Jesus, protect us all and allow us to rescue my brother safely. Aleatha could not help but feel a chill of apprehension as they approached the castle door. She pulled her shawl tighter around her shoulders. She had been to the castle only a handful of times and the imposing structure never ceased to send shivers down her spine.

Her father, seeming to sense her fear, put his arm around her shoulders and pulled her closer to him. He kissed her on the top of her head and whispered, "Come, my brave girl. Let us go rescue your brother."

Tears filling her eyes, Aleatha smiled up at her father, but his face was set toward the gate. His simple nod to the soldiers standing guard was all that was needed to grant them passage into the castle. Aleatha watched her father in amazement as he urbanely greeted familiar servants and lingering courtiers as if he were on his usual mission for the queen. Fear their true mission would be somehow discerned by everyone they met drove all etiquette from her memory. It took all of the control she possessed to remember to smile and curtsy when introduced.

The time it took to make their way to her father's medical chamber seemed interminable. Tristan and her father had determined it would be safer if Dr. Medellin were to give the queen her sleeping draught before they began their rescue attempt, since it would make one less enemy to worry about.

At last, Dr. Medellin led her into the tiny room he used to prepare medicine for the queen and closed the door behind them. He guided her to the bench just inside.

"I will not be reminding that witch I have another child for her to steal," he explained bitterly as he turned to his drugs.

He mixed an extra strong sleeping draught for the queen and left the room, closing the door between Aleatha and the queen's chambers behind him. Voices floated in from the queen's chambers, but the door was closed too tightly for Aleatha to make out the words. Nervous energy would not allow her to sit still for long, so she stood and crossed the room to her father's work table. She scanned the shelves of vials, wondering what each drug contained in them did. Since her only visits to the castle had been for unavoidable court functions, she had never been brought up here before. Her father had wanted to keep her away from what he felt was the "immoral influence of the court."

The voices on the other side of the door rose, especially the deep-toned one she recognized as her father's. She glanced to the door. Had they been exposed? Perhaps the queen suspected her father planned to free Lucas tonight and refused to take the draught, or worse, threatened to call the palace guard on him. Feet rooted to the floor, Aleatha listened as her father's strident voice came closer to the door.

With a final angry shout, Dr. Medellin tore the door open, stomped into the room, and yanked the door shut behind him.

"The gall of that woman. To think she would dare threaten me!"

"Father! What happened?" Aleatha grabbed his arm as he pushed past her in the tiny room. "Are we discovered?"

Dr. Medellin looked at her as if he had nearly forgotten she was there. He gave a harsh laugh. "No, of course not, that blind witch thinks she has me under her thumb. She would never expect me to try anything. She had the audacity to ask me to use my 'considerable influence' over Prince Tristan to persuade him to surrender in exchange for Lucas's life. She threatened to pick off members of my family one by one until he was apprehended." Dr. Medellin rubbed his hand over his eyes and lowered his voice as he said, "She told me she knew our family were the only people the prince truly cared about." He paused and looked up at Aleatha, confusion written on his face. "She fears him, Aleatha, more than I have ever seen her afraid of anyone in my entire life."

"You were wrong about Tristan. Can you not see that now?" Aleatha asked, her hands still on her father's arm.

With a grunt and a shake of his head, Dr. Medellin turned to gather a few supplies. "We need to hurry. Our hour is nearly up."

Choosing not to press her advantage, Aleatha decided rather to meekly follow her father out the door and down the hall.

How are we ever going to find my brother? She wondered as they made their way down to the dungeons. *And what condition he will be in when we do find him?* There was no way to know if he had been injured during the kidnapping or if he had been mistreated since he had been put in the dungeon. She shuddered. The queen had a reputation for treating her prisoners poorly. She glanced at the bundle of medicines and bandages her father was carrying, her father's concern for Lucas's injuries increasing her own.

The air began to grow dank and the fetid smell of death and human waste lay heavy on them as they descended the dark stairway leading into the dungeons. Her steps began to slow.

"If this is too much for you, my dear, I could send you home." Her father looked back at her, his low voice filled with concern. "There are a few servants here I trust enough to see you safely through the city."

Not trusting herself to speak, Aleatha shook her head. Apart from keeping her father on task, her part was small, but important. If any guards were left after Tristan's diversion, she was to plead weakness to distract the remaining men. Her short time in this awful place convinced her she would not need to pretend much.

"Who goes there?" a deep voice demanded from the bottom of the dark stairs. The owner of the voice held a blazing torch in one hand, blinding Aleatha and Dr. Medellin as he used it to check their identities.

"Gifford, it is I, Dr. Medellin." Dr. Medellin raised a hand to his eyes to shield them from the blinding light. "I have come to check on my son, to make sure you are not disobeying the queen's orders not to harm him."

"We ain't touched 'im, Doc, I swears to that." Gifford lowered his torch and leered at Aleatha, his grin marred by several missing teeth. "Oo's the pretty wench?"

"My daughter, and you will do well to treat her as you do the queen." Receiving a snicker from the raggedy guard, Dr. Medellin amended himself, "Better than you do the queen."

"You got it, Doc." Gifford flung one last rotted grimace at Aleatha and turned to lead them down the hall.

Though Gifford continued to babble as they walked, Aleatha focused her attention on their escape route. Tristan had said the guardroom would be the first one on the bottom of the stairs. A quick glance into the torch-lit room as they passed the doorless arch revealed at least five more men in there. The men must have noticed her, too, since whistles and jeers followed her as she scrambled to catch up to her father.

"I guess the Lord Devon ain't got the queen's orders not to touch the young man," Gifford said as he winked at Dr. Medellin, "or else 'e's just figuring the queen's orders doesn't apply to 'im, likes always."

"What do you mean?" Aleatha asked sharply, coming up beside her father.

"I'm sorry, me lady, but 'e was down 'ere asking your brother about the whereabouts of the young prince." Gifford shrugged. "Seems 'e's lost 'im and the queen's like to 'ave Lord Devon's head, she is. Ain't none to gentle about 'is questioning neither."

Aleatha's worried gaze met her father's grim one for a moment as they both quickened their pace.

"If Lord Devon has harmed my son, I will be sure he answers to the queen." Dr. Medellin blustered as he turned back to their talkative guide.

"I'd like to see that, I would." Gifford laughed as if Dr. Medellin had told a joke. "But you can see to your son yerself, 'e's right in there."

Gifford took the torch and set it in the sconce beside the heavy wooden door of the dungeon cell Lucas occupied.

Dr. Medellin peered in the small barred window near the top of the door. "Unlock the door," he ordered, "and leave it open as long as we are in there. I will not have you frightening my daughter."

"Wouldn't want to do that, now would I." Gifford flashed Aleatha another jagged grin as he fumbled with the ring of keys around his waist. Finding the one he wanted, he opened the door and swung it wide.

"Lucas!" Aleatha cried in dismay as she saw her brother lying on the bare floor in the center of the room, motionless. She dashed to Lucas's side, her father close behind.

Lucas opened his eyes with a start and pushed himself up to a sitting position. He blinked at Aleatha and Dr. Medellin with bleary eyes. "Aleatha, Father, what are you doing here?"

"We have come to take… we have come to check on you," Dr. Medellin corrected himself, laying his hand on Lucas's shoulder. "Are you all right?"

"A little sore, probably bruised." Lucas put a hand to his side and winced. "But I think I will be fine."

"Lord Devon?" Dr. Medellin asked, motioning for Lucas to remove his tunic so he could examine his injuries.

"Yes, he was in here earlier asking about Tristan." Lucas pulled his tunic over his head slowly and groaned. "He wanted to make sure he did not leave any noticeable marks, I guess the queen ordered him to leave me alone."

"What were you doing on the floor?" Aleatha asked, relieved he seemed all right.

"I had to get some rest." Lucas wrinkled his nose and pointed to the pile of straw in the corner. "That mess of rags and straw is infested with vermin. I would not think of sleeping there." He gave Aleatha a tight grin. "Sorry to worry you, but I did not exactly expect visitors."

"We are getting you out of here," Dr. Medellin whispered, bending his head close to Lucas's ear as he continued to examine his bruises, "as soon as Prince Tristan distracts the guards."

Lucas looked at Aleatha, an eyebrow arched in bewilderment. "Father and Tristan… together?" He mouthed to her.

Putting a finger to her mouth, Aleatha shook her head. "Later." She mouthed back.

"I think you will be fine." Dr. Medellin sat back and gave his son one more appraising look. "Nothing worse than some ugly bruises to go along with your pain and stiffness."

A noise of commotion in the hall interrupted them. Gifford stuck his head in the door. "I got to see what that's about. I'll just be down the hall. Don't you go nowhere now." His laughter echoed down the hall as he walked away.

Aleatha's pulse quickened as she looked at her father and brother. Soon, they would be doing the impossible: escaping from the castle dungeons.

Chapter 30

Protect us all, Lord, and allow us to free Lucas, Tristan prayed as he sat against a wall in a shadowy alley and calculated the time for him to begin his distraction. As the hour he'd promised Aleatha and Dr. Medellin neared the end, he stood with a sigh and wove his way down the darkened streets toward the castle. Reaching the end of the street, he turned sharply down the final alley before the castle. He had thought hard about where his vantage point should be when he revealed himself to the palace guards. Too near, and they would be on him before he had a chance to lead them on a chase. Too confined and he ran the risk of being trapped.

Stacking a pile of empty crates and barrels, he climbed to the flat roof of one of the nearby buildings. All of the buildings were close together here, some close enough to touch, most close enough to leap from one to the next. If the street became filled with soldiers, he would still have a chance to escape across the rooftops. Keeping low to avoid being silhouetted against the moonlight, he crawled across the rooftop to the edge of the building. Peering over, he could see the two soldiers standing guard on either side of the massive wood doors of the castle. One man's head bobbed as if he were falling asleep. The other slouched against the wall beside the door.

The doors opened a crack and another man slipped out and shoved it closed behind him. The newcomer stormed over to the dozing soldier and backhanded him across the face with enough force for the sound of the impact to reach Tristan's ears. The newcomer screamed at the careless guards, his voice deep and clear, even at that distance.

Devon.

The guards' eyes, white in the moonlight, widened in fear as Devon continued. He was furious with the guards for their negligence and threatened to kill them in horrible ways if Prince Tristan eluded their grasp.

"Prince Tristan will show himself before dawn, I am sure of it," Devon snarled, snapping at the two men like a rabid dog, "either to surrender or to make an ill-advised attempt to break out the prisoner." His voice took on a nearly demonic tone, one that sent a stab of terror into Tristan's chest. "I personally would prefer Prince Tristan made the attempt to rescue his friend rather than surrender. The queen has ordered he not be harmed if he surrenders. If Prince Tristan is caught attempting a desperate rescue, he is mine. This time I will make sure there is not enough left of his mangled corpse for his God to resurrect!"

Cold fear gripped Tristan's heart. If he were caught this time, there would be no second chances. He took a deep breath. Many people were counting on him. He would not let them down. *Heavenly Father, give me courage.* He stood and stepped onto the edge of the rooftop so he was illuminated by the moonlight.

"Devon!" he shouted down to the trio of men, forcing steel into his voice. "I demand you release Lucas Medellin. It is me you want."

"Your Highness! I was beginning to wonder where you were." Devon bowed low in his direction, his voice mocking. "I thought perhaps you took our little conversation in the desert to heart. That Brutus is not worth the sacrifice of your royal blood. He was taken in an attempt to sell your whereabouts to one of my spies."

The last thing he needed now was a tete-a-tete with Devon over Lucas's loyalty. He just had to attract attention to himself long enough to draw the guards out of the castle. "I have come to negotiate for his release."

"The terms are your life in exchange for his, Prince." Devon nodded to the guard on his left, who immediately ducked inside. "Hardly a worthy trade for a man who was willing to sell you for a few coins."

Still pressing the suggestion of Lucas's betrayal. There was no way he was going to allow these doubts to take root, not this time. He threw a wary glance around him before responding. The missing guard opened the door to the castle and soldiers poured out after him. Devon would never engage him in conversation for so long without ensuring he could not escape. "How can I be certain you will honor the terms of the trade?"

"You will have to take my word as a man of honor, Your Highness," Devon said. Even at this distance, Tristan imagined he could see the corners of his mouth curl maliciously.

"Lucas would go free and I would be delivered, *unharmed*, to my mother?" Tristan shifted his feet. He was running out of time, voices below him indicated several men were at the front of the building trying to figure out how he got up there. It would not take them long to find his makeshift staircase.

"Certainly, Your Highness, all according to the terms of our agreement. I am a man of my word."

A cry behind him warned his hiding place was compromised; the soldiers would be on him in a few minutes. Tristan gritted his teeth and stood firm as every fiber of his being told him to run now. *They need to be a little closer.*

"Come, Prince, what will it be?" Devon called from below. "Is my word not good enough for you?"

If Prince Tristan is caught attempting a desperate rescue, he is mine. Devon's comments only moments earlier came back to him. He had every intention to discourage Tristan from surrendering so he could do as he pleased to him without incurring Queen Brigitte's wrath. Tristan drew himself to his full height. So be it, he just would have to make sure he was not caught. The first soldier's head rose over the edge of the rooftop. It was time. He turned back to Devon, his voice clear as he answered, "No, I do not believe it is."

With that he turned and ran across the flat rooftop, leaping the space between it and the next one easily. Devon's angry cries pierced the clear air as the soldiers' rapid footsteps behind him punctuated each word.

The greatest game of fox and hounds in the history of Boldaria had begun.

*****

The commotion down the hall from where Lucas was imprisoned had become an all out ruckus. The Medellins waited anxiously as an authoritative voice barked out orders and the chaos gave way to organization. A few minutes later and all was quiet. Lucas's father gave his son's shoulder an encouraging squeeze, stood, and crossed the room to the open doorway.

"Guard! I say, Gifford, what is going on?" Dr. Medellin called down the hallway to a figure standing at the bottom of the stairs, staring up after the soldiers.

"Lord Devon and Captain Brogan are gathering men to hunt down the young prince." Gifford turned and walked toward him, his shoulders slumped. "I got picked to stay here."

"Tristan?" Aleatha stood and gasped dramatically.

"Not to worry. They will have 'im here soon enough." Gifford stopped in the doorway and snorted. "Maybe you could say hello to 'im yourself."

"No! They cannot." Aleatha shoved past Gifford in an apparent desperate attempt to stop the soldiers leaving.

Gifford grabbed her arm as she brushed by him. "See here now, missy…"

"*You* see here!" Dr. Medellin growled, hitting the unwary guard first on the shoulder, and following up with a solid blow to the head. Gifford slumped to the floor at his feet.

"Good hit, Father," Lucas said, biting his lip against the pain as he rose from the floor. "Though Aleatha's acting was a bit overdone."

Both his father and his sister were at his side in a moment.

"Do you need help, son?" Dr. Medellin took Lucas's arm to lend him support.

"No, I am fine, really. Just a little sore."

"Are you sure you are all right?" Aleatha asked from his other side.

"I am sure," Lucas said, offering a weak smile as proof.

"Good." She hit him playfully on the shoulder. "This is for your comment about my acting. Yours was not all that good a few days ago, if I remember."

As Lucas rubbed his shoulder and scowled at his sister, Dr. Medellin shook his head, crossed the room, and peeked into the hall. "Come on you two, it is time to get out of here. I do not know how long the prince can keep up his distraction." He grabbed a torch out of its sconce and led his children down the hall to the guard room. Pausing at the edge of the open arch, he peered around it and waved them on. Once in the room, he went straight to the left wall and searched for the release for the secret door. Lucas and Aleatha waited, nervously glancing between their father and the hall.

"No, Father, Tristan said a little right of center, not left," Aleatha whispered, going to his side to help.

"You do it, then," Dr. Medellin growled testily and stomped to the opposite side of the room to a wall-mounted weapons rack. It was nearly empty, since most of the weapons had gone with the soldiers hunting for Tristan, but he managed to grab swords for both him and Lucas and a rather long dagger for Aleatha.

"Hurry, Aleatha, I hear footsteps!" Lucas whispered, as he took the sword his father offered him.

"I found it!" She pushed against the wall with first one hand, then two. Her whisper became frantic, "I... I am not strong enough! It is stuck."

"Dr. Medellin, I knew you would be down here visiting your son," a melodious voice interrupted, "but I assumed you all would be in his cell, where I had him placed."

The trio spun to face the owner of the voice. In the doorway of the guardroom stood Queen Brigitte. A member of the castle guard stood in her shadow.

"You should be sound asleep." Dr. Medellin took a step forward and guided his two children behind him, his sword ready in front. "I saw you drink your sleeping draught not ten minutes ago. You should be insensible until morning."

"I am not as naïve as you seem to think I am," Queen Brigitte replied dryly. She lifted her skirts and stepped further into the room, allowing her man to enter, ready for her orders. "I know your love for your family; I was certain you would try to rescue your son, regardless of what my fool son did. I merely appeared to drink the draught." She motioned for her man to stay still as she moved closer to the Medellins and frowned at Lucas. "Devon didn't hurt you too badly, did he? He tends to get a bit overzealous at times."

Lucas glared at her silently. Dr. Medellin stepped back and ground his heel into Lucas's foot, prompting a tight, "No, Your Majesty," from his son.

"Leave my children out of this," Dr. Medellin demanded. "My family has never done anything against you. I have been your faithful servant for the last two decades."

"You have feigned allegiance to me for the last two decades because you feared me," the queen corrected with a dismissive wave, "just as everyone else in my kingdom. However, at home, you have trained your children to hate me, to be traitors to this realm. You have even encouraged them to join the rebellion against me. Is that the behavior of a *faithful* servant, Doctor?"

"We are not traitors to this realm," Lucas snapped. "We support the true king, King Tristan!"

"Be quiet, Lucas," Dr. Medellin hissed.

"That is precisely my point," Queen Brigitte said, her careless voice growing hard. "My son should be ruling beside me, not opposed to me. Not only have you poisoned your children against me, but you have succeeded in turning my own son away from me. His loyalty to you and your family was so complete I was forced to send him away with Devon in an attempt to break the hold you had over him."

"The lifetime of cold-hearted brutality that led you to make the decision to order your own son tortured to bend him to your will is what turned him from you, not me," Dr. Medellin countered, his passion getting the better of him. "My family simply showed him the love he always craved from you."

"Love makes weak rulers," Queen Brigitte mocked. "Tristan's weak, fool of a father believed he loved me. Look where that got him. Every foolish decision he made was out of 'love' for the people of Boldaria. I mean to make my son the strong ruler his father never was, whatever it takes." She looked at them as if she were a lion sizing up its prey. "No matter how much pain I have to cause him.

"So this is the girl my son is so infatuated with." She stepped over to Aleatha and took the girl's chin in her hand. "I suppose she *is* attractive. Perhaps I have been going about this wrong. A woman's influence over a love-struck man can be very powerful. I will allow you to marry my son, just as long as you remember who your ultimate allegiance belongs to."

Aleatha pulled free of the queen's grasp and glared at her, fear glittering in her eyes.

"You," the queen addressed the guard. "Kill the boy; his influence over the resistance and my son are too great. Dr. Medellin, too. He has become more dangerous than he is useful. Perhaps with them out of the way, the power they and their God have over my son will end. The girl on the other hand…" She gave Aleatha another appraising look and turned away. "I will have Devon spend some time with her. Perhaps he can turn her where he failed with my son."

"You will not touch my children!" Dr. Medellin thundered. He lunged toward the queen with his sword raised to strike.

With a swift, smooth motion, the queen turned, drew a dagger from the folds of her dress, and drove the dagger into Dr. Medellin's unprotected stomach.

Aleatha's scream echoed through the dungeon chambers as her father staggered backward and dropped his sword to the ground with a clatter. Tears streaming down her face, she knelt beside him as he sank to his knees.

Lucas's medical training took the fore as he, too, knelt beside his father, his own sword dangling limply from his hand.

"Foolish, Doctor," Queen Brigitte scolded. "Did you really think I would be unprepared for an attack? Though I did expect the attempt to be from your impetuous son rather than you. I really did not think you had the courage." She gave her guard a withering look. "Must I do everything? Take care of the boy and put the girl in his cell to await Lord Devon's return."

The queen's order burst the weak dam that held back Lucas's emotions. With a cry of rage, he lifted his sword and rushed toward the soldier, his fury augmenting his moderate swordfighting skills. The battle was over before it even started.

Lucas swung his sword in a vicious arc and severed the soldier's head from his body.

"I guess I really do have to do everything myself," the queen sighed in irritation. She stooped, picked up the dead soldier's sword, and stood with it held defensively in front of her. "I can assure you, young doctor, I am much better with a sword than that imbecile."

The first heat of passion was gone, and Lucas had no illusions about the outcome of a cold-blooded fight with the lethal queen. He bit his lip and copied her pose. *Lord, help me!*

She lunged for him, stepping carelessly past Dr. Medellin's body. Her sword was nothing more than a liquid silver blur as Lucas tried desperately to ward off her attacks. With a sharp motion, she drove her sword into Lucas's left bicep.

Crying out in pain, Lucas moved his sword hand instinctively toward the wound, leaving himself unprotected. His heart seemed to stop as he realized his mistake too late to ward off the queen's deathblow.

The deathblow never came. The queen froze in her tracks, eyes wide with surprise, and wilted before him. She fell face down at his feet with her own dagger sticking out of her back. Dr. Medellin stood over her with his hand clutched to his stomach and a look of vengeance on his face. A shudder coursed through his body, his eyes rolled back, and he slumped to the floor.

"Father!" Aleatha cried, leaping forward and catching him in her arms. She stumbled beneath his weight, but succeeded in lowering him to the floor and cradling his head in her lap.

A quick glance was all it took for Lucas to be certain the queen would no longer be a threat to them. His father had driven the dagger between the queen's shoulder blades and directly into her heart. She died before she hit the floor. *Good riddance,* he thought, as he turned his attention to his father.

"Is she *dead*?" Aleatha squeaked, glancing at the motionless body of the queen.

"Most certainly," he answered as he assessed his father's condition with a trained eye. "But right now I could not care less. I'm only concerned about Father." His father was conscious, but his eyes were dull with pain and his torn tunic was darkening quickly with blood.

"Father, we need to get you into the passages before more soldiers come. Can you get up?" He was taking a great risk moving his father, but it could not be helped. He needed to get him to a place of relative safety so he could dress the wound.

"I think so."

"But, I couldn't get secret passage open, remember?" Aleatha spoke up worriedly.

"Stay with him, I'll take care of it." Lucas stood and crossed the room to the wall. He placed his hands over the small rock his sister had been pushing on and leaned against it with all his weight. The secret door ground open in its track, revealing a dark passage.

"Help me get him inside," Lucas ordered his sister. "We need to be out of sight before anyone discovers the queen." He did not need to tell her what would happen to them if they were caught with the queen's body. Regicide was punished without mercy or room for explanations.

Together they assisted their father up and through the gaping hole in the wall. He was breathing heavily and his weight sagged against their shoulders.

"Did Tristan say how to close this thing after we are through?" Lucas asked Aleatha as they helped their father to the floor a short distance inside the opening.

"I will take care of it," she said with a sniffle. "You take care of Father."

"Give me your shawl. I need to tie up Father's wound."

Without hesitation, Aleatha handed him her shawl and turned to the inside of the wall beside the opening. The lever on the inside was easier to find and operate. She had it closed in a matter of moments and returned to her place beside Lucas next to the prostrate form of their father.

His expert hands working quickly, Lucas tore open Dr. Medellin's tunic to expose the bleeding wound, removed his own tunic, and ripped it into smaller pieces to use as a bandage. He pressed a folded pad of cloth against the wound and slid another under his father's body carefully, tying Aleatha's shawl around his father's waist to keep the bandages in place.

"Where were you supposed to meet Tristan?" Lucas asked Aleatha as he worked, his voice low and business-like.

"At the other end of the tunnels." Her voice nearly broke as she stared at her wounded father. "The door between the castle passages and the underground tunnels is locked on this side. Someone needs to remove the peg that is keeping the door from opening."

She caught her trembling lip between her teeth. "How do you think he will take the news of the queen – his mother's – death?"

He really had no idea how Tristan would react. Lord Devon had planted and nursed many doubts about the Medellins' faithfulness in Tristan's mind, as well as promoting the queen's love for him. *Would this only serve to prove Lord Devon's accusations?* Lucas sighed. Even if Tristan did retain his faith in his friends, he was bound to be grief-stricken. She was his mother, in spite of everything.

"We'll worry about that when the time comes," Lucas answered. "You bring him back here. Father will need help going any further."

"Lucas… will he be all right?" Aleatha choked out as she stood, her eyes fixed on her critically injured father.

Will he, Lord? Lucas stared down at the unconscious figure of his father for a long while before answering. "I do not know, Aleatha," he finally answered with a catch in his voice. "I just do not know."

Chapter 31

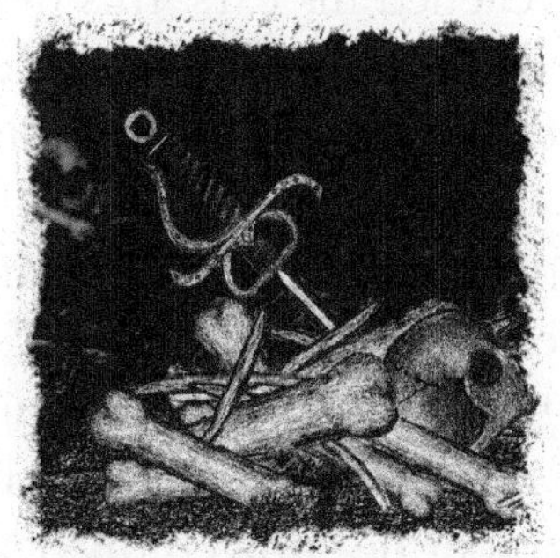

Tristan leaned back against the alley wall and laid his head back on the cold stone. His shoulder throbbed and his chest burned as he gulped air. He had no idea how long he had been running, only that it had not been nearly long enough. He needed to give the Medellins as much time as possible before he lost the guards chasing him for good. His injuries at Devon's hand in the not so distant past and his battle with Dr. Medellin's poison more recently had left him weak. His forced breaks had become longer and closer together throughout the night. The last time, the guards had nearly caught up to him.

He peered around the corner into the street. It was still clear, giving him a few more desperately needed moments to rest. He had led the palace guards on many merry chases as a child, though none with such high stakes. The few times he had been caught, the consequences were unpleasant, but obviously never fatal. A chill ran up his spine as he remembered Devon's threats. He had to widen the gap between him and the soldiers without losing them.

A nearby shout told him it was time to move again. He scrambled up a mound of rubbish piled against the wall, straining his tired arms to pull himself onto the roof. By alternating running on the ground and running along the rooftops, he had wound his way toward the city gate. It not only allowed him to cover more ground, but it allowed the soldiers a better view of him which in turn made his distraction more effective.

Another shout reached his ears, this time a command. Intuitively, Tristan dove to the hard surface of the rooftop and flattened himself down as a flurry of crossbow bolts rained overhead.

"Keep him pinned down, men!" Captain Brogan roared from the ground below. "He is ours now."

Heart pounding, Tristan crept along the rooftop on his stomach, the stone rail on the edge of the roof hiding him from view. The moment he showed his head over the edge, he would be fired upon. Even if he could make it over the edge onto the next building without getting shot, the soldiers only had to move a few feet to keep him pinned to that roof. At the terrible snail's pace he was forced to travel, they would catch him in a matter of minutes. He stopped and lay still. Silence greeted him; worried him. Surely they should have sent someone up to fetch him by now. He quickly surveyed his forced battlefield. The sword he had brought, anticipating the chance of running into trouble, was useless here. If he stood to use it, he would instantly be pierced by a dozen quarrels.

"Prince Tristan, you have nowhere to go," Devon said, his pleased voice sounding like a tiger preparing to pounce on its unfortunate prey.

Desperate, Tristan glanced around the rooftop. Some of the rooftops he had been on were bare, but many were used by their owners as a summer room or storage. He realized with a glimmer of hope this was one of the latter. Crates and barrels lined the edge of the roof away from the street. He rolled toward them.

"You have accomplished nothing, my young prince," Devon taunted as Tristan crawled along the rows of crates searching for a place to hide. "I realized shortly after you began to lead us on this merry little chase around the city exactly what you were trying to do. Surely you did not believe I would be fooled? I sent some of my men back to the castle to take care of whoever you had trying to break young Medellin out. They are now dead, you will soon be captured, and Lucas Medellin will burn at dawn."

Aleatha and Dr. Medellin, killed? Tristan's blood turned to ice in his veins. *No, Devon could not know that or he would have certainly mentioned Aleatha's name.* Devon was bluffing, though Tristan guessed the part about sending soldiers back was true. The Medellins could be fighting for their lives right now. Tristan felt a strong urge to take his chances fighting it out with the soldiers now and go help them, but he would be dead before he could even get off the roof. His only chance was to hide until the soldiers left. *There!* A large, empty barrel had fallen to its side, allowing him to creep inside without exposing himself to the archers.

"I suppose I should offer you one last chance of surrender," Devon said. His voice took on a tone of smoldering hatred. "But I think I will rather enjoy making sure I correct the mistake I made nearly two months ago. Tonight you die, Prince Tristan, as slowly and as painfully as possible."

A sudden onslaught of intense memories from the past year washed over Tristan. *Heavenly Father, give me strength*, he prayed, forcing himself to focus his mind away from Devon and on making his hiding place as secure as possible. Squeezing into the cramped space, he used his feet to turn it so the opening faced into the row of crates, hiding him from view. It certainly would not protect him if Devon and his men decided to search thoroughly. He could only pray they did not.

Soon, the sound of heavy footfalls sounded on the rooftop. Tristan caught his breath. The footsteps stopped and a voice called down to the men waiting on the ground, "He ain't here, Lord Devon. Ain't no one here."

"It cannot be!" Devon roared in rage. "You told me he was pinned down."

"He was, my lord," Captain Brogan answered. "He has to be there."

"Take your men to search the area. I will look myself," Devon snapped.

A grunt was followed by more footsteps as Devon mounted the roof and crossed its length, cursing the poor soldier who stood by, Tristan, and Tristan's God.

"Did you search the crates?" Devon growled at the other man.

Silence. Tristan assumed the soldier was too afraid to speak.

"Fool!" Devon's sword sang as he slid it from his scabbard.

Tristan clenched his teeth, certain the soldier was about to pay for his oversight with his life. Instead of the wet sound of razor sharp metal cutting through human flesh, he heard the dry knocking sound of Devon driving his sword into the crates and barrels one by one.

As the sound moved closer to his hiding place, Tristan's heart thundered in his chest. He could not run, and the confined space of the barrel would not allow for him to shift out of the path of the sword. It would be better to go down fighting than to be skewered in the barrel like a fish. Gauging the sound of Devon's movements to time it so he hit Devon with the barrel and give himself a momentary edge, he braced his feet against the wall of crates blocking the opening of the barrel he was hiding in. Devon was beside him now. He bit his lip and placed his hand on the hilt of his sword. A few more steps to go.

"Lord Devon! The prisoner, he's escaped," a frantic voice called from the ground below.

"What?" Devon thundered. Pounding footsteps crossed the roof to the edge facing the street. "That is impossible. No one has ever escaped the dungeons before."

"I know, sir, but he did, somehow. There was a sword fight. Blood everywhere. Tad is dead and Gifford is out cold." The soldier paused, as if steeling himself for worse news, "And the queen, my lord, she's dead, too. Had her own dagger in her back."

Silence ruled the night as everyone processed the implications of the soldier's news.

My mother is dead? Tristan dropped his head against the back of the barrel, his eyes wide with shock. The first emotion that hit him was a wave of relief. Perhaps now the nightmare would end. The relief was quickly replaced by a rush of guilt. The queen was his mother.

She cares for you… in her own way. Devon's words returned to him. Still, he found it hard to muster anything more than regret for a relationship he never had.

"The Medellins murdered her," Devon called out, both for the benefit of the soldiers and, presumably, Tristan. "Hunt them down. Take them alive if possible, if not, kill them."

I must get to my friends before Devon's men do. Tristan felt his pounding heart skip a beat.

"What did I tell you, Prince?" Devon shouted, his voice directed back toward the barrels, "They killed your mother. How long will you persist in your belief in their loyalty? Until you find Lucas Medellin's dagger in your own back?"

In spite of himself, Tristan felt Devon's deeply planted doubts rise up like banished ghosts. Lucas's ultimate betrayal had been a common theme in the desert, one he had nearly succumbed to. Nearly, but not quite. He shook his head to clear the doubts. The Medellins held no love for his mother. Dr. Medellin had made his view quite clear when he sided with Lord Blakemore. Had Dr. Medellin taken advantage of the attempt to free Lucas to carry out the underground faction's plot? Even if he had, that did not mean Lucas was involved.

Frustrated by Tristan's silence, Devon made an irritated noise and stomped back across the rooftop. "Captain Brogan, gather the men and meet me at the castle."

"What about the prince?" the soldier's fading voice indicated they were going over the side of the roof.

"Prince Tristan will have to wait." Devon cursed. "He and I will meet again, and next time it will take more than a miracle to save him."

*****

After the sounds of the soldiers to died away, Tristan spent several more anxious moments in his cramped position to be sure no one was waiting for him. Finally, he pushed against the wall, scraped the barrel against the rooftop, and slid out. Stretching his arms and legs first, he began to crawl quickly across the rooftop. The moon still illuminated the night around him, and he did not want to take any chances. He was only a few houses from an ivy covered section of the city walls he could climb down to meet Aleatha and the others at the tunnels.

Worry spurred him on. The soldier had said there had been a lot of blood. There was no way to know if one of his friends had been wounded in the battle. Despite his best efforts to teach Lucas, his friend was still only a barely passable swordsman and, as far as he knew, Dr. Medellin had no skill with the sword whatsoever.

How could I place them in that kind of danger? Even if they escaped unharmed, the entire army of Boldaria would soon be searching for them. He stood to his feet and began to run, crouched over, across the rooftops. He needed to return to them as soon as possible. He reached the top of the city wall and looked over, but saw no one. His mother's murder would keep all the guards near the castle or the gates for a little while longer.

Moving as one familiar with his actions, Tristan scrambled down the side of the wall, clung to the thick ivy, and dropped the last few feet to the ground. Breaking into a full run, he crossed the short expanse of lawn to the woods. The thickness of the trees obscured most of the light from the moon, giving Tristan barely enough light to pick out his old path through the woods. He raced through the darkness, tree branches grasping at his clothes and roots threatening to trip him as his feet flew over the ground as fast as he dared. He pulled up short at the edge of a small clearing. Four horses stood tied to a tree, whinnying and snorting softly, but he saw no signs of human life. He crossed the clearing to a large fallen tree leaning on a pile of rocks. The entrance to the underground tunnels sat nestled in the rocks under the overhanging branches of the tree. Getting on his hands and knees, Tristan crawled under the branches and fumbled with the hidden door. Pulling the door open, he lowered himself down a ladder carved into the stone wall of the tunnel and his feet hit the muddy floor with a splash.

The tunnel was dark, cold, and silent. Tristan's worry grew. There was no sign of the others, not even a flicker of light or movement indicating the presence of anyone in the tunnels with him. Trailing his left hand along the damp stone wall, Tristan made his way blindly up the tunnel toward the door that led to the castle's inner passages, praying someone had been able to get it open, otherwise his friends would be cut off from all help.

Hope filled his heart as a faint flickering glow lit the end of the tunnel. He rounded the final corner to see a torch set in a sconce in the wall beside the door. The door was open and Aleatha was just coming through. Her skirt was muddy and smeared with blood and her face was streaked with tears. She turned as he rounded the corner and her body sagged with relief.

"Tristan!" she cried, as she ran to meet him and threw her arms around his neck. "We have been worried sick."

"Things did not go as well as I had planned," he responded mildly, embracing her. She seemed unhurt, praise the Lord. "Lucas and your father, where are they?"

A shudder coursed through Aleatha's body as she buried her face and muffled a sob in his shoulder. "Lucas is with Father in the castle passages. Father has been asking for you. Lucas says he… has not much time."

The news hit Tristan like a punch in the stomach. Dr. Medellin was the only father he'd ever had. The contrast to his reaction to the news of his mother's death brought another twinge of guilt, but he pushed it aside. The Medellins had always been his family. "Take me to him, quickly."

Aleatha gripped Tristan's hand in her own as she led him through the heavy stone door back into the castle passages. A faint glimmer of torchlight guided them to the narrow passage where Dr. Medellin lay propped against the wall, Lucas kneeling beside him.

"Tristan!" Lucas lifted red-rimmed eyes as he heard them approach. "I was beginning to fear you had been captured."

"I nearly was," Tristan answered as he joined his friend beside Dr. Medellin and Aleatha knelt next to him, "but my story can wait. How is your father?"

"He will never make it out of here." Lucas's voice was unsteady as his tenuous hold on his emotions threatened to slip. "I thought perhaps I could save him, but there is… there is nothing more I can do."

"Lucas?" Dr. Medellin whispered as his dim eyes searched for his son's face.

"I am here, Father," Lucas took his father's hand tenderly, his eyes glistening in the torchlight. "We all are."

"Tristan?" Dr. Medellin's eyes drifted to Tristan. "I am sorry. About everything. I misjudged you, sorely. Please, will you forgive me?"

"Of course I forgive you, Doctor." A knot rose in Tristan's throat. Dr. Medellin had not called him by his given name since his return. Even to his untrained eye it was clear Dr. Medellin was failing fast. "You need to rest. Conserve your strength so we can get you out of here."

Dr. Medellin's laugh was little more than a cough. "I know better than any of you I am not going anywhere, in spite of my son's expert care." He focused on Lucas's face again. "You did all anyone could do, I am very proud of you. You will do a wonderful job… wherever you decide to practice." His gaze shifted to Aleatha as he continued, "I am so sorry, Sweetheart, I just wanted what was best for you. I overreacted, can you ever forgive me?"

Tears spilled down Aleatha's cheeks as she bit her quivering lip and nodded.

"Tristan?" Dr. Medellin leaned his head back against the wall and closed his eyes. His voice was fading and unsteady. "Take good care of my Aleatha."

Dr. Medellin's words hit Tristan like a thunderbolt, burying him in an avalanche of grief and joy. He had given up hope of ever receiving his blessing, but finally receiving it now, in this way, made his heart ache for the relationship he had lost with the man who had accepted him into his home as a son. "I… I will, sir, you have my word."

"Joanna..." Dr. Medellin whispered his wife's name. "Tell her... I'm sorry...Our time together was too short."

With a small sigh, Dr. Medellin sagged against the wall. Aleatha clutched her father's shirt in her hands, buried her face in it, and smothered her sobs in his motionless chest. Lucas held his father's lifeless hand tightly in both of his, the dam of emotion he had been holding back breaking into unashamed sobs. Tristan could only continue to stare at Dr. Medellin's vacant expression as tears streamed freely down his face. How he wished he could turn back the clock to the time a little more than a year ago when the Medellins' home had been a place of joy and peace. Since his return, he had only brought it pain and suffering. Perhaps if he had never returned, things would have continued as they were. He shook his head slowly, willing away the doubts that threatened to oppress him. This was not his fault; his mother and Devon deserved all the blame. With God's help, he would make sure Devon paid the penalty for his actions. His mother already had.

Minutes passed, perhaps hours. In the darkness of the passages there was no way to be sure of the time. The three of them sat beside Dr. Medellin's body, consumed with grief. Tristan stirred, brushed his sleeve across his eyes to dry them, and laid a hand on Lucas's heaving shoulder. "We need to go. We must be back to Chapman's before dawn."

"We cannot leave him here."

"Chapman has horses waiting for us at the tunnel's exit. If you help me, we can carry him out to one of them."

As Lucas struggled to his feet, Tristan laid his hand on Aleatha's back, caressing her gently across her shoulders. "Aleatha, we must be going."

Aleatha sat up slowly and looked at him dumbly. Her eyes were red and puffy and her disheveled hair framed her face in thin wisps. Even in her grief, she was beautiful. He brushed a few strands of hair away from her face as he helped her to her feet. She stood silently as Tristan and Lucas each slid their shoulders under one of Dr. Medellin's limp arms and carried him out. When they reached the door separating the castle passages from the underground tunnels, they paused for a moment to rest. Tristan took a moment to place the locking peg into a hidden recess on the outside of the door to allow them access again if they needed it. Reaching the horses, they tied Dr. Medellin's body to one and made their way back to the Chapman estate.

Chapter 32

At dawn the next morning, Chapman held a private funeral for Dr. Medellin in a grove at the edge of his estate. The funeral was short, as no one could risk being outside long after the events of the previous night. As soon as it was over and everyone was safely back inside, Tristan allowed the Medellins some time together, following Chapman to his study at the merchant's request.

"I know you and the Medellins do not need another problem at this moment," Odell Chapman said, knitting his brow as he considered his words, "but I am afraid it is no longer safe for you to be seen here. There were men here last night looking for you. I was able to allay their suspicions for now, but it will not be long before they return."

Another weight seemed to rest on Tristan's shoulders. He had known it would happen eventually, but after last night he wanted nothing more than a short reprieve from the running and the danger. "Lucas and I will return to the Morrison home as soon as it is safe to leave."

"That will work for you, but not for the women. It is too small and the risk of being in town is great. I would offer that Aleatha and Lady Medellin stay here if I did not fear Lord Devon would make an attempt to take them as well."

Heavenly Father, how do I protect those I love from Devon's wrath? Tristan clasped his hands behind his back and crossed the room, looking vacantly over the immense shelves of books that covered the walls. There was a sharp knock at the door and Lucas let himself in. His expression was grim and dark circles lined his eyes from lack of sleep.

"Perhaps after all that has happened, I can convince Aleatha and Lady Medellin to leave the city." Tristan mused.

"Mother has already decided to go to her sister's in Shanksdale," Lucas offered, wincing as he lowered himself into an empty chair. "She actually began packing after you and Father left the house last night. She leaves within the hour."

"Would your sister go with her?" Tristan asked as he cast a concerned glance at his friend. His arm was bandaged from an injury sustained either in the sword fight or during his capture, but no other injuries were apparent. In all the commotion since the rescue, Tristan had not had an opportunity to ask Lucas about his time in Devon's custody. That he had suffered was without question, but Tristan worried about how badly Devon had treated his friend for his sake.

"There is no way you will convince Aleatha to leave with her." Lucas answered as he waved away Tristan's look. "Mother is trying already." He rolled his eyes. "They are still arguing up there."

Tristan turned to Chapman. "Can you have one of your servants make sure Lady Medellin gets to Shanksdale safely?"

"I believe one of my men has a cousin in Shanksdale," Chapman recalled. "I will see if he would be willing to escort her there"

"I will let her know." Lucas gripped the arms of the chair and pushed himself up to standing.

"I would like to tell her goodbye myself." Tristan turned to follow as Lucas walked slowly to the door. "Perhaps I can also talk to Aleatha about a safer place to stay."

Lucas nodded silently, his troubled thoughts obviously somewhere else. "Tristan… about last night. Your mother attacked us. Father only killed her to protect Aleatha and me. She was going to kill me and send Aleatha away with Lord Devon. You must believe my sister and I have never plotted against you or your mother."

Tristan gave his friend a long, careful look. Lucas did not meet his gaze and his hands were clasped together so tightly his knuckles were white. Clearly his friend dreaded his reaction to Queen Brigitte's death, but the simple explanation was likely enough to be true. The queen's own wickedness had brought about her death.

"I believe you," Tristan assured him softly. The thought of Lucas lying lifeless on the dungeon floor and Aleatha in Devon's hand sent a chill of fear down his spine. "And I thank God He spared me the choice between the lives of my friends and the life of my mother. I do not know if I would have had the strength to make that decision."

Relief filled Lucas's face as he clasped Tristan's hand in both of his. "I… I know Lord Devon put great effort in casting doubt on my faithfulness. I admit I feared how your mother's death would appear. I just want you to know you have my complete loyalty, both as your subject and your friend. I would never betray you."

Tristan pulled his friend toward him and clapped his arm around him in a brief embrace. Pulling back, he held Lucas at arm's length. "I do know that, Lucas. You and Aleatha have ever shown me love and loyalty. The doubts Devon planted may always linger, but with God's help I will never allow them to take hold."

A tight smile split Lucas's face. "Thank you. You have no idea how that has weighed on my mind since last night. I had best see to Mother now."

"Prince Tristan, a moment, if I may." Chapman spoke up as Lucas left the room. The heavyset man closed the door behind Lucas and continued, "I did not want to say anything in front of Master Medellin, since he would only delay his mother's leaving for safety, but there may be another option for Lady Aleatha. One that might be satisfactory to everyone involved."

"If you have any ideas, I am open to them," Tristan said. "I am afraid she is not going to like any of mine."

"I spoke to the minister this morning after the funeral. He would be willing to perform a private wedding ceremony for the two of you tonight here at my house. She could go with you wherever you went and you could be sure she was safe." Chapman looked at Tristan. "It will not be without risk, though. Any delay in getting you to another place of safety increases the chance you will be discovered here. I need not tell you what will happen if Lord Devon discovers you here."

No, he does not need to tell me. Tristan rubbed his jaw. There was nothing he would like better, but was it what was best for Aleatha? "You will be putting your home at risk."

"No more than I have by sheltering you here up to this point," Chapman said, dismissing his concern. "I am also taking the liberty of sending Celia to a neighbor's until you are gone. If you are that concerned about it, perhaps the minister would agree to have the ceremony at his church. It is small, but private, and not far from here."

Hope smoldered in Tristan's tired soul. Perhaps this was the solution after all. He would speak to Aleatha as soon as possible. The discussion would be little more than a formality, since there was no doubt in Tristan's mind Chapman's suggestion would be acceptable to everyone involved.

* * * * *

After a few hours sleep, the little wedding party began its preparations. A servant was sent to take provisions and Aleatha's meager belongings to the Morrison house where she would join Tristan for their wedding night. Chapman assigned some of his servants to assist Aleatha: finding her a dress, braiding her hair, even providing her with a bouquet of flowers. Tristan bathed, pulled his black hair into a short ponytail, and dressed in the rich clothing he had worn away from the castle. He strapped his father's jeweled scabbard and sword to his waist, then at Lucas's insistence, he placed his coronet on his head. He examined himself critically in the mirror. He looked strong, regal, but inside he felt like jelly.

I wonder if all bridegrooms feel this nauseating mixture of nervousness, excitement, and fear. Taking a deep breath, he threw a cloak over his shoulders, covered the glittering gold circlet with his hood, and followed Lucas out of the room to join the little wedding procession on its way to the chapel.

The sun had set and the overcast sky blotted out all light from the moon. Chapman led the way, holding a lantern in front of him to guide them. They reached the small clapboard church without incident, slipping through the darkened doors and down the center aisle to the stooped, elderly minister waiting at the altar for them. A pair of lit candelabras stood on either side of the altar, the only light in the whole church besides Chapman's lantern. Tristan untied the strings of his cloak and tossed it over a nearby pew.

The minister's widened eyes traveled from Tristan's coronet to his sword, each sparkling brilliantly in the flickering candlelight. He bowed low as he stammered, "Do you expect trouble, my king?"

King? Tristan raised an eyebrow and glanced at Chapman questioningly.

"Reverend Prestwick is one of us that looks forward to your reign, Highness. Perhaps with a bit more… foresight than most," Chapman clarified.

Reverend Prestwick looked up at Tristan, following with an explanation of his own, "Your mother's reign has seen much persecution against any who dare speak against her, especially those who would seek to worship God outside of her state controlled churches."

Now Tristan understood. The Medellins were affiliated with a dissenting church, as were many others in the resistance. He himself had held little regard for his mother's brand of Christianity, and had spoken loudly against her cruelties toward the dissenting churches, obviously gaining this old minister's reverence. "There may be danger, Reverend, I will not deny it. It is best to be prepared."

"I have had no use for swords myself, but I will say I am glad for the protection tonight." The old man chuckled. "Your mother will be none too glad if she finds out we are defying her wishes here tonight."

Reverend Prestwick actually seems to relish the prospect of defying my mother, Tristan realized, finding himself beginning to like the elderly minister. "All the more reason for us to get started, then."

Aleatha's hand slipped around his left arm. As she placed his right hand over her own hand, he turned to look at her. He blinked once and his heart began to pound faster as he allowed his eyes to drift admiringly over her. She was wearing a white dress, cut in a simple style, but the bodice was overlaid with lace and sparkling glass beads traced the neckline and waist. A single string of pearls hung from her neck and a pair of matching earrings dotted her ears. Her long brown hair had been braided, the braids were wrapped in a circlet around her head, and her head was crowned with a wreath of daisies. *She has never looked more lovely.*

As Aleatha blushed at his open admiration, Tristan raised her hand to his lips and kissed it gently. Turning to the minister, he said, "Whenever you are ready."

"Please face each other." Reverend Prestwick stepped behind the pulpit and laid his hand on the Bible.

Following Reverend Prestwick carefully, Tristan took both of Aletha's hands and gazed into her golden brown eyes as he pronounced his vows of devotion to her. Each of their vows held a richness of meaning brought out by the knowledge they could be tested further in the near future. Everything he had, poverty or the wealth of a kingdom; everything he was, a fugitive or a prince; belonged to her, for as long or as short as God might allow him to live on this earth. As she repeated her vows in turn, he read in her eyes a fierceness that highlighted her determination to stand by his side through whatever lay ahead.

"Have you any token of your love?" Reverend Prestwick asked Tristan.

Tristan shook his head. The lack of a ring was an unfortunate – almost embarrassing – omission, but one that could not have been remedied at such short notice, at least not without drawing attention to the wedding.

Lucas cleared his throat and stepped forward, his hand outstretched. Resting in the palm of his hand a tiny circle of gold glittered in the candlelight. "Mother gave this to me before she left. It was hers, but she wanted Aleatha to have it. Especially now that…" Lucas's mouth twitched and he cleared his throat again. He placed the ring in Tristan's open hand and stepped back without another word.

Reverently sealing the marriage in the name of the Father, Son and Holy Ghost, Tristan slid the ring down Aleatha's thumb, forefinger, and then her middle finger before finally slipping it into place on her third finger. He and Aleatha bowed their heads together as Reverend Prestwick prayed for God's blessings on the new couple.

"Amen," Reverend Prestwick finished his prayer and raised his head. "I now…" he broke off with a gasp, his eyes focused on something behind the small wedding party.

An amused snicker came from behind them following Reverend Prestwick's reaction. Tristan placed his hand on his sword as he prepared to face the intruder. A sharp point digging into his spine stopped him before he could even get his sword out halfway.

"I would strongly recommend you put the sword back in its place, Your Highness." Devon's voice was low and deadly, allowing no room for argument. "Unless you want your friends to die here and now."

"Tristan!" Aleatha cried out as she was pulled away from Tristan's side, her cry cut off by a firm hand pressed over her mouth.

Gritting his teeth angrily, Tristan slammed the sword back into its scabbard and raised his arms. He turned slowly to face Devon. There were six soldiers, as far as he could see. One each stood behind Lucas and Chapman, their razor sharp swords held to his friends' throats and their hands clamped over his friends' mouths. Two others flanked him, the points of their swords mere inches from his body. One slipped past him to guard the elderly Reverend Prestwick. Beside Devon and Captain Brogan stood the sixth man, holding Aleatha as she struggled vainly against his arm wrapped around her waist and his hand covering her mouth.

"Let them go, Devon," Tristan ground out. *How could I have been careless enough to allow them to slip in unaware?* "I am the one you want."

"But I do not want you. Your mother wanted you, but your friends put an end to that." Devon's black eyes flashed and devilish grin split his face. "*I* want you to suffer unimaginable torment as you die knowing the one you love more than anything in this world, more even than your very life, is in the hands of your greatest enemy."

Tristan's heart thundered in his chest as he flashed a glance to Aleatha. Her eyes were wide with horror and her struggles had become frantic. Lucas attempted to cry out angrily, but his voice was muffled by the soldier's hand.

"I will not let you touch her!" Tristan took a step toward Devon, only to be stopped by a sword digging into his stomach.

"I do not see how you have much choice. I spent nearly a year listening to your description of her great faithfulness and beauty. After all that time, I find myself intrigued," Devon said. Evil pleasure lit his face as he turned to Aleatha and stroked the side of her face with his hand. She froze at his touch, tears filling her terrified eyes. "She is quite lovely." Devon dropped his voice menacingly as he added, "Do not worry, I will take good care of her."

With a cry, Tristan lunged toward Devon with almost animal-like rage, dodged the swords guarding him, and pulled his own sword free of its scabbard before he even took a full step. The soldiers were on top of him in an instant. He fought fiercely, savagely, as the soldiers pummeled him with their fists and the hilts of their swords. The force of their blows hammered him to the floor until he was too dazed to even raise his head. The soldiers jerked him up from off the ground. This time a soldier held each of his arms as Captain Brogan held his sword to his chest. Tristan's coronet and sword lay at his feet and blood ran from his nose. A wayward strand of black hair fell over one glowering eye as he panted, "Devon, if you harm her, so help me, I will kill you myself!"

"I am afraid that will be impossible, since I intend to make sure you do not survive that long," Devon said, sneering as he turned to go. "Take her out of here," he ordered the soldier holding Aleatha as he passed.

"What do you want done with him?" Captain Brogan grunted, flicking his eyes toward Reverend Prestwick, but never taking his sword from its place over Tristan's heart.

"Kill them all, but make it sporting." Devon turned back to them with a sinister smirk on his face. "I wish for Prince Tristan to have time to relish the knowledge his precious Aleatha now belongs to me."

Panic gripped Tristan's heart like a vise as Devon and Captain Brogan followed the soldier carrying the struggling Aleatha out the doors of the church. *Dear God! Not Aleatha. Do not let him hurt Aleatha.* Helplessness and rage threatened to swallow all reason. Clenching and unclenching his hands beside him, he struggled to steady his breathing and clear his mind.

Guide my sword as I fight to defend myself and my friends, Tristan prayed as the soldiers beside him and his remaining friends stepped back, poised to fight. He took a deep breath and dove for his sword, scooping it up in his right hand, then rolling to his feet to face his former captors. This was going to be the fight of his life, and the life of the woman he loved hung in the balance.

Chapter 33

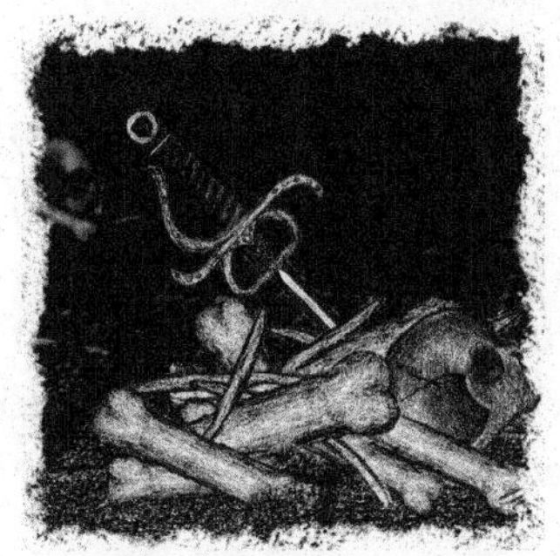

"Please, someone, help!" Aleatha cried to the crowd gathering outside in spite of the lateness of the night. Pulling against the soldier's grasp, she looked from one man to the next. Every man averted his gaze, unwilling to interfere. The soldier jerked her around to face away from the crowd as Devon and Captain Brogan came out of the church. Two more soldiers carrying blazing torches stood guard on either side of the door.

"Barricade the door," Devon commanded the soldiers, "and torch the place. I want no one to escape."

"But sir, my men inside," Captain Brogan objected.

"Do not worry about them," Devon said with a cruel chuckle. "Unless I overestimate the young prince, most of them will be dead by his sword long before the fire gets to them."

A displeased look on his face, Captain Brogan instructed his men to obey. Each set the torch he held against the dry siding of the church and stepped back.

"No! Please, no!" Aleatha screamed as the flames began to lick up the side of the church. *Please, Jesus, will you not do something?* What had been the best moment of her life was quickly becoming its biggest nightmare.

"What do you want us to do with her?" Captain Brogan jerked his thumb over his shoulder at Aleatha.

The evil smirk Devon had given Tristan twisted his mouth again as he walked toward Aleatha and stopped less than an arm's length away from her.

Pull yourself together. Aleatha ordered herself. She fought the shrinking feeling she felt at his stare and forced herself to stand tall. *You are Princess Aleatha now, even if it is only for a moment. Make Tristan proud.*

She shuddered as Devon made no attempt to be discreet as his eyes traced every curve of her body. Hot tears flooded her eyes, but she blinked them back. *I will not allow this monster to affect me.*

"Quite lovely indeed. Perhaps Prince Tristan has some taste after all." Devon stroked her cheek with the back of his hand.

"Take her back to the castle," he finally answered Captain Brogan. "I have my room ready for her. Any wench good enough for Prince Tristan is good enough for me."

"You will not dare touch me," Aleatha retorted, trying to mask the tremor in her voice. "I am Princess Aleatha now, Prince Tristan's wife. He will survive your little death trap and come for me."

"You need not concern yourself about that, my lady." Devon leered at her. "Even if Prince Tristan were to survive, which is highly unlikely, I mean to make sure he will never want to have anything to do with you again."

*****

Inside the church, Tristan crouched, facing off against two of Devon's soldiers. He had been trained in sword fighting from his youth and was more than a match for his opponents, but his nagging concern for Aleatha distracted him.

Parry, turn, duck… a desperate swing of an opponent's sword swished over his head. *Heavenly Father, save Aleatha!*

Jab. A short stab at his other opponent's knees brought the soldier down temporarily. A third soldier joined the fight. *Please do not let that devil harm her.* Fear for Aleatha began to overwhelm him. He had spent a year with Devon – a year of torment. His mind flooded with the terrible things Devon could do to her.

As yet another soldier engaged his sword, Tristan found himself backed against one of the church's support pillars. He forced himself to focus. *I cannot rescue her if I am dead.* He slashed his sword in a wide arc to drive back his opponents. A quick thrust and one of his opponents doubled over. Tristan pulled his sword back and the soldier fell to the floor at his feet. The other two stepped back, giving Tristan a moment to take stock. His sword flicked back and forth rhythmically as he kept the men at bay. The acrid smell of smoke reached his nostrils and a dull haze crept into the building.

Devon means to be certain no one survives, Tristan realized, feeling a twinge of pity for the soldiers Devon was obviously willing to sacrifice.

Tristan spun to avoid the thrust of his opponent's blade. A quick parry and a thrust to the chest and a second opponent fell. The rhythm of his sword slowed as he only had to keep up with one opponent. *If we are going to escape, we need to get out soon, before the whole building burns around us.*

Taking a quick look around him, he scanned the room for the other three men. He spotted Reverend Prestwick first, his body lay contorted on the ground in a spreading pool of blood. Guilt gripped Tristan's heart. Reverend Prestwick had told them he had never used a sword. He had probably gone down as soon as the fighting started.

Parry, turn. Tristan focused his attention back on his opponent. The soldier had mounted an aggressive offense. The man was good, but seemed to be holding back. Fear and hesitation filled his eyes.

"Please go," Tristan admonished. "I do not want to kill you."

"If you don't, Lord Devon will," the man ground out, "and I would rather take my chances with you, Highness."

The soldier's sword flashed and Tristan parried. Tristan felt a sting in his arm as the blade slashed his left bicep. Gritting his teeth against the pain, Tristan delivered a quick thrust of his own. The soldier collapsed. Tristan looked down at the man with true regret. He hated taking any life, especially when Devon was his real enemy.

Free from all opponents, Tristan peered into the smoky sanctuary. Odell Chapman was locked in a close fight to his left. A soldier lay at his feet, but sweat glistened on Chapman's face and his movements seemed sluggish and choppy. Tristan rushed to aid his ally. As he saw Tristan approaching, a hard look crossed the soldier's face and he drove his blade into Chapman's gut. Chapman doubled over with a look of agony and collapsed over the soldier he had slain earlier.

With speed motivated by anger and grief, Tristan crossed the distance between him and Chapman's murderer. He engaged the soldier aggressively, pushing him back until the man was bent backward over a pew. Tristan looked for an opening for his blade. He needed to finish quickly and find Lucas before it was too late. *Heavenly Father, help it not to be too late already.*

A moment of hesitation on his opponent's part was all he needed. A flash of his sword and the soldier folded over the back of the pew.

"Lucas!" He turned his attention back to the search for his friend. The smoke was thick and the heat from the fire was nearly unbearable. The building was beginning to groan as its supports were weakening from the blaze. If they were going to have any chance of getting out, they needed to go soon.

A cry at the back of the church caught his attention and he dashed down the aisle between the rows of pews toward the sound. The smoke grew thicker the nearer he came to the entrance and flames licked up the support pillars on either side of the doors. Lucas lay on the floor, his sword several feet away from him. The soldier stood over him with the hilt of his sword in both hands and the blade pointed downward over Lucas's chest.

"No!" Tristan cried as he ran toward his friend. *Heavenly Father, please, no!* First Aleatha, now Lucas. He was trapped in a nightmare.

As the soldier raised his sword and prepared to plunge it down, Lucas raised his arm over his body in defense. A sob tore from Tristan's throat. He was only a few feet away, but it was enough. He was going to be mere seconds too late.

A loud cracking sound caused Lucas's attacker to turn slightly. A portion of the roof came crashing down, sending a shower of ash and sparks over them. The soldier lifted his arms to shield his face. That moment of distraction gave Tristan the time he needed to cross the gap between them. With a shout of surprise, the soldier raised his sword to cross Tristan's.

"Lucas, get out." Tristan coughed. The air was getting too thick to breathe. He kept his eyes on his opponent, forcing himself to focus through his growing fatigue. A false move now would mean both their deaths.

"I have to check the others." Lucas scrambled to his hands and knees, crawling to stay beneath the smoke.

"They're dead," Tristan called after him, "get yourself to safety."

As Lucas disappeared into the smoke, Tristan turned his full attention to his opponent. *I need to finish now and get Lucas out before the whole building comes down.* His sword flicked in and out like the tongue of a snake as he pressed his opponent back, closer to the burning rubble behind him. Sweat and smoke burned his eyes and the toxic air choked him with each breath he took. He spotted his opening and took it. His final opponent fell at his feet.

"Lucas!" Tristan shouted into the smoke. The ceiling above him groaned again. "Lucas, we have to go..."

The ceiling gave with a loud snap and a crash. A searing pain struck him across the back, driving him to the floor. The room swam as he tried to push himself to his feet. The heat from the burning ceiling beam was unbearable and the weight across his back hindered his already labored breathing. He struggled to free himself, but his right arm and sword were both buried under the burning rubble.

"Lucas," he rasped. All he could see was smoke. For all he knew, Lucas had fallen, too. As he hovered on the edge of consciousness, he cried out to God, *Help Aleatha. Please, do not allow Devon to touch her. She is yours now...*

The flames crept closer to him as he finally slipped into unconsciousness.

Chapter 34

Aleatha woke with a start. She lay on her stomach on a plush bed. The pillows from the bed were scattered on the floor in front of an ornately carved door. The room was lavishly decorated in satins, velvets, and gold. The royal crest was carved into head of the bed, gilded with gold, and inlaid with jewels.

Where am I? The palace certainly, but which room? The opulence and richness of the room seemed excessive, even for what she imagined royalty would enjoy. Assuredly more than Tristan would desire. Lord Devon must have had her taken to the queen's room.

Panic flooded over her as memory of the previous night returned. She buried her face in the silky covers of the bed and stifled a sob. Her eyes burned and her throat was raw from screaming. After the soldiers had locked her in the room, all the bravado she had put on in front of Devon melted away. She had screamed until she was hoarse and flung all the pillows off the bed against the door before she finally sobbed herself to sleep.

Dear Jesus, please allow Lucas and Tristan to live. She clung desperately to her last shred of hope. Only God could save Lucas and Tristan… and her. Tears began to soak the blankets again as she thought of Tristan. Barely a bride, she had been forced to spend the wedding night alone, the captive of another man. She had been dragged away from her husband before she had even had a chance to kiss him. She clutched the covers closer to her, soaking them with her tears. At least Devon had not bothered her last night.

A gentle caress down the calf of her leg startled her. She rolled away quickly. Devon stood at the foot of the bed leering at her. Pushing against the bed with her hands and heels, she backed away from him against the cold, gilded headboard. She had not heard him come in. Fear welled up inside her as she remembered his words from the night before.

"Good morning, Lady Aleatha." He laid a cloth-wrapped bundle on the bed without taking his eyes off her. "I would ask if you slept well, but I can see you did not. Pity, you will need all your energy for the events I have planned for today."

"Tristan will come for me." Her voice was raspy and she sounded desperate, even to herself.

"Even if Tristan had survived last night, why would he come for you?" Devon grinned wolfishly. "Why would he want anything to do with you at all?"

"What do you mean? I am his wife, why would he not come for me?"

"You spent your wedding night in another man's bed. The bed of his mortal enemy, no less."

"It was not like that," Aleatha whispered. Fear clutched her heart as she saw the way Devon had arranged things. "Tristan will believe me."

"Will he? Husbands are notoriously jealous men. Especially husbands with beautiful wives." Devon's eyes traced her body as he added almost to himself, "Prince Tristan certainly did have good taste in women."

He shook his head and shrugged. "It really does not matter. You need not worry about him anymore."

"What…" Aleatha's mouth grew dry. She licked her lips, swallowed and tried again. "What do you mean?"

"I am afraid I bring you bad news." Gravity settled on Devon's face. "How can I break this to you gently?" Devon paused as if thinking. He continued, a malevolent smile twisting his mouth, "Prince Tristan is experiencing firsthand the eternal faithfulness of his God."

"No. Tristan is not dead. You are lying," Aleatha said, her hoarse voice quivering. She pulled her knees up and hugged them to her chest. *This can not be happening. Surely God would not allow it.*

"I thought you might not believe me, so I brought proof." Devon deftly uncovered the bundle at the foot of the bed. He revealed a fire-blackened sword and a tarnished, disfigured circlet of gold. "Recognize these?"

Tristan's sword and coronet, I would recognize them anywhere. She tried to speak, but a lump closed off her throat. Finally, she managed a strangled, "Where did you get these?"

"My men found these in the church with all that remained of your husband's body. It seems both your husband and your brother perished in the blaze last night."

Tristan and Lucas… dead? Aleatha closed her eyes and rested her forehead on her knees. It could not be true, and yet, Devon seemed so confident. Her heart raced and her breathing quickened as she fought back the overwhelming panic rising up inside her. Tears burned her eyes, but she refused to lose control in front of this murderer. *Please, make him leave. I cannot hold on much longer.*

"First your father, then your husband and brother, this has been a hard week for you," Devon said, feigning sympathy as he walked around the bed to lay a hand on her back. "I suppose I can give you an hour to grieve before you start to get ready."

Aleatha shrugged his hand off her back and looked at him. Her mind barely registered what he was saying. *How can he possibly know about my father?* She blinked as his last statement sank in. "Get ready? For what?"

"Our wedding, of course," Devon replied, watching her reaction with pleasure. "There is a lot for you to do to be ready for tonight."

"I will not marry you," Aleatha sobbed. Her eyes burned as they filled with the tears she had been holding back.

"Have it your way." Devon shrugged. A wicked challenge filled his eyes. "Though, I think you might change your mind. You see, I intend to have my bed back tonight. I have decided to insist you keep me company. I am simply offering you the chance to make it legal, but that is up to you. I do not intend to force you to marry me."

Aleatha dropped her head back onto her knees and wept. Each sob tore itself from her chest with such force her body began to ache. She felt Devon's hand caress her back again, but had no energy to shake off his touch.

As he left she heard him say one last time, "It really is your choice, Lady Aleatha."

But it is not. I really have no choice. Aleatha realized as terror gripped her. *Dear Jesus, I really have no choice at all.*

* * * * *

When Tristan awoke, his face felt like he had a bad sunburn again, and his body ached as if he had been beaten by Devon. Defensively, he kept his eyes closed and regulated his breathing, hoping to gain a few minutes before Devon began his torments again.

"Tristan, it is Lucas, wake up," Lucas's voice called to him. "We are safe now."

Groaning, Tristan pushed his hands against the floor to sit up. His throat, eyes, and lungs still burned from the smoke.

Devon. The memories returned in a flash. *That devil has Aleatha.* He tried to rub his face with his right hand. Cloth rubbed across his skin. He looked in surprise at his bandaged hand.

"Your hand was burned, not too badly, but badly enough I decided to bandage it," Lucas explained. "You have other burns, cuts, and minor injuries, but nothing that will not heal."

Lucas's own hair and eyebrows were scorched, his skin was covered in soot, and his eyes were red from smoke. His hands were bandaged, as well.

"How about you?" Tristan rasped. "You look awful."

"Too bad you cannot look in a mirror," Lucas retorted. "I can tell you you are not winning any prince charming competitions today." His serious expression returned. "My hands were slightly burned pulling you from the rubble. I… I nearly did not get you out of there. I do not know what I would have done if I had lost you, too."

"We have to go after Aleatha." Tristan gritted his teeth. He looked around his surroundings for the first time. They were back at the Morrison house. "How long has he had her?"

"I estimate it to be about noon," Lucas answered. He looked down at his injured hands and lowered his voice. "Ten or twelve hours?"

Tristan closed his eyes and groaned again, this time from anguish rather than pain. "Do you realize what that devil could to her in that amount of time? You saw the way he looked at her in the church…"

"Stop, please," Lucas begged, his soot smeared face contorted with grief. "Remember, she is my sister as well as your wife."

"Some husband I turned out to be," Tristan grumbled. "I lose my wife to my worst enemy before the minister even finishes pronouncing us man and wife. I have to go to her."

"There are extra swords in the main room. Ours were lost in the fire," Lucas said. He snorted and added, "though I question what good they will do us. I was already not all that good with my hands, but I will certainly not be able to do much with these burns. If I take my bandages off, I at least can bluff; your right hand is too burned to even hold a sword."

"I am a moderate swordsman with my left." Tristan gave a modest grin. "I probably could hold my own with anyone for a while. Anyone, except perhaps Devon."

"Then, as much as we would both like you to face him, we will have to make sure you are ready first." Lucas left the bedroom for a moment and returned with two swords in their scabbards. He passed one to Tristan. "Now we need a plan to get in."

"If they have not discovered the tunnels we used before, I can get us in and out." Tristan pulled the sword out of the scabbard and examined it.

"And if they have?"

"We will have to risk it." Tristan pressed his lips together tightly as he slid the sword back into its scabbard. "Even a few soldiers are better than the whole castle guard. The problem will be finding Aleatha before Devon finds us."

"Is there anyone loyal to you in the castle that might help? A servant, perhaps?" Lucas suggested.

"Perhaps," Tristan said pensively, rising to his feet. "I will think about it as we go. We have wasted enough time already. I can only pray we can rescue Aleatha before it is too late."

"And that we can get out of there safely a second time," Lucas murmured as he followed Tristan out of the room.

Chapter 35

"Lady Aleatha?" A soft voice and a gentle knock interrupted Aleatha's desperate prayers. She crossed the room and opened the door to a chambermaid looking at her compassionately. "Lord Devon said it is time for you to get ready."

Dear Jesus, what do I do? Devon had promised to make her his wife either by the law or without it. She shuddered. Could she truly go through with a wedding to Devon? What if Tristan still lived? She had thought he was dead before. Surely she could not trust Devon's word. *Perhaps Tristan will still come for me.* Tears filled her eyes as reality struck. *No, Tristan truly is dead this time. He would never have left behind his sword and coronet if he were not.*

"Lady Aleatha?" the chambermaid repeated. "Lord Devon told me to remind you to hurry if you are to be ready for tonight." The girl sighed. "I know Lord Devon may not be the most appealing husband, but 'tis better to be a reluctant bride than a forced concubine."

She was right. As hateful as her words were, they were true. Aleatha gripped her hands together tightly and look down at them. "What do you need me to do?"

"I have drawn you a rosewater bath, my lady." An eager smile on her lips and an excited sparkle in her eyes brightened the chambermaid's face. "After that, I will rub you down with special scented oils, do your hair, and help you dress. Lord Devon has provided you the most beautiful wedding dress ever."

A lump in Aleatha's throat threatened to choke her as she stood to allow the chambermaid to help her remove her own tattered, dirty wedding dress. The removal of her dress seemed to signify the removal of her old life.

"May I see my dress for a moment?" She held the dress to her for a moment, willing herself not to collapse again into a heap of sobs. She tore a length of ribbon from the sleeve, laid the dress on the bed, and slipped her mother's ring off her finger. Using the ribbon, she tied the ring securely around her neck. She was not going to let Devon get his hands on her ring, her true wedding ring.

The chambermaid looked at Aleatha as if she were wearing a snake around her neck. "Lord Devon will not like you to wear that, Lady Aleatha. He asked me to make sure you took it off."

"It is off now, is it not?" Aleatha's lips curved defiantly. If Devon thought she was going to submit to him easily, he was mistaken.

Crossing the room, she slipped off her undergarments and stepped into the bath the chambermaid had drawn. She took a deep breath as she slid into the steaming water. It smelled like her rose garden at home. Closing her eyes, rested against the back of the tub, and clutched her wedding ring in one hand. *Dear Jesus, help me to have the courage to act in a way that would have made Tristan proud.* The tiny reminder of her true husband clutched in her hand gave her the strength to face Devon.

"May I wash your hair?" the chambermaid asked "It smells of smoke and is full of snarls."

Aleatha held her head still as the girl finished unpinning her tangled braids. "What is your name?"

"Mary, my lady," the chambermaid answered as she ran her fingers gently through Aleatha's hair, loosening the knots.

"Know this, Mary. I do not marry Lord Devon willingly tonight." Aleatha turned and really looked at the girl for the first time. She was only slightly younger than herself with blond hair and expressive, blue eyes. "Last night, he interrupted my real wedding, murdered my husband and brother, and burned the church to the ground. I was brought here by force and I marry Lord Devon by coercion."

"Please, my lady, do not speak so of Lord Devon." Fear shone in Mary's eyes. "He hears all that goes on in the castle, some say in the whole kingdom."

"I am not afraid of his hearing me." Aleatha settled back into the tub. "He knows I do not marry him willingly."

Mary combed through Aleatha's hair and washed it thoroughly. She reached for a towel beside the tub. "You will want to get out before it gets cold."

Reluctantly, Aleatha stood, stepped out of the tub, and took the towel from Mary. "Thank you, Mary, but there are some things I prefer to do for myself."

"Then I think, perhaps, this might be one of them." Mary reached over and picked up an ornate glass bottle with an amber-colored liquid inside. "Scented oil. It was brought over from the middle-east. Devon insisted you use it. If you wish, you can rub it on while I fix your hair."

Aleatha took the bottle from Mary and pulled out the glass stopper. The scent was richer than any she had ever smelled. She jammed the stopper back in. Devon was trying to buy her with expensive gifts. She handed it back over her shoulder to Mary. "This had to cost a fortune. I will not use it."

"Lord Devon insisted. He said you were to do things his way, or not at all." Mary bit her lip as he pushed the bottle back toward Aleatha. "Please, my lady, do not cross him."

With a scowl, Aleatha took back the bottle. She did not want to do this at all, much less his way. If he pushed her too far, she might change her mind about cooperating and take her chances with him tonight. She shuddered. *No, this was the only way. Girls are forced into unhappy marriages all the time,* she reasoned. *There is no wrong in my agreeing to one to save my honor.*

She pulled the stopper again and rubbed the oil on her body. She used the smallest amount needed to cover her skin, stopped the bottle, and set it aside.

"Finished? Good, so am I." Mary stood and crossed the room to a bundle of clothes lying across a chair. "I will help you dress. These undergarments can be a bit tricky." She picked up an elaborate white corset and a shift.

Aleatha groaned. She had only worn a corset a few times when she had been to a ball or other formal affair at the palace, her father had been adamant against them as unhealthy. Every moment it had been on had been torture. *I should have known I would be required to wear one now.* She sucked in a sharp breath as Mary expertly yanked the strings of the corset and tied them. Struggling to breathe, she allowed Mary to help her with her stockings and the elaborate underskirts.

"Now for the dress, my lady." Mary gently lifted a heavy, white satin dress from the chair. The dress was covered with embroidery, pearls, and clear sparkling jewels.

"Are… are those diamonds?" Aleatha gasped.

"Yes, my lady." Mary looked at the dress admiringly. "It is a dress any woman would be proud to be wed in."

"If the woman were proud to be wed in the first place," Aleatha responded. "Come, I am certain I will need help putting that on. It looks as if it weighs fifty pounds."

"It is heavy," Mary admitted as she helped Aleatha pull the dress over her head. She buttoned the dozens of tiny buttons up the back of the dress. "I heard it took the dressmaker a whole year to make it. The queen commissioned it for the Prince's wedding…"

The blood drain from Aleatha's face. Tears filled her eyes. "This was to be for Tristan's bride?" she whispered, her voice a cross between a question and a statement. In another lifetime this would have been her dream rather than her nightmare. The same dress, the same care in her appearance… a different groom. Her willpower waned. How could she go through the ceremony with Devon? *Dear Jesus! What am I to do?*

"Oh! I am sorry, my lady," Mary said, her voice filled with dismay. "I should have known better than to..."

"Forget it, Mary," Aleatha responded hoarsely. "None of this is your fault. Please, let us just get this over with."

"Just the make-up now, my lady. Good thing, too. We are almost out of time."

While Mary applied the make-up to her face, Aleatha stood patiently. As much as she hated the whole process, she was beginning to wonder what she looked like. She had been facing away from the only mirror in the room the whole time she was getting dressed.

"There. You look like a princess, Lady Aleatha, a real princess." Mary's voice was filled with awe as she added, "and I might say, a lot more lovely than a lot of the princesses I see around here."

"May I see?"

"Certainly." Mary helped her turn to face the mirror.

Tears filled Aleatha's eyes and she covered her mouth with her hand to stifle a cry. She looked regal, like a real princess, as Mary had said. Her hair was pulled up around her head and held in place by several jeweled pins and a large jeweled comb. Her face had just the right touch of make-up and the dress truly was elegant. *I wonder what Tristan would think?*

"Now, none of that. You will spoil your face." Mary pulled out her handkerchief and dabbed at Aleatha's eyes. "Oh, I almost forgot the jewels."

She crossed to the chair, pick up a velvet-covered box, and hurried back. She set the box on a nearby dressing table, opened it, and pulled out a finely crafted diamond necklace. She clasped the intricate network of gold and jewels around Aleatha's neck and placed the matching earrings in Aleatha's ears.

"There, I can see why Lord Devon chose you, Lady Aleatha. There is no lady in the whole kingdom more exquisite than you, even if I do say so myself."

This is the fairy tale wedding Tristan and I should have had, not some clandestine nightmare. Aleatha blinked back the tears that swam in her eyes. *Oh, Lord Jesus, why have you allowed things to happen this way!*

A knock at the door interrupted her thoughts. Without waiting for a response, Captain Brogan opened the door.

"Lord Devon requires the presence of his bride," he announced, leering at her. "I see you decided to cooperate. Good. I am sure Lord Devon will be pleased. Come on, mustn't keep your bridegroom waiting." He turned to Mary. "You, come along. Lord Devon needs another witness."

Aleatha's courage ran from her like water as she followed Captain Brogan numbly down the corridor, down several flights of stairs, and down another corridor. It all seemed like a horrible nightmare, a nightmare she could not force herself to wake up from. Stroking her hand down the skirt of the wedding dress, she felt the smoothness of the satin and the sharpness of the tiny diamonds covering the fabric.

What would I give for the plain dress and the secret ceremony of the last night! Consumed by her thoughts, she walked into the back of Captain Brogan, who had stopped before a large, ornate pair of double doors.

"We are here, my lady," Captain Brogan said, gesturing exaggeratedly to the door.

It took a moment for Aleatha to process where "here" was. She gave a small gasp and placed her hand over her mouth.

"The throne room?" She had never actually been in the throne room before. "Why here?"

"With Queen Brigitte dead, Lord Devon will soon be the next king. He felt the throne room was the only fitting place for him to wed his queen," Captain Brogan said with a wide grin, evidently enjoying her discomfort. He pushed the door open and gestured for her to enter the room.

Her stomach turned at the suggestion of her being the next queen beside Lord Devon, and she hesitated in front of the door. Captain Brogan prodded her into the room and onto the lush red carpet trailing from the door to the throne. The vastness of the ornate room made Aleatha feel very small and afraid. Her nervous gaze swept the empty space - empty except for herself, the two people behind her, and two people before her. On the throne at the end of the path of red carpet sat Lord Devon in full royal splendor. A minister in fancy ecclesiastical robes stood beside him watching with a frown.

"Welcome, my dear," Devon said. He stood from the throne and smiled at her. "We've been waiting for you."

Feeling as if she were walking to her own execution rather than to her wedding, Aleatha swallowed hard and headed up the red carpet runner toward the front of the throne room.

Her expression must have revealed the dread she felt, because the minister's frown deepened. Hoping to find a little sympathy in the cleric, she turned her eyes to him pleadingly. "Please, sir, don't allow this to happen. Surely you can't perform an unwilling wedding."

"The Cardinal leads the state church. He will do precisely as I tell him if he wishes to retain his position when I am king," Devon said, casting a fierce look at the minister. He took a step toward Aleatha and trailed his fingers down her arm in an intimate caress. "Besides, I am not forcing you," he reminded her slyly, "I left the choice entirely up to you."

"Let us get started." He turned to the minister with a suggestive grin on his face. "I wish to have some time with my new bride before I turn my attention to the queen's funeral and my coronation."

Shrugging off his touch, Aleatha let her passion gain control over her tongue. "Everything you have was stolen from the rightful king," she snapped. "If Tristan were here, you would not be so smug."

"But your handsome prince is not here," Lord Devon returned. His tone was glib, but fear lurked in his eyes. "He will never get in my way again. His throne is mine. You are mine. In a few moments nothing he could do would change that."

A faint spark of hope kindled in her heart, as she caught the fear he was hiding. "You fear Tristan might be alive. That is the reason for your haste. You wish to be sure he cannot upset your plans."

"Prince Tristan is dead. I showed you the proof this morning," Devon assured her confidently, all trace of fear vanishing. "I swore to him I would take care of you. I am nothing if not a man of my word."

"Lets just get this over with," Aleatha retorted sharply, covering the flood of despair that drowned her final hope. With Tristan dead, so was any chance she would be rescued from the fate Lord Devon intended for her.

Chapter 36

"Take her hands," the cardinal instructed, nodding to her with a solemn frown.

As Devon took her hands in his and began his vows, visions of the night before flooded into Aleatha's mind. Tristan, her husband, his dark eyes gazing lovingly into hers as he recited his vows from the very depths of his heart. Devon's words repeated vacantly after the leader of the state church and his eyes leering at her as he spoke seemed a mockery of the sacred ceremony of the previous night. It was so wrong, almost as if she were defiling Tristan's memory by even standing here now.

Her stomach tightened. *I cannot do it, no matter what Devon does to me.*

"Lady Aleatha?" the minister prompted. "I asked you to repeat after me."

"No." Aleatha raised her chin and looked Devon in the eye. "I will not go through with it. I love Tristan, I will not betray his memory by participating in this sham."

Mary stifled a cry of dismay and the minister gasped while Devon made a low, guttural threat. His hands tightened like vises on Aleatha's own and his eyes stared daggers of hate into hers.

"Unlike the world out there, here your cooperation, though desired, is entirely unnecessary," Devon said coldly. "Captain Brogan, the ring."

Scowling at Aleatha fiercely, Lord Devon took the ring from Captain Brogan, gripped Aleatha's left hand tightly in his, yanked it toward him, and jammed a heavy circle of braided gold onto her finger.

"By my supreme authority, I pronounce you man and wife." The cardinal touched them both lightly on the head. "You may kiss your bride."

Devon pulled Aleatha toward him roughly and embraced her tightly. She pulled back as far as she could and turned her face from him.

"You will submit to me!" he snarled, grabbing her chin with his hand and turning her to face him. Pressing his lips to her mouth, he kissed her long and passionately, seemingly unbothered by her struggling. Finally, he stepped back, released his hold on her chin, and looked at her possessively. "I wonder what Prince Tristan would think if he could see you now, Lady Aleatha Gautier."

The blood rushed to Aleatha's face as anger choked off all words. Her only response was to spit in Devon's smug face.

Devon roared in rage as he released his grip on Aleatha and backhanded her forcefully across the face. The force of the blow knocked Aleatha to the floor and brought tears to her eyes. Pressing her hand to her stinging face, she managed to look up defiantly at Devon standing over her.

"Now see here," the cardinal protested taking a step forward. A glare from Devon drove him back to his place.

"Take her to my room," Devon snapped at Mary. "I will be up to deal with her shortly."

As the young chambermaid timidly helped her to her feet, Aleatha held her head proudly. Her fear of Devon's threats was eclipsed by her own feeling of triumph. No matter what Devon did to her now, she was assured she had done nothing to shame the memory of her true husband. She only hoped, if he could see her from heaven, he was proud of her.

*****

Tristan and Lucas finally left the underground tunnels and entered into the labyrinth within the castle walls. So far, they had seemed to be undetected. Either Devon had not discovered how Tristan had gotten Lucas out, or he was so confident they had died in the fire he had not placed any guards on the entrance to the tunnels.

"The kitchen," Tristan whispered as they stopped at a panel in the wall. "The head cook has been my ally since I was a child. If we can catch him alone, perhaps he can tell us something."

Lucas raised the torch he was holding so Tristan could locate the catch on the door and slide it open.

Sliding the door open a crack, Tristan peeked into the kitchen. The passage opened into the pantry. The head cook stood right in front of him, facing a row of shelves to the side. The rest of the kitchen staff bustled around in the kitchen. Tristan opened the panel a bit further and whispered cautiously, "Elwyn, do not turn around and do not make a sound."

Elwyn stiffened. "Prince Tristan!" he said hoarsely. "Lord Devon told us you were dead."

"Let him think that," Tristan answered. It was certainly in their best interest if he did. "Where is Aleatha?"

"In Lord Devon's room, I'd imagine," Elwyn responded. "Your mother's old room. But…"

"But what, Elwyn? Tell me quickly." Tristan steeled himself against whatever fearful news Elwyn had, even as his heart pounded with dread.

"She… spent the night there. Lord Devon announced their engagement this morning. The wedding just ended, my prince. Lady Aleatha is Lord Devon's wife now. The cardinal presided over the ceremony. Lord Devon will be going to join her at any moment."

Tristan heard Lucas mutter a sharp imprecation behind him, but kept his own voice steady as he urged, "Tell no one you saw me, Elwyn. I am trusting my life, and the lives of my friends, to your loyalty."

"You can count on me, my prince," Elwyn replied as Tristan disappeared back into the passage and slid the panel closed behind him.

"He forced her to marry him, Tristan," Lucas insisted. He looked at Tristan, clearly concerned Elwyn's news would rekindle his friend's old doubts about Aleatha's faithfulness. "You know that."

"I know, but we need to rescue her before he forces her to do anything else," Tristan responded grimly, mounting the narrow stairs two at a time. Fear clutched his heart at Elwyn's words. *She spent the night in his room.* This morning Devon had announced a hasty engagement and a hurried wedding. Perhaps they were already too late. *Please, Heavenly Father, protect my wife,* he begged as he raced up the passage stairs, turning on each landing sharply as Lucas followed behind.

"We stop here." Tristan stepped off the staircase and into the narrow corridor before they mounted another flight.

"Why? Your mother's old room is still another flight up."

"We know that floor will be busy," Tristan explained as he hurried down the corridor. "Probably guarded, and we may need the locations of the passages to remain secret for our escape. There is an exit here in the suite used by visiting royalty. I doubt if Devon has time to entertain heads of state while he plots the takeover of the kingdom."

He stopped abruptly and ran his fingers deftly over the wall beside him. Another panel slid aside. He peered into the room, and turned to Lucas. "Leave the torch here. I can come back for it once we have Aleatha. You are going to want both hands free."

Lucas placed the torch in its sconce beside the door and followed Tristan into the empty room.

Tristan quickly crossed the room to the door. "Have your sword ready. We are not far from the stairs, but we will have to make a dash for it. Be ready to defend yourself if someone sees us."

"If we are spotted, I will try to hold them off while you go after Aleatha," Lucas whispered as he pulled his sword from his scabbard. "I will follow as soon as possible."

Getting to Aleatha was imperative, but Tristan did not like the idea of leaving Lucas behind. "If that happens, I will come back as soon as I have Aleatha safely in the passages."

Turning back to the door, Tristan opened it a crack to glance down the hall and make sure they were safe. The way seemed clear, so he threw the door open the rest of the way and ran toward the stairs at the end of the hall with Lucas close behind him.

"You there, halt!" a voice commanded behind them just as they reached the foot of the stairs.

"It is only one. Go, I will follow as soon as I can." Lucas turned to face the soldier.

Tristan laid a hand on Lucas's arm. "God be with you," he said as he mounted the stairs.

"You, too," Lucas called back after him. "Bring back my sister."

*****

The stairs were vacant and Tristan quickly made his way to the top. He paused only for a moment to make sure the hall was clear before running as hard as he could toward his mother's old room at the other end. He had to get there before Devon did. Reaching the door of the room, he paused to catch his breath and survey the situation. Silently, he opened the door a crack and peered inside. There was no sign of Devon. Tristan's breath caught in his chest. Aleatha was sitting on the bed facing the door. She was dressed in a silky, pure white chemise and one of his mother's chambermaids was brushing out her waist-length brown hair. His gaze rested on her face. Her eyes were red-rimmed from crying and her jaw was set in determination.

Aleatha is preparing to give Devon the fight of his life, Tristan observed with grim amusement. His amusement faded to rage as Aleatha turned her head to dismiss the girl behind her. An angry red mark stood out on her flushed face. Tristan seethed. *Devon will pay for daring to lay a hand on my wife.*

Ducking into an empty room, Tristan waited for the chambermaid to exit the room and pass out of sight. Then, taking one last glance down the hall, Tristan quickly opened the bedroom door and stepped inside, closing the door behind him.

Aleatha stood, her body and countenance tense, clearly expecting Devon. Her expression shifted to disbelief, to relief, and then to joy as she realized who had entered the room.

"Tristan!" she cried, running to embrace him. "Lord Devon told me you were killed in the church last night. He showed me your sword and coronet as proof."

Pulling her close, Tristan kissed her passionately on the lips, a long, breathtaking kiss meant to replace the one Devon had interrupted the night before. "Do I feel dead to you?" he quipped as he looked down into her face.

Tears welled up in her eyes as Aleatha shook her head.

"Did Devon do this?" Tristan's voice hardened as he stroked the red mark on her face with his thumb.

"He forced me to kiss him after the ceremony and I spit in his face. It barely stings now," Aleatha assured him with a look of pride on her face.

Her expression clouded. "We have to get out of here. Mary went to go get Lord Devon. He will be here at any moment."

"He is here already," Devon spoke from the doorway. "And I am afraid I am going to have to ask you to get you hands off my wife, Prince Tristan."

Turning to face Devon, Tristan pulled Aleatha behind him with his right hand and drew his sword with his left. His eyes darted to the location of the hidden panel beside the bed. He had only ever used the passage in his mother's room once. If he could not remember where the catch was before Devon decided to draw his sword, they might never make it out of the castle.

"I am not your wife, you devil," Aleatha retorted. She turned to Tristan. "He tried to force me to marry him. I did not take the vows; he could not make me."

"Now, my dear, let's be honest. You practically threw yourself at me. Actually begged me to allow you to be my queen," Devon amended fiendishly. "You wasted no time aligning yourself with the man in power."

"Everyone in the castle knows she spent the night here in my room." Devon turned to Tristan, his voice taunting, "She slept in my bed, no less. Everyone knows what happened, no matter what she tries to tell you. Of course she would lie to you; she fears to lose your love. I warned you she was not worthy of you, Prince."

"Nothing happened. Devon was not even there." Aleatha gripped his arm as she pled, "Please believe me!"

"Aleatha is my wife. I married her first. By law, that makes your marriage void." Devon's accusations about Aleatha's character were just the same song sung to a different tune. Tristan shut them out and began backing Aleatha toward the wall. They could not afford to get caught in one of Devon's mental games. They just needed to get out.

"If your marriage was legal to begin with," Devon challenged, his black eyes glittering.

Tristan gritted his teeth and steeled his mind for the battle of wits Devon insisted on playing. He took another step back toward the wall. "I am not in the mood for your games. You know as well as I do Aleatha is my legal wife. You have no claim to her."

"If you are legally wed." Devon took a step closer to Tristan. He still hadn't drawn his sword, choosing instead to push his psychological advantage. "Where are your witnesses?"

"Lucas will be here soon," Tristan replied, unflinching. Concern struck him. Lucas should have been there already. *Please, Father, grant Lucas the strength to defeat his enemy.*

"That is only one," Devon contended, "by law you need two."

"You had the others killed, you monster!" Aleatha cried. She tried to take a step forward, but was restrained by Tristan.

"What proof do you have?" Devon directed his question to Tristan. "And what about the queen?"

"What about her?" Tristan flung back, his voice holding more bitterness than he intended. "She ceased to have any control over me when she ordered you to kill me. Besides, she passed away before we were married."

"I seriously doubt you got her permission before she died," Devon said with a smirk. His eyes flickered to the door as Lucas entered behind him, but darted back to Tristan. "By law you need her permission before you marry."

"Only if I married before I turned twenty-one," Tristan returned, nodding to Lucas, but never taking his own eyes off Devon. "Which I did a few weeks ago, unless you have forgotten."

"Turned twenty-one and crowned king," Devon persisted. He stepped closer to Tristan. "Which has not happened yet, unless *you* have forgotten."

Tristan grew cold. Devon's arguments were beginning to plant doubts in his mind. *Heavenly Father, help me!* He pushed the doubts away and raised his sword to Devon's throat. "Lucas, take his sword and tie him to a chair."

Moving quickly, Lucas disarmed Devon, pulled a cord from one of the curtains, and tied Devon to a chair. Devon submitted, looking oddly triumphant for a man in his position.

"We cannot go back the way we came; the guards are right behind me." Lucas looked at Tristan and narrowed his eyes. "Are you all right?"

"Take Aleatha. I will follow behind." Tristan ignored Lucas's question and turned. He took the last few steps to the back of the room and faced the wall for a moment, his body shielding his actions from view as he played his fingers over the wall, searching for the catch. Suddenly the wall slid aside to reveal a dark passage.

"Finally," Aleatha said, her shoulders sagging with relief, "we are safe!"

"But you will not be happy, my dear," Devon provoked, finally addressing someone other than Tristan. "Your prince is a man of honor. He will never touch you as long as there is any doubt of the legality of your marriage. He would never risk laying a hand on another man's wife."

Aleatha stopped on the threshold of the passage and turned to glare at Devon. "The only one who has any questions is you," she snapped.

"I am sure the magistrate would have plenty of questions if I were to bring my wife before him on a charge of adultery. Would you not agree, Prince Tristan?" When Tristan did not respond, Devon pressed harder, "Would you put your beloved Aleatha at risk of a public hanging, Your Highness?"

Tristan shuddered inwardly at the mental image Devon's word had painted, but steeled his body against any response. He would have to deal with the doubts Devon had created later. Right now they just needed to leave. "I am through playing your games, Devon. Lucas, Aleatha, go!"

"You will never touch her, Prince," Devon called after him as Tristan followed his friends. "Your honor will not allow it."

"At least you will not touch her either," Tristan said softly as the panel slid closed between them.

Chapter 37

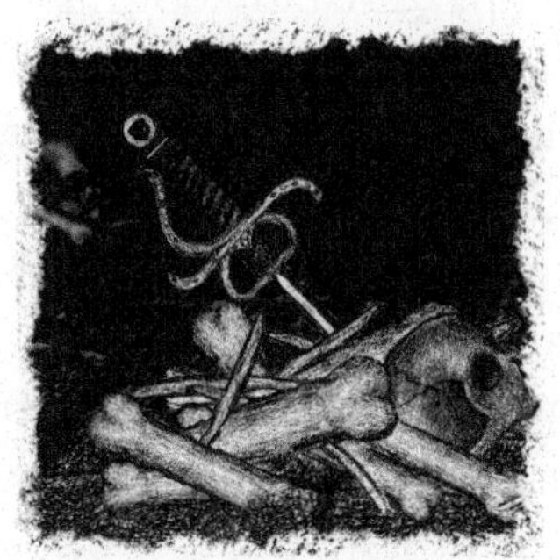

The darkness in the passage seemed to swallow them as the panel slowly choked off the only source of light they had. Fumbling in the dark, Tristan grabbed one of Aleatha's hands. "Lucas, take her other hand. I can navigate these passages blind, but we all have to be away from here before someone frees Devon and he figures out how to open the panel."

"Got her."

Tristan tiptoed down the narrow passage as quickly as he felt the other two could handle in the dark, gritting his teeth against the delay. They needed to hurry, to run. They had to be in the underground tunnels before Devon could flood the passages with soldiers or they were as good as dead.

"Stairs," he whispered. Their progress slowed to a crawl as his friends picked their way down the unfamiliar steps. The flickering light from the torch Lucas had left behind grew stronger as they drew closer. Dropping Aleatha's hand, Tristan dashed forward, dashing down the familiar stairs. He scooped the torch up and returned to his friends. "Hurry now. We have little time."

Aided by the torch, they descended two more narrow flights of stairs, turning at each landing with nearly dizzying speed.

"Tristan," Lucas hissed, nodding to the wall separating them from the main staircase. The rhythmic sound of many feet tramping on the stairs just feet away from them caused them to stop short.

"Soldiers, going up," Tristan kept his voice as low as he could. If they could hear the soldiers, he did not want to take a chance on the soldiers hearing them. "Devon must have managed to summon them."

Fear hastened them along and they quickly reached the dungeon level. A faint thundering behind them indicated the soldiers had breached the passages and were closing on them. Tristan clenched his teeth. It could take the soldiers all night to search the passages for them, but if the soldiers discovered the entrance to the underground tunnels before them, they would never get out. He led his friends down the narrow corridor toward the exit panel. So far, the corridor was clear. Stomping feet above their heads told them the soldiers were searching the ground floor corridors. That might buy them a few minutes. If they could get out before the soldiers saw them, they should have a few hours before the soldiers managed to figure out the location of the hidden exit panel, if they ever figured it out at all.

He stopped before the bare stone wall, his fingers feeling over the rocks for the secret catch. The panel slid back silently. A dank, earthy smell greeted them as they crossed the threshold into the underground tunnels. Waiting for his friends to pass, Tristan closed the panel, turned, and searched the area around the door with his torch. His fingers traced every line of the stones as quickly as possible.

"What are you looking for?" Lucas whispered urgently. "The soldiers will be here soon!"

"Relax." Tristan allowed a small smile to reach his lips. He had found it. The soldiers could not reach them now. Wiping aside some cobwebs, he pulled a metal peg out of a hidden recess to the right of the panel and slid it into a barely noticeable hole beside the panel. "It is locked now. I was not sure if I could remember how to find the peg. Even if they find the exit, they will be unable to follow us now."

Lucas's mouth twitched wearily and some of the tension melted out of his body.

"We are finally safe?" Aleatha asked, though she did not loosen her desperate grip on her brother's hand. "They cannot catch us?"

"For now." Tristan turned his gaze down the damp tunnel. "We still need to make our way to the Morrison house as soon as possible. Tomorrow, we can search for a place outside of town."

Pushing briskly past his friends, Tristan led them into the muddy tunnel. He pulled his lips into a grim line. While they were in the castle, he had been too busy running to think about Devon's words. Aleatha's question had brought the nagging doubts Devon had created back with the force of a tornado. Aleatha's abduction had shaken him more than he would have admitted even to himself, but Devon's threats forced him to face his fears head on.

Are we truly safe? No. Not while Devon lives. As long as Devon hunted him, his friends lives were in danger, too. The mental image Devon had created of Aleatha hanging from a gibbet flashed vividly through his mind. He sucked in a sharp breath. Allowing those thoughts to rule him admitted Devon to be the winner. If Devon could not kill him and his friends, he meant to make sure they could never lead happy lives. *Heavenly Father, help me defeat these fears,* Tristan cried silently as he sped Aleatha and Lucas instinctively though the tunnels he had frequented as a child.

"Tristan," Lucas panted behind him. "You have to slow down. Aleatha can barely keep up."

Glancing back at Aleatha, who clutched her brother's hand like a lifeline, Tristan slowed. Concern gripped him, he had not realized he was pushing her too hard.

Perhaps I could carry her. The image of her limp body hanging from a rope forced itself into his mind. He clenched his teeth, turned back to the tunnel ahead of him, and pressed forward, more moderately now. Did he even dare touch her, much less take her to be his wife? Devon's suggestion that Aleatha had begged to be his wife had brought back the doubts Devon had hammered into him in the desert, but only faintly and easily banished. Tristan refused to believe Aleatha was that duplicitous. Devon's assertion that Tristan's own marriage was invalid and Devon's was binding was a greater worry. Could Devon really do as he had threatened? He could, and ever so much more. As long as Devon lived, Aleatha was in danger.

Perhaps I should send her to her mother until this is all over. I cannot be a danger to her if she is nowhere near me. He should have done that to begin with. He had allowed his desire for her to overcome his better judgment. He sloshed through a particularly deep puddle of water. They were nearing the end of the tunnel, but he could not help feeling like they were miles away from true safety.

"Tristan?" Aleatha's voice called behind him. He turned to see her trudging toward him, the hem of her chemise lifted just above the water, a worried look on her face. "Are you all right? You seem very…" She broke off with a cry as she stumbled and fell into the water.

Tristan sprang to her without a thought, scooping her out of the water and into his arms in the time it took to blink. She was soaked to the skin and her chemise clung to her body. The warmth of her skin seeping through the filmy fabric to Tristan's unbandaged hand sent a charge of electricity from his fingertips to the pit of his stomach, igniting a fire of desire that threatened to consume his resolutions for his wife's safety.

Setting her to her feet on the other side of the pool quickly, he snatched his hands from her as if he were in danger of being burned.

"Lucas," he appealed to his friend, his voice low and husky. "Take her, please."

With a nod and a questioning look, Lucas wrapped his own cloak around his shivering, bewildered sister.

His heart still pounding, Tristan tore his eyes away from Aleatha and continued toward the exit. His hands still tingled and his shirt was damp where he had held her pressed against his chest. He realized now sending her away was the last thing he ever wanted to do, even only for a short time. *But her safety takes precedent over my desires, does it not?* Tristan rubbed the wet spot over his heart with his hand. Suddenly he was not sure that was true at all.

* * * * *

"Lucas, take Aleatha to my room," Tristan commanded as they entered the tiny Morrison house, not looking at either of them. "Make sure she is all right after tonight's adventures. I will sleep out here tonight."

Lucas raised an eyebrow at his friend's odd request. But then, much of Tristan's behavior since they had left the castle had seemed odd. *Surely he does not believe Lord Devon's accusations against Aleatha.*

"Tristan, please." Aleatha stepped forward and gripped Tristan's arm in both her hands. Her voice was on the verge of cracking. "Can I not stay with you? Do not do this."

Tristan laid his free hand on hers with a look of pain in his eyes. "I am sorry, Aleatha," he rasped as he gently lifted her hands from his arm and turned to Lucas. "Please, Lucas. I need some time alone."

Lucas opened his mouth to retort, but clamped it closed again, deciding to save his comments for after he took care of Aleatha. Without a word, he turned and led his sister away.

When Lucas got her to the room, he set her gently on the bed and looked her over appraisingly. She looked more exhausted and upset than physically hurt. Still, he had no way to know what Devon had done to her before they had arrived.

"Are you all right? Do you hurt anywhere? Other than here." He turned her face slightly to look at the mark on her cheek. It would leave a nice bruise by morning.

"I am wet, dirty, tired," She looked down at her trembling hands as she answered, "and scared, but otherwise I am unhurt. Lord Devon truly did not do anything to me. I need a brother, Lucas, not a doctor."

"You need not be afraid of Lord Devon," Lucas assured her, sitting on the bed next to her and laying his arm across her shoulders. "If he ever gets near you again, either Tristan or I will take care of him. I can promise you that."

"Like you did at the church?" Aleatha's eyes welled up with tears. She clutched her brother's cloak more tightly around her.

"It will never happen again," her brother promised, hugging her closer to his side. "Tristan and I will die before we see you in that monster's hands!"

"Would Tristan?" The tears ran freely down her face. "After last night?"

Lucas started and looked at his sister with wide eyes. "What are you saying? You know Tristan as well as I do. He will never allow Lord Devon to touch you."

"I am not afraid of Lord Devon," Aleatha confessed. "I am afraid of Tristan."

Lucas's surprise turned to shock. Tristan had been rude, but he had not noticed anything that would cause Aleatha to feel threatened. Had his father's fears that Tristan would turn out like his mother affected her also? "You know Tristan loves you. He would never lay a hand on you!"

"That is exactly what I am afraid of," she choked. "You heard Lord Devon as we left. Tristan will not dare take me as his wife. If he even still wants me, after last night."

"What do you mean, if he still wants you?" Lucas stared at his sister. It was becoming clear that, though Lord Devon may not have hurt her physically, he had managed to affect her thoughts and feelings. "No matter what Lord Devon said, Tristan still loves you."

"No," Aleatha said. Her voice was nearly inaudible. "You heard the terrible things Lord Devon told him. I did not beg Lord Devon to marry me. Lord Devon was not even with me last night. But… I do not think Tristan believes me. Did you not see him in the tunnels? He wanted nothing to do with me. He is so disgusted with me he would not even touch me. When he helped me out of that pool, he passed me off to you as if he could not get rid of me fast enough. And the look in his eyes…"

Lucas choked back a laugh. He laid one hand gently on his sister's shoulder and used the other to turn her face to look at him. "I did see everything. I can assure you, based on those events alone, that Tristan *does* want you. I think your perception was a little distorted by your time spent with Lord Devon."

"What do you mean?"

"Think back. You were wearing only your chemise and soaked to the skin. Why do you think I made you wear my cloak?" Lucas grew serious. "You are Tristan's wife; he loves you and desires you very much. Trust me."

"Oh." Aleatha's voice was small as color flamed to her face. "But… why did he act like he could not wait to get rid of me?"

"I will not pretend Lord Devon's words did not have some affect on him," Lucas admitted. "Give him some time to sort things out."

Aleatha nodded slowly. Her deep frown showed it was not exactly what she wanted to hear, but it would have to do. "Thank you, Lucas."

"You get changed and try to get some rest. Doctor's orders," Lucas insisted as he stood. Aleatha had packed a small bag of her things and he had made sure it had been moved from the Chapmans' before the wedding. She would feel better in clean, dry clothing. "In the meantime, I will go see if I can talk a little sense into my wayward brother in law."

Chapter 38

Lucas closed the door gently behind him and found Tristan kneeling on the floor, deep in prayer. He hesitated at the doorway, unsure if he should interrupt. Concern for Tristan gnawed at him. Though Lucas believed all he had said to his sister, he had not told her everything. He knew a little more than she did about what Tristan had been through and feared the affect Devon's words may have had. Tristan's battle to believe in Aleatha's faithfulness had been a hard one. Had Lord Devon's words rekindled those conquered doubts?

Tristan lifted his head and looked at him. "It is fine, Lucas. You may come over," he said as he sat back on his heels. "Is Aleatha all right?"

"She is scared, and a little bruised, but she will be fine." Lucas sat on the floor next to his friend and looked at him carefully. "What she really needs is her husband."

"I hurt her. I could see it in her eyes." Tristan drew a deep breath. "She must think I hate her."

Lucas bit his lip. "Do you?"

"No!" Tristan's eyes widened. "You of all people should know that."

"Then go to her. She is the one who needs to hear it." Lucas laid a hand on Tristan's shoulder. "Lord Devon told her he would make sure you would never have anything to do with her. I am afraid your conduct since we left the castle has only served to prove that to her."

Tristan blanched and gripped folded his hands tightly in his lap.

"She heard what Lord Devon said to you," Lucas continued." We both did. After the way you treated her on the way over here, she fears you believe Lord Devon's lies about her. She is convinced you despise her." A smile twitched at the corner of Lucas's mouth as he added, "She was especially convinced by your reaction when she fell in the pool. I believe she said you were disgusted by her and could not get rid of her fast enough."

Tristan's face blazed a deep red and a small, embarrassed smile touched his lips. "I suppose I could not get rid of her fast enough at that. Though 'disgust' would be the opposite of what I was feeling."

Seriousness crossed back over Tristan's face. "I choose to believe her, in spite of what Devon said, but what do I do about Devon's threats? I know he is wrong. His marriage to Aleatha is a sham. Though I fear he may have the law on his side. With Odell Chapman and Reverend Prestwick dead, you are the only witness I have. That scares me. Aleatha is in enough danger already. Perhaps I should send her somewhere safe, like to Shanksdale with your mother, until this is over."

"When will it be over, Tristan?" Lucas asked wearily. "A week? A month? A year? How will it end? Lord Devon nearly killed us both yesterday. What if he succeeds next time? What if you are never able to come for her?"

Tristan stared at the floor, but did not answer.

"Even if Lord Devon is able to do everything he threatened to, how is that worse than what he already has tried to do to Aleatha? How would sending her away make her safer?" Lucas continued, "She is your wife now; should she not have some say in your decision?"

"You are right, of course," Tristan acknowledged. He rubbed his hands over his face. "I just cannot get the picture Devon painted out of my head. Aleatha… hanging from the gallows…"

"I know. Believe me." Lucas shuddered. He hated to admit Devon's words had an effect on him also. He had just been so focused on Aleatha and Tristan he had not had time to think about it. "I am not telling you to act like everything is fine, just to go to her."

"What do I say?" Tristan looked expectantly at Lucas. "I do not even have it all sorted out yet."

"Show her you love her. Hold her," Lucas counseled. "I think the two of you will figure out something."

*****

Tristan took a deep breath as he paced the floor outside the house's single bedroom. *Heavenly Father, give me wisdom.* He knew what he wanted to say to her; what he wanted to do. There was nothing he desired more than to take Aleatha as his wife, and Devon could burn for all he cared. He stopped and stared at the door as he rubbed the back of his neck. But he did care, more than he would like to admit even to Lucas. With God's – and Lucas's – help, he had come a long way since his time in the desert, but he still feared Devon and the power he had to make his life miserable. Devon knew Aleatha and Lucas were all he cared for in the world. He was tempted to abandon his right to the crown, if that would protect them, but he could not. God had placed him in this position for a reason. Besides he doubted Devon would leave them alone until he was sure Tristan could never be a threat to the throne.

What do I do? he prayed as he began pacing again. He wanted what was best for Aleatha; he just did not know what that was. *Talk to her, tell her everything. She is your wife now,* a gentle answer crossed his mind. Resolved, he stopped pacing and faced the door. He knocked. *Give me grace.*

"Yes?" Aleatha's voice, muffled by the door, called to him.

"Aleatha? It is Tristan. May I come in?"

He heard the faint sound of her catching her breath, followed by a long silence. He bit his lip. Perhaps she was not going to let him in. He had not considered that possibility.

It cracked open and Aleatha peered out, her eyes red rimmed and her face pale. She did not speak.

"May I come in?" he repeated earnestly. "I need to talk to you."

She hesitated, as if the idea of them being alone in her room was still foreign to her, and sighed deeply. "I suppose we had best be done with it," she replied. Her weak voice belied the set of her jaw. She held the door open long enough for him to enter, and closed it behind him.

Tristan considered her carefully as she crossed the room and sat on the end of the bed. She had bathed and braided her brown hair behind her. She was wearing a pale blue robe and her feet were bare. A sash tied in a bow at her waist accented her slim figure. A bit of blue lace at the point where the robe crossed over her chest hinted at a matching chemise beneath.

Tristan caught his breath. Any words he had been about to say flew out of his mind. He was alone with Aleatha in her room, *their* room. His heart rate quickened as he realized the feelings he felt now, the desires suddenly engulfing him, were not only normal, but right and good. She was his wife now.

He took a step toward her; then stopped. Aleatha looked up at him, her eyes wide. A mix of emotions played across her face: uncertainty, fear, confusion. No pleasure, no anticipation. Her expression reminded Tristan why he had come in the first place. He averted his gaze and swallowed hard. *Give me strength.* This was going to even be harder than he had thought. Her eyes followed his every move as she waited for him to speak first.

Sitting on the edge of the bed beside her and gently taking both of her hands in his, he allowed himself just a moment to stroke the back of her hands with his thumbs. He looked up at her, forcing his eyes to her face and away from the bit of blue lace that still threatened to distract him.

"We need to talk about what happened today." He paused. Aleatha's jaw tightened and her lips pressed together in a tight line. A determined look entered her eyes. He continued, "Back there at the castle…"

She pulled her hands out of his and stood suddenly. Tears rimmed her eyes, but her voice was firm. "Stop, Tristan. Before you go any further, I have something I need to say."

Too taken aback to speak, Tristan nodded.

"Lord Devon told me he would do everything he could to make sure you would have nothing to do with me. He did do nearly everything." She turned her back to him, a shudder coursing through her body. "Spending the night in his room, the wedding, his words to you before we left: I know how it must look."

Opening his mouth to interrupt, Tristan stood and took a step toward her. He could see where she was going.

She quickly turned to face him, her hand held up. "I am not finished. I could see in your eyes Lord Devon's words meant something to you. Lucas says I … misinterpreted… some other things, but that was clear. I just need you to trust me; to take my word over Lord Devon's."

Reaching forward, Aleatha grabbed Tristan's hands in hers and held them to her heart. She looked up at him, her eyes pleading with him. "I did not take any marriage vows, I did not intentionally kiss him, and I certainly did not sleep with him, willingly or otherwise. I love you, and I have been entirely faithful to you."

Tristan licked his dry lips and swallowed. All he could think about was his hands pressed against her chest. He gently pulled his hands free, determined to try one more time to concentrate on why he came, though the reason was becoming fainter in his mind.

Aleatha looked down at his hands, and back to his face, his actions clearly misunderstood. Tears filled her eyes and her voice cracked as she whispered, "Please, Tristan, please, do not put me away."

A sense of gravity forced itself back into Tristan's mind as Aleatha's words underscored the reason he had come. He gently took her hands in his again, this time keeping them carefully in front of him. His voice was husky as he asked, "Is that what you think I want to do?"

Aleatha bit her lip, but did not answer.

"I love you, no matter what that devil may or may not have forced you to do. No matter what, Aleatha." He dropped one of her hands, cupped her chin lightly in his hand, and lifted her face as he assured her, "But I do believe you."

A sob escaped her lips and she threw herself into his arms, burying her face in his chest. Her hands gripped his tunic as great sobs tore from her throat.

Thank you, Heavenly Father, for Lucas's advice. Tristan held her and stroked her back with one hand. He had not realized how much Aleatha had needed him. Gradually, her sobbing slowed and faded to a sniffle.

After gently kissing her on the top of the head, Tristan pulled her back away from him and looked down at her seriously. "You were right about one thing, Devon's words did have an effect on me, just not what you imagined."

Fear flashed across Aleatha's eyes, but she allowed Tristan to lead her back to the bed. He gently set her on the end of the bed and sat beside her.

"I do love you, more than anyone else in this world. That is why his threats scared me," Tristan said. He clenched his jaw. "Devon has the power to do the things he promised, and much more. Things you could not even begin to imagine. I just do not want to put you in any more danger."

Understanding lit Aleatha's eyes. "I knew the danger when I agreed to marry you." She reached up and stroked his face. "Lord Devon may be powerful, but he does not really worry me." She paused, looking into his eyes intently. "But he does you. What power does he have over you?"

For a moment Tristan was silent. He had not told her anything about what had happened during his time with Devon. He suspected Lucas had told her some, but he doubted even that was much. He took a deep breath. She would need to know sooner or later. Standing, he pulled his tunic over his head.

"Tristan!" Aleatha protested. "What are you…" She broke off with a gasp and leaped to her feet at the sight of the scars crisscrossing his chest. "Lord Devon did… that?"

Pressing his lips together grimly, Tristan turned his back to her. The scars on his back were far worse than the ones on his chest.

With a cry, Aleatha took a step toward Tristan. She reached out her hand and gently laid it on top of the raised lines on his back. "I had no idea."

Tristan turned to face her again, circling his arms around her waist. "For nearly a year Devon put me through every form of torture his twisted mind could come up with. All with one goal in mind: to bend me into complete subjection to his – and my mother's – will. I almost died more times than I care to count. We were in a battle for my mind, my sanity, and my very soul. Perhaps we still are."

He pulled her closer to him and she laid her head against his bare chest. He gently stroked her hair as he continued, "But for the grace of God, I would have lost all of it. When I face Devon, the old battle returns. Even though he no longer has much control over my body, he still seeks control over my mind. He knows I cannot bear to lose you, Aleatha. I fear the things he could do to you to hurt me."

Aleatha lifted her head and looked at Tristan's face. "The God that brought you out of that year is the same God I serve. Lord Devon has no power over me except what God allows. Lucas told me you only survived what you went through because of your faith in God. Have faith in Him now. You may not be able to protect me from Lord Devon, but you do not have to. God will take care of me. I will be just as safe by your side as I would be anywhere else."

She was right; he was allowing his fear of Devon to overpower his faith in God. *Forgive me, Heavenly Father. Strengthen my faith.* He looked down at Aleatha. *Thank you, for giving me such a wonderful wife. Protect her as I do what I believe You would have me do.*

He gently cupped her chin in his hand and tilted her face to his. "You are right. Thank you," he whispered. The apprehension and fear in her eyes had been replaced by love and desire. He leaned in closer, Devon's threats forgotten, at least for tonight.

Chapter 39

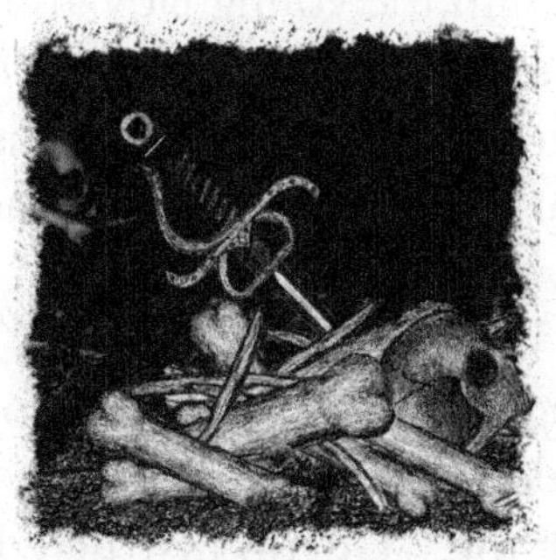

In his room at the castle, Devon paced the floor at the foot of the gilded bed, fury fueling each step. The floor was littered with shards of broken pottery and scattered décor, anything he had been able to lay his hands on and throw in his anger. Prince Tristan had cheated death again, and had managed to sneak into the castle and cheat him of his prize. He cursed Tristan and his God loudly. Devon had never believed in a higher power; he only believed in his own power to get what he wanted. However, Tristan's continued survival seemed to testify of a supernatural power on the young prince's side.

How do I win against a deity? Devon stopped his pacing long enough to hurl another priceless vase against the wall with a cry.

No, Devon thought, clenching his fist and composing himself, *Prince Tristan and his friends have only been inordinately lucky. The next time I get my hands on him, I will make the young prince kneel and worship me, before I separate his head from his body. We'll see if his God will resurrect him then.*

A timid knock sounded at the door.

"What?" Devon roared, flinging the nearest object, a jade statuette, at the door. The statuette broke into several pieces and skittered across the marble floor.

"I have the spy you summoned," Captain Brogan called through the protection of the door.

Devon smiled. He had nearly forgotten he had ordered Captain Brogan to bring him the queen's spy in the resistance. His own spies told him the young lady and Lucas Medellin were close. Perhaps he could use her to get to the prince's best friend, and through him, to the prince himself. Besides, she was the daughter of the resistance's last leader, if anyone knew where the prince was hiding, she would.

"Bring her in," he ordered.

The door swung open and Captain Brogan shoved a frightened, disheveled Celia Chapman into the room.

"Leave her with me," Devon instructed. He smiled at the terrified girl. "I have important matters to discuss with her."

Captain Brogan's mouth twisted into a leering grin as he nodded and stepped back out into the hallway, closing the door behind him.

Devon crossed the large room as he looked over the girl. He had barely given her a second look when the queen had met with her before. *She is attractive. Quite attractive.* Celia's eyes widened as he came close to her and she stepped back against the closed door. *Not nearly as attractive as my own wife, though. This girl will be the means of bringing my wife back to me.*

"Please, Lady Celia, take a seat," he gestured broadly to the lush sitting area behind him. "You have nothing to fear from me. I wish only to discuss a business proposition with you."

The fear in her eyes lessened only slightly as she lifted her skirts, scurried to the nearest armchair, and sat down.

"I was quite sorry to hear about your father," he purred sympathetically, as he sat on the arm of the chair next hers. "His wines were the best in the land."

Celia began to tremble as tears streamed down her face, but she kept silent. Clearly the news of her father's death had reached her already.

"I have no quarrel with your family," he assured her. "As long as you remain my faithful servant, I will make sure you and your brother remain safe. Serve me well and I may even be able to make sure your brother is promoted to the castle guard. Do you understand?"

The poor girl nodded miserably.

"Do you know where your father hid Prince Tristan?" Devon demanded, watching her sharply for any sign of deception.

"I think so." She bit her lip and fear filled her face again. "But Lucas and Aleatha, they'll be with him." Her words tumbled over one another. "Aleatha has been my best friend since we were girls, and Lucas…" she broke off as a blush rushed to her face.

"I don't have anything personally against the Medellins, that was Queen Brigitte," Devon said slyly. "In fact, I am even more anxious Lady Aleatha be returned to me unharmed than you are, since she is my wife."

Celia gave him a startled look, but wisely chose to keep her opinion to herself.

"I want Prince Tristan out of my way and I want Lady Aleatha back in my arms." Devon said, leaning forward. "Lead my men to them and I will allow you to lure Lucas Medellin out of the house and out of danger. Use any pretense you like."

As if considering his words, Celia looked down at her hands silently. "If I lead you to Prince Tristan, you will allow Aleatha and Lucas to live?"

"You and your young doctor can live happily ever. My wife and I can live happily ever after." He gave her a piercing gaze and added, "Your brother and his wife can live happily ever after."

A large tear rolled down her face and landed in her lap.

"Do we have an agreement?" Devon asked coldly.

Celia sniffled and nodded, not meeting his gaze.

Leaning back, Devon smiled. Within a few hours Prince Tristan would be out of the way and the throne and Lady Aleatha would be his.

*****

A light, but frantic knock on the door woke Lucas early the next morning. He quickly jumped up from his makeshift bed on the floor and crossed the room to the door. Gripping the hilt of his sword with his right hand, he demanded, "Who is it?"

"It is Celia. Lucas is that you?" a trembling female voice answered.

Celia. A sick feeling gripped him. *Has she heard about her father?* He threw the bolt on the door and let Celia in. One look at her tear streaked face told him she had.

"I am so very sorry, Celia," Lucas said compassionately as he took her hand and closed the door behind her. His sympathy seemed to break the weak dam that held back her emotions and she threw her arms over his shoulders and began sobbing into his neck. Surprised, Lucas awkwardly tried to comfort her, rubbing her back as she wept.

"A messenger came and told me about last night," she sobbed. "I heard you had escaped and I knew I could find you here. I… I just cannot believe he is gone!"

Her weeping renewed and large tears slid down Lucas's neck as he held her. Gradually, her crying quieted and she pulled away from him.

"Thank you, Lucas, I needed that, but it is not really why I came." She sniffled, pulling herself together with great effort. "The underground resistance has called an emergency meeting to vote on someone to replace Father. Lord Blakemore is pushing to be elected. I thought you ought to be there."

"Tristan and Aleatha are still asleep." Lucas said, glancing at the still closed bedroom door. "I hate to wake them after the last few days, and I do not dare leave them alone." Though he feared Tristan and his sister would never be safe if Lord Blakemore had his way.

"They will be safe here, will they not?" Celia asked, her teary eyes pleading. "Is that not the whole purpose of staying here anyway?"

She had a point. Her father had hidden Tristan here because he believed it was free from detection. Besides, he did want to be sure a man favorable to Tristan's cause took Chapman's place, certainly not Lord Blakemore. "I just need to let Tristan know where I am going."

Celia placed a hand on his arm. "I thought you did not want to wake him. We will be back again soon, maybe even before they wake up. Come on, they will probably not even notice you are gone."

"Fine, but we must hurry back." Lucas looked back at the bedroom door apprehensively. "I do not want them worrying about me."

*****

Tristan lay awake in his bed. His eyes were closed and his breathing steady, but his mind was alert and his body tense for action. His attention was focused on the sounds of heavy footfalls in the other room. Not Lucas, he had grown accustomed to the sound of Lucas coming and going by now. Soldiers, by the sound of it. Several of them. He rolled toward Aleatha, still asleep in the bed next to him, and pulled her close to him.

"Tristan?" she mumbled. She cuddled closer to him. "Is it morning?"

"Shh," Tristan whispered in her ear. "Do not speak, just listen. We have been discovered. As quietly as you can, I want you to hide under the bed. Do not come out until you are sure it is safe. No matter what happens. Promise me that."

"What are you going to do?" Her body tensed with alarm.

"I have my sword. I will hold them off as long as I can." Tristan turned her face to his, placed a lingering kiss on her lips, and rolled away from her. He quickly pulled on his pants and grabbed his sword as she scrambled under the bed. "Whatever happens to me, remember I love you. I will not let them take you from me again."

He positioned himself by the door, throwing a final glance back at the disheveled bed to be certain Aleatha was not visible. *Heavenly Father, protect her.*

At that moment, the door swung open, hitting the wall behind it with a bang.

"Captain, I found him!" the soldier cried as he lunged forward to engage Tristan's sword.

Tristan's only chance was to keep the men out of the room. He could only pray he was good enough to hold them off with his left hand; his right was still bandaged and felt even worse this morning. The doorway was narrow and only one or two men could fight him at a time. He dodged the soldier's sword and plunged his own into the man's chest. He drew it back and allowed the body to fall on the threshold with a dull thud. When Tristan looked up, two more soldiers stood in the doorway in his place. His sword darted in and out between the two men.

They are novices, he realized thankfully as he slashed his sword at one to drive him back and sent his remaining opponent to join the other body on the threshold.

Angered, the third soldier jumped toward him to avenge his partner's death, his sword tearing a shallow gash across Tristan's right arm. Tristan let out his breath in a hiss and parried the soldier's attempt to finish him, sending the soldier to suffer his partner's fate instead.

A fourth soldier mounted the pile of bodies, crossing Tristan's sword from above. Tristan found himself on the defensive for the first time, his sword flashing like lightning to keep the man from advancing into the room. The soldier pressed forward, his own sword matching Tristan's speed. Tristan was forced back away from the door and the soldier jumped down toward him just as Tristan brought his sword up. The fourth soldier joined the growing heap at Tristan's feet.

"Prince Tristan," Captain Brogan called to him from the other side of the doorway. "I offer you terms of surrender."

Tristan pulled himself up to his full height and smirked at Captain Brogan, his breath coming fast and hard, but his guard up for any tricks. "No surrender, Captain. I seem to be doing quite well on my own."

"Come, Prince," Captain Brogan said with a sneer. "You are wounded and quite clearly tired. I still have many men to send in. How much longer can you hold out?"

Truly, not much longer at all. Tristan admitted to himself. He was already beginning to feel faint. The fire, lack of sleep, and his injuries were taking their toll. Still, there was Aleatha to think of; he had to hold out as long as he could. "Devon will certainly kill me at the castle. I may as well die here."

"What of the girl – your 'wife'?" Captain Brogan scanned the room for Aleatha. "I am quite certain you have her hidden in there somewhere. When you fall, I will command my men to run you through the heart, just to be sure you are truly dead. We will then tear this building apart, down if needed, to find her and bring her with us."

He is right, I cannot hold out forever. Tristan blanched. His fate would be the same whether he fought to the death here or died by Devon's hand at the castle. If he died here, however, Aleatha would be taken. Perhaps she could be allowed to go free.

"If I surrender, do you swear you and your men will leave her alone? No searching for her, no waiting outside for her, nothing. Would you swear no harm would come to her?" he asked through clenched teeth.

"I would swear by Lord Devon's soul, may he live forever." Captain Brogan placed his hand on his heart in mock reverence.

"Swear by something that matters," Tristan scoffed. He knew from years in the palace what was important to Captain Brogan. "Swear by the life of your daughter. What is she now? Four? Five?"

Captain Brogan turned a deep shade of purple. "It is my daughter's life already if I fail to bring you in."

"Then it is in your best interest to swear honestly," Tristan said blithely. "Choose quickly, Captain. I feel a second wind coming on. Would you like to face me next?"

"I swear. Now surrender," Captain Brogan ordered harshly.

"Say it. Swear by the life of your daughter nothing will happen to Aleatha," Tristan persisted. He was not about to take any chances.

"I swear by the life of my daughter nothing will happen to your precious Aleatha," Captain Brogan growled, his hand resting on the hilt of his sword. "Now surrender, or I will run you through myself."

"I surrender, Captain Brogan." Tristan allowed his sword to drop to the ground beside him as he raised his hands above his head.

With a grunt, Captain Brogan stepped over the bodies on the threshold and walked cautiously to Tristan. He circled him once, his hand still resting on the hilt of his sword. Standing before Tristan again, he looked him over and slid his sword from its scabbard.

Tristan took a deep breath and held his head high. So he truly would run him through here. *Heavenly Father, please, not in front of Aleatha. She has suffered enough.*

Turning the sword in his hand, Captain Brogan rammed the pommel of his sword into Tristan's stomach. Tristan gasped, doubling over from the pain. Waves of nausea rippled through his body. Another fierce blow struck him on the side of the head, driving him to his knees. Fighting to maintain consciousness, he pressed his hands against the floor to steady himself as the room spun around him.

He struggled to catch his breath as Captain Brogan called to the remaining soldiers. "You and you, take him. The rest of you, gather the bodies."

"What about the girl?" one of the soldiers asked as he yanked Tristan to his feet. "Do we hunt for her?"

"You swore," Tristan ground out. Blood trickled from the wound caused by the blow to the side of his head into his eye and he blinked to clear his vision. "My life for hers."

"So I did," Captain Brogan agreed maliciously. "She may go free, as I promised, and you will face Lord Devon, as you promised. I hope he kills you slowly and painfully for all the trouble you have caused me."

* * * * *

Lucas and Celia had nearly reached the edge of town when Celia began to cry softly.

Lucas slid his arm across her shoulders and pulled her closer to him. "Your father was a good man," he said gently.

"It is not that," She covered her face with her hands and wailed.

If it is not about her father, then what would upset her so badly? Lucas looked at her, bewildered. He took her by the shoulders and shook her gently. "Celia, Celia! What is wrong? Are you all right?"

"Oh, Lucas! I am so sorry." She tore herself away from him, her hands still covering her face. "I have done something terrible. Father would be so ashamed of me!"

"What have you done?" Lucas caught his breath as fear gripped him.

"The queen's was forcing me to spy for her. She knew we were seeing each other. She threatened to kill my brother John and his family. Lord Devon summoned me again early this morning," she broke off with another wail. "I am sorry; I had no choice."

"Tristan and Aleatha," Lucas realized, his heart pounding. He grabbed Celia's arms, turned her to face him, and shook her again, a little less gently. "What did you do? Be quiet and tell me everything."

She swallowed hard and rubbed at the tears streaming down her face. "I led the soldiers to the house and tricked you into leaving with me. I was supposed to make sure Prince Tristan was unguarded. I am sorry. Please, please forgive me. I had no choice. He would have killed my brother and his family!"

Speechless, Lucas stared at his sweetheart in disbelief. *How could she have betrayed us?* He clenched his teeth and turned back the way they had come. She didn't matter now. Perhaps if he ran he could get there in time to help Tristan and Aleatha. "I am going back."

"You cannot." Celia grabbed his arm. "There were more than twenty soldiers. You will only be killed with them."

Lucas pried her fingers from his arm and looked at her coldly. "If you have any remorse for what you did, do not try to stop me."

Celia did not answer, but simply followed behind Lucas as he ran.

Half block from the Morrison house, Lucas pulled up short. A hiss of breath escaped through his clenched teeth. He ducked around a corner and pulled Celia back after him.

We are too late. Cautiously, he peered around the corner. An army had stormed the house. Lucas counted ten men on guard, and at least another half dozen escorting Tristan from the building. Tristan looked as if he had put up a fight. Blood smeared his bare chest and arms and stained his pants. A trickle of blood flowed from a gash on the side of his head, matting his hair. Tristan's held his head high in defiance.

Good. Tristan survived. Now where is my sister? Lucas scanned the soldiers pouring from the battered doorway as they began to move down the street away from the house. Captain Brogan followed, carrying Tristan's sword. Lucas scanned the soldiers again, including the ones on guard. He still saw no sign of Aleatha.

"I do not see Aleatha," Celia whispered, "maybe she escaped."

"Maybe," Lucas replied. He was not sure what to think. Tristan did not look as if Aleatha had been killed or captured. The sight of Tristan's sword in the hands of the commander could indicate Tristan had surrendered rather than allow Aleatha to be harmed.

Please, Lord, allow her to be unharmed. As soon as the soldiers had turned the corner, he stepped out of his hiding spot. He had to get inside that house. He was not going to let his sister down again.

Chapter 40

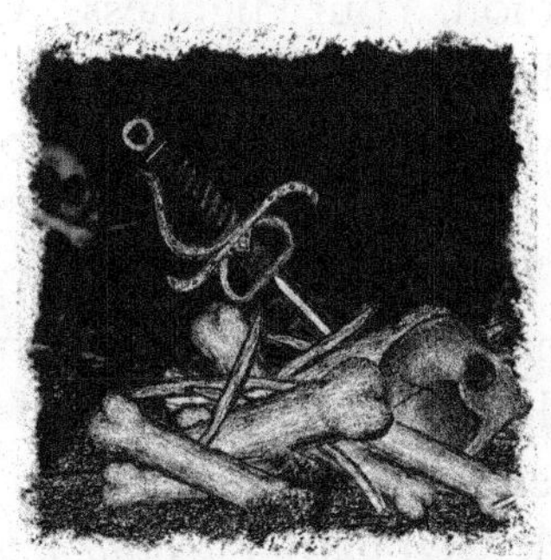

As the soldiers turned onto the main street, Captain Brogan stopped and led Tristan back to the corner, within clear sight of the Morrison house.

"What are we doing?" Tristan asked.

"There is something you might want to see," Captain Brogan answered slyly and pointed back at the house.

Dale Blakemore stood near the back of the house, shifting from one leg to the other as if he were waiting for something.

Some hiding place, Tristan thought, looking daggers at Dale. *How many more people know about it?*

Dale's shifting stopped as the back door swung open and Aleatha came running out. She ran right into Dale's waiting arms. Tristan wetted his lips, waiting for her to extricate herself from Dale's embrace. She did not. Instead, she returned the embrace, burying her face in Dale's neck.

"Your faithful wife," Captain Brogan mocked. "You sacrifice your freedom – probably your very life – for her, and she runs right into the arms of her lover."

Jealousy burned in Tristan's heart as he watched Aleatha and Dale. He tried to excuse Aleatha's actions, to maintain his faith in her fidelity, but the flames of jealousy threatened all rational thought.

I should have killed Dale back at Aleatha's party when he was asking for it. He stopped himself. *What am I thinking? I know I am playing into their hands, but this time I am seeing it with my own eyes!*

"It is very common, Your Highness," Captain Brogan said, pretending sympathy, "marry for position; keep your true lover on the side. Many a man has fallen for the lies of an unfaithful wench."

Heavenly Father, help me! Tristan tried to push back the rage and jealousy that threatened to swallow him. The Scripture "Charity believes all things" repeated itself in his mind. He tried to force himself to believe the best of Aleatha, but the doubts pushed back even harder. *Aleatha, what are you doing?*

"Look, your faithful friend returns," Captain Brogan scoffed again, pointing back at the house. "Nice of him to make sure he was out of the way when my men showed up."

As Lucas and Celia ran up to the house, Lucas called out, but Tristan and Captain Brogan were too far away to hear the words. Dale answered, without letting Aleatha out of his embrace.

"I think you have seen enough." Captain Brogan took Tristan by the arm and led him away. "When you see Lord Devon, you should thank him for allowing you to see what your 'friends' really are."

"You set them up," Tristan accused, as he tried to defend his friends actions even to himself. "That is why you knew to turn back."

Captain Brogan shrugged noncommittally, enjoyment on his face. "Perhaps, but they seem to have played into my hands quite willingly. Would you not agree?

Tristan did not reply. The image of Aleatha falling into the arms of another man played unbidden in his head, searing the memory into his mind's eye.

*****

Aleatha had waited under the bed for what seemed an eternity after the soldiers had left. She had wanted to scream when Tristan had agreed to surrender in exchange for her safety. She had wanted to sob when she saw his sword hit the floor and the Captain pick it up. She nearly had lost all control when they had beaten him and led him out of the room. The only thing that had kept her quiet was her promise to him.

Now her chest ached with pent up emotion and her eyes burned from unshed tears. The last three days had been like a pendulum swinging from one extreme to the other, from heights of joy to depths of fear and despair. As Aleatha crawled out from under the bed and stood to her feet, a thought hit her with the force of the roof collapsing on her head. *I will likely never see Tristan again.*

The room swam before her. Fighting for consciousness, she steadied herself on the bed. She had to find Lucas, or someone who would know what to do. Her stomach turned as she looked around the room spattered with the blood the dead soldiers had left behind. She stepped gingerly around the stains as she made her way to the door, gagging and pressing her hand to her mouth at the sight of so much blood. She stopped to grab Lucas's cloak to throw over her chemise. Reaching the doorway, she paused. The threshold where the soldiers had fallen was slick with a pool of blood too large to be avoidable.

She retched as she realized she would have to walk through it to get out. Closing her eyes, she took as large a step as she could over the blood. Still, she felt the dampness beneath her foot.

Dizziness washed over her again and she steadied herself on the door frame. I have to get out of here. Another step and she was clear. She swallowed back her emotion one last time and quickly scanned the room for a sign of her brother.

Where was he when we needed him? The main room was empty. *Who else should I go to?* The only people she knew to trust were the members of the underground resistance, but she had never been to their meetings. Her only connections to them were Chapman and Dale.

Dale. She pulled at the ends of her long hair. She knew where to find him, but would he help? She had to go to someone. Deciding, she turned to go out the back. She did not dare use the front in case the soldiers were still out there. Throwing the door open, she dashed out, hoping to make it across the street without being seen. As soon as she stepped into the open, she slammed right into the arms of a man waiting outside the door. She stifled a scream.

"Aleatha?" Dale asked, surprise in his voice. "Are you all right? I saw soldiers…"

"Oh, Dale, they took Tristan!" With those words, all the emotion of the past hour rushed over her. She buried her head in Dale's shoulder and sobbed, sagging against him as darkness overcame her.

*****

As soon as the soldiers were out of sight, Lucas and Celia rushed around the back of the house to find Dale holding an insensible Aleatha. His expression was one of both uncertainty and irritation.

"Dale!" Lucas called as he neared. "Is Aleatha all right?" His heart raced. His sister was not moving. *Dear Lord, if those monsters have harmed her...*

"She seems unhurt," Dale answered, "but I think all the strain was too much for her. She fainted."

"I will take her back to the house." Lucas held out his arms, but Dale did not loosen his hold on Aleatha.

"He had no right to do this to her, Lucas." Dale's voice was low and angry. "If he truly cared for her, he would not have put her through this."

Tristan, Lucas thought as understanding dawned. He looked at Dale coldly as he said, "The soldiers took him. He would never have left her willingly."

"She told me. Right before she collapsed," Dale retorted, rage flashing in his eyes. "I hope that devil does kill him, for Aleatha's sake."

It certainly would not hurt your purposes either. Lucas's own anger rose as he stepped forward and lifted Aleatha out of Dale's arms. She moaned, but did not regain consciousness. "Do not dare let Aleatha hear you say that. She chose Tristan happily."

Dale set his jaw and let his arms drop to his side, but did not respond.

"Let us get Aleatha inside long enough to make sure she is all right," Lucas suggested, moving toward the door. "We can discuss a better hiding place after that."

With Dale and Celia following close behind, he carried Aleatha back toward the door, stopping short at the trail of bloody footprints his sister had left. He shot a glance at Dale.

"I will check the house," Dale offered grimly, stepping past Lucas and disappearing inside.

When he returned, his face was flushed with anger. "She cannot stay here, not even for a moment. The main room is bathed in blood and the bedroom looks like a battlefield. She had to walk through it to get out here."

He glanced back over his shoulder into the open doorway and growled under his breath, "I hope some of it is his, the brute. He had no right…"

"Enough, Dale," Lucas warned. Concern hit him. Tristan had been wounded, but it had been impossible to tell how badly. In any case, if they did not get to him soon, Dale's wishes would come true.

His sister moaned and stirred, but she still did not awaken. He held her closer to him. *Aleatha needs my help first, then I will try to rescue Tristan. It is what Tristan would want anyway.* "Where do we go? I do not dare take her back to our house."

"Take her to mine," Dale volunteered. "She will be safe there until we can decide what to do next."

Lucas hesitated. Dale's home was built like a castle. She would certainly be safe from Lord Devon's men there, but he was also concerned about Dale. "I doubt that is a good idea. You make no secret you still covet her hand."

"Do you have a better idea?" Dale snapped. "I will not say anything to her. If it would make you feel better, I will disappear as soon as we get there. She need not even see me. I would never do or say anything that would hurt her. Believe me."

"There really is not any other choice, Lucas," Celia appealed, placing her hand on Lucas's shoulder.

Lucas shifted Aleatha's weight in his arms. She was getting heavy. "Fine. Let us go quickly. I do not want her to wake up here."

Chapter 41

The soldiers threw Tristan into the deepest part of the dungeon. They gave him no food or water, or even a cloak to ward off the dank chill of the cell. They had not even bothered to dress his wounds. That meant this would be his last chance. With his mother dead, there would be no offer of his allegiance for his life. As all that stood between Devon and the throne, his fate was most certainly death. Devon could not afford to allow him to live as a threat to his reign. How, though, that was another question. A public, humiliating execution celebrating the conquer of a failed resistance? A quiet, slow poisoning like the one his mother had dealt his father? Or perhaps the sufferings of a forgotten traitor left to die in the depths of the royal dungeon from starvation and infection. Knowing Devon, it would more likely be a slow, painful battle for his very soul before Devon finally ended his life as mercilessly as possible. Tristan shuddered. *Had it not been for Aleatha, I would have died fighting back at the house.*

Aleatha. Visions of his last sight of her flashed through his mind. He pulled his knees to his chest, crossed his arms on top of them, and rested his head on his arms. Aleatha, his beautiful Aleatha, in his rival's arms. Certainly it was all a plot, some scheme cooked up by Devon to crush him once and for all. He had seen what Devon had wanted him to see; narrated by Devon's man to make sure he interpreted his friends' actions the way Devon wanted him to interpret them. Aleatha, the unfaithful bride, just as Devon had always asserted. Lucas, the treacherous friend, leaving him defenseless in the hands of the castle guard. He knew it had been arranged. He wanted to believe the best, and yet… The doubts were strong, so very strong.

Heavenly Father, help me to conquer these doubts. Help me to remember Devon has no power over my mind. He can do to my body what he will, but I commit my mind to you.

Vivid images of Aleatha embracing Dale rushed into his mind again. A lump rose in his throat, threatening to choke him. *And Lord, I know I am going to see you soon. Please help this not to be my final memory of my dear wife.*

Realization hit him with the sharp force of the pommel of Captain Brogan's sword. He had come a full circle. Had he truly lost all of the ground he had gained over his fears in the last few weeks? Had he so little faith in his friends and his God to fall back into the same pit of despair that had threatened to destroy him after his escape from Devon? If he had, Devon had already won. Lucas and Aleatha had proved their loyalty to him in a thousand ways since he returned. He refused to allow a carefully orchestrated scene to cause him to doubt it now. Devon only had the power over him that he allowed him to have.

He took a deep, painful breath, determined not to permit Devon to control him. Not now, not ever, no matter how painful the death Devon had planned for him. Pushing the images out of his mind, he chose instead to focus on preparing for the battle he was about to face. It would be a battle for his soul and he could not afford to enter it already weakened.

I will say of the Lord, He is my refuge and my fortress: my God; in him will I trust. A verse of scripture came to his mind. *Heavenly Father, I put my trust in you, the ever faithful God. Give me the strength to stand strong before Devon, even to death, however awful he can make it.* Peace filled his heart even as the burden of his despair was lifted from his shoulders. The tension flowed from his aching muscles. The pace of the last few days had taken their toll on him and he realized he would not have the strength to face Devon without a little rest. His tortured mind finally eased, he slipped into a dreamless sleep.

With a clang, the door to his cell swung open and slammed into the stone wall behind it. Tristan jerked his head up. Three soldiers stood in the doorway. One carried a torch; the other two carried drawn swords. *Devon is taking no chances.*

"Take him." The soldier carrying the torch gestured to Tristan. "Careful now, if he escapes, it is worth all our lives."

The two men yanked Tristan to his feet, holding his arms on either side. Both kept their swords drawn, but one held the blade of his sword to Tristan's stomach as they walked. "If you even think about escaping, Prince, we will be bringing you to Devon in two pieces."

Tristan set his jaw grimly, steeling himself for the battle ahead. As Boldaria's rightful king, he was all that stood between Devon and absolute power. He could expect no mercy from his enemy, not even the relative mercy of a quick death, only Devon's final attempt to destroy him as completely and painfully as possible.

Heavenly Father, I commit my mind and soul to you. Please allow me to hold onto my faith in you and my friends until the end.

* * * * *

After assuring himself Aleatha and Celia were safe at Dale's, safety that included having Dale place guards on the building, Lucas directed Dale to take him to Lord Applegate's home. Celia had been truthful about one thing, the resistance was preparing to choose a new leader. Dale had confirmed they were meeting right now, and that his father was expected to succeed Chapman as the leader of the underground. He had also pointed out something Lucas did not need reminded of, that Lord Blakemore was not likely to place a high priority on rescuing Tristan if he were elected. Lucas gritted his teeth as he urged his horse faster. He had to get there before the vote if there was to be any chance of rescuing Tristan.

He reigned in his horse outside the house, dismounted, and threw the reigns over a hitching post before the horse could even come to a complete stop. Crossing the yard to the servant's entrance of the dark house, he knocked firmly and gave the password when prompted.

"Master Lucas," the doorman stammered as Lucas brushed past him. "We thought you were dead."

"Clearly I am not. Have they voted yet?"

The man shook his head. "Lord Blakemore was nominated only a moment ago. No one else seems interested."

Lucas pushed into the crowd as Dale hovered in the back. It was much larger than any of the other meetings he had attended. Circling the back of the room stood a large number of men in tattered clothes, some he recognized as men he had treated in the Shambles. Lord Blakemore stood to one side of the aged Lord Applegate as the councilman addressed the crowd.

"Are there no other nominations?" Lord Applegate scanned the crowd, waiting for a response that never came. "All right then. All in favor of Lord Bryce Blakemore as the new leader of the resistance?"

"Wait!" Lucas broke through the crowd to the front. His words tumbled out rapidly as he said, "Please, Lord Applegate,

Prince Tristan lives, but has been captured by the castle guard. We must save him."

"Prince Tristan is a threat to this kingdom," Lord Blakemore responded icily. "There will be no rescue. Certainly not once I am in charge."

"This group once voted against Lord Blakemore in Prince Tristan's favor," Lucas turned to face the buzzing crowd, pleading boldly over the din of voices, "Surely there would be a man willing to lead it forward in an attempt to rescue Boldaria's rightful king." He took a breath and waited as the room grew silent. Setting his jaw, he and turned back to Lord Applegate. "Sir, we both know Lord Blakemore would sooner see Prince Tristan dead than rescued. If he will not lead the men to rescue him, I will."

"Are you volunteering to lead the resistance, young man?" Lord Applegate encouraged.

Lucas's heart pounded. He had not intended to do that at all, but if that was what it would take, so be it. "I will do whatever is necessary to save my friend, and my king."

"What will it be then?" Lord Applegate addressed the murmuring crowd. He held up his right hand, gesturing to Lord Blakemore. "A vote for Lord Blakemore and his plan to depose Lord Devon?" He raised his left to Lucas. "Or a vote for the young doctor and Prince Tristan?"

The room thundered with the response. The support for Lucas was overwhelming. The men from the Shambles, having thrown in with the resistance when the queen announced the capture and planned execution of their beloved Young Doc were the loudest in their vote.

Dale pushed through the roaring crowd, crossed to Lord Applegate, and whispered in his ear. Lord Applegate raised his hands for silence. "A messenger has brought grave news. Lord Devon has declared himself king and has announced the coronation will take place this evening after the queen's funeral." He looked to Lucas, a grim look on his face. "I am afraid that does not bode well for Prince Tristan."

Icy fingers gripped Lucas's heart. No, they could not be too late. Perhaps Devon had delayed killing Tristan, choosing to toy with him a while longer. He held onto that slim hope, knowing if they did not get to the castle before the coronation, Tristan's chances sank from extremely slim to none. "I can get us into the castle. Once there, we can stop Lord Devon's coronation, even if we are too late to save Prince Tristan. All I need are a few men willing to hazard themselves for the cause of Boldaria."

A chorus of voices rose as volunteers stepped forward. Lucas had come looking for a few men to help him in a rescue; he would be leaving with an army to follow him as he led an assault on the castle itself.

* * * * *

The soldiers led Tristan into the throne room, closing the doors behind them before leading him down the rich scarlet runner. Devon sat on the throne, dressed in his richest clothing and accented with a few pieces of jewelry belonging to the crown jewels. The coronation crown sat on a pedestal to his right and a pair of crossed swords sat on a pedestal to his left. Tristan cast a quick glance at the swords as the soldiers forced him forward, gauging his chances of grabbing one and fighting his way out. It would be suicide, especially with the two soldiers still behind him, but it would be far better than the death Devon had planned for him.

"Sorry to have kept you waiting, I was busy preparing for your mother's funeral this evening," Devon said, adding smugly. "I suppose since the Medellins murdered her, that would finally make you King Tristan now, would it not, Your Majesty? At least until I am crowned this evening.

"It looks as if you put up quite a fight." Devon stood, clucking his tongue in his mouth as he circled Tristan, his expression clearly pleased with Tristan's battered appearance. "My men say you sacrificed yourself for the Lady Aleatha.

How truly noble. Too bad she proved herself unworthy of your devotion. I did warn you repeatedly about her faithlessness, my king."

Heavenly Father, be my shield, Tristan prayed, staring straight ahead as the image of Aleatha in Dale's arms threatened to force itself back into his mind. He refused to play this game anymore. No more banter, no more replies. He would not allow Devon's words to have any power over him.

"Did you not even wonder why young Medellin was not around when my men came?" Devon mocked, settling back onto the throne carelessly. "Your 'faithful' friend betrayed you, leaving you alone while my men stormed the building. I warned you about him also, my king."

Anger at Tristan's calm silence grew evident on Devon's face. "You cannot deny it anymore, not even to yourself. You saw with your own eyes. Young Medellin returning as soon as my men left. Lady Aleatha falling into the arms of her lover. Surely you see the truth now."

"Your accusations mean nothing to me, Devon," Tristan said, his voice clear and his eyes still straight ahead. "You do not control me anymore. I saw what your men wanted me to see, but I choose to trust in the faithfulness of my friends. Nothing you say will change that."

Rage flashed across Devon's face as he leaped to his feet, but faded quickly. When he spoke again, his voice was cold and deadly, "It does not matter now, since we both know I cannot let you live. Take comfort in knowing that, since you will not allow me to enjoy our little game of wits, I will be forced to get my enjoyment watching you die slowly and painfully over the next couple hours." He took a step forward, his face inches from Tristan's, the hate and wrath burning darkly in his eyes. "I have won, King Tristan. Your throne is mine. Your castle is mine. And, yes, even your precious Aleatha is mine."

Tristan bit back a sharp retort, but was unable to keep a flicker of emotion from his face.

Devon caught his weakness and pounced. "Your God failed you. Your friends failed you. I am your master, whether you care to admit it or not. You only continue to live because I will it. I can have your friends brought to me at my whim. In fact, I had already intended to have Captain Brogan bring my wife back to me as soon as I had finished with you. Perhaps you will be more cooperative if I have your 'faithful' friends brought here now."

The familiar feelings of terror and helplessness crept into Tristan's heart. He had prepared himself for any pain Devon had planned to inflict on him, but how could he stand by and watch while Devon tortured his friends in front of him? *Heavenly Father, protect them.* He drew a shaky breath and drew himself up to full height. "They are in God's hands now; He will protect them from you."

"Just as He has protected you?" Devon mocked. "Take him back to the dungeon, and bring me the young doctor and my wife," Devon ordered the soldiers. He looked at Tristan maliciously. "I have a few hours to kill."

Chapter 42

As Devon turned back to the throne, Tristan lunged for one of the swords, pulling it swiftly from the table and pointing it at Devon. Devon's own sword was in his hand at the same moment, crossing Tristan's lightly.

"Stay back." Devon motioned to the soldiers advancing to his defense. He looked triumphantly at Tristan, as if even this was part of his plan. "The king knows he has no chance against me, especially using his left hand."

Devon was right. Even using his right hand, it would be a hard battle. Tristan pulled the bandage off his right hand with his teeth, never taking his eyes – or his sword – off Devon. He flexed his injured hand. It hurt more than ever now that the bandage was gone, but it would have to do. He switched hands, wincing as his burned fingers closed around the hilt of the sword. *Give me the victory,* he prayed as his sword clashed with Devon's.

The enemies locked swords, parrying, slashing, ranging around the throne room as if caught in a deadly dance where one false step could be fatal. Tristan felt his confidence grow as he realized they were evenly matched, though he found Devon's constant smile bizarre and unsettling.

"How is your hand, Your Majesty?" Devon taunted. "Better is it?"

Tristan flicked his eyes to his hand, then back up to Devon, his eyes widening. The pain in his hand *had* seemed to numb since he had started. His stomach clenched. *How could Devon possibly know that?*

"Soon your whole hand will be numb, and that will be only the beginning," Devon said, his voice filled with devilish satisfaction. "The numbness will spread quickly because the hilt of that sword you are holding is coated with a potent and deadly poison."

Tristan started, nearly dropping the sword from his hand as if it were a live snake. His momentary distraction allowed Devon to find an opening, plunging his sword toward Tristan's chest. Tristan twisted away at the last moment, the tip of Devon's sword catching his side, tearing a jagged, bloody line across his bare ribs.

"You lie," he shot back, even as intense nausea gripped his stomach and he knew Devon truly was not lying.

"I told you I would see you dead before my coronation." Devon stepped out of the reach of Tristan's sword. "Soon the numbness will rob you of your ability to fight. In your final moments, pain will be more excruciating than any you experienced by my hand in the desert, but you will be conscious to enjoy every second."

A shudder coursed down his back as Tristan swallowed back his nausea. He looked at his hand in alarm, it had grown so numb he could no longer feel the sword gripped in his fingers. He drew a labored breath, determined to keep fighting as long as he could. If this was the way God intended for him to go, perhaps He would at least allow him to be able to take Devon with him. He switched hands again, hoping to gain time. The raw burns on his right hand would only speed the absorption of the poison. He lunged toward Devon, crossing swords again, desperation fueling his attack.

Just give me one opening, he prayed as Devon pushed him back. His vision was clouding and his breaths came in short gasps. Sweat glistened over his body and burning droplets slid down into his eyes.

A noise from outside the throne room drew Devon's attention to the door. "Find out what that is," he hissed to his men. "I will not be disturbed now."

Hoping to use the distraction to his advantage, Tristan jabbed his sword toward Devon's stomach. He was too slow; Devon batted his blow away easily. Devon was just toying with him now. The torturer's face glowed in wicked delight as he effortlessly parried every move Tristan made, never attempting to strike a blow of his own. He was clearly biding his time for the end, an end that would not be much longer in coming. The numbness had leached from Tristan's hands to his entire body.

Tristan stumbled and fell to his knees, retching violently as he fought for each staccato breath. He tried to stand, but a sudden wave of dizziness forced him back down again.

"I had hoped you would last longer," Devon said disappointedly as he lowered his sword and looked down at Tristan. "I neglected to allow for your injuries when I decided how strong to make the poison." He knelt, his face inches from Tristan's bowed head. "Your God has forsaken you. You belong to me, body and soul. I am your god. Acknowledge me as supreme and perhaps I will end your misery now."

As Devon threw his head back in a cruel laugh, Tristan saw his chance. He could barely hold his sword and his blurred vision only gave him an outline of Devon's body to aim for, but he prayed it would be enough. Summoning all his remaining energy, he threw himself forward, using the force of his weight to replace his waning strength as he drove his sword deep into Devon's unprotected chest. The impact tore the sword from his nerveless hand and he fell prostrate on the floor.

Devon looked down at him, then at the sword. Disbelief, rage, and dismay all played across his face as he worked his mouth soundlessly. He sat back on his heels, his hand clawing at the sword sticking from his chest as his eyes rolled to the back of his head and he collapsed to the floor.

Thank you, Heavenly Father. Tristan closed his eyes as he fought to breathe. The numbness had spread over his whole body and he felt intensely cold, as if his blood had frozen in his veins. He was dying, but at least his friends would be safe.

* * * * *

Fifty armed men stood behind Lucas at the door between the tunnel and the castle passages. The plan was simple, the men would flood the castle from all levels, sparing any who would surrender, rescuing Tristan if possible, and stopping Devon at all costs. He had broken the men into four groups, one to storm each of the floors of the castle, including the dungeon level. He himself would lead the group to the main level, believing it to be most likely where Devon would be found and perhaps Tristan with him. Lucas's heart thundered in his chest as he knelt to pull the peg Tristan had used to lock the door behind them.

What am I doing here? I am a doctor, not a warrior. Yet here I am leading an assault on the castle. His stomach tightened as his nervous fingers fumbled over the wall to find the catch. *There!* He paused and looked over his shoulders at the three other leaders standing directly behind him. "Remember your instructions, bring me Lord Devon, alive to stand trial for his crimes if possible, and report to me immediately if Prince Tristan is found, regardless of his condition."

Even he was forced to admit there was little hope of finding Tristan alive, but he clung to that slight hope tenaciously as he pushed the catch and allowed the door to slide aside. Like a silent tide, the small army flooded the tunnels, pouring into each level and overwhelming the few soldiers set to guard against them. Lucas led his own little team to the main level, pausing before the very door he and Tristan had used to access the kitchen. He turned to the man behind him, looking into his eyes sternly.

"Swear to me you will not raise your own hand against him." He had been forced to take Dale with him, in order to appease Lord Blakemore's twice supplanted faction, but that did not mean he had to trust him. That was why he placed him in his own group, so he could make certain he held to his instructions.

"I will not kill him in cold blood, if that is what you mean. I am not a murderer," Dale shot back. "No matter what my father may expect."

Did Lord Blakemore truly order his son to kill Tristan? Lucas narrowed his eyes, but did not press the issue. They needed to move, now. He led his men through the passage door and secured the kitchen and the loyal servants. They surged from room to room, finding little resistance even among the soldiers, who held no love for Lord Devon. The loyal soldiers, and even many of the servants who could find arms, joined with Lucas's group.

They met with their first real resistance outside of the throne room. Captain Brogan stood on guard outside the door, sword in hand, glaring at them. The two soldiers standing to either side of him looked much less confident as they gaped at the swelling band of men.

"Surrender, Captain," Lucas challenged, pointing his sword at Captain Brogan. His eyes darted to the two frightened soldiers behind the captain. "All who swear allegiance to Prince Tristan will be spared, those who resist will be killed or taken and tried as traitors."

"Certainly, young Medellin, I have found it to be in my best interest to keep myself on the winning side." A mocking grin twisted Captain Brogan's mouth. He took his sword by the cross guard and offered the grip to Lucas. "Though, perhaps I ought to pledge my sword to you, since Lord Devon has killed the prince, and you certainly will never allow Lord Devon to live. Long live King Lucas?"

All hope drained from Lucas. *I am too late.* Tristan had nearly sacrificed everything to save him only a few days ago, but he had been unable to do the same for his friend. He swallowed back a lump swelling in his throat and blinked his burning eyes. There would be time to grieve later, once the man who had killed Tristan had paid for what he had done. He took a deep, ragged breath, forcing strength into his voice as he took Captain Brogan's sword from him. "I may lead this group, but it will be up to the people to choose their king."

"Where is Lord Devon?" Dale asked, stepping forward. When Captain Brogan indicated the throne room door, Dale turned to Lucas. "With your permission?"

"Take four men with you," Lucas ordered. There was no way he would give Tristan's murderer a chance to escape. "Take him alive if possible, to stand trial before the people."

Dale motioned to a few members of the group to follow him as they cautiously entered the throne room. A few moments later, he returned. His mouth was set in a grim line, but a glint of exultation sparkled in his eyes as he looked at Lucas. "I think you should come in here."

"Keep him here," Lucas said as he passed Captain Brogan's sword to a nearby member of his group. He followed Dale back into the throne room. In the center of the room, surrounded awkwardly by Dale's four men, lay two bodies.

"This is the way we found them," Dale informed Lucas. "It looks like the prince took care of Lord Devon for us before he died."

Rushing down the runner of red carpet toward the bodies, Lucas felt his stomach clench. He barely gave Devon a cursory glance; the sword sticking straight out of his chest and his sightless eyes told him all he needed to know. His full attention was on Tristan's body lying prostrate beside Devon's.

A sob caught in Lucas's throat as he knelt beside his friend. *First Father, now Tristan. What good is being a doctor if you can not even save the people you love?*

Tears blurred his vision as he examined the body. Tristan's hair was matted with sweat and a fresh gash in his side still seeped blood, but the cause of his friend's death was not readily evident. Tristan's bare torso was slick with perspiration and his body was already cool to the touch as Lucas gently rolled him onto his back. A flicker of movement caught Lucas's attention. He could have sworn he saw Tristan's eyes opening. His heart nearly stopped as he found himself looking, not into the empty eyes of a corpse, but the pain dimmed eyes of a man only nearing death.

"Tristan!" Lucas nearly shouted for joy. *He is not dead, not yet. Perhaps there is a chance I can save him.* He examined Tristan hastily. His pulse was slow and weak and his breathing shallow. He did not have much time. "Can you tell me what happened?"

Tristan licked his lips and struggled to speak, his words slurred and barely audible, "Poison… so cold… cannot feel…" His eyes closed again and a shudder coursed through his body.

"No, please, hold on!" Panic gripped Lucas. His best friend was slipping away fast. Lucas stood. *Father trained me almost obsessively in the remedies for many poisons, but can I get it to him in time?*

He turned to Dale, whose look of exaltation had been replaced by one of displeasure. Lucas could not tell if Dale's displeasure was over the fact his rival lived, but he was not about to risk Tristan's fragile life on Dale's jealousy. "Swear to me on your love for Aleatha you will not harm him," he demanded, staring into Dale's eyes.

"I swear I will not touch Prince Tristan in any way, for good or ill," Dale answered sullenly.

Frustrated by Dale's animosity, but satisfied Tristan was in no danger from him, Lucas dashed from the room, shoved his way through the crowd still gathered outside the door, and practically flew up the stairs to his father's medical chamber. Standing before the row of cabinets, Lucas scanned the labels on the vials.

Tristan's symptoms seem consistent with Monkshood poisoning, the same poison King Justin died from. Father recommended the use of Foxglove as a remedy for Monkshood. He snatched a vial from the shelves and darted down the hall. *Help me to be in time.* Even as he ran, he knew it would take a miracle for Tristan to survive. Only the God who had spared him when Lord Devon tried to kill him before could spare him now.

Tristan's screams of agony echoed through the halls before Lucas even reached the throne room. The murmuring crowd parted before him as the Red Sea before Moses as he rushed to the door.

The poison is in its last stages. Gritting his teeth, he forced aside the fear that threatened to debilitate him. He raced to Tristan's side. Tristan's body convulsed in pain as great cries tore from his throat.

Dear Lord, Lucas prayed as he pulled the tiny cork on a vial of medicine, *if he must die, at least spare him this suffering.* There was not time for precision, Lucas simply poured the medicine directly into Tristan's open mouth, gauging the amount as well as he could visually. For a moment there was no improvement as Tristan's cries became more frantic, then he fell into an eerie silence, his eyes closed and his thrashing body stilled.

"Is he dead?" Dale asked, his eyes wide with horror as he stared at Tristan's colorless body.

Alarmed himself, Lucas laid a hand on his patient's chest. He let out a long breath and finally relaxed. Tristan's heart rate had steadied and his breathing was stronger. "No, only unconscious, praise God. He will need to be cared for carefully for a few days, but I think he is going to make it."

Chapter 43

Tristan stood before the mirror, nervously smoothing his sapphire blue tunic and adjusting the belt of his scabbard for the tenth time. With a sigh, he dropped his arms to his sides. He had been in bed for three days, but the simple task of getting dressed still tired him out. He sat on the foot of his bed and rubbed his face with his hands. Perhaps he should have called for Jackson or one of the other servants to help him, but he had rather gotten used to the independence. A knock at the door caused him to look up.

"Come in."

"Everything is ready." Lucas stuck his head in and frowned at Tristan's pale face. "Are you sure you are up to this?"

"Whether I am or not, I doubt the people will understand any further delay." Tristan set his jaw and stood. He looked at

Lucas, his eyes twinkling with a teasing glint. "Though perhaps they would be satisfied with King Lucas instead."

Lucas pressed his lips together in a tight line, his hard glare telling Tristan he did not appreciate his attempt at humor. The national unrest had grown each day as the people demanded a king. Lucas, as leader of the resistance had been faced with an ultimatum: either produce Prince Tristan or a new king would be appointed. Aleatha had informed Tristan the overwhelming majority were pushing for Lucas himself to be crowned, which caused Lucas no little distress.

Lucas opened his mouth as if to retort, then closed it abruptly. His look softened as if he remembered Lord Devon's accusations about his loyalty, his eyes searching Tristan's. "Tristan, please believe me when I tell you I have no desire for your throne."

"I know that, my friend." Tristan laid a hand on Lucas's shoulder. He did, too, without any doubt. It was as if his final stand against Devon had banished all his tortured thoughts from his mind. With Devon gone, perhaps he could finally have peace. "Is Aleatha ready?"

"Ready and waiting. She could not be more thrilled," Lucas said cheerfully. "This means a lot to her."

"To me, also," Tristan admitted as Devon's accusations about their wedding resurfaced. Perhaps some things had not been as completely banished as he would like, but shortly any doubt about the legality of their marriage would be taken care of. "Better not keep her waiting."

Within minutes, Tristan had taken his place in front of the throne room with Lucas beside him as his best man. All sides of the scarlet runner leading down the middle of the room were crowded with people and in front of him stood Lord Applegate. As the leader of the Royal Council, he would preside over both the wedding and the following coronation. To Lord Applegate's right stood two pedestals with sapphire pillows on top. Resting on the pillows sat the coronation crowns for the King and Queen of Boldaria.

A hush settled over the crowd as the massive doors at the other end of the long room spread open. Framed in the arched doorway stood Aleatha, her face glowing with anticipation. Lady Medellin walked beside her daughter, her eyes red with bittersweet tears as she performed what should have been her husband's duty of giving the bride away. Tradition required the bride's nearest male relation to give the bride away, but Tristan had insisted Lucas be his best man and had extended the honor to Lady Medellin, an honor gratefully accepted by both Aleatha and her mother.

Tristan allowed his eyes to follow each graceful movement his bride made as she glided down the center of the room toward him. She was wearing the elaborate jeweled bridal gown originally prepared for Prince Tristan's bride, now being put to its proper use. In her hands was a bouquet of freshly picked daisies and a wreath of the same flowers crowned her tightly braided brown hair. He looked at her appreciatively, perhaps even a bit possessively. After everything they had been through, she would finally be indisputably his. Her eyes caught his gaze and she blushed deeply.

"Who gives this woman to be married to his man?" Lord Applegate intoned as the two women reached the front of the throne room.

"Her brother and I do." Her mother bit her lip and added, her voice quivering, "With the blessings of her late father." She turned to Aleatha, embraced her, and kissed her on the forehead before stepping aside.

Taking her place beside Tristan, Aleatha passed her bouquet to Celia. Tristan still was not sure what he thought about making his mother's spy Aleatha's maid of honor, in spite of the fact she had been Aleatha's friend since they were girls; but Aleatha had insisted on putting the past behind them, reminding him his mother and Devon had been very persuasive. He could not even begin to argue with that, so there Celia stood.

Tristan took Aleatha's hands in his as Lord Applegate led them through the vows. In spite of the fact he had spoken these very same words just a few short days before – or perhaps because of it – Tristan was struck by the realization that their love and devotion for each other had already faced nearly every challenge mentioned in the vows and had come out even more solid in the end. If that was any intimation of things to come, they certainly would live happily ever after.

If you like this book, please give me a good review.

Visit my website: https://authorjessicajoiner.weebly.com

Follow me on Facebook: Author Jessica C. Joiner
@JCJAuthor

Follow me on Twitter: @JCJAuthor

Follow me on Pinterest: Author Jessica C. Joiner

CPSIA information can be obtained
at www.ICGtesting.com
Printed in the USA
BVOW03s0220031117
499453BV00001B/6/P